AND THE MISS RAN
AWAY WITH THE RAKE

This Large Print Book carries the
Seal of Approval of N.A.V.H.

RHYMES WITH LOVE

AND THE MISS RAN AWAY WITH THE RAKE

ELIZABETH BOYLE

THORNDIKE PRESS
A part of Gale, Cengage Learning

GALE
CENGAGE Learning®

Detroit • New York • San Francisco • New Haven, Conn • Waterville, Maine • London

GALE
CENGAGE Learning®

Thorndike Press® Large Print Romance.
The text of this Large Print edition is unabridged.
Other aspects of the book may vary from the original edition.
Set in 16 pt. Plantin.

LIBRARY OF CONGRESS CATALOGING-IN-PUBLICATION DATA

Boyle, Elizabeth.
  And the Miss ran away with the Rake : rhymes with love / by Elizabeth Boyle. — Large Print edition.
    pages cm. — (Thorndike Press Large Print Romance)
    ISBN 978-1-4104-5728-8 (hardcover) — ISBN 1-4104-5728-1 (hardcover) 1. Nobility—England—Fiction. 2. Upper class—England—Fiction. 3. Love-letters—Fiction. 4. Mate selection—Fiction. 5. England—Fiction. 6. Large type books. I. Title.
PS3552.O923A83 2013
813'.54—dc23   2013002935

Published in 2013 by arrangement with Avon Books, an imprint of HarperCollins Publishers.

Printed in the United States of America
1 2 3 4 5 6 7 17 16 15 14 13

To my readers,

This, my twentieth book, is dedicated to each and every one of you.
To those of you who have been with me since the beginning and to those of you who have found me along the way.

Your letters, notes, e-mails, encouragement and friendship have taught me more about the power of storytelling than anything else.

Thank you for being at my side through the good days, and especially through the trying ones.
You hold my heart and appreciation.
Bless you all,
Elizabeth, your devoted fan

Dear Reader,

In a tiny corner of England, there was a village that boasted a curse. Now, most places would rather ignore the fact that they were cursed, but not Kempton. Their curse made them unique, and they clung to it with a stubborn resolve.

Who was to argue with a curse that left every maiden born of the village a spinster for the length of her days? And woe be it to the man who dared marry one of Kempton's ladies. The last courageous fellow, a Mr. John Stakes, tempted the powers that be and married Agnes Perts. A man with such a last name should never have given the Fates such an opening, nor should he have left an unsecured fire poker in the wedding chamber.

Just saying.

And while no one was quite sure how the curse had happened or how to resolve it, Miss Theodosia Walding had once let slip at the weekly meeting of the Society for the Temperance and Improvement of Kempton that she'd been researching the matter in hopes of freeing the village from this plague, and she'd found her investigations met with abject horror.

She never made such an impertinent, and

quite frankly ridiculous, statement ever again.

But this is not her story. It isn't even the story of the rather remarkable lady who is thought to have broken the curse, Miss Tabitha Timmons, the now infamous Kempton spinster, who inherited a fortune from a wayward uncle (aren't all fortunes inherited thusly?), went to London and got herself betrothed to a duke.

Yes, *a duke.*

But since Tabitha and her scandalous nobleman are as yet unmarried, and the duke hasn't shown up with some sharp object imbedded in his chest or been found floating face down in the millpond, no one can say definitively that the Curse of Kempton is broken.

However, one intrepid miss from Kempton, Miss Daphne Dale, is about to take her own stab at finding a perfectly sensible husband.

No pun intended.

The Author

PROLOGUE

Sensible gentleman of means seeks a sensible lady of good breeding for correspondence, and in due consideration, matrimony.

An advertisement placed
in the Morning Chronicle

Earlier in the Season of 1810

"No! No! No!" Lord Henry Seldon exclaimed as their butler brought a second basket of letters into the morning room. "Not more of those demmed letters! Burn them, Benley! Take them out of my sight!"

His twin sister, Lady Juniper, the former Lady Henrietta Seldon, looked up from her tea and did her best to stifle a laugh as poor Benley stood there, wavering in the doorway, grasping a large wicker basket overflowing with correspondence. "Set them beside the others and ignore his lordship, Benley. He is in an ill humor this morning."

Ill humor? Try furious, Henry would have told her. Instead, he vented his anger toward the true object of his ire. "I am going to kill you for this, Preston."

Preston, being Henry and Henrietta's nephew, who was also the Duke of Preston and the head of their family, ducked behind his newspaper at the other end of the table, feigning innocence in all this.

If only he was innocent in deed.

Hardly. Currently, he was the bane of Henry's existence. Not only had Preston's rakish actions — having ruined no less than five young ladies in the past few weeks — put the duke on the "not received list" but now that taint had spread to Henry and Hen, for suddenly they'd joined the ranks of "barely received."

Guilty by association, as it were.

"You cannot kill Preston," Hen said, wading in. She wiped her lips with her napkin and set it down beside her breakfast plate. "You are his heir. It would be bad form."

"Yes, bad form indeed, Uncle," Preston said over the top of his paper. Preston only called Henry "Uncle" when he wanted to vex him further — there being a difference of only six months in age between the three of them — Preston's grandfather having added the twins to the nursery at an indecently advanced age.

And making Henry the uncle to one of London's most notorious rakes.

So if Preston wanted to play proper nephew, then Henry would oblige him by glaring back, taking the bait against his better judgment. "Bad form was what you and that idiot friend of yours, Roxley, displayed when you placed that ridiculous advertisement in the *Morning Chronicle*."

That one small advertisement, a drunken joke, had now garnered an avalanche of responses.

Henry was being buried alive in letters from ladies seeking husbands.

"You should be thanking me," Preston pointed out. "Now you can have your pick of brides without ever having to set foot in Almack's."

"Thanking you? I don't want to get married," Henry declared. "That is your business. Why don't you marry one of these tabbies?"

Preston glanced up, an odd look in his eye. "Perhaps I've already found my own tabby."

"Oh, there's a lark," Henry sputtered. "Are you telling us that you intend to marry that vicar's daughter you've been dallying after?"

11

Before Preston could answer, Hen chimed in, "You should be thankful, Henry, that Preston didn't place that unfortunate jape in the *Times.*" Her lips curled into a smile before she took one more sip from her tea and settled back in her seat. "Personally, I found Preston's ad rather dull myself."

"Dull?" Preston complained, snapping his paper shut and eyeing his aunt. "I am never dull."

"Then tedious," she corrected. "I can't imagine anyone replying to such nonsense, let alone want to marry a man who describes himself as 'sensible.' " She glanced up at Benley, who was placing the basket of correspondence next to the one that had arrived earlier. "Just how many lonely hearts are there in London?"

"This will make over two hundred, my lady," Benley said, warily eyeing the collection that carried with it a competing air of rose water and violets. "My lord," he said, turning to Lord Henry, "Lady Taft's footman would like to know how you are going to settle the bill for the outstanding postage. Her ladyship is quite put out at having to pay for a goodly number of these — apparently the newspaper has now reached the outlying counties."

Hen's eyes widened. "The letters are arriving at your house?"

"Yes, they are," Henry told her.

"I wasn't so foxed that I'd use this address," Preston supplied. "Can you imagine the clamor and interruptions?" He shuddered and returned to his paper.

"Which is exactly why Lady Taft is not amused," Henry said. "I promised her when she took my house for the Season that it was the quietest of addresses."

The house in question, on the very respectable and previously sedate Cumberland Place, was a large residence that Henry had inherited from his mother, though he had yet to live in it. He, Preston and Hen (when she was between husbands) lived quite comfortably in the official London residence of the Seldons on Harley Street, just off the corner of Cavendish Square. With such a good address and all the comforts of a ducal residence, Henry saw no reason to strike out on his own.

Besides, he could collect an indecent amount of rent for his well-situated Mayfair house — though now even that was in question. He glared at his nephew again, but Preston was too busy studying his newspaper to notice.

Probably examining it for more gossip about, what else, himself.

Really, who wouldn't blame Lady Taft for threatening to quit the lease, what with a bell that was ringing constantly from the steady arrival of these demmed letters?

All addressed to *A Sensible Gentleman*.

Well, right now he felt anything but sensible.

Henry shoved his seat back from the table and got to his feet. Crossing the room in a few quick strides, he caught up the first basket and strode over to the fireplace.

"Good heavens!" Hen exclaimed, jumping up. "Whatever are you doing?"

Even Preston put down his newspaper and gaped.

"What does it look like?" Henry said, poised before the grate. "I am going to burn the lot of them."

Hen dashed across the room, a black streak in her widow's weeds, and yanked the basket from his grasp. "You cannot do that."

He tried to retrieve it, but this was Hen, and she was quite possibly the most stubborn Seldon who had ever lived. She turned so the basket was out of his reach and glared at him.

"The ladies who wrote these letters did so with great care. They are expecting responses. You cannot just burn them to suit

14

your mood," she said, looking down at the basket of notes she held. "You must reply to them. All of them."

Too busy hoping that the overwhelming *eau du floral* rising from the pages would leave his sister overcome, Henry gave scant regard to what she was saying. All he could hope was that when Hen was out cold on the floor, he'd have enough time to consign them to the flames before she came to.

But not even the happy image of these annoying reminders of Preston's prank roasting over the coals could overshadow what Hen was saying.

What she wanted him to do: answer them.

Henry stilled. Answer them? *All* of them?

A notion that Preston found quite amusing. "Yes, Henry, I quite agree," the duke said. "You wouldn't want to disappoint so many ladies. That would hardly be sensible."

Henry ignored Preston and faced down his sister. "You can't seriously expect me to write to all those women?"

"But of course! Each one of these poor, dear souls is awaiting your answer. Most likely watching the post as we speak."

He let out a graveled snort at the image of lovelorn spinsters all over London — and from the return addresses, a good part of England — sitting by their front doors in hopes true love was about to arrive in a scrap of paper, sealed with a wafer. "That is ridiculous."

"It is not," Hen said, in that tone of hers that Henry knew all too well meant she would brook no opposition. Hen carried the basket to the table and began sorting through the feminine appeals. "Do you recall what I was like when Lord Michaels was courting me and how distraught I was when I did not hear from him for two days straight?"

Both Henry and Preston groaned at the mere mention of that bounder's name.

Michaels being her second husband. There had been three to date — with her most recent venture, Lord Juniper, having died suddenly nearly six months earlier. Hence the widow's weeds and the onset of Hen's sentimental side.

"I had no idea if he loved me or not," she declared, clutching a few of the letters to her breast, as if to make a desperate point. That is until the competing florals doused over the letters made her sneeze and she had to surrender the missives back into the basket.

"Didn't stop you from marrying him when he did bother to show up," Henry muttered. Then again, he'd never approved of Lord Michaels. A mere baron and barely that.

Hen sniffed. "Be that as it may, those two days, when I knew not what he was thinking, those were the longest, worst two days of my life."

"Really, Hen? Isn't that doing it up a bit? The *worst* two days of your life?" Henry shook his head and glared at the basket of letters. They were making this the worst week of his life.

"You must answer these," she repeated, wagging a finger at her brother. "If only to let these ladies know that they have been deceived, just as you were, and you are most sorry for any distress this will cause them."

"Make Preston apologize," Henry told her, pointing toward the real culprit in all this. "He placed the ad."

"Yes, well, you know he will never do that," Hen said with a dismissive wave.

"And I wouldn't have placed it if you hadn't been so prosy that night," Preston complained. "Going on and on about how I'd ruined the family's good name." He picked up his paper. "I would remind you both, we are Seldons. We have never had a good name."

"Exactly," Henry said, latching onto the notion with an idea of his own. "When these ladies discover who has written them, and they nose it about how they've been ill-used by a Seldon, don't you think, Hen, that this will only go to sully our family name further? Might even leave you cut from Almack's."

Both he and Preston eyed her speculatively. For while Preston was in name the head of the family, neither of them naysaid Hen. Not if they knew what was good for them.

And it very nearly worked.

Nearly.

"There is no reason for you to sign your own name," she pointed out. "Sign it . . ." She tapped her fingers against her lips and then smiled. "I know! Sign it 'Mr. Dishforth.' "

"Dishforth!" Henry exclaimed, for it had been some time since that name had been uttered under their roof.

"Dishforth! Of course! I don't know why I didn't think of it myself, Hen," Preston said with an approving nod. Of course he would approve. Dishforth — Henry's invention when they were children — had become Preston's shining hero. If something got broken or the apple tart disappeared and all that was left was a plate of crumbs, the always culpable and ever rapscallion "Mr.

Dishforth" was blamed, much to the annoyance of their nannies and tutors.

Dishforth had been the cause of any number of tragedies. And now, it seemed, he could take the reckoning for this newest one.

"That doesn't get you off the hook, Preston," Henry told him. "You are going to answer those letters."

"Trust me to do that?" Preston said, waggling his brows and winking at Hen.

"Preston won't have the time, Henry. You'll have to see to this yourself," Hen advised her brother. And her nephew.

"He won't?"

"I won't?"

"No," she replied. "I don't see why you are complaining, Henry. I know very well you will assign the task to your secretary and be done with the matter."

Henry had the good sense to look sheepish, as this was what he had planned from the very first moment she'd suggested he respond to the letters.

Not that Preston was going to escape her wrath either. Looking the duke in the eye, she said, "You will have nothing more to do with this, as you are going to be too busy finding a wife. A respectable lady to bring your reputation — and ours — up out of the gutter."

"Good God, Hen! Not this again," Preston moaned. "What if I told you I had already discovered such a paragon? The perfect lady to be my duchess."

"I wouldn't believe you," Hen replied, arms crossed over her chest.

Henry grinned over his sister's shoulder at Preston, only too pleased to see the tables turned on the scalawag of a duke. For once.

But Henry hardly got the last laugh in.

As Hen was dragging Preston from the morning room, the duke turned and pointed a finger at his uncle. "Best answer those quickly. Lady Taft is known to gossip. Terrible shame if it were nosed about Town that you've been advertising for a wife." He waggled his brows and was then led off by Hen to whatever fate she had in store for him.

For a moment, Henry spared his nephew a twinge of guilt — what bachelor wouldn't at the sight of a fellow comrade being led to his demise? — though his sympathies didn't last for long. Not when he realized that Preston would find it all that much more amusing to spread his joke about Town, albeit via Lady Taft.

Bother him! He would do just that. Probably get that jinglebrains Roxley to spill what they'd done and then he, Henry, would be the laughingstock of London.

He hadn't even considered that horror.

Now in a regular pique over the mere threat of this humiliation becoming public knowledge, Henry realized he needed to nip it all in the bud.

And quickly.

Going to retrieve the first basket, he noticed one of the letters had fallen to the floor, the wax seal having come loose and the page wide open.

Inside, a vivid, albeit feminine, hand caught his eye, her bold script jumping off the pages.

Dear Sensible Sir,
If your advertisement is naught but a jest, let me assure you it is not funny. . . .

Despite his mood, Henry laughed. This impertinent minx had the right of it. There was not one funny piece to the entire situation. Glancing at the letter again, he realized most of the first page was a censorious lecture on the moral ambiguities of trifling with the hearts of ladies.

A composition that would scald even Preston's thick skin.

Not even realizing what he was doing,

Henry sat down at the table, entirely engrossed in the lady's frank words. Pouring himself a fresh cup of coffee — for while Hen and Preston loved tea, Henry much preferred coffee, and Benley always made sure there was a pot on hand — he propped his feet on Hen's chair and read the entire letter. Twice.

And laughed both times. Good God, what a handful of a minx. He tossed the letter down on the table, but his gaze kept straying back to the last lines.

However, if your wishes are truly to meet a sensible lady, then perhaps . . .

He paused and looked at that one word. *Perhaps.*

No, he couldn't, he thought, shaking his head. But then he glanced at the letter again and, against every bit of sense he possessed (for Preston had been correct about one thing; Henry was overly sensible), he called for Benley to bring him a pen and some plain paper.

CHAPTER 1

Miss Spooner,

I will be frank. Your reply to the advertisement in the paper displayed exactly how little you know of men. No wonder you are as yet unmarried. Either you are a frightful scold or the most diverting minx who ever lived. I suppose only time and correspondence will abate my curiosity.

> A letter from Mr. Dishforth
> to Miss Spooner

London, six weeks later

"Miss Dale, you appear flushed. Are you coming down with a fever? That will never do, not here at Miss Timmons's engagement ball!" Lady Essex Marshom declared, turning to her recently employed hired companion, Miss Manx. "Where is my vinaigrette?"

While the beleaguered young woman dug through a reticule the size of a valise to find one of the many items Lady Essex insisted Miss Manx have on hand at all times, Daphne did her best to wave the dear old spinster off.

"I am most well, Lady Essex," she told her, sending a look of horror over at her best friend, Miss Tabitha Timmons. The last time Lady Essex had pressed her infamous vinaigrette into use, Daphne hadn't been able to smell a thing for a week.

"You do look a bit pink," Tabitha agreed, a mischievous light flitting in her brown eyes.

Daphne bit back the response that came to mind, for ever since Tabitha had gotten herself engaged to the Duke of Preston, she'd become as cheeky as a fishwife, displaying none of her previous sensible nature.

This is what came of marrying a Seldon.

Daphne tried not to shudder right down to her Dale toes, for here she was in the very heart of Seldon territory — at their London house on Harley Street, where Tabitha and Preston's engagement ball was being held.

But Daphne couldn't begrudge Tabitha her happiness — there was no arguing that Preston had her glowing with joy. And the engagement had brought them all back to London. Where all Daphne's hopes lay.

Ones that rested upon a certain gentleman. And tonight, Daphne carried high expectations she would be . . . would be . . . She glanced over at her dear friend and whispered a secret prayer that when she found her true love, she might be as happy.

And how could she not with Mr. Dishforth somewhere in this room?

Yes, Mr. Dishforth. She, Daphne Dale, the most sensible of all the ladies of Kempton, was engaged in a torrid correspondence with a complete stranger.

And tonight she would come face-to-face with him.

Oh, she would have stared down an entire regiment of Seldons tonight if only to attend this ball. To find her dear Mr. Dishforth.

"Who looks a bit pink?" Miss Harriet Hathaway asked, having just arrived from the dance floor looking altogether pink and flushed.

Meanwhile, Lady Essex was growing impatient. "Miss Manx, how many times do I have to remind you how imperative it is to keep one's vinaigrette close at hand?"

Harriet cringed and asked in an aside, "Who is the intended victim?"

Tabitha pointed at Daphne, who in turn mouthed two simple words.

Save me.

And being the dearest friend alive, Harriet did. "It is just Daphne's gown, Lady Essex. That red satin is giving her a definite glow. A becoming one, don't you think?"

Bless Harriet right down to her slippers, she'd tried.

"She's flushed, I say," Lady Essex averred. Then again, Lady Essex also liked any opportunity to bring out her vinaigrette and had even now taken the reticule from Miss Manx and was searching its depths herself. "I won't have you fainting, Daphne Dale. It is nigh on impossible to maintain a ladylike demeanor when one is passed out on the floor."

Tabitha shrugged. It was hard to argue that fact.

Yet Harriet was ever the intrepid soul and refused to give up. "I've always found, Lady Essex, that a turn about the room is a much better means of restoring one's vitality." She paused and slanted a wink at Daphne and Tabitha while the lady was still engrossed in her search. "Besides, while I was dancing with Lord Fieldgate, I swore I saw Lady Jersey on the other side of the room."

"Lady Jersey, you say?" Lady Essex perked up, immediately diverted. Better still, she failed to remember that she should probably be chastising Harriet for dancing with the roguish viscount in the first place.

"Yes, I am quite certain of it." Then Harriet did one better and looped her arm into the spinster's, handed the hated reticule back to Miss Manx and steered the old girl into the crowd. "Weren't you saying earlier today that if you could but have a word with her, you'd have our vouchers for next Season?"

Just like that, the hated vinaigrette was utterly forgotten and so was Daphne's flushed countenance.

A Lady Jersey sighting trumped all.

With Harriet and Lady Essex sailing ahead, Daphne and Tabitha followed, albeit at a safe distance so they could talk.

"You are taking a terrible risk," Tabitha whispered to Daphne. "If Lady Essex were to find out —"

"Sssh!" Daphne tapped her finger to her lips. "Don't even utter it aloud. She can hear everything."

It was a miracle as it was that the old girl hadn't discovered Daphne's deepest, darkest secret — that she'd answered an advertisement in the paper from a gentleman seeking a wife.

There it was. And the gentleman had answered her. And then she had replied in kind. And so the exchange had gone on for the last month, all anonymous and mysterious and most likely beyond the pale and ruinous if anyone discovered the truth.

Certainly if Lady Essex found out that such a scandalous correspondence had been carried out right under her nose, the only notes Daphne would be composing would be answering the messages of condolences for Lady Essex's fatal heart ailment.

"Do you think he's here yet?" Tabitha asked, looking around the room.

Daphne shook her head, glancing as well at the crush of guests. "I have no idea. But he'll be here, I just know it."

Her own Mr. Dishforth. Daphne felt that telltale heat of a blush rising in her cheeks. At first their letters had been tentative and skeptical, but now their correspondence, which was carried out in a daily flurry of letters and notes, had suddenly taken a very intimate turn.

I would write more, but I have obligations this evening at an engagement party. Dare I hope my plans might intersect with yours?

Daphne pressed her fingers to her lips. *An engagement party.* Which could only mean

28

he was here. At Tabitha and Preston's ball. Her Mr. Dishforth.

Wear red if your plans take you to such a festivity, and I will find you.

So she'd donned her brand-new red satin gown and come with breathless anticipation of finally putting the mystery of Mr. Dishforth's identity to rest.

Which would also stop Tabitha and Harriet from worrying over the entire situation. When they'd discovered what she'd done — *was* doing, rather — they'd been shocked.

"Daphne! How could you? An advertisement? In the paper?" Tabitha had said, clearly taken aback. "You have no idea who this Dishforth might be."

Harriet had been more to the point. "This bounder could be exactly like that horrible man in Reading last year who advertised for a wife when he already had one in Leeds. Why, he could be one and the same!"

Daphne had cringed, for her Cousin Philomena, who'd been intercepting the letters being sent by Mr. Dishforth and passing them along to Daphne, had made the very same argument. Twice.

"You won't tell Lady Essex, will you?" she'd begged. Lady Essex did not take her role as their chaperone in London lightly. If she caught wind of this illicit correspondence — given the spinster's strict notions of suitable *partis* and proper courtship — Daphne's chance to discover Mr. Dishforth's identity would be lost.

Forever.

But luckily for Daphne, her friends, who were more like sisters to her, had agreed to keep her secret as long as she allowed them to have the final say in Mr. Dishforth's suitability before Daphne did anything rash.

As if she, a proper and respectable Dale, of the Kempton Dales, would do anything less.

Still, Daphne shivered slightly as she recalled that last line from Mr. Dishforth's recent missive. The one she hadn't read aloud to her friends.

I will be the most insensible gentleman in the room. Insensible with desire for you.

Smiling to herself, she stole another glance around the room, hoping beyond hopes to find some way to distinguish the man she sought from the press of handsome lords and gentlemen who filled out the distinguished guest list.

"Daphne, don't look now, but there is someone ahead who is paying you close heed," Tabitha whispered.

Indeed there was. Daphne tried to be subtle as she looked up, well aware that any gentleman in this room could be him.

But immediately she shook her head. "Oh, heavens no!"

"Why not?" Tabitha asked.

"Look at the cut of that coat. It is not Weston," Daphne said. No, complained. For if any of the three of them knew fashion, it was Daphne. "My Mr. Dishforth" — for he was her Dishforth — "would never use that much lace. And look at the overdone falls of that cravat." She shuddered. "Why, with all those wrinkles it looks as if it has been tied by a stevedore."

Tabitha laughed, for she was well used to Daphne's discerning and mostly biting opinions on fashion. "No, no, you are correct," she agreed as the rake sidled past them, casting an appreciative glance at Daphne's décolletage.

Not that such a glance wasn't to be expected. The gown was a bit scandalous and Daphne had ordered it in a moment of passion, wondering what Dishforth would think of her, so elegantly and daringly attired.

Lady Essex came to a stop to gossip with

an old friend, and Harriet drifted back toward them. "Now quickly, who is on your list, Daphne? Let's find your Dishforth."

Daphne plucked the list from her reticule. From the moment she'd learned that Mr. Dishforth was attending Tabitha's engagement ball, the trio had scoured the invitation list for possible suspects.

"Lord Burstow," Tabitha read over her shoulder.

The three of them glanced over at the man and discovered their information hadn't been entirely correct.

"However did we get him so wrong?" Harriet whispered.

"He is well over eighty," Tabitha said, making a *tsk, tsk* sound.

"And the way he shakes, well, he'd never be able to compose a legible note, let alone a letter," Harriet pointed out.

They all agreed and struck him from their list, once again going back to their investigation.

"Tell us again what you do know," Tabitha prodded.

Daphne, with Harriet's help, had assembled a thick dossier on everything she knew about Dishforth. A compilation that would have rivaled the best produced by Harriet's brother, Chaunce, who worked for the Home Office.

"First and foremost, he is a gentleman," Daphne said. "He went to Eton —" a point he had mentioned in passing. "And his handwriting, spelling and composition all speak of a well-educated man."

That fit most of the men in the room.

Daphne continued on. "He lives in London proper. Most likely Mayfair, given the regularity of his posts."

"Or at the very least," Harriet added, "has been in London since the appearance of his advertisement."

"Nor did he quit Town at the end of the Season," Tabitha pointed out.

Daphne suspected he might be a full-time resident of the city. "His letters are all delivered by a footman in a plain livery."

"Sneaky fellow," Harriet said. "Livery would be so helpful."

Oh, yes, Mr. Dishforth was a wily adversary to track down. The address his letters were sent to had turned out to be a rented house situated quite nicely at Cumberland Place — something the trio had discovered while they'd been purportedly walking in the park.

"It is too bad we have yet to meet Lady Taft," Tabitha mused, glancing around the room, referring to the current occupant at that address. They had been able to learn — with the help of Lady Essex's well-thumbed edition of *Debrett's* — that her ladyship had two daughters and no sons.

Sad luck that, for it meant that Dishforth most likely resided elsewhere. Then again, Daphne was using her Great-Aunt Damaris's address for her letters to avoid Lady Essex's discovering the truth.

"If we do not find Dishforth tonight," Harriet said, "then tomorrow we knock on Lady Taft's door and interview her butler as to why her ladyship acts as Dishforth's intermediary."

"Or who her landlord might be," Tabitha suggested.

"No!" Daphne exclaimed, for she held a secret hope for a much more romantic venue for their first meeting. And storming the portals of Lady Taft's rented house did not fit into that scenario.

Of course, all of what Daphne knew about the man assumed that he was being completely honest with her. That his letters were not as fictional as his name.

Certainly she'd been honest with him.

Mostly so. Certainly not her name. For she had replied as Miss Spooner, the name of her first governess. It had seemed the perfect pseudonym at the time. Hadn't her own Miss Spooner eloped one night with a dashing naval captain?

Still, it wasn't only her name that wasn't true. Daphne shifted uncomfortably, for she hadn't been absolutely honest with Mr. Dishforth. She hadn't mentioned her lack of finishing school. Or how she loathed London.

But some things were best not admitted in a letter.

And good heavens, if everyone was completely honest in courtship, no one would ever get married.

Woolgathering as she was, Daphne hadn't noticed that Lady Essex had returned.

"Miss Dale, you appear undone." The old girl studied her with those piercing blue eyes of hers. "Positively flushed, I say. Miss Manx, my vinaigrette—"

"I am quite well," Daphne rushed to reassure her.

"It is most likely the heat in this room," Lady Essex declared. "A ball in July — I never! Do you suppose this Owle Park of Preston's will be so stifling?"

"No, Lady Essex, not in the least," Tabitha assured her. "Owle Park is most delightful. Large, airy rooms and a wonderful view of the river."

"A river? That is promising, as long as it

isn't spoiled with all the heat," she said. "Young ladies are not to their best advantage when they are damp with the heat. Ruins good silk." She shot Daphne a significant glance, for earlier the lady had declared her red silk too hot — which had been Lady Essex's polite way of saying "utterly improper" — and had suggested a more modest muslin for such a warm evening.

But Daphne had been determined. She was going to wear red, and when both Tabitha and Harriet had remarked how pretty and engaging Daphne appeared in her new gown, the old girl had relented.

For if there was one thing Lady Essex wanted for Harriet and Daphne, it was for them to show well. She was taking great delight in claiming full credit for Tabitha's engagement to Preston, and she now had her sights set on a triple play, but only if she gained excellent matches for Daphne and Harriet.

"I hope you will be attentive to the right gentlemen, Daphne Dale. No more of this missish and particular behavior you've displayed of late," Lady Essex said in no uncertain terms and probably loudly enough for half the ballroom to hear. "And bother your lack of dowry. Men tend to ignore those things when a lady is as fetching as you are. If I had but possessed your hair and fine eyes, I would have been a duchess."

"Is that why you turned down the earl, Lady Essex?" Tabitha teased. "You were holding out for a duke?"

"Not all of us can be as lucky as you, Miss Timmons!" the lady declared. "A duchess, indeed! And Preston's bride, no less. The Seldons must be in alt over Preston finally getting married. And to think we all shall be there."

Daphne shuddered as she always did when she heard that name. There was nothing that set a Dale's teeth to rattling like that one single name.

Seldon.

How it was that the rest of English society didn't see them in the same light as every Dale did was beyond Daphne.

"Miss Dale, would you please find a way to smile over Miss Timmons's happiness," Lady Essex chided.

"Oh, just say it," Tabitha told her. "You wish I wasn't marrying a Seldon."

"I know I would never marry thusly," Daphne said diplomatically, because she had resigned herself to the notion that her dearest friend was wildly in love with Preston, and he with her.

If only . . . he wasn't a Seldon.

"Daphne," Lady Essex scolded, "that feud has dragged on for how long? A century?"

Nearly three, actually, but Daphne wasn't going to correct her.

"I would think the Dales and the Seldons could forgive and forget!" Lady Essex said. "It is all very tiresome. Besides, Tabitha is far better off marrying Preston than that odious Barkworth her uncle thought to force her to marry."

Tiresome feud, indeed! Daphne was only glad her mother wasn't here to hear such a thing. More so, that she wasn't here to see her only daughter attending a Seldon ball — against her mother's express wishes.

"Never fear, Lady Essex," Tabitha said, looping her arm into Daphne's and continuing their stroll around the room, "when I am married, Daphne will have no choice but to fall in love with the Seldons as well."

"How right you are," Lady Essex agreed. "Once she has attended the house party at Owle Park and seen your happiness in marriage, all this nonsense between the Seldons and the Dales will be forgotten. For by then, she will have found a husband as well."

Owle Park. Daphne glanced away, the very mention leaving her at odds. The Duke of Preston's country home. The Seldon family seat. A house as marked to the Dales as if it had been an annex to Sodom and Gomorrah.

"You are coming to the house party?" Tabitha pressed. What she really meant to ask was, *Are you coming to my wedding?*

Daphne stilled. Her parents, while delighted that Tabitha was making such an advantageous match, remained dead set against spending a fortnight in enemy territory.

In a Seldon house.

In such *a place,* her mother had said with a deep shudder.

Though they hadn't been so ill-mannered to say it thusly in Tabitha's hearing.

"I have been discussing the matter with my mother," Daphne told them. Discussing it was not quite the right way to describe the situation.

When Daphne had broached the subject, her mother had gone straight to her bed and spent two straight days encamped there, crying and wailing over the request, certain that taking her only daughter, her *unwed* daughter, to a Seldon house party was akin to consigning her to the nearest house of ill-repute.

Everyone knew the Seldons practiced the worst sort of debauchery, but out in the country? Well away from the prying eyes of society, who knew what sort of depravity they would witness, be subjected to . . .

We will all be ruined. Or worse, her mother had wailed and complained to her sympathetic husband.

What exactly "worse" implied, Daphne didn't know. She only hoped that Tabitha wouldn't soon regret her marriage into such a notorious family and especially to its infamous duke. And his equally notorious relations — whom Daphne had managed to avoid meeting thus far.

"Of course she is coming to your wedding," Lady Essex said, handing her fan to Miss Manx. "If your mother can see fit to allow you to attend the engagement ball, surely she will set aside her own prejudices and allow you to attend the duke's house party. Why, half the *ton* is mad for an invitation, and the other half is just plain mad over not getting one. Your mother is no fool, Daphne Dale."

That might be true, Daphne wanted to tell Lady Essex, but her mother was a Dale through and through — both by marriage and birth. Her disdain of the Seldons was born not from a lifetime of distrust but from generations of enmity.

"At least you are here tonight," Tabitha said, smiling. "She didn't forbid you to

40

come to my engagement ball."

Daphne pressed her lips together, for her mother had not exactly given her permission to attend.

Quite the opposite.

Certainly she had meant to keep her promise to her mother when she'd left Kempton and come to London with Tabitha that she would not spend a moment more than was necessary in the company of the Seldons.

Certainly tonight would suffice as "necessary," with the likelihood of meeting Mr. Dishforth so close at hand.

Even if it meant enduring a dance with Preston's uncle, Lord Henry Seldon.

Oh, it was a wretched notion, though.

"You're thinking about Lord Henry, aren't you?" Harriet said, giving her a nudge with her elbow.

"Please do not pull such a face when he comes to collect you," Tabitha added.

"I wasn't thinking of Lord Henry, nor am I pulling a face," Daphne lied, forcing a smile onto her lips.

"You are and you were," Harriet said. Sometimes there was no getting anything past her.

"Traitor," Daphne whispered.

"Not my feud," Harriet replied with a shrug.

Meanwhile, Tabitha stood there, arms crossed and slipper tapping impatiently.

"Oh, bother both of you!" Daphne said. "Yes, I promise I will appear the most gracious and contented lady in the room when I have to dance with *him.*"

"I don't see what has you in such a state," Harriet said. "From what Roxley says, Preston's uncle is a most amiable fellow. A bit of a dullard, really."

"Tsk, tsk," Lady Essex clucked. "Whatever are you doing, Harriet, listening to that rapscallion nephew of mine? His opinions hardly hold any credit. And Miss Timmons is correct, Miss Dale, you cannot go to the supper dance pulling such a face. Just dance with Lord Henry and be done with the matter."

"How many times do I have to explain it?" Daphne huffed with a sigh of exasperation. "He's a Seldon. If my family discovers I have danced with him, supped with him . . ."

She stopped herself right there.

Every time she thought of dancing with Lord Henry, she saw quite clearly every Dale Bible across England being opened and her name being vehemently scratched out.

And in some cases gouged out.

Great-Aunt Damaris would waste no time in ordering a new one in which would be inscribed a reordered family lineage.

One that did not include Daphne.

"Daphne, I do not know what has come over you," Tabitha scolded. "I thought you'd come to like Preston."

"Oh, he seems to have come around," she admitted, "but I think that has more to do with your influence, Tabitha, and nothing to do with his inherent Seldon nature."

"Inherent Seldon nature?" Harriet's nose wrinkled. "Listen to you. You sound like the worst sort of snob."

Daphne took offense. "I am no snob, just well versed in the Seldon family history. Even Lady Essex will tell you that blood runs thick."

Lady Essex pressed her lips together, her brows deeply furrowed, for indeed she did believe thusly, but she could hardly admit such now. Instead, she made every appearance of searching the room for her previous quarry, Lady Jersey.

"Again, I have to ask, why must I dance with him?" Daphne grit her teeth and lips into a tight smile, if only to appear slightly

43

amenable.

"It is Seldon tradition," Tabitha repeated for about the fourth time, "that whoever is standing up with the bride dances at the engagement ball with whoever is standing up with the groom."

Harriet chimed in quickly. "And you will do so because Tabitha is our dearest friend. And we will not have her happiness marred in any way whatsoever." Her words were both a reminder and a bit of a scold.

"You could dance with him," Daphne pointed out. For wasn't Harriet as much Tabitha's friend as Daphne was?

"I told you, I already promised that dance to another," Harriet said, folding her arms across her chest. "And it is only one dance."

"It is not just one dance," Daphne pointed out. There was also the supper arrangements. She had to dine with him. "You both know that my mother would not approve."

"Your mother is in Kempton," Harriet pointed out. "And we are here in London."

"Gracious heavens, Harriet," Lady Essex declared, squinting at a spot across the way. "There is Lady Jersey! And here I thought you'd made it up to keep me from pressing my vinaigrette upon Miss Dale." She made a very pointed glance at the three of them, a warning to say that nothing, nothing, got past her, and then said, "Come now, Harriet, Miss Manx, we shall secure those vouchers for next Season — if they become necessary." Again the sharp glance that spoke quite pointedly to the fact that she would prefer Harriet and Daphne to get on with the business of finding suitable *partis* and stop dragging their heels.

Tabitha sighed. "I am ever so glad to have found Preston. . . . Goodness, speaking of him, there he is being buttonholed by Lady Juniper. Probably over the seating arrangements. Again."

Daphne glanced in that direction and found Tabitha's soon-to-be groom indeed cornered by an elegantly clad lady in mauve — the aforementioned Lady Juniper. Preston's aunt and Lord Henry's sister.

Tabitha glanced back at Daphne, her desires clear.

"Yes, yes, go save him," Daphne told her friend. "I will be safe and sound right here."

"If you find him" — meaning Mr. Dishforth — "bring him to me immediately." Tabitha wagged a finger in warning. "Don't you dare fall in love at first sight and run away with him before I grant my approval."

"Tabitha, I am far too sensible for such a thing. I promise, when I find my Dishforth, I will not run away with him." She crossed her heart for good measure.

Satisfied, Tabitha hurried across the room to make her rescue while Daphne took a moment to study one and all filling the Seldon ballroom. She was probably the first ever Dale to cross into this unholy space.

So far, so good, she mused, considering she'd been here nearly an hour and had yet to be ruined. Or sold to an Eastern harem.

Oh, Tabitha could swear up and down that there was nothing out of the ordinary in the Duke of Preston's residence. Yes, the Red Room was a bit ostentatious, but only what one would expect of a ducal enclave.

And certainly, Daphne had to concede, there were no odd remnants of the Hell Fire Club or some other league dedicated to debauchery laying about in open view.

Those damning bits of evidence, she suspected, were kept in the basement.

She made a cautionary note to herself: Do not go in the cellar.

Then again, considering she'd risked everything by coming here tonight, the cellar might be the least of her worries. Especially if her family found out what she'd done.

But in her defense, she'd come to the ball with the noblest of intentions. Because *he* was going to be here. Her Mr. Dishforth.

And after tonight, theirs would no longer be a love affair of merely letters.

Oh, she knew exactly what was going to happen. She was going to look up and their eyes would meet. He would smile at her. No, grin with delight that he'd discovered her.

In that so-very-magical moment they would know. Just know they had found their perfect partner.

Dishforth would be dressed elegantly, but sensibly. No grand waterfall or scads of lace, just a well-cut Weston coat, his sterling white cravat done in a simple, but precise, Mailcoach, and he'd be handsome. Perhaps even as handsome as Preston.

Oh, she'd concede that much about a Seldon. Preston was a good-looking devil. But all the men in his family were reputed to be too well put together by any measure.

Daphne sighed. Still, if Mr. Dishforth was even half as grand . . .

Then she glanced up, telling herself it was all naught but a ridiculous, fanciful dream.

And it was just that, a silly fancy, until she looked across the ballroom and it happened exactly as she thought it ought.

"Ho, there," the Earl of Roxley called out as Henry tried to slip unobtrusively into the ballroom. He usually arrived promptly at social gatherings, but tonight, Henry was late. And to Preston's engagement ball, no less.

Hen was going to be furious with him.

Nor was the earl making his entrance any less discreet.

"Ah, hello, Roxley," Henry said. He wasn't overly fond of Preston's gadfly friend, for he could never get a full measure of the man. Yet here he was — as if they had been boon companions since they were in short pants. Of course, with Preston about to be married, the earl was probably looking for a new comrade-in-arms, as it were, to join him in his capering about Society.

Henry shuddered at the thought of such foolishness and was about to make his excuses when he did a double take at the earl.

A man about Town.

Good heavens, Roxley was just the man to help him, for the earl was a regular font of knowledge when it came to the *ton,* especially as to the ladies.

More to the point, finding one.

So Henry brightened a bit. It was, after all, Roxley and Preston who had placed that demmed ad in the first place; now Roxley could help him finish the matter. Ironic and fitting.

"How nice to see you, old man," Henry said, trying to smile.

"Of course," the earl replied, slapping Henry on the back as if that was their usual form of greeting. "Have I missed anything?"

"Wouldn't know," Henry told him. "I just arrived."

"You?" Roxley declared, taking a second long look at Henry. "Rather out of character, my good man."

Truer words. There was a lot about Henry that was out of character of late. Because of her. Miss Spooner.

The earl continued. "Preston mentioned you'd been skulking about recently. Asked me to keep an eye on you."

"Me?" Henry shook his head. "I never skulk."

"So I told Preston," Roxley avowed. "But here you are, prowling about the edges of your own ballroom. If I didn't know better, I'd say you were looking for someone."

Oh, good God! Was it that obvious? Still, Henry tried to brazen it out. "Whyever would you say such a thing?"

And then Roxley — who usually appeared half-seas over and made little to no sense — became all too sharp-eyed, rather like that harridan aunt of his, Lady Essex. "Why because you've checked the door three times in as many minutes, and you've surveyed the dance floor twice. Who is she?"

"No one," Henry tried. "You must be —"

"My dear man, don't try and flummox me. I make my living telling bouncers. Who is she?" And then he stood there, poised and ready for Henry's confession.

Henry pressed his lips together, for certainly he hadn't told a living soul what he'd done — answering that letter and engaging in a correspondence with some ridiculously named chit, Miss Spooner. At least Henry hoped that wasn't her real name.

Nor did he want to make a confession to the likes of Roxley. Yet something was different about the earl tonight. Perhaps it was because he hadn't arrived in a cloud of brandy, and the man's eyes were sharp and clear.

"I . . . that is . . ." Henry began.

Roxley held up a hand to stave him off. "Will have to wait. There's my aunt. In full sail with Lady Jersey in her wake." He shuddered. "I'm doomed if that pair catches me." He edged into the alcove behind them, then opened the door to the gardens just wide enough to slip out. "Good luck with your search. I fear I must step out for the time being." He went to leave but then turned around and added, "A word of advice — whatever it is you were about to confide, don't tell your sister." He nodded across the way and then was gone.

Henry glanced in that direction and spied Hen and Preston engaged in what appeared to be a terse conversation. Most likely a continuation of the debate he'd interrupted earlier this morning. Even as it played out once again in his thoughts, he still couldn't believe what his family expected of him.

"Preston, the only solution is to see that he doesn't meet her. Not right away." Then Hen had glanced up and found Henry standing in the doorway and her mouth had snapped shut.

"Who doesn't meet whom?" he'd asked.

Hen cringed, but to her credit, she recovered quickly as she shared a glance with Preston that said all too clearly, *Do not say another word.*

Why was it, when Hen was conspiring, she seemed to forget that they were twins, and, as such, he knew all her tricks? Henry had no doubt exactly who was one of the parties that was to be kept separated.

Him.

But what lady Hen was trying to keep him

from? Usually his sister was dragging all sorts of debutantes and misses and Lady Most-Excellently-Bred past him for his inspection.

Now there was a woman she didn't want him to meet? She would have managed to pique his curiosity if not for his overriding passion to discover the identity of Miss Spooner. Still, it wouldn't do to let Hen think she'd managed to gain the upper hand.

Not this time.

"Come now, Hen, are you saying that some breathtaking Incognito is going to be in our home tonight and you don't want me to take up with her?" Henry winked broadly at Preston.

"Nothing of the sort," Hen informed him.

Henry's gaze narrowed as Preston and Hen exchanged a pair of guilty glances.

"Out with it," he told them, folding his arms across his chest. "You know how I deplore surprises."

"You tell him," Hen ordered Preston. As the oldest (having arrived mere minutes earlier than Henry), she thought it her right to delegate the worst of whatever needed to be done.

"Me?" Preston shook his head, exercising his position as head of the family. "It would be best coming from you."

Hen wasn't so easily cowed, and had her argument at the ready, even as she made her literal escape by crossing the room to the sideboard. "It won't be best any way around it. Besides, she is your responsibility. Certainly not mine."

This was followed by a discerning little sniff, the one Hen made when she discovered herself straying into lowly waters. Having been born the daughter of a duke, his sister was not one to step down from her lofty perch of privilege willingly.

Henry turned back to Preston, brow cocked and waiting for a response.

Steeling his shoulders, Preston came out with it. "One of our guests tonight is a Dale —"

Henry barked out a laugh. A Dale! How utterly preposterous. And he continued to laugh until he realized neither his nephew or sister were joining him. "You're jesting," he'd said to Preston, giving him a slight punch in the arm.

He must be.

Preston sighed. "No." There was nothing in his stony expression that might hint at a late or belabored joke.

Then again, this wasn't something a Seldon would find amusing.

"But she cannot —" Henry began.

"She is —"

"Here? Tonight? Are you certain she's a —" Henry couldn't bring himself to say it. Utter that wretched name.

Hen suffered no such lack of conscience. "A Dale. Yes, that is the point. We are to have a Dale in our midst, and apparently we had best get used to it." This was finished with a wrinkle of her nose and a pointed glance at Preston, which meant the blame lay squarely at his feet.

"What a pile of nonsense," Henry told them. "Turn her away." Never mind that he couldn't believe she'd even dare set foot in this house.

She might be a Dale, but both Seldon and Dale knew better than to mix.

Yet Preston shocked Henry when he said in reply, "I fear it is not that easy. I am slightly indebted to Miss Dale —"

Henry stilled and then shook off such a notion. "Indebted? Now you are joking —"

"No, I'm not —" Preston added. Emphatically. Too much so.

"It is as Preston says," Hen added. "A most unfortunate situation." She turned to Preston. "I am glad Father isn't here to see this day. Inviting a Dale to our house! Unthinkable."

One word stood out in Henry's mind. *Invited?*

"You don't mean —" he began to stammer.

"Yes, I fear we do," Hen replied with the air of one who'd stepped into something while exiting her barouche. "Preston insisted she be invited to the ball tonight and . . ." His sister looked to be attempting to swallow the words lodged in her throat. Instead, they came out in a rush. "And the house party."

"Noooo!" Henry gasped, rounding on the duke. Head of the household be damned, this was beyond the pale. "Preston, you cannot —"

But apparently Preston could. And then the rest of the truth had come tumbling out. She was Tabitha's dearest friend — and here Henry had thought the vicar's daughter quite respectable. Then worse yet, the news that this Dale chit was standing up with Tabitha at the wedding.

"Which means . . ." Preston began, slanting another guilty glance at Hen.

As if she might help him. Instead, Hen made a loud, indignant *"harrumph"* and washed her hands of the entire affair.

"I have to dance with her," Henry had ground out. Oh, there were many things

Henry was not, at least in the eyes of his Seldon relations — a rake of the first order was one of them — but he was an expert on Seldon family history and tradition.

And even now, all these hours later, Henry knew he was bound by honor to do as he was asked.

That didn't mean he had to like it.

Looking across the ballroom at Preston and Hen, Henry frowned. He had no choice but to dance with this Miss Dale. But to his benefit, he still had two hours in which to find his Miss Spooner, her recent words luring him into the crowd.

Do you ever look across a room and wonder if I am there, so close at hand, and yet unseen?

Henry paused and turned to search the faces of the sad little array of leftover wallflowers lining the ballroom walls, but none of them seemed to fit the image he'd fixed in his mind.

Miss Spooner, where the devil are you? he thought as he waded into the crush, her words swirling through his thoughts.

Do you think we will ever truly meet? Do we dare? Mr. Dishforth, I want ever so much to meet you, yet . . . I fear you might be disappointed in me. . . .

Yes, he understood that sentiment. For while their correspondence had been of a sensible nature — favorite books, taste in music, current politics — it had been easy to put off a face-to-face meeting. For all he knew he could be exchanging letters with one of Roxley's maiden aunts . . . or Roxley himself, given the earl's perverse sense of humor.

Yet in the last sennight everything had taken a decidedly different turn.

One that could hardly be deemed sensible.

I laid awake last night and wondered how we might meet.

He hadn't meant those words as anything other than a passing comment, until she'd replied.

I too. In the wee hours before dawn, I found myself drawn to the window, parting the curtains and wondering which roof might be yours. Under which eaves you slept. Where I might find you . . .

The very vision of this intriguing minx

searching him out in the last hours of darkness had left him with more than just a restless night.

He'd written her specifically about his attendance at this ball. That he wanted to see her wearing red (for she'd professed it her favorite color) and that he would find her.

Glancing over at Preston again, buttonholed as he was by Hen, he decided not to rescue his nephew after all. Instead he began his search for Miss Spooner.

If he found her before the supper dance, this wretched Miss Dale could go hang for all he cared. Tradition or no.

All he had to do was hope that Miss Spooner — whatever her real name — had been invited, though it seemed that every member of the *ton* still left in London was crammed into their ballroom.

But all too soon he realized his search might not be as simple as he'd once thought. For as it turned out, it seemed half the ladies in the *ton* had taken his suggestion "to wear red."

Red muslin. Red silk. Even a red velvet. Red in every hue.

"Good God!" he muttered. Then again, how was he to have known red was the most popular color of the Season? That was what came of having a sister who was perpetually in widow's weeds. A man had no sense of fashionable colors save black, gray, and her current choice of mauve.

He continued through the room, nodding in greeting to friends and acquaintances alike, rather amused that not a month ago most everyone in this room had turned their backs on the Seldon family over Preston's antics.

Now the duke's engagement to the very respectable Miss Timmons had erased years of misdeeds in the eyes of Society.

Henry shook his head. He'd never understand the fickle nature of . . .

His thought went unfinished, for in that moment, the crowd parted and his gaze fell on a young lady across the way — a lithesome vision he'd never seen or met, wearing red silk, a mane of pale blonde hair tumbling down to her bare shoulders in a tempting waterfall of curls.

Then this unknown vision turned, as if tugged by his very examination, and looked at him.

Her eyes widened, just a bit, and then she smiled. Ever so slightly, and he felt as if he'd been harpooned, struck down as it were, the haunting lines from one of Miss Spooner's latest missives echoing through his stricken thoughts.

Mr. Dishforth, I am taken aback by your words, your unfettered desires. I know not what to say. But when we meet, I have no doubt I will find the words and the means to express my affection for you.

Henry tried to breathe, but apparently when one met their destiny, one stopped breathing.

Good God! It had to be her. Miss Spooner.

He didn't know how he knew it, but he did. His elusive little minx, with her tart replies and her winsome secrets, was here. Standing across the ballroom.

Practical to a fault, Henry didn't care how the Fates had done this, just that they had, and he wasn't going to let something as ethereal as chance or serendipity steal her away before he could.

Lord Henry, the most respectable and sensible Seldon who ever lived, suddenly found his inner rake and strode across the ballroom.

However, it was one thing to discover one could be rakish, and quite another to pull it off.

For when he came face-to-face with the

lady, he hadn't a single notion of what to say.

What if she wasn't Miss Spooner? Demmed if he was going to make an ass of himself.

Still, what if she was?

There was only one way to find out.

So beyond all propriety, and all good manners, he simply bowed. And when he straightened, he said the only thing that came to mind.

"May I have this dance?"

CHAPTER 2

Your words, Miss Spooner, dare I say it, your confession, have me captivated. I long to find you — though we have promised not to do so until we both desired it thusly. Instead I spend my nights searching for you in the only way I can, prowling every ball, soirée, even the theater, God help me — hoping for a meeting that would instead be in the hands of the Fates, so that I might take your fingers in my grasp and raise them to my lips and whisper for you and your ears only, "At last, my dearest Miss Spooner, we meet."

A letter from Mr. Dishforth
to Miss Spooner

"May I have this dance?"

Daphne nodded — for how could she speak?

She, Miss Daphne Dale, the most practical spinster to have ever come out of Kempton, found herself stricken with the most formidable ailment a lady could suffer.

Love at first sight.

It isn't love, she tried telling herself, for she couldn't even be certain this man was the one she sought.

But no matter, this was the gentleman her heart wanted, her body seemed to recognize without even the most sensible of reasons.

Why, it was a ridiculous notion, and yet . . .

She set her hand on his sleeve, her fingers trembling slightly until they came to rest on the wool of his jacket. There, beneath the smooth fabric and the linen shirt beyond, lay hidden the solid warmth of his muscled arm.

No dandy, no slight fool, this one. The same shiver that had run through her when she'd first read Dishforth's advertisement in the paper once again stole down her spine, like a harbinger, the coursing notes of a spring robin.

Here I am, it sang.

Falling in step beside him, Daphne moved toward the dance floor in a bit of a daze. Whatever was she to say? However could she ask him if he was Dishforth? Never mind that she was accepting his request for

63

a dance without the benefit of a proper introduction.

And when she slanted a glance up at him, this handsome rake with his stone-cut jaw, a tawny mane of golden brown hair, and deep, dark blue eyes that held a potent light, she just knew he must be the man she'd been destined to discover this spellbound night.

For when Daphne looked again, her errant imagination took over, and all she could envision was this rake tipping his head down to steal a kiss from her lips.

In his arms, she'd be unable to resist. His lips would touch hers, and the very thought left her insides coiled with a longing that she'd never experienced.

He, and he alone, would know how to unravel this knot, with his kiss, with his touch . . . his fingers undoing the laces of her chemise . . .

Daphne nearly stumbled. Whatever was wrong with her?

Then the music struck up, and he took her hand in his, while his other wound possessively around her hip. His touch sent shock waves through her, echoing what she'd suspected moments before. . . . This man could put her in knots of desire and then unravel her tangled senses with his touch.

He held her close, and Daphne should have protested . . . might have . . . but tonight seemed so full of promise and adventure that she allowed herself to forget all that was proper and necessary.

What had Dishforth written?

Have you ever wanted to dance where you may?

Yes, she had. So many times. And now she would.

She tucked up her chin, daring anyone to naysay her, and smiled at her partner as he began to swing her through the first notes.

"You are quite daring, Miss . . ." His words trailed off, as if he was waiting for her to give him the introduction he should have sought before asking her to dance.

"Am I?" She certainly wasn't going to let this magical moment end with the horrible discovery that this wasn't her Dishforth. He must be, for whyever else would this particular man have her aquiver?

"Yes, you are quite daring."

Daphne, who had never had a daring moment in her life — up until a few moments ago — felt her insides light up, as if all the candles in London had been illuminated at once.

The man holding her grinned. "Dancing with a man to whom you have not been formally introduced." There was no censure in his words, only a twinkle of mischief in his eyes. "I could be anyone."

"Hardly."

His brows rose, and he made a good effort to appear affronted, yet the light in his eyes said something altogether different. "Hardly? Who am I then?"

"A gentleman," she replied, for certainly there was something very familiar about his features. As if she knew who he was but couldn't quite place the face.

"How can you be so certain?" He tugged her a little closer. Closer than was proper, for now she was up against his muscled body, intimately so.

Stilling her pounding heart, Daphne tipped up her chin as if to say he wasn't going to change her mind. "You wouldn't be here if you weren't."

"You don't know the Seldons very well or you wouldn't say that," he teased.

She laughed — for here was someone who shared her opinions. "You cannot hide who you are," she told him. "Besides, I have the distinct feeling we've met."

"I don't see how."

"What do you mean?"

"I would remember meeting you." His brow furrowed. "Still, I am at a loss as to how we haven't met."

Daphne brightened. Here was an opening to start her queries. "I've been in London most of the Season," she told him, in complete agreement and a bit puzzled as to how this could be. All this time in Town, and how had she not noticed this man? "And you?"

"Yes, of course," he said with a nonchalant shrug, as if the answer was obvious. "I live here in London."

Check number one in the "he-is-Dishforth" column.

"You live here?" she repeated, just to be certain.

"Yes, quite close, in fact." He smiled as if he'd made a joke. Though one that ran right over Daphne's head, for she was too busy putting a check in the "lives-in-Mayfair" column.

Quite honestly, if Daphne hadn't fallen in love with the man in the first moment she'd spied him, he was certainly doing his best to secure her affections.

A house in Mayfair . . . If ever there was a way to a practical girl's heart.

Daphne couldn't help herself. She sighed.

"And you?" he prompted.

"Pardon?" she managed. Apparently this sharing of information was going to be *quid pro quo.* Unfortunately, Daphne had been too busy giving in to the speculation that if he had a house in Mayfair, a country estate was most certainly assured. . . .

Daphne bit her lips together to keep from grinning. Truly, she shouldn't be too obvious.

"Do you live in London?" he repeated.

She shook her head. "No." When he appeared rather crestfallen over this, she added quickly, "As I said before, I came for the Season. I've been here since May."

This brightened his countenance. "And now that the Season is over?"

"I've found reasons to stay."

"Reasons? Might those reasons be regarding a certain gentleman?"

"They may," she said, smiling at him.

The man glanced around the room, making a grand show of searching for someone. "Need I worry he'll arrive and take grave offense to me holding you so close?" As if to prove his point, he moved her even closer.

Oh, good heavens, if Lady Essex found her lorgnette before she found her vinaigrette . . .

"I do believe he is already close at hand," Daphne advised him.

"Indeed?"

"Indeed," she told him.

"Is he a gentleman?"

She nodded.

"Like me?"

She smiled, "Yes, most certainly like you."

"I don't think we ever truly established that I am indeed a gentleman," he reminded her.

"I know you are."

"How so?"

Daphne leaned back a bit and took a critical glance at his ensemble. "A coat reveals everything about a man."

"It does? What does mine reveal?"

"The cut is excellent but not overly fussy. The wool is expensive and well dyed. The buttons are silver, and the diamond in your stickpin is old. An heirloom, I would venture. Tasteful, but not overly large or showy."

"Which means?"

"You are no Dandy whose tastes exceed his income. You prefer sensible and well-made over the latest stare. You have an excellent valet, for your coat is perfectly brushed and your cravat well tied. I have no doubt you're a man of breeding and refinement. A gentleman."

His eyes widened in amusement. "Indeed?"

"Indeed," she replied, her insides quaking. Was she flirting? She'd never flirted before in her life. Coming from a family of extraordinary beauties, the sorts who inspired poetry and duels and heated courtships, Daphne had always considered herself quite ordinary. And far too practical to flirt.

But not when this man looked at her.

"You are a forward minx," he was saying, shaking his head.

"Not in the least," she shot back. Daphne had to wonder if he was testing her. . . . She raced through all the lines she'd memorized from Dishforth's letters.

Which meant nearly every one.

Would Dishforth make such an assessment? More so, would he be inclined to like her being brazen?

She truly didn't need to worry, for this man, this unknown cavalier, leaned down and whispered into her ear, "I find you perfect in every way."

He lingered there, ever-so-close, as if he might be about to kiss her. If she dared turn her head, tip up her lips, would he?

Already his warm breath was sending shivers down her spine, as if his hands had traced a dangerous line down her back and freed her from the confines of her red silk, leaving her naked to his touch.

Naked? Daphne tried to breathe. What was wrong with her? Dishforth was expecting a sensible, respectable partner.

I opened my window tonight and called to you, softly and quietly, certain the breeze would carry my plea to you. And then I waited. For you to come and stand beneath my sill and implore me to follow you. I would, you know. Follow you. Into the night.

Well, mostly sensible and respectable, she conceded. In her own defense, she'd written those lines far too late into a sleepless night, and after one too many comfits.

They swirled and turned about the dance floor. Near the edge of the crowd, beside that invisible line which divided the dancers from the rest of the crush, stood Tabitha and her beloved Preston.

Daphne and her partner whirled past, and in a blur, she watched first Tabitha's mouth fall open, then Preston's.

There wasn't even time to mouth the words, *I think this is him.* But if the expression on Tabitha's face, a mixture of amazement and shock, said anything, Daphne felt

71

assured she'd uncovered the man she'd risked so much to find.

Then her partner echoed her very thoughts. "I have been searching for you, my little Miss Conundrum."

He had?

"You have?" she gasped, then tried desperately to rein in her hammering heart, all the while adding another check to her list.

He'd been looking for her. If that wasn't enough evidence . . .

Daphne, don't get ahead of yourself, that ever-present voice of reason warned.

"Of course," he told her. "That is why we needed no introductions."

None whatsoever, she mused as she looked into his deep blue eyes, which shone with a rich, dangerous desire for her and her alone.

He was all but telling her who he was.

But not quite.

Straightening, she returned his sally. "I rather thought you had avoided propriety in an attempt to circumvent my chaperone."

He peered at the edges of the ballroom. "A regular old dragon, is she? I had rather thought the invitation list a tad more exclusive."

She laughed. "She is well disguised, but don't say I didn't advise you. She's ever so fearsome."

"I stand warned," he said, again scanning the room as if he thought to catch sight of this fierce creature.

"Would she have stopped you from asking me to dance?"

His brow furrowed. "How fearsome are we talking? Is she the fire-breathing sort, or just the more common menacing type, all scales and teeth?"

Daphne giggled. "Oh, most decidedly fire-breathing."

He nodded. "I'll make a note to fetch my suit of armor before you introduce me."

She saw her opportunity and leapt in. "And to whom would I be introducing her?"

Yet her partner was just as wily. He shook his head and refused her even a tidbit. "That is up to you to discover, that is if you haven't guessed."

"That won't do," she told him.

"It won't? You don't want to discover who I am?"

"Oh, yes, I would love to know who you are, but it will be ever so difficult to identify you once my chaperone has burnt you to a crisp."

This made the rogue grin widely. "Then you must endeavor to discover who I am before that unfortunate occurrence, if only to let my family and friends know of my brave demise."

"And again, whom should I inform?"

"I doubt very much I need to tell you," he replied. "I daresay you already know who I am."

"I might," she admitted.

He leaned down and again his lips were right above the curl of her earlobe. "I knew you in an instant."

The Earl of Roxley edged over and filled the space vacated by Daphne.

Harriet glanced over her shoulder. "My lord."

"Miss Hathaway." He smiled at her. "Enjoying your evening?"

Harriet nodded and tamped down the retort that was even now fighting for an airing.

I'd enjoy it far more if you'd ask me to dance, you lowly cur.

Yes, well, unfortunately ladies were not allowed to be honest in their interactions with gentlemen.

Of course that implied she was a lady and Roxley was . . . Well, Roxley was what he was.

He leaned closer. "Twice, Harry?"

She tucked her chin up and ignored the way his words ruffled her spine.

"I'm surprised you noticed, considering you've been absent most of the evening. What is it, my lord, a lack of willing widows to hold your interest?"

Roxley ignored her barb and continued on. "I'll not say it again; he is not fit company."

Of course he was speaking of Fieldgate.

She slanted a glance up at the earl, a look that she hoped did to him what his whispered words did for her. "What a relief."

"How is that?"

"If you are not going to speak of it again, then I shall no longer have to listen to your tiresome lectures." She smiled and turned her attention back to Daphne, who was dancing with a handsome fellow. And given the bright smile and warm light in her eyes, Harriet suspected she had found her Mr. Dishforth.

"Harry, I'm warning you —"

Harriet lost her patience, wrenching her gaze away from Daphne and her mysterious partner and glaring up at the Earl of Roxley. "Then do something about it, my lord."

Shoot the fellow. Tell my brothers. Declare yourself.

All the things she wanted him to do.

But what she got was his silence.

His lips pressed shut, his glance flitted

away and then he leaned against the wall and pretended he hadn't heard her.

Yes, there it was. If he wanted to have a say in her life, he would have to do something.

But he wouldn't.

And for the last three months they had met over and over again and danced on the edge of this very precipice time and time again.

So Harriet danced with Fieldgate and ignored Roxley's complaints.

Daphne whirled past them, and Roxley straightened up.

"Is that Miss Dale?" he asked.

"Yes," Harriet said, turning her gaze back to Daphne to see what had alarmed Roxley so.

"With Lord Henry?" Roxley continued.

"Lord Henry?" Harriet rose up on her tiptoes. "Is that who that is?"

"Yes." Roxley shook his head.

"Lord Henry who?"

Roxley turned his wide-eyed gaze to Harriet. "Lord Henry Seldon. As in Preston's uncle." He let out a low whistle and went back to watching the couple sail about the dance floor.

"Seldon?" Harriet whispered. "Oh, no!"

"Whatever are they doing together?"

"I don't think they know who the other is," Harriet told him, rising again on her tiptoes and looking around for Tabitha.

This was going to be a disaster.

"Their ignorance won't last long." The earl nodded over at his aunt, Lady Essex, who was watching the couple dance with a light of impending doom in her eyes. Then he tipped his head in the other direction at a woman in half-mourning, who appeared in the same state of rare horror. "Lord Henry's sister, Lady Juniper. She looks ready to roast him alive."

"If only they didn't have to discover the truth," Harriet mused. "They look quite enamored."

"Enamored? You can see that from here?" Roxley rose up to his full height to get a better look at the pair.

"Yes, of course I can," Harriet told him. "See how he looks at her."

The earl shrugged. "Might be merely the cut of her gown that has him in such straits." Then he glanced over at Harriet. "Besides, what do you know about a man's regard?"

"If you haven't noticed, I am no longer the little girl you liked to tease. And I am not so young as to not see when a man is looking at a woman just as Lord Henry is looking at Daphne. He is enamored."

Roxley shook his head. "Harry, you made more sense when you asked me to marry you all those years ago."

"I never asked —"

He grinned. "No, I suppose you didn't ask . . . ordered is more like it. You were rather a bossy minx as a child. Still are, all these years later."

"Roxley —" she began, the warning clear.

"You aren't going to lay me low like you did the last time I refused you?"

Harriet crossed her arms over her chest and willed herself not to do just that.

Lay him low.

But that didn't stop her from smiling. "Did I?" she asked, all bright and innocent.

"Yes, you did," he shot back.

"Ah, I remember it now." She tipped her head and smiled again. "But it seems you have a better recall of the events, since you persist in reminding me of it every time we meet."

"Of course I remember it. A most humbling moment, if I must say."

"Oh, isn't that doing it up a bit?" Harriet said. "You were twelve. I daresay you've been made a worse fool of since then — and all on your own, I might add."

"You would. Still, it's demmed embarrassing to be flattened by a little girl."

"Then you shouldn't have refused my of-fer." Harriet smirked, for that thrust was almost as satisfying as her original facer had been.

But the thing about boxing is that one's opponent can always surprise you.

Roxley leaned closer. "Then ask again, Harry."

"I shall not," she vowed, though much to her chagrin she shivered as she held fast to the words that nearly sprang from her lips.

Oh, Roxley, please marry me.

"You know you want to," he said, all smug and all-knowing. Of course it had been that same condescending air that had gotten him into trouble as a twelve-year-old.

"I'd rather flatten you," she told him, crossing her arms over her chest and hold-ing the words inside her heart with a will that matched his.

"I daresay you would."

Oh, yes, she would.

Roxley straightened, tuugging at the edges of his immaculate coat.

He nodded out at Daphne and Lord Henry. "Care to make a wager as to whether or not Miss Dale and Lord Henry's dance comes to something?"

"I hope it does," Harriet said, wishing her words hadn't come out with that wistful note. A leftover result of having had Roxley so close at hand.

He always did this to her — left her insides a tumbled pile of knots. Of desires unfulfilled . . .

Roxley, damn his hide, edged closer to her, as if he knew exactly how he made her feel. "You have a romantic nature, Harry. Who would have suspected as much?"

"Someone should have a chance at happiness."

And she wasn't talking about Daphne and Lord Henry.

He knew her? He claimed to know who she was. . . .

"Indeed?" Daphne managed, breathless and teetering on the edge of something she'd never imagined before. Feeling a bit off kilter to be at this disadvantage.

"Indeed." It wasn't just a word but a pronouncement. A possession. He knew her, and he wanted her.

"How so?" she asked.

"You sparkle, where the rest of the ladies in the room merely shine."

Daphne, who'd never been flirted with in her life, drew back a little. "I do not sparkle."

"Your eyes do," he whispered into her ear.

Did he know what the heat of his breath did to her senses as it teased across her ear, her neck? The way it sent coils of desire through her limbs?

He continued on, "I always knew one day my heart would be stolen by a lady with eyes in just your very shade."

"You mean blue?"

He shook his head, grinning at her practical response.

"Like larkspur or bluebells?" she offered. Truly, she'd always thought the poets and their flowery comparisons were naught but a pile of foolish flummery, but right now, the notion of being compared to anything romantic, like the attributions regularly laid at the feet of her Dale cousins, was just too tempting a notion.

"Not in the least," he said, putting a damper down on her moment of wonder. But not for long. "Your eyes are the shade of intelligence, able to pierce a man's heart with merely a glance. As they have done so to mine."

He thought her intelligent? Daphne would have found the words to say something, blurt out her name, beg to know if he was indeed her Dishforth, but in that starry moment she spied Lady Essex out of the corner of her eye.

And the old girl didn't look amused.

"Oh, dear," she muttered.

"What is it?" he asked, turning his head in that direction.

"No, don't," she said, tugging him in the opposite way and nearly running them into another couple. "Don't look!"

"Whyever not?"

"My chaperone. She doesn't look pleased," Daphne whispered, stealing a cautious glance over his shoulder, then back up at the man holding her. "Who are you?"

"I can assure you, she has nothing to fear from me. Besides, she had best get used to seeing me holding you thusly." And with that he tugged her scandalously close.

"Oh, you mustn't," she told him, even as her body nestled closer to his. To the sturdy wall of his chest, to the steady confines of his arms, against the lean, long muscled length of his thighs.

Oh, yes, you must.

But even as Daphne tried to will herself to maintain a position of decorum, the man holding her suddenly straightened, his gaze locked on the opposite corner of the room.

"Good God, what now?" he muttered.

"Is it my guardian?" she asked, turning to glance in that direction.

He whirled her around, making it impossible to pin-point the source of his dismay. "No, worse. My sister appears to be in a fettle over something."

"Your sister?" Daphne brightened. For here was another check in the "Yes-I-Am-Dishforth" column. For on more than one occasion, Mr. Dishforth had mentioned his sister.

"Yes, my sister. But don't ask for an introduction. I daresay she could out-dragon your chaperone."

"She could try," Daphne told him, knowing all too well what sort of adversary Lady Essex made.

"Whatever has her in such a stew?" he mused.

Daphne couldn't offer an answer, for Lady Essex and Tabitha were bearing down on them through the crowd.

It was then that Daphne realized the set was finishing. The last notes wheezed out, so quickly ending their dance — *their first dance,* she corrected — that Daphne came to a tumbled stop. Instead of a graceful pause, she slammed into his chest, hands splayed out over his waistcoat, leaving her fully and completely aware of every bit of the man who'd claimed her.

Stolen her heart.

No wonder poor Agnes Perts had been

willing to risk madness and marry John Stakes all those years ago. Even if they'd only had one night together.

Well, half a wedding night.

For to be held like this, Daphne discovered, was the most perfect madness. Her fingers curling over the muscles beneath her hand, her hips swaying slightly, seeking desires as yet unknown.

But oh, the promise . . . it left her breathless. She looked up and into his deep, dark blue eyes and found herself trapped with no wish to ever break this spell.

And whoever he was, Dishforth or no, it mattered naught. He could be anyone for all she cared.

Or so she thought as she glanced up at him, ready for this man who had so quickly stolen her heart to steal so much more.

Henry caught the delightful armful of muslin that came tumbling up against him. She'd been as caught unaware that the music was ending as he'd been.

But not so insensible of the woman in his arms.

From the moment he'd spied her across the ballroom, he'd suspected she was Miss Spooner. Who else could she be?

Now, in the course of a dance, she'd given

him all the evidence he needed.

She had been in London for the Season. Demonstrated Miss Spooner's sharp wit and keen intelligence, both in her words and the bright, sharp light in her eyes.

Though definitely a spinster — he gauged her to be nearly, if not so, at her majority — she wasn't so far up on the shelf to make one wonder why it was a beauty like her wasn't married.

He drew a deep breath and thought about her letters, her words. Tart, opinionated, strong-willed.

Those traits in a lady were enough to scare off most gentlemen.

Not him.

Gathering her closer, Henry glanced up to gauge which of the matrons coming closer might be her fire-breathing chaperone.

And how much time he had left to risk.

"There is much that needs to be said between us," he told her, gazing down into those bright blue eyes. He'd always imagined her thusly — fair and lithe.

"Is there?" she asked, smiling slightly. "I rather thought we'd said all that was necessary."

"True enough," he agreed, his blood running thick and hot with her pressed up against him.

Good God, whoever was this minx? Not that it mattered, for whoever she was, she left him insensible with desire. For a thousand utterly irrational reasons, he wanted her, would have her.

Henry could sense the others closing in around them — Hen coming up from behind, Preston and Tabitha moving toward them.

And somewhere, her scaly, fearsome chaperone was beating a path to them.

To make matters worse, here they were, still in the middle of the dance floor. The music had ended, the other couples had scattered throughout the room, and while the crowd had exhaled and moved in to fill up some of the empty space, there was still a wide circle around them.

Leaving a daunting number of curious gazes fixed on them. Enough to give the London gossips a full dish of cat lap on the morrow.

Suddenly the fact that half the *ton* was watching him — Lord Henry Seldon — and not his errant nephew was a bit unnerving.

That is, until he looked into her starry gaze.

And the light there said she thought him the most rakish, perfectly ruinous gentleman alive.

"I should find your chaperone," he managed. Not that he meant it.

"Must you?" she whispered, even as she nestled a bit closer. "What if —"

Her question hung there for a moment, sending this tremor of warning through him.

It isn't going to be this easy . . .

Yet here she was, in his arms, and everything about her perfect . . . and perfectly willing.

I am yours, her lips, parted, moist and pert, seemed to whisper.

Never in Henry's life had he ever been the rake, never been Seldon enough to manage even a trifler's reputation. Having lived all his life in Preston's shadow — as the spare heir, as the sensible Seldon (for in his family that was a worse crime than a scandalous reputation) — he'd never fit in.

Even Hen had all her notorious marriages to maintain her stake in the family tree.

Not that Henry had ever truly minded. He'd never wanted to be the duke, had thought all the scandals more bothersome than essential, and Hen's penchant for dashing off to the altar? He nearly shuddered.

No, Lord Henry Seldon had been quite content to be rather normal.

Boring, even.

Yet not when this slip of muslin looked up at him with that very dangerous light of desire. Something sparked inside him that he'd never thought he'd inherited.

Now, damning every bit of propriety he possessed as he glanced at her lips, he had only one thought.

To kiss her.

Claim her. Then he'd carry her off to Gretna Green if he must, if only to have her always.

Fire-breathing dragon of a chaperone notwithstanding.

Then it happened all at once.

Later he would realize that the warning note in her voice before that "what if" had been the Fates' way of saying, *Be careful what you wish for.*

Or rather, *Who you desire.*

"Daphne!"

"Henry!"

"My goodness, unhand her, you bounder!"

That remark, he assumed, came from the chaperone.

As they broke away from each other, Henry swore that something fragile and most rare broke, as if snipped away before it ever had a chance to grow, to fully wind around them, bind them together.

Ridiculous notion, he thought immediately, glancing at her, and yet she was already lost, looking one way and then the other as the barrage of questions and outrage continued.

"What the devil are you doing?" Preston demanded, glancing first at Henry and then at the lady, his expression bordering on horror.

"Daphne, whatever are you about?"

But it was her chaperone who shocked him as she rounded Hen and pushed her way to the forefront. "Daphne Dale! I will have answers! You were supposed to dance with Lord Henry for the supper dance. Now that will make two dances, and there will be talk." The hawk-eyed matron shot him a stony glance that said she blamed him. Entirely. "As if there won't be already."

Not that Henry was really listening, for he'd rather come to an abrupt halt over one thing.

Her name.

Daphne Dale. His gaze shot back to her. Oh, good God, no!

"Lord Henry?" his once perfect miss was managing to say. Her words came spitting out as if she'd found a pit in a cherry tart.

A very sour one. "As in Lord Henry *Seldon*?"

She backed up, her hands brushing down her arms, sweeping away whatever vestiges of him might be still lurking about, her nose wrinkled in dismay.

Not that he felt much better. What the hell sort of spell had she cast to leave him so blind? How had he not seen it? The disingenuous beauty, the deceptively fair and frail features . . . of course she was a Dale.

"Henry, explain yourself," Hen was saying as she tugged him off the floor and into the folds of the crush of guests.

"Daphne, come with me at once," Lady Essex said at exactly the same moment, carting off her charge with an air of indignation that suggested Daphne had missed the last tumbrel to her execution.

She cast one last glance at him before the crowd enveloped her, and the furious, scornful shame in her eyes tore at Henry's heart.

It was as if she was suddenly the dragon to be feared.

As if she had the right to be angry.

Well, he'd like to remind her that this was *his* home. A Seldon home. Whatever was she, a Dale, doing here in the first place?

If he didn't know better, he'd swear she'd

gone out of her way to beguile him on purpose. Lured him to her side, teased him into believing . . . tipping her smile just so he might . . . might . . .

Good God! He'd nearly kissed her. Right in front of the entire *ton.*

Meanwhile, Hen was the epitome of fury and composure, smiling to their guests while her fingernails dug into his sleeve. "What were you thinking? How could you not know who she was? I only hope Aunt Zillah didn't notice you out there making a cake of yourself with one of them. Why, it would be —"

Ruinous. Yes, he knew.

"How was I supposed to know?" he said in his own defense. Better that than confessing the truth: that he'd thought Daphne Dale was someone else. Against his better judgment, he looked over his shoulder toward her. Not that there was any sight of of the minx, save the whisk of her red skirt as she was pulled from the room by her chaperone.

Henry shook that vision from his thoughts. Shook her from his heart, even as it clamored for him to fetch her back. Demand answers of her.

Gain that kiss . . .

No. None of that. There would be no kissing that minx. Vixen. Witch.

That starry-eyed miss who'd stolen his heart.

No, he reminded himself, "she" had a name.

He only wished she hadn't *that* one.

CHAPTER 3

Do you think it is possible that we have met? Have seen each other and not known who the other truly was? Could such a thing be possible, for I think I would know you, sir, anywhere.

Found in a letter from
Miss Spooner to Mr. Dishforth

"The supper dance is next," Harriet said happily, rocking on the heels of her slippers as she scanned the crowded dance floor.

"Don't remind me," Daphne groaned. If anything, she was becoming desperate. For every tick of the clock that left her search unresolved, every dance that left her lacking an answer, she remained under the threat of having to dance with *him.*

Lord Henry Seldon.

She still wasn't quite past her shock that the man she'd thought — nay, would have sworn — must be Mr. Dishforth was none other than Preston's uncle.

His *Seldon* uncle.

Harriet hardly batted an eye. "Have you considered, Daphne, that Lord Henry might be your Mr. Dishforth?"

Daphne tried to speak, but the words choked in her throat.

Her Mr. Dishforth a Seldon? Wasn't it bad enough she'd considered, even been willing, to let that ne'er-do-well kiss her?

"No, he cannot be," she told her friend. "I am sure of it."

"How unfortunate." Harriet shrugged and continued scanning the crowd around them.

Unfortunate? Daphne would call it a blessing.

Nor did she want to recall the delicious sense of wonder that had unfurled inside her limbs as Lord Henry had held her, gazed down upon her. The hard strength of his chest beneath her hands, the steady drum of his heart.

Daphne shuddered. This was exactly the madness she had hoped to escape when she'd started corresponding with Mr. Dishforth.

A sensible courtship, that's what she'd sought.

Which certainly meant not letting some dratted man leave her at sixes and sevens, what with his rakish charms and lies.

No, somewhere in this room was a sensible, reliable, perfectly amiable man, and she meant to find him. But when she looked up, all she spied was a portly fellow heading in her direction, and she edged behind a large red velvet curtain to escape his wandering gaze.

Harriet glanced over her shoulder. "What are you doing back there?"

Daphne sighed and stepped out of its protective shadow. "Hiding from Lord Middlecott."

"Whyever won't you dance with him?" Harriet asked, propping herself up on her tiptoes and taking a measure of the baron, who was prowling the crowd for his next choice.

"There isn't a prayer that he is Dishforth," Daphne replied, maintaining a position well out of the man's line of sight.

"Is that because he isn't as handsome as Lord Henry?" Harriet teased.

Daphne cringed, for there was some truth in that statement. However, it wouldn't do to give an ounce of credit to Harriet's impertinent opinions. "No. It is because he's only just come to London. Which rules him out as a possible candidate."

"And you thought Mr. Ives, that rather

rapscallion Mr. Trewick, and that poor vicar
—"

"Mr. Niniham," Daphne supplied.

"Yes, Mr. Niniham, might be Dishforth?"
Harriet echoed. "You will dance with him, a
vicar with barely enough income to keep
you in hats, and two fellows who aren't
worth a snap, just in hopes that one of them
might be *him*."

"Yes," Daphne told her, though she'd
been quite relieved the poor vicar had
turned out to be in no way, shape or form
her Dishforth.

Oh, she'd been so confident when she'd
strolled into the ball earlier. So sure she'd
find her dearest, genuine Mr. Dishforth.

But that had been before . . . before *he'd*
ruined everything.

Now every time she tried to recall her list
of parameters for identifying Mr. Dishforth,
the only thing that rose up in her mind was
the image of an arrogant, tall, and excep-
tionally handsome man — one with leonine
features, a tawny shock of hair, a piercing
gaze and a sure stance.

Daphne's brow furrowed. For what she
envisioned was the very image of Lord
Henry.

Lord Henry, indeed!

Her dismay must have been all too obvious, for here was Harriet studying her. "Good heavens, Daphne, whatever has your petticoat in a knot?"

Daphne straightened and pressed her lips into a line. "Harriet Hathaway! What a singularly vulgar thing to say!"

Harriet hardly appeared chastened. Quite the opposite. "Oh, don't start parroting Lady Essex to me. I know you," she shot back, arms crossed over her chest. "So what is it?"

"Him!" Daphne said, nodding across the way.

Harriet glanced up. "Lord Henry?"

"Yes, of course, Lord Henry! The man is wretched. I deplore him."

"Didn't look that way earlier," Harriet said. "The two of you looked quite cozy."

"He tricked me," Daphne avowed. Though she knew that was only partially true. She'd tricked herself. "He lulled me with his charm."

Harriet's eyes widened, a slight smile tugging at her lips. "So what you are saying is that Lord Henry is charming . . ."

Daphne found herself being herded toward a confession she wasn't going to make.

Ever.

"He can't help it," she said, mostly in her own defense. "Look at him over there now, flirting with Miss . . . Miss . . ."

Oh, bother, it was impossible to think of the girl's name when her gaze kept straying to Lord Henry's bright smile. And never mind that she knew exactly where he was. She was willing to concede that the Seldon males were overly handsome and eye catching.

Most likely every woman in the room knew exactly where that Lothario stood.

It was their curse, *their charm.* Daphne cringed at that last thought. Lord Henry Seldon was too charming.

"That's Miss Lantham," Harriet supplied.

"Yes, well, poor Miss Lantham. For there she is getting her hopes up that he's taken notice of her, and he won't. For in about two minutes he will be on to his next conquest."

Harriet cocked her head to one side as she looked at Daphne. "And you would know this because . . . ?"

"Because that is exactly what he did to me. At least what he attempted to do," she said. "I can hear him right now. 'Oh, Miss Lantham, I would remember meeting you — how is it I have yet to have the pleasure of your acquaintance?' "

Harriet laughed at her imitation.

But Daphne wasn't done; she nodded at

the pair across the way, and when Miss Lantham began to chatter, she filled in the words for Harriet.

Miss Lantham: *"Lord Henry, I avow I've always wanted to meet you."*

"And I you, Miss Lantham," Daphne added, with a deep rakish voice.

Miss Lantham: *"I have a very large dowry I would love to show you."*

Lord Henry: *"I possess a great fondness for large dowries and ladies who delight in sharing."*

"Daphne, you are being wicked," Harriet complained as she laughed. "Do stop, or you'll have Lady Essex over here to discover why we are having fun and not out dancing with the Lord Middlecotts of the world." Having composed herself, Harriet dared not look over at Lord Henry, but in his defense she said, "I hardly think he is as bad as all that."

"He is an unpardonable rake."

Harriet looked sideways at her. "Daphne Dale, I've never known you to be prone to such dramatics. Lord Henry is no rake. By all accounts, he's considered quite dull."

Against her better judgment, Daphne glanced across the room where he still stood charming Miss Lantham.

Dull? Hardly.

Not for all the silver in the King's treasury would she admit the treacherous thoughts that had sprung to mind when Lord Henry raised his heart-stopping gaze and turned ever-so-slightly to look at her.

As if he'd known she'd been watching him.

Wrenching her gaze away, Daphne feigned indifference. Her insides were a little more difficult to tame, for her heart raced, and something wild and tempting uncoiled inside her, teasing her to look again.

Well, she wouldn't.

"Whoever is your partner for the supper dance?" Daphne asked her friend, hoping this would change the subject.

"Oh, just Fieldgate," Harriet said, casting the name aside with a breezy wave of her hand.

"Fieldgate!" Daphne made a *tsk, tsk.* "But you've danced with him twice tonight. I hope Lady Essex hasn't noticed. She's already vexed that I'll be dancing with Lord Henry twice, but another round with Fieldgate? Harriet!" She wagged her finger at her friend. "She'll complain to Roxley."

"I know," Harriet said, a slight grin tipping her lips.

"You deplore the viscount, Harriet."

"I do indeed."

"And Roxley avows he is a scandalous,

scurrilous fellow."

"Precisely his appeal," Harriet said, once again smiling like a well-pleased cat.

Daphne shook her head. "You'll push Roxley too far."

"Not far enough," Harriet said, glancing around for the earl, who was even now across the room chatting with a tall, well-dressed widow. The sight did nothing but bring a glower to Harriet's face. "And what about you? Are you ready to risk England's welfare and dance with Lord Henry a second time, or shall I stand warned that such a happening will most likely bring down the realm?"

"You shouldn't tease," Daphne told her, though when Harriet said it, it did sound rather ridiculous. "The Seldons are an egregious lot. Any Dale would tell you so."

"Harrumph!" Harriet snorted. "However did this ridiculous feud get started?"

"I haven't the least notion," Daphne replied. She actually did know, but it was a very private matter. And not spoken of. Not by Dale or Seldon.

At least not in public.

"Daphne! There you are," Tabitha said, having appeared out of the crush. "My goodness, you've been difficult to catch up with. If I didn't know better, I would swear

101

you've been hiding behind that curtain —
which can only mean you haven't found
him."

Oh, but I have, her errant and newfound
desires cried out. *He's right over there.*

Daphne fixed her gaze on Tabitha and did
not indulge in another glance across the
ballroom.

Tabitha, taking her friend's silence and
distraction all wrong, linked her arm in
Daphne's and began towing her along the
edge of the ballroom. Harriet brought up
the rear.

While it may appear a sisterly and af-
fectionate move, Daphne was not fooled.
Her friends were herding her toward her
next partner. The last dance on her card.
The one she'd been ordered to fill with a
solitary name — and rebelliously she'd left
blank.

The supper dance with Lord Henry.

"Whyever must I do this?" Daphne complained.

Heaving a sigh, Tabitha launched right in.
It seemed she was quite prepared for this
last protest. "Because it is Seldon family
tradition. A sign that both families are in
agreement over the marriage."

"Rather ironic, don't you think?" Harriet

mused. "The two of you leading the way —"

"Yes, yes, very amusing," Daphne shot back. "If Preston can scoff at the Kempton curse, whyever is he holding fast to this tradition?"

Tabitha smiled. "It is considered a blessing, a sign of good luck on the marriage. Don't you want that for me?"

Daphne clenched her teeth. Oh, bother. Tabitha would have to say something like that.

And now it seemed Daphne would have no choice. Even when she'd left the supper dance blank on her card solely because she had held out every last hope that when she discovered the identity of Mr. Dishforth he would take Lord Henry's spot.

Nay, demand it.

Miss Dale, it is my privilege, my right to claim this dance. Save you from this knavish Seldon.

At least that was how she'd imagined it.

Unfortunately for Daphne, all she had to show for an evening of accepting one dance after another was a pair of sore feet. She'd quite worn out her new slippers.

She took a moment to look down and mourn their loss. Daphne did so love a pretty pair of shoes.

"Oh, dear!" Tabitha exclaimed. "It appears Lady Essex is over there badgering Lady Juniper again. Most likely about the buntings for the wedding ball. Do you mind? I must extract her from Lady Essex's clutches before Preston intervenes — you all know what happened the last time he crossed swords with Lady Essex."

They all smirked. For the lady liked to remind one and all that the Duke of Preston had once kissed her.

Though not in that way, she was wont to add.

"No, I don't mind in the least," Daphne said, glancing over toward the garden doors.

It would hardly be her fault if she missed her dance with Lord Henry because she needed a breath of fresh air. . . .

"Don't you dare, Daphne Dale," Tabitha warned, having taken two steps and then turned back.

"Dare what?" Daphne exclaimed, wrenching her gaze away from the lure that the open doors offered, the deep shadows of night enveloping the roses and graveled paths.

"Go hide in the garden to escape your dance with Lord Henry. I will not have this evening ruined by your lack of attendance at the supper dance. You must be there to lead it off with Lord Henry — it means everything to Preston. Besides, if you refuse, there will be talk."

"I think their first dance together covered that issue quite nicely," Harriet said with a well-meaning smirk.

Daphne's gaze flew up. "I hardly think . . ."

But the look that passed between Tabitha and Harriet said it all. Oh, goodness, it hadn't looked as bad as all that, had it?

Apparently so.

But gossip? Daphne stifled a groan, for the last thing she needed was *on dit* about her attendance at this ball bandied about London. A Seldon ball. She was still a bit in horror that someone might let drop to Great-Aunt Damaris that they'd spied her niece dancing the night away.

With Lord Henry Seldon.

She might be able to explain away her attendance — for Tabitha's sake and all. But a second dance? Unforgivable.

"Daphne? Do you promise?" Tabitha said, giving her a little shake to rattle her out of her reverie.

Harriet crossed her arms over her chest and shot her pointed stare. "I'll see that she makes it over to his lordship," she said, more to Daphne than Tabitha.

"Traitor," Daphne whispered.

"Again, not my feud," Harriet replied with a shrug.

Meanwhile, Tabitha stood there, arms crossed and slipper tapping impatiently.

"Oh, bother both of you!" Daphne said. "Yes, I promise."

"I do not know what has come over you," Harriet scolded as she had to tug Daphne back into their ambling pace around the room. "I thought you'd come to like Preston . . ."

But Daphne wasn't really listening. She was taking one last scan of the crowd around them for any man who might possibly be Mr. Dishforth. Much to her chagrin she found her wandering led her right back to one man. Lord Henry.

Ah, yes, there he was, having moved on from his previous conquest of Miss Lantham to charming a pair of impressionable and utterly innocent twins.

"Harrumph." Daphne shook her head as the girls took turns fluttering their fans and batting their lashes in hopes that Lord Henry could discern one from the other.

Not that he would probably care.

"Which of you is Lucinda and which is Lydia? No, don't tell me. I prefer to guess."

"Giggle."

"Giggle."

"Hmm. I believe it could take a man an entire lifetime to discern between the two of you."

"You aren't making up the conversation again, are you?" Harriet asked over Daphne's shoulder.

Daphne blushed a little. "No."

"Yes, you are," Harriet contradicted.

"I might be," Daphne conceded as the dialogue continued unabated inside her head.

"Ah, the problem with twins is that I find it hardly fair that I must choose."

"Must you, Lord Henry?"

"Oh, aye. Must you choose?"

"I don't even want to know what is going on in that diabolical mind of yours," Harriet avowed, shaking her head.

Daphne glanced around the room. "I would like to know where their mother might be, for she's left them utterly unguarded."

"Perhaps they are not here in London with their mother."

"Then a companion? Or a maiden aunt?" Daphne turned to her friend. "You have no idea what he is capable of."

"And you do?" Harriet asked, as if she would like Daphne to enlighten her.

Which she was not going to do. Notching

up her chin, Daphne turned her gaze back at the identical pair, look-alikes right down to their matching gowns and gloves. Oh, bother, there must be, at the very least, a guardian nearby, perhaps one with a penchant for pistols.

For if Lord Henry was called out, then sadly she would have to forgo the pleasure of partnering him for the supper dance.

"He hardly seems as bad as you would like me to believe," Harriet said, nudging into Daphne's reverie, one that had Lord Henry face down on a grassy meadow, with the retort of a pistol still echoing through the early morning shadows.

Daphne turned to argue but just as quickly bit back her remarks. For if she was to point out that Lord Henry Seldon had spent the entire evening prowling about the ballroom, dancing with every woman he could charm — which was any bit of muslin his lustful gaze fell upon — Harriet would only too gleefully point out the obvious.

Whyever were you watching him if you know he isn't the man you want . . . ? Unless . . .

Unless nothing!

And luckily for her, now that she knew exactly who he was, she was quite immune to his charms.

Unlike that silly pair of girls who stood

there, gazing up at that handsome, roguish son of a duke with stars in their eyes.

"Oh, Lord Henry, say that again . . ."

"Oh, yes, Lord Henry, tell us that witty story over and over . . ."

Daphne would never be so misled, not again. Not by him.

"Brace yourself if you are determined to be stubborn about all this," Harriet warned. "Here he comes."

"Why must I dance with him?"

"Because Tabitha is our dearest friend. And we will not have her happiness marred in any way whatsoever," Harriet said as both a reminder and a bit of scold. "And it is only one dance."

Yet for some reason, that thought — one dance — made Daphne's heart beat a little faster, her insides quake and tighten.

Ridiculous, truly. Quite insensible.

"Oh, don't look like that," Harriet was saying. "It scrunches up your brow in the most unbecoming way — you look older than Miss Fielding."

Daphne immediately smiled, for Tabitha's sake and so as to avoid any further unflattering comparisons, especially since Miss Fielding was three years her senior. It would never do to be thought of as that ancient and still unmarried.

Even if she was from Kempton.

"Do make the best of it," Harriet continued. "Show these Seldons that the Dales possess all the manners and grace you keep declaring is the difference between your families. Besides, you know not who else might be watching you."

Daphne stilled. But of course! Dishforth! Perhaps he was here still — or had been delayed and was even now set to arrive. Oh, yes, he'd been delayed. That was it. Nor would he find her scowling like an old maid, even when faced with Lord Henry's glowering visage, which made him resemble some stone-carved mythical beast.

Albeit a rather handsome one.

Daphne buttoned down her resolve, as well as the odd rabble of passions he evoked. One dance. That was all.

And the supper . . .

Clearly Lord Henry found this situation as distasteful as she did, for he did nothing to hide the disdain in his glance.

So why was it, as she stared into his stormy gaze, that all she could think of was a line from one of Dishforth's early letters?

We are all bound by our lot, by tradition, are we not, Miss Spooner? But don't you long to be free of it all? Free to choose? Free to dance where you may?

Dance where you may . . . She would dance with Lord Henry — under duress — but very soon she would find Mr. Dishforth, and they would dance where they may and no one would naysay her choice ever again.

"Miss Hathaway," Lord Henry said, bowing low to Harriet. As he rose, he sent a scant glance at Daphne. "Miss Dale."

The greeting came out in a tone one might use upon finding a beggar curled up on one's front step.

Ignoring his complete lack of manners — truly, what did she expect? — Daphne pasted a bright smile on her face, the most regal tilt to her chin and sent a slight flutter of lashes at Lord Henry, if only to disarm him.

She was, after all, a Dale.

"Lord Henry," she replied with a mixture of bright charm and an equal dose of disdain.

Harriet cringed, having recognized the same polite, yet terse, tones Daphne took when she locked horns with Miss Fielding over some point of order in their weekly meetings at the Society for the Temperance and Improvement of Kempton.

"I believe we are expected to begin this dance," he said, glancing over his shoulder at the parties forming. "But, if you . . ."

Daphne shot a glance at Harriet to see if she had heard the implication behind Lord Henry's statement.

If you refuse me, Miss Dale, it will not break my heart.

Unfortunately for Daphne, Harriet stood stonily at her side, an ever-present reminder, her conscience, per se, that she was not allowed to give in to what she wanted more than anything.

To avoid this dance.

"Apparently it is a Seldon tradition," she said, reminding him that this was not a situation of her making. It was a slippery slope, a moral equivocation.

She didn't dare glance over at Harriet, but she heard all too clearly her snort of derision.

No, Harriet wasn't buying her dissembling in the least.

"Yes, tradition," he agreed, sounding no more pleased about it than she. "Are we not all bound by it?"

Daphne stilled. Good heavens, he almost sounded like . . .

Then Lord Henry did her the favor of proving himself utterly unworthy of the title of Dishforth, dispelling any further comparisons.

"Well, shall we get this over with?" he asked as the music started.

Get this over with? Daphne wrenched herself out of her woolgathering and let the full impact of his words come to rest. *Get this over with?* Why, she'd never been so insulted. He should be so lucky to be able to dance with a Dale.

And she would show him just how lucky he was.

Holding Miss Daphne Dale, Henry quickly surmised, was akin to holding a rosebush.

One with a generous portion of thorns that had previously been hidden beneath her beauty.

If only she wasn't so demmed pretty. That was the real problem, Henry told himself. Lithe and fair, Miss Dale's gown — some tempting creation of silk that clung to her every curve and left her looking like one of the Three Graces come to life — was enough to make any man mad with desire.

And how ironic that it was red. He nearly shuddered. Now every time he tried to envision his Miss Spooner, all that came to mind was this tempting chit.

Worse, the supper dance had them hedged

in — for nearly everyone was dancing. Even Roxley's old aunt, Lady Essex, was being squired about the floor by some aging gallant.

So here he was, forced to dance with an utterly desirable lady, one who would most likely leave him pricked and bleeding by the time the musicians got out the last note.

Certainly the expression on her face suggested that such a fate would not be beyond her means.

He tried smiling in the face of his predicament.

"You needn't feign any affection you do not feel, Lord Henry. Not for my sake," the blunt little snip told him.

So much for putting her at ease in hopes she might rein back the worst of her thorns.

"Affection is hardly the word I would use," he replied, not caring that he was being an ass. Besides, he had a few choice things he could say about her behavior earlier.

"Then may I be frank?" she asked.

As if she wasn't planning on being so anyway. He just nodded, for it was a rather ridiculous question.

"Lord Henry, you know who I am, and I know *what* you are —"

114

What he was? Of all the rude, presumptuous —

"Well, yes, I am under no delusions that you, as a Seldon, cannot help your predilection to vice and debauchery —"

Him? He was the most sensible Seldon who had ever borne the name, yet, holding this impossible miss, this woman who had more charms than a lady deserved, he had the insensible urge to take up Preston's newly retired rakish mantle and prove Miss Dale right.

That he was truly a Seldon. A rake of the first order. Might send her scurrying back to Kennels . . . No, Kempling . . . Oh, bother, whatever that village of spinsters she'd come from. Well, they could have her back with his blessing.

Perhaps he could take up the matter in Parliament and see about having a wall constructed around the village so no more of its ladies descended upon London.

"— so let us make the best of this situation, and when this evening is over, we can go our separate ways," she said, as if that settled everything neatly and properly.

As if she'd been the paragon of virtue and he the devil incarnate.

Then, to make things worse — if one could imagine this entire tangle going much further down the well — he detected what could only have been a shudder running through her limbs.

Whatever did she have to shudder about?

He straightened slightly, ruffled by her implications, for they pricked at his pride. He'd spent his entire life being tarred with the Seldon brush — that he must be a rake, that he must be inclined to vice, and he had thought he'd risen above such implications.

"Miss Dale, believe me when I say I am merely trying to make the best of this situation," he told her, smiling this time for the sake of Aunt Zillah Seldon, who looked ready to storm the dance floor and pluck Henry from these ghastly straits.

Good heavens, she was in her eighties and could barely cross the room without her cane, let alone manage to weave and wind her way through an entire floor full of swaying couples.

Then he glanced down and realized he hardly appeared the willing gentleman — he had Miss Dale out nearly at arm's reach and was dancing with the measured grace of a twelve-year-old lad.

While Miss Dale, despite his clod-footed handling, moved with the grace of a lady born.

A lady, indeed. He'd show one and all

what sort of *ladies* the Dales produced.

As they swung around the next turn, Henry hitched her up close. Scandalously close.

Miss Dale's mouth opened in a wide moue, and her brows? They now arched like a pair of cats on points.

Well, she did assume him to be quite the rake. And he hated to disappoint a lady.

Ignoring her outraged expression or her attempt to step from his grasp, he said, "I know that Miss Timmons is ever so disappointed that you will not be attending the wedding." He smiled as if the very idea was certainly not breaking his heart.

"Yes, well, we both know that such a thing is impossible," she replied, not at all looking at him.

"Quite so, which makes your attendance this evening ever so surprising."

"It was a last-minute decision," she told him. "For Tabitha's sake." Then she glanced away, as if she could wish herself halfway to Scotland rather than be here. In his arms.

Henry rather liked her dismay. Served her right. Coming here and pretending to be . . . Well, never mind that. . . . After all, he'd been only her first in a long string of conquests this evening. He'd seen how she'd taken great delight in accepting nearly every gentleman who'd asked her to dance and then summarily dismissing them after.

Not that he'd been watching her. Not in the least.

"Ahem," she coughed.

He glanced down at her and wished he hadn't. For here she was, all blue eyes and fair complexion. And how hadn't he noticed before that delicate spray of freckles on her nose? So very kissable and so tempting.

"Yes, Miss Dale?" he managed.

"Must you hold me so close?"

He leaned a bit to one side and studied his own stance for a second. "Am I?"

"Yes," she complained, followed by a stony glance that said what the lady refused to say in public. *Let me go, you great pondering ape.*

He smiled, tucked her ever so slightly closer, and hoped she knew exactly what he meant.

Not in your life.

While he thought she might make a scene — which would definitely guarantee her a one-way mail coach ticket back to wherever it was she came from, ruin dripping from her hem — at that moment, as she surveyed the crowd around them, she fluttered those long lashes of hers as if she'd suddenly remembered something very important.

And instead of sending him off with a flea in his ear, she did quite the opposite.

As they swept along the edge of the dance floor, the lady's entire demeanor changed.

She smiled brightly as her gaze swept from one man to the next — all the way down the line.

And her captivated audience gazed back in appreciation.

Henry's brow furrowed. Normally it didn't bother him to have the *ton*'s rakes and Corinthians eyeing the armful he'd gained for a dance. It left him able to smile over the lady's shoulder with a look that said all too clearly:

Mine if I want her. . . .

Yet when he looked down at this minx, this lady who was causing more than one jaw to drop in admiration, he realized two things:

Firstly, Miss Daphne Dale had every asset necessary to leave a man aching with desire.

And secondly, she would never be his.

Much to his chagrin, that notion — that she was well out of his reach — left him a bit off kilter.

Not that he wanted Miss Daphne Dale. Certainly he wasn't mad like Lord Norton Seldon, the last known member of his family foolish enough to cross the firmly established lines between the Seldon and Dale clans, but there was just no arguing that she was a tempting piece of muslin.

He saw her as he had earlier, looking up at him with eyes shining — alight all for him. He rather liked the way she tipped her head as she glanced just over her shoulder, letting the waterfall of curls pinned atop her head fall all the way over her bare shoulder . . . a teasing sort of glance that made a man consider how she would look being tossed atop his bed . . . those glorious blonde tresses freed and falling all about her shoulders . . . over her naked . . .

Henry wrenched his gaze away, righting his errant thoughts as quickly as he could.

How he'd ever thought her to be his sensible Miss Spooner, he didn't know.

Not that Miss Dale seemed to care what her come-hither glances and bright smile might do to a man. In fact, if he didn't know better, he might think she was posing for another.

Another?

He glanced about the room and tried to gauge who this fribble might be. Not that her previous partners could be considered. A beggary lot of dull sticks for the most part. Ives. Niniham. Trewick. And that dull vicar Hen had insisted be invited.

120

Yet she'd turned down Middlecott, considered to be the catch of the Season. Odd choice that, given that the man was as rich as Midas and rumored to be ready to set up his nursery.

So if she wasn't looking for a title and fortune, then what was she after?

He cast one more glance down at her rosebud lips, pursed and ready to be kissed. Henry didn't know what came over him, but he hitched her up a little closer.

Thorns and all.

Oh, and how those thorns bristled. Her brows arched higher, and in tones dripping with censure, she said, "I'll have you know, I am nearly engaged, and you are being entirely impudent by insisting on holding me thusly."

Of all the self-important, pompous Dale presumption. As if he was holding her solely for his benefit.

Which he wasn't. Not in the least.

"Nearly engaged?" he wondered aloud. "Whatever does that mean? Could it be the man can't make up his mind, or you haven't let him get a word in edgewise?"

Her bright smile tightened, and her lashes stopped that delectable flutter. And he should have realized the next thrust from this slight English rose would be straight into his gut.

"What would you know of love, Lord Henry?" she returned. "Being a Seldon and all. From what I hear, a Seldon's forte is to ravage and run."

She would bring Montgomery Seldon into all this.

Rather than acknowledge her sniping comment — good heavens, that incident had happened during the reign of Charles the Second, but leave it to a Dale to carry it about — he asked, "And is this paragon of yours here tonight? I wouldn't mind knowing whose wrath I should be fearing."

Her brow furrowed, her lips pressed together.

What? No answer? Henry knew a mystery when he held one, and Miss Dale's "engagement" had all the hallmarks of a most intriguing one.

"Well, is he here or not?" he pressed. "It is a simple question."

"Ours is not a simple engagement," she shot back.

Of course it wouldn't be. The fellow must be stark raving mad. Perhaps they had refused to let the poor blighter out of Bedlam to attend this evening's festivities.

For certainly if Henry had known what was in store for himself, he would have gladly exchanged places with the fool.

"Not that I would expect you to have any understanding of such a relationship," she was saying.

"A relationship?" he mused aloud and immediately wished he hadn't.

"Yes, I thought the word would be foreign to you," she shot back. "And having seen you at work this evening —"

"At work?" What the devil did that mean?

Oh, she told him.

"Lord Henry, I have not been blind to the fact that you've flirted and flitted your way through every innocent in the room this evening —"

He hoped she didn't count herself amongst them. There was nothing innocent about a lady who wore such a gown.

"— but it is refreshing to discover that I am not the only one immune to your rakish charms —"

She thought he had charms? Never mind that. More to the point, she'd been watching him.

Just as you were watching her . . .

"— true love," she continued, "a meeting of minds and hearts is not found in such trivial pursuits as flirting and dancing."

"You don't like to dance?" he said. And to prove his point, he held her closer and swung her tightly through the crowd.

Something fluttered in her eyes, a mischievous light. She loved to dance. Just as he did.

Yet she was also just as stubborn. "There are not so many opportunities at home for such festivities."

"Ah, yes, in . . . where is it you are from?"

"Kempton," she told him, her chin notching up slightly.

He nodded. "Preston mentioned the place. Something about all the ladies being cursed. Should I worry for my safety?"

"Only if we were to marry," she shot back, and was it him, or did her gleeful note imply she'd rather like to see him married to a Kempton bride?

And end up just like all the rest of the village grooms, spending their honeymoons napping in the graveyard.

"That will never happen, I assure you, Miss Dale," he replied.

She sighed, with a bit of resignation. "The curse is naught but a myth."

"Yes, well, I hope so," he told her. "For the sake of your unknown gentleman and my nephew. I would hate to have Preston turn up his toes with a fire iron sticking out of his chest —"

There was a flash of annoyance in her eyes.

So she didn't like her hometown curse being bandied about or mocked. Yet it was so perfect an opening . . .

"— leaving me in the demmed uncomfortable position of having to inherit," he finished.

"You wouldn't want the dukedom?" This surprised her, as it did most people.

"Heavens, no," he shuddered. "I have other plans for my future."

She didn't ask what those were, and he didn't elaborate.

He could imagine the delight she'd take in laughing at his desires for a comfortable, sensible life in the country, well away from London and the *ton.*

Speaking of his future, he glanced down at the tempting beauty in his arms and knew that *sensible* would never be a word attributed to her.

"Now whatever is the matter?" she asked, once again wiggling in his arms to gain some distance between them.

If only she knew what that did to a man — her breasts pressed against him, her hips moving to and fro.

Or perhaps she did.

"Your gown," he said.

She glanced down at it. "It is the first stare of fashion. Why, there are three other ladies wearing very similar dresses — though I should complain to the modiste, for she said it was the only one like it in London."

Henry laughed at her consternation. "You needn't worry; you far outshine them. I doubt any man in the room noticed the others."

Then he realized what he'd said. Confessed, really.

Her eyes widened and then narrowed as she regarded him warily. "If you are trying to charm me yet again —"

"I wasn't trying to charm you before —"

"You weren't? Whatever was all that you were doing?"

"A grave error," he told her, growing a bit annoyed — mostly at himself.

Every moment spent arguing and bear-baiting with Miss Dale was just more time lost and with it his hopes of finding Miss Spooner before he was forced to hie off to the country for Preston's house party and wedding.

It would be a good month before he returned to London, and where Miss Spooner would be then or if she would still be in Town, he knew not.

He had to find her tonight.

"A grave error?" Miss Dale repeated. "Dancing with me was a grave error?"

If he had been paying more attention, he might have heard the warning note in her voice. It was one that Norton Seldon had ignored and one Montgomery Seldon should have heeded . . . and saved ensuing generations of Seldons from wagonloads of grief.

"I'll have you know, you should be honored," she told him, thorns coming through the silk. "I haven't trod on your foot, like that simpering Miss Rigglesford did — twice — and I've managed to hold up my end of this . . . this . . . *conversation,* unlike that tongue-tied nitwit Lady Honoria, who you seemed to find so amusing. No one finds her amusing, Lord Henry. No one. You, sir, have been lucky beyond measure to dance with me. Twice, I might note."

"Lucky?" he sputtered. "As if this is some boon to me? To be cast with one of your lot?"

"One. Of. My. Lot?" she bit out.

"Yes, lot. Dales! Stubborn, prideful, braggarts," he told her.

"Seldons!" she shot back. "I am too much a lady to give your gaggle of relations their due."

"Are you sure about that?"

If ever there was a question a man wished he could take back, that was one.

127

Her eyes darkened with fury. No simpering gel like Miss Rigglesford, or rigidly dull chit like Lady Honoria, or like any other Bath-educated, perfectly mannered London lady.

Kempton-born, and Dale to the bone, Miss Daphne Dale wrenched herself out of his arms and went to leave him mid-dance, mid-turn, as everyone was executing a complicated step.

It was uncalled for, it was a cut direct. It was a ruinous move on her part.

But her timing couldn't have been more perfect. For the ruin, it turned out, was to be all his.

For when she gave him the heave-ho, he wasn't prepared for her flight and found himself floundering forward, his feet tangled and hung up.

He would have sworn he'd been tripped. Or perhaps he'd just trod upon her silken hem.

Not that the *how* mattered, for all of sudden, one moment she was there, and the next she was casting him off and he was falling, his hands flailing out to catch hold of something to keep him from toppling headfirst into the tight knots of dancers.

And find something he did. His outstretched hands came right into a lady.

More to the point, the very front of a lady's gown.

Lady Essex's, to be exact.

After that, the evening was naught but a blur for Lord Henry.

Though it all came into sharp focus when the Earl of Roxley came ambling into the upper reaches of Preston's town house a few hours before dawn and found the duke and Lord Henry on their second decanter. Or maybe their third.

Well, perhaps not sharp focus, for Henry was well into his cups. Then again, he had much to forget.

Miss Dale, for one thing. And then that entire mishap with Lady Essex. And the hullabaloo the lady had raised. And the peal Hen had rung over him for his disgraceful behavior.

Accosting a spinster! Why, it was beneath even a Seldon.

Henry tried to forget, but it was nearly impossible. For along with Hen's scolding chorus still ringing in his ears were Lady Essex's shrill screams.

Oh, good God! He'd all but mauled Lady Essex Marshom. The room began to spin around him.

And now added to that whirl was Lord Roxley. Or rather two earls. It was rather difficult to discern when one was this top-heavy.

"Ah, Roxley," Preston called out, waving him toward the sideboard. "How fares your aunt?"

The earl shuddered at the question, as if he wished the entire evening could be dismissed so easily. Teetering over to the sideboard, he poured himself a measure. Then, eyeing it, he tipped the bottle of brandy yet again until the glass was almost full.

Preston shot the nearly overflowing glass a second look. "As bad as all that?"

"Worse," Roxley avowed. "She's demanding satisfaction. Wants me to name my seconds. My aunt seems to think that only my shooting Lord Henry on some grassy field will 'regain her lost honor.' "

"Did you point out that I am the better shot?" Henry said.

Roxley nodded. "Unfortunately, she's quite willing to take the risk."

CHAPTER 4

Have you not wondered why the Fates considered bringing us together? I fear at times they could also have a change of heart and pull us apart. Promise me we shall endeavor to avoid their snare, my dearest Miss Spooner.

> Found in a letter from
> Mr. Dishforth to Miss Spooner

Daphne was doing her best to forget the previous evening. Not that Lady Essex was likely to let her.

Where the lady should have been scandalized and overwrought, Roxley's aunt was instead in alt. The tempest had put her in high demand with every gossip in London, and there was nothing Lady Essex liked more than being the center of attention.

Of course, the Dale clan might applaud Daphne's scandalous part, saying it was only what a Seldon deserved, but then the inevitable questions and recriminations would come.

What the devil were you doing there in the first place?

And whatever would she say?

That she'd been corresponding with an unknown gentleman, who, she had discovered, was going to be attending the ball and she couldn't help herself, she'd gone into the Seldon lair if only to discover her Prince Charming?

Yes, that would be about as well received as the gossip that was surely going to land on Aunt Damaris's doorstep before nightfall — that her niece was a dreadful harridan.

Caused the scene of the Season! some catty relation would come to tell the dowager of the Dale clan.

Though Daphne couldn't imagine who would be brave (or foolish enough) to drop such a cannonball into Aunt Damaris's gilt salon.

Which, in itself, might buy Daphne a few days.

Perhaps even enough time to discover Mr. Dishforth's true identity before she would be shunted off to Kempton, never to be allowed back in London again.

Which was the last thing Daphne wanted or needed. So she'd made her excuses to

Lady Essex and fled Roxley's town house, claiming an obligation to visit her Great-Aunt Damaris one more time before she returned to Kempton.

If anything, she hoped beyond hope that when she got there, she would find a note, a few lines, anything from Mr. Dishforth.

Oh, Mr. Dishforth! Whatever was she going to tell him?

Daphne hurried through the streets of Mayfair, her ever-faithful maid, Pansy, trotting along behind her, her cheeks pink with the heat and the pace.

Not that she could hope to outrun the gossip, but perhaps she could head it off before it turned into an insurmountable storm.

Daphne paused at a corner to wait for traffic and considered how she might explain her wretched behavior to him.

To Mr. Dishforth.

Well, there were only two words to justify what she'd done.

Lord Henry.

Ruinous, awful man! Daphne could not think of him without shivering. No, it wasn't shivering, more like shuddering, she corrected herself.

For shivering had an entirely different intimation.

And not one she wanted to share with Lord Henry. Not in the least.

"Horrible man," she muttered as she started across the street.

"My pardon, miss," a stuffy-looking fellow huffed in reply as he hurried past.

Daphne blushed a bit, especially when Pansy looked over at her with that puzzled, censorious expression she seemed to be wearing much of late.

And feeling a bit of remorse, Daphne knew eventually she would have to admit the truth. Lord Henry couldn't be blamed entirely. For one thing, she had tripped him.

Not deliberately. Not intentionally.

Well, maybe a little.

Daphne drew herself up straight. Annoying, wretched man. Why, he was the very epitome of all that was wrong with the Seldons and had been wrong for centuries. Too handsome. Too full of his own worth. And much too handsome.

Oh, dear, she'd listed that twice. Well, it needed to be, she told herself as she rounded the corner onto Christopher Street.

No man should look that sinful; it made him capable of driving a perfectly sensible lady to make a complete cake of herself in a crowded ballroom.

Well, never again, she vowed. Never again

would she be swayed by a tall, handsome, overly charming man. Not whatsoever.

And as if the Fates meant to test her resolve, she looked up and came to a complete halt. For there, hurrying down the steps at the far end of the block — on Great-Aunt Damaris's steps, to be exact — was a tall figure in an elegantly cut jacket of navy superfine, a tall beaver hat atop his head, the brim obscuring his face.

Just the sort to make a lady's heart do that odd double thump if only to ensure she'd taken notice.

Yes, Daphne had noticed.

This striking Corinthian paused for a moment at the end of the steps, adjusted his hat to a jaunty tilt and then continued in the opposite direction with a determined stride, his walking stick tapping out his hurried pace.

For some reason, her boots found themselves planted to the sidewalk. She could only stand there on the curb, not even caring that she was gaping like a veritable country rube.

Out of the blue, she found herself thinking it was exactly how Lord Henry might stroll along — the very same self-assured line of his shoulders, the steady stride, as if he owned the very sidewalk.

Goodness! How ridiculous, she told herself, a bit piqued that at every turn he seemed to invade her thoughts.

Now she was even seeing him where he shouldn't be.

Besides, she told herself, studying this object of curiosity, he didn't possess Lord Henry's arrogance. No, certainly not. This man held himself with an air of composure and aplomb that would captivate any woman.

So, whatever was such a man doing visiting Great-Aunt Damaris? Firstly, he was too tall and too dark to be a Dale.

"Who are you?" she whispered, not even realizing she had said the words aloud until this mysterious stranger, who was about to round the corner at the end of the block, paused, as if he had heard her question.

Then, to her shock, he turned slightly and glanced over his shoulder.

Oh, my! Oh, goodness . . . Her thoughts jangled together as his features slowly came into view, until —

"Do you mind?" a voice blared at her as a large fellow shouldered past her. Tall and wide enough, it turned out, to completely blot out her view. "Don't you have anything better to do?" the old gentleman scolded. "Foolish chits! The same every year! Filling

136

the streets like a baffled horde of dimwits."
He huffed and continued down the block,
and by the time she could see past him, the
corner where the gentleman had stood was
empty.

He was gone.

"Bother," she muttered. Then, realizing
there was only one way to find out who he
might be, she hurried down the street to
Number 18 and had barely gained the first
step when the door flew open.

"Oh, heavens, Daphne!" Cousin Philomena Dale exclaimed. "You just missed
him."

"Him?"

Her cousin didn't answer immediately,
having come down the steps only to herd
Daphne and Pansy back up them with great
haste. "Come in, come in," she said.

Pansy, now that her mistress was in good
hands, scurried off for the kitchens, while
Phi plucked off Daphne's hat and pelisse,
chattering on in a blur of "ooh's" and
"ah's," which were punctuated by a chorus
of "him" and "shocking" and "ever-so-
thrilling's."

By the time they had gotten seated at the
window bench, Daphne was dizzy, but it
seemed so was Cousin Phi, who wasn't
more than a few years older than Daphne

but, having failed at finding a husband, now resided at Number 18 as Great-Aunt Damaris's companion.

A fate no one would envy her for, though Phi seemed to consider it a boon and took the old lady's complaints and tirades in patient stride and with nary a lament.

Better still, Phi had only been too willing to help Daphne with her correspondence with Mr. Dishforth — for no one had a more romantic little soul than Cousin Philomena.

"If only you had arrived just a few seconds earlier, why, you would have met *him*," Phi was saying, looking once again up and down the street, clearly disappointed to find the block empty.

"The man? The elegant one I saw coming down the steps?" Daphne asked.

"Yes, yes, him!" Phi exclaimed, her eyes wide.

"Who was he?" Daphne asked, for it wasn't all that unusual for Great-Aunt Damaris to have callers. She was a bit of a legend in the Dale clan, and cousins and relations from all corners came to beseech her for advice.

Which the lady doled out with a heavy hand and no lack of sarcasm.

All good advice comes with a price, she was

wont to say.

Great-Aunt Damaris had the effect of leaving one feeling scalded, but better for the experience.

"Who was that, she asks! It was *him*!" Phi said, as if that explained everything.

Daphne paused for a second and then felt a tremor of horror. Great-Aunt Damaris hadn't made good on her threat of ordering the Right Honorable Mr. Matheus Dale to Town on some flimsy pretense.

She'd brought it up each time Daphne had visited, claiming the two of them would suit and had a matchmaker's fire over the notion.

Advice Great-Aunt Damaris could offer in plentitude; matchmaking, however, was not her forte.

"Not Matheus," Daphne whispered to Phi, who was once again looking out the window.

Phi shook her head. "No, not Cousin Matheus," she said, making a moue of displeasure. Obviously this push of Great-Aunt Damaris's to find a Dale cousin to marry the esteemed Mr. Matheus Dale had been tried before.

"So if it wasn't Matheus, then who?" Daphne prodded, settling into the window seat, where she and Phi always had their hasty "coze" before Great-Aunt Damaris realized, with the uncanny sense of a cat, that someone was in the house and would have Daphne summoned upstairs.

Phi's expression brightened. *"Him!"* Then she lowered her voice, which was a good idea, for any Dale worth their salt knew — or at least swore — that Great-Aunt Damaris could hear conversations uttered all the way up north in the family's Scottish hunting box. "Oh, bother, Daphne. You truly have to ask?" Still, Phi leaned closer and whispered in a voice barely audible, "It was your Mr. D."

Daphne's mouth fell open. That man . . . that elegant, self-assured, handsome man (at least he'd seemed handsome at that distance) was her Mr. Dishforth?

"No!" Daphne said, glancing back at the door, restraining herself from jumping up and setting off after him.

After all, it was her lack of restraint that had plunked her right down in the scandal broth.

"That was him?" she managed.

"Yes," Phi said. "Oh, I'm ever so glad you did see him." Her cousin's face wore a dreamy sort of expression, as if she'd just witnessed a miracle.

Daphne reached over and caught Philomena by the arm — if only to steady her own racing nerves. "Are you certain? The man wearing the superfine jacket and the tall beaver hat was Mr. Dishforth?"

Phi nodded. "Yes, and he carried a silver-tipped walking stick. A most elegant one. Oh, Daphne, he is so handsome, and he must be ever-so-rich."

Rich? Visions of a large rambling country house once again danced through Daphne's thoughts.

Handsome was one thing, but Daphne wasn't so impractical as to not realize the benefits of falling in love with a wealthy man. "And he came here?"

"Yes. And I met him," Phi declared. "He came to the door, and luckily for you, I was downstairs checking the salver for Herself."

"Herself" being how most everyone in the family referred to Great-Aunt Damaris.

"He came here?" Daphne's heart raced. "Where was Croston?" Great-Aunt Damaris's butler would certainly have had a thing or two to say to his mistress about an unknown gentleman calling.

"Downstairs," Phi said, her eyes wide with the luck of it. "Checking on tea. And luckily I caught the door before *he* pulled the bell."

He. Mr. Dishforth. Daphne still couldn't get over it, the image of the handsome stranger now burnt into her memory. "What did he want?"

Another foolish question, for Daphne knew all too well what Mr. Dishforth desired. Wanted. Had written so boldly.

My darling Miss Spooner, we cannot ignore that some day, some day very soon, we shall have to meet. I long for the moment when I first set eyes on you.

And Phi wasn't so innocent not to see right through the feigned query, the desires behind it. "You, of course. He came calling to meet you." She sat back and eyed her cousin with a look that was nothing less than incredulous.

Daphne opened her mouth to say something, yet nothing came out.

"Yes. Shocking, indeed," the practical Phi said, echoing Daphne's feelings precisely. Then Phi's brows furrowed and her voice lowered noticeably — for Croston wasn't above tattling. "You said he wouldn't come calling."

"He promised not to," Daphne shot back. But then again, after last night . . . *Oh, no!*

What if, somehow, he'd discovered that she, Miss Daphne Dale, was his "dearest girl" after all and had been horrified by the scene she'd created.

Perhaps he'd come to call — in person, no less — to wash his hands of their entire affair.

Daphne shivered. It was no affair. Their letters were just that, letters.

An affair implied something so much more . . . well, personal. Physical.

And why was it that when that word *physical* came teasing through her thoughts, she recalled Lord Henry's arms around her?

Lord Henry holding her close . . . Lord Henry about to . . .

Dear heavens, had Dishforth seen her with that Seldon scoundrel? Seen her lingering in his embrace? However would she explain that she'd thought that rakish devil was him?

"Don't look so despairing, Daphne," Phi told her. "I know you are jumping to every conclusion but the correct one."

The correct one? The note in Phi's words lent some hope to the entire scenario.

"Tell me everything," Daphne said. *"Everything."*

Phi basked in her moment of importance. "He is the handsomest man I have ever seen. Far more handsome than Cousin Crispin."

More handsome than even Crispin, Viscount Dale? Was such a thing possible?

Then Daphne noticed something important. "Phi?"

"Yes?" Her cousin winked owlishly at her.

"Where are your spectacles?"

Phi touched her nose and, realizing she didn't have them on, plucked them out of her apron pocket and quickly slid them on. She blinked a few times, then glanced at Daphne as if seeing her anew.

Which she was.

"My, don't you look lovely today!" Phi enthused. Then she must have seen Daphne's speculative expression. "I know what you are thinking, and yes, even without my spectacles, I can discern a truly handsome man."

"If you say so —"

"I do," she insisted, ruffling a bit. "Now where was I? Oh, yes, sorting out the salver — just in case one of *his* letters had been mixed in — when I heard someone coming up the steps. His boots made such an impressive sound — so strong a stride. Immediately I knew."

Daphne nodded in understanding, thinking of the steady, purposeful beat of Lord Henry's heels as he'd danced with her.

Though the comparison was not to be taken very seriously. Lord Henry could hardly hold a candle to Mr. Dishforth.

Especially now that she'd seen him. Well, sort of.

"I got the door just as he was about to ring the bell," Phi said.

"Thank goodness!" Daphne exclaimed, having been curious as to how Great-Aunt Damaris had not been awakened.

"Yes, precisely," Phi agreed. "Then he bowed — most elegantly —"

"Of course," Daphne agreed, envisioning him doffing his top hat and making his bow.

"And then he introduced himself," she said. "And asked to see you. Well, not you, but Miss Spooner. 'I am here to see Miss Spooner,' he said and in such a commanding voice, Daphne." Phi sighed. "Yet he was ever-so-considerate at the same time. I nearly swooned."

"Truly?" For Phi was the most practical of all the practical Dales.

Phi spoke in hushed tones of awe. "His voice is like the finest plum cake. Rich and deep and ever so tempting."

Daphne sat back and eyed her cousin. She had the sudden suspicion that Phi had taken to reading those ridiculous *Miss Darby* novels that Harriet swore were the most romantic stories ever written.

"Yes, well," Phi continued when she realized Daphne was gaping at her, "suffice it

145

to say your Mr. D is handsome, mannerly and speaks in the most heavenly tones."

"But what did he want?"

"Well, you!" Phi said. "He wanted to see you. He was most insistent."

Daphne let out the breath she'd been holding. "Whatever did you tell him?"

"That you were not here. That you had gone out of Town." Phi sighed. "Which is nearly the truth, for you are still planning on returning to Kempton when the others go to *that house party,* are you not?"

"That house party" being the one at Owle Park.

Phi was a Dale down to her bones in her dismay.

"Yes," Daphne told her. "I am returning to Kempton. On the afternoon coach, the day after next."

Phi nodded approvingly, for she'd been on hand when Great-Aunt Damaris had lectured for a full hour on the follies and ruin of associating with the Seldons, including instructing Daphne on how to extract herself from her friendship with Miss Timmons now that Tabitha was to be so tainted in her marriage to one.

"You might want to find some way to delay your return," Phi said, "for he would not take 'no' for an answer when I said you

146

were unavailable."

Daphne shivered. Handsome *and* forceful. "Whatever did you do?"

"Gave him the letter you asked me to post yesterday. And wished him a good day." She shrugged. "I had to get him out of the foyer as quickly as possible before Herself caught wind of him . . . or worse, Croston came up from the kitchen."

Daphne's mouth dropped open at Phi's presence of mind.

"Thankfully, he was enough of a gentleman to take no for an answer," Phi continued, smoothing out her skirt.

Unlike how Lord Henry might have handled the matter, Daphne found herself thinking, imagining him in the foyer and not leaving well enough alone, bursting into the parlor and giving Great-Aunt Damaris the fright of her life.

Before the old girl gave him one of her own.

Goodness, Daphne thought with a shake, would that man never stop invading her thoughts?

Thank goodness Mr. Dishforth was nothing like him.

Save the handsome part.

A handsome Mr. Dishforth, a wealthy Mr. Dishforth. This gave Daphne some smug satisfaction.

Oh, if only she'd been able to find him last night at the Duke of Preston's ball before she'd met with such humiliating disgrace. Then she could have danced with him and snubbed the Seldons, one and all, from the sanctuary of Mr. Dishforth's solid and steady embrace.

And she would never have had to suffer through Lord Henry's insufferable opinions.

"Are you sure about that?" she could almost hear him mock.

"Oh!" Phi burst out, straightening up and digging into the pocket of her apron. Her actions jolted Daphne out of her woolgathering. "But that wasn't all."

There was more?

"He asked me to pass this on to you." Phi held it close for a moment longer. "He said he had written it just in case he could not meet you in person."

Of course he had. Mr. Dishforth was not only a romantic; he was also a practical man who always had the forethought to plan ahead.

It was one of a myriad of reasons Daphne was already in love with him.

Phi continued to hold onto the letter, slowly presenting it, as if she was offering a chest of jewels, ones she truly didn't want to surrender.

Daphne barely breathed as she reached out for the now familiar thick paper, the address written in that strong, bold hand she liked to trace with her finger.

Miss Spooner
18, Christopher Street
Mayfair, London

"Open it!" Phi said, as breathless as Daphne.

"Yes, yes," she said, suddenly reluctant to do so. Especially in front of Phi.

What would she say if it held more of those bold, passionate sentiments that his letter of the other day had carried?

But the news, she soon discovered, was of a different sort.

My Dearest Miss Spooner, I have put off telling you this, and I had hoped to tell you all this last night — may I say this frankly, shall we forget last night? —

Forgotten, Daphne would have told him most emphatically.

I am under an obligation to leave Town and will not be back for a month, perhaps longer. I am to attend a house party in the country. Please, after last night, if you are still inclined to correspond with me, address your letters to Owle Park, Kent, . . .

Daphne sucked in a deep breath. Owle Park?

"What is it?" Cousin Phi begged, squinting down at the page.

"He is going to the wedding."

"He is going to be married?" Her cousin straightened, clearly outraged and ready to pitch herself head-long into a plot to exact revenge.

Daphne reached over and pulled her back. "No, no! He is *going* to a wedding." Then, remembering where she was, she lowered her voice. "Tabitha's wedding."

Phi paused as she made all the connections, then her mouth fell open. "Dear heavens!"

"Whatever am I to do? Mother has forbidden me from going. Aunt Damaris said she will have me removed from the family annals if I even consider attending."

Cousin Phi straightened. Then she said something that shocked Daphne right down to her boots. "There is nothing left for you to do but go. You must."

150

Had Cousin Phi just urged her to go to the wedding? A Seldon wedding?

"How do I dare?" Daphne whispered.

Phi leaned closer. "If you had met Mr. Dishforth, as I have, you wouldn't even ask that question."

CHAPTER 5

Does it matter what is on the outside,
when there is a heart beating inside, a
soul full of longing as it waits to discover
its own grand passion?

> Found in a letter from
> Mr. Dishforth to Miss Spooner

Owle Park, Surrey
A sennight later

Henry came down the main staircase early
for breakfast. More to the point, before the
rest of the guests arose. Benley would have
the newly arrived London papers at the
ready for him, and he could eat his kippers
and eggs in peace.

Which would be difficult to find — solitude, that is — in the next fortnight, what
with Owle Park overflowing with guests.
Carriages had arrived in a steady stream the
previous day and late into the night, the
last-minute guests hurrying to stake their

claim at what gossip columns were calling "the only house party of note."

Thus, no one had turned down an invitation.

Especially since the engagement ball — specifically the supper dance, or that "scandalous dance," as it had been dubbed. One night and he'd become an object of speculation and gossip, a position for which he was ill-fitted.

That had always been Preston's role in the family, not Henry's. But now that the duke had become utterly respectable with his engagement to Miss Timmons, the curious had pinned their avid interest on Henry.

And all because of *her.* That demmed Miss Dale.

Not that Henry didn't feel a bit of guilt over all of it. Perhaps he had provoked her.

Ever-so-slightly.

Still, there was no arguing that her flight from the dance floor had put a crown on his head as the most Seldon of all Seldons, and there was just no removing it — not if the invitations that had suddenly flooded the foyer at Harley Street afterward were any indication. Offers, vouchers and notes from ladies — married and otherwise. All addressed to Lord Henry Seldon.

Not Preston. Not Hen. Him.

Apparently a man who inspired such wrath from a lady demanded a closer inspection.

Overnight, he'd become London's most notorious rake.

Henry didn't realize it, but he'd come to a stop on the landing, and one of the newly hired maids scuttled past him, all wide-eyed and curious, as if she were viewing such a creature for the first time.

A rake!

He felt like calling after her, "Boo!"

Instead, he shook his head and continued down the steps, the house around him silent at this unfashionable hour, save for the whispered movements of the servants as they readied the house for the day's activities.

Which he would have to take part in — at Hen and Preston's insistence. Penance, he supposed, for the debacle at the engagement ball.

He would have been much happier to have stayed in Town and come down the day before the wedding and then return to London immediately after, but no, now that he'd become the latest *on dit* there had been naught to do but flee to the country.

At least Owle Park afforded him one benefit. No Miss Dale.

That thought should have been some comfort to him, but it only showed that the impudent, wretched bit of muslin continued to invade his thoughts. What with her winsome smiles, her bright eyes and fair features.

And her utterly vexing behavior.

Well, thankfully, her stubborn pride and Dale bloodlines had kept her from accepting the invitation to Preston's wedding and house party — no matter that she was supposedly Miss Timmons's dearest friend.

But being in the country also left him at a disadvantage; he could hardly press forth with his search for Miss Spooner while he was stuck here rusticating.

His jaw worked back and forth. There hadn't been a letter or a note from the lady since that night.

The night Miss Dale had ruined everything.

And as it was, every time he thought of that miss, he couldn't but help compare her to Miss Spooner.

Which left him imagining her as Miss Dale's true opposite — dowdy, plain, without an ounce of grace — like the creature who'd answered the door at Christopher Street.

For a moment, Henry had feared he'd

need to put his own words to the test.

Does it matter what is on the outside . . .

The owlish girl — no, make that spinster — who had answered the door and regarded him with a mixture of suspicion and awe had left him a bit taken aback. That is until he discovered she wasn't Miss Spooner.

Thank God, he'd nearly cheered, even as she'd taken his letter and efficiently sent him packing.

Must be a relation, he realized, for she had the same sensible and determined air that echoed through the pages of Miss Spooner's letters. He'd also been struck by the thought that there was something very familiar about the gel, as if he'd seen her before — a family resemblance perhaps to his Miss Spooner — but the only person who kept coming to mind was Miss Dale.

Henry grimaced. Miss Dale, indeed! Wouldn't that be a nightmare?

No, he wanted a steady, reliable companion to spend his days with.

But what about your nights? a wry voice teased. *Who would you rather spend your nights with?*

Never mind that the first image that came to mind was Miss Dale, her hair unbound and that sylvan, delectable figure of hers wrapped only in his sheets, enticing him to abandon his sensible nature and come while away the night in the pleasures that only a creature of her nature could offer.

It was an image that had haunted him since that night.

Why, he'd even thought he'd seen her following him in London when he'd gone to discover Miss Spooner's identity. Ridiculous notion — but that was what Dale women and their insufferable beauty did to sensible men.

Yes, a proper, sensible miss was exactly what he needed to extinguish this restless fire Miss Dale had lit inside him.

With that resolution firmly planted in his heart, he turned the corner at the bottom of the stairs and noticed a single note in the salver. He might have just walked right past, for it was probably no more than some titillating bit of gossip dashed off and left for one of the footmen to deliver to the intended party, but the handwriting stopped him cold.

And not just the handwriting, the name to whom it was addressed:

Dishforth

Glancing around, if only to ensure there was no one looking, Henry's hand snaked

157

out quickly and snatched it off the silver plate. He gaped down at the single folded page written in none other than Miss Spooner's sure hand.

How the devil . . .

Taking another surreptitious glance around the open foyer and reassured that no one else was about, he slid his thumb under the wafer, wrenched the folded sheet open, and read the single line it contained.

As it turns out, I was invited as well.

Tucking neatly into her laden plate, Daphne sighed and glanced around the comfortable morning room. She found it unfathomable that this welcoming corner of Owle Park — what with its rococo ceiling, white wainscoting, celery paint and gilt trim here and there — was the design of a Seldon. Even the sparkling morning sunshine pouring in from the long windows at either end of the room cast such a bright, friendly glow that it made it nearly impossible to believe she was so deep in enemy territory.

Owle Park. The hereditary home of the Seldon heirs. She'd tamped down a momentary bit of panic by reaching over and putting her hand atop Mr. Muggins's wiry head. The Irish terrier, Tabitha's beast of a dog, had greeted her last night like a long-lost friend and had yet to leave her side — for which Daphne was grateful.

"Out on our own, aren't we?" she whispered to him as she scratched behind his ears.

Mr. Muggins let out a grand sigh and tipped his head just so, willing to listen to her troubles as long as she continued to hit *that* spot.

"Dishforth is close at hand," Daphne said, happy to have someone to confide in, even if it was just Mr. Muggins. "He's here, within these walls."

That very thought should have been enough to bolster her spirits, but there was one other consideration.

While Dishforth may indeed be at Owle Park this very moment, so was Lord Henry Seldon.

Daphne pressed her lips together and sighed. Wretched, awful man.

She couldn't help it. Every time she thought of him, she reminded herself that he was exactly that.

A wretched, awful man.

Speaking of the devil, his deep voice sputtered from the doorway. "Oh, good God! What are *you* doing here?"

Daphne and Mr. Muggins both looked up

to find the very fellow standing in the doorway.

"Lord Henry." Daphne tipped her head slightly in greeting, while inside her thoughts clattered about like a shop bell.

Whatever was he doing up so early? She had assumed that when they — she, along with Lady Essex, Harriet and Lady Essex's nephew, the Earl of Roxley — had arrived so late the night before and there had been no sign of him, he'd most likely already been engaged in whatever rakish and devilish exploits a man of his reputation and proclivities pursued.

For some reason the very notion of him with another woman piqued her in ways she didn't like to consider.

Instead, she'd lent her consideration and pity toward the poor deluded lady who was the object of his attentions.

But that didn't explain what he was doing up so early and looking as if he was in top form — brushed and dressed, his gaze sharp and piercing. Hardly the appearance of a man who'd been out carousing the hours away.

"Miss Dale, where did you come from?" he demanded as he came into the room and stopped at the far end of the table.

"London," she replied smoothly, despite

the flutter of emotions inside her at the sight of him. "Don't you recall, we met there but a week ago."

He flinched. "I had heard you declined Preston's invitation," he replied, glancing around the empty room and frowning.

She wasn't any more pleased to be alone with him than he was. "I changed my mind."

"Of course you did," he said, looking ready to throw up his hands in despair . . . or throw her out.

Daphne reached for Mr. Muggins and tried to look braver than she felt. Whyever did this man leave her so . . . so . . . undone? And certainly she couldn't let him inspire another scene like the one that had transpired at the engagement ball.

No, no, that would never do.

Stealing another glance at him, with his brow furrowed, his blue eyes dark with something she suspected was not a welcoming light, she thought it might help to remind him of her position here. "I know Tabitha will be ever so glad to see that I was able to come down with *Lady Essex*."

As she suspected, Lord Henry looked ready to cast up his accounts at the mention of the spinster's name.

But the devilish man wasn't completely undone. Composing himself quickly, arms

161

crossed over his chest as if he hadn't the least notion what she was talking about, he said, "And your family? They approve of you being here? I'd think they'd be up in arms."

Now it was Daphne's insides that quaked. "Not in the least," she lied. "They trust I will not be tempted by your family's notorious predilections." Pausing for a moment to look again at his handsome features, she added hastily, "Which I won't."

"Thank God for small favors," he shot back, his deep tone ruffling down her spine with its rich notes of irony, while his gaze raked over her and dismissed her all at once.

"Are there more Dales due to come after you?" he asked, having obviously warmed to his subject: her removal. "A rescue effort so to say? Should we expect the odd catapult to be wheeled over from Langdale?" he said, making light of the Dale property that adjoined Owle Park.

The property resided in by Crispin, Viscount Dale.

That was the one snag in all this. Crispin. She just needed to avoid him. Which would be easily done, since he would never set foot on Seldon land.

Unlike her.

Daphne felt a frisson of guilt but once

again pushed it aside. There was more at stake here than deeply held family obligations.

"No, I hardly think that will be necessary," she said. "I don't believe my stay will be overlong."

"No?" Good heavens, he needn't sound so hopeful.

"No," she acknowledged, not saying anything more, returning to her breakfast with a determination to ignore the man and concentrate on her plans to find Dishforth.

For she hadn't much time to accomplish her task.

Daphne had no idea how long Phi could hold up her end of the bargain and stall the family from discovering the truth — that she wasn't, as her mother believed, continuing her sojourn in London at Great-Aunt Damaris's home. Which meant the grand dame of the Dale clan had to be kept under the impression that Daphne had returned to her parents' house in Kempton.

Given that it would take a week or so for the letters to cross and recross, as long as Phi could intercept any damaging correspondence and no one reported Daphne's whereabouts or repeated some gossipy report from the night of the ball, Daphne would have just enough time to discover

Mr. Dishforth, fall utterly in love with him, and then return to London or Kempton betrothed to the perfect gentleman.

At least that was the plan. She glanced down at Mr. Muggins for reassurance.

The dog had his eyes on the plate that Lord Henry was filling over at the sideboard.

She ground her teeth in frustration. Did he have to stay? Then she reminded herself — this was his family's house, and she was the interloper.

When he noticed her staring at him, he asked, "Whatever are you doing up so early?"

"I prefer to arise at this hour." She glanced over at him. "As do you, it seems."

"Yes, I had thought to avoid the wedding hordes." His glance at her and Mr. Muggins was telling.

Or the stray unwanted Dale.

Daphne smiled blandly, as if she hadn't a clue what he might mean.

Then he turned, plate in hand, and faced her. "Why?"

"Why what?"

"Why?" His jaw set. "Miss Dale, your being here is inexplicable."

"And yet, here I am."

"Again, I ask why?" he pressed.

He would.

"Tabitha, of course." She glanced away, because she didn't trust herself. Lord Henry was many things, but the man was no fool and his sharp gaze had a way of piercing her — leaving Daphne with the sense he could see right through her gown, straight to her very heart.

"And your family approves?"

"But of course," she lied again. "My lord, let me be frank —"

"I prefer it," he said emphatically.

"As do I," she told him. "I am here for Tabitha and Tabitha only. Once she and Preston are wed, I will return to London . . ." Or to wherever her furious family decided to banish her. She suspected a prolonged visit to Dermot Dale would be in order, never mind that Dermot had the distinction of being the only Dale ever to be convicted and transported to Botany Bay.

A moment of panic struck her. *I wonder if they have modiste shops in New South Wales?*

She steeled herself to such a fate and looked Lord Henry directly in the eye. "So you can see, you will not have to suffer my company any more than a fortnight, and then we shall never see each other again."

She waited for him to add some comment.

An "Amen!" or "Thank God." Or the one probably closest to the surface of his sharp tongue, a heartfelt "Good riddance."

But he did not. Much to her amazement, he nodded and sat down in the chair across from hers. "Then if that is the case, Miss Dale, might I suggest that we pledge to keep our distance?"

"You mean keep to our separate corners, as it were?" she asked, glancing tellingly down to the other end of the table.

"Yes, exactly," he said, completely missing her point.

"An excellent proposal," she agreed.

"Nothing I would like more," he said, then tucked into his breakfast.

Daphne paused, then cleared her throat. *"Ahem."*

He glanced up and blinked at her as if he had already forgotten her presence. "Yes, Miss Dale?"

"You can start by moving."

He glanced up. "Excuse me?"

"Moving, my lord."

"Wherever to?"

"The other end of the table." She nodded down to the far end. The one well away from her.

"But I am settled here. I always sit here."

"Yes, that may be so, but this was your

idea, your proposal." She dabbed her lips with her napkin. "It hardly seems gentlemanly to insist on such an arrangement, then require a lady to move."

She eyed him yet again, sending a skeptical, scathing glance that said she highly doubted he was capable of such a gentlemanly concession.

Henry's eyes narrowed, murderously so, but even still, he picked up his plate and stomped down to the end of the long table, well away from her.

And once he was well settled, she handed Mr. Muggins the last of her sausages and arose, having suddenly lost her appetite. As Lord Henry gaped at her, Daphne left the morning room at a serene pace despite the glowering storm cloud rising behind her.

Daphne spent a good part of the morning in the quiet of the library, comparing the guest list she'd purloined from Tabitha's desk drawer to her own list of possible candidates. She'd come quickly to the conclusion that she had her work cut out for her, for nearly half a dozen of the gentlemen assembled could be the man she sought.

"Bother, Mr. Muggins! However will I narrow the field?" she asked the now ever-present terrier.

Mr. Muggins scrambled to his feet, his ears at attention, and it was only after he'd raced to the door that Daphne heard the telltale click of Tabitha's sensible boots.

Her friend poked her head in the library. "Here she is, Harriet," she called out. And to Daphne she said, "We have been hunting for you all over. Whatever are you doing?" she asked as Harriet appeared at her shoulder.

"What else? Trying to discover who Dishforth might be." Daphne quickly folded her papers and notes into her notebook, tying it shut.

"Perhaps you'd need only look as far as Lord Henry," Harriet suggested.

Daphne bristled. Not this again. Ever since Tabitha's engagement ball, Harriet had been unrelenting in her conviction that Lord Henry must be Mr. Dishforth.

"How many times must I say it, Harriet? Lord Henry is not my Mr. Dishforth."

"But at the ball —"

"Yes, yes, I might have been misled into thinking he was Mr. Dishforth, but can't you see how wrong I was?"

Tabitha and Harriet exchanged a pair of skeptical glances.

"Daphne," the future duchess began, "why

168

don't I ask Preston if he knows —"

Daphne cut Tabitha off in an instant. "No! You mustn't! What if he were to mention it to Lord Henry?"

"Might clear this all up," Harriet muttered under her breath.

Daphne ignored her, as did Tabitha.

"The night of the engagement ball was mortifying enough —" Daphne began. "Please, Tabitha, I beg of you, don't mention any of this to the duke."

"I won't," her friend swore.

Seeing the outright pessimism on Harriet's face, Daphne had no choice but to continue on. "I was merely caught up in the romance of a ball and the very idea of meeting him. If I had been in a more sensible frame of mind, I would never have made such a mistake. The very idea! Lord Henry, indeed. Why, it is too ridiculous to consider."

"Yes, well," Tabitha mused, slanting a glance at Harriet. "Might I suggest that instead of hiding in here, you resume your search in person. We are all summoned outside." She moved forward and plucked up Daphne's notebook, handing it off to Pansy, who was hovering behind with Daphne's hat and a shawl at the ready.

"Whatever is going on?" Daphne asked as

Tabitha hustled her and Harriet through one long hall, and then another.

"House party obligations," Harriet filled in from behind.

Daphne was about to protest that she had better tasks at hand than tea on the lawn or embroidery when Tabitha led them out the front door and down the steps.

To her amazement, the entire house party stood about the wide gravel mews of Owle Park. Out along the curved drive that lay beyond sat a collection of carriages, gigs and carts awaiting whatever the duke had planned.

But more to the point were the gentlemen.

Daphne's gaze flitted from one to the next. "Is this all of them?"

Tabitha's eyes sparkled with amusement. "Yes. Much more revealing than guest lists and entries copied from Debrett's."

"Now all you must do is find him," Harriet added, waving at Lady Essex, who was standing near another elderly matron.

It was at that moment that Daphne's gaze came to an unwanted halt on Lord Henry.

He was strolling about through the throng of guests, and she could see why she might have mistaken him for Dishforth. There were glaring similarities between Preston's uncle and her true love — certainly they shared the same sure stance and confident bearing she'd witnessed the other day on Christopher Street.

If only she had seen the man up close, for the more she looked around, she realized nearly all the men in attendance carried themselves thusly.

Good heavens, it was just her luck to be at the house party with every handsome man in England. So much for going by Phi's near-sighted description.

"Have you been introduced to all of them, Tabitha?" she asked.

"I have," she offered but said nothing more.

Harriet nudged her with her shoulder. "Stop being a tease and tell us who they are. Before Daphne trips you."

Tabitha smirked. "She wouldn't dare try that stunt twice."

Daphne ignored them both and marched down the steps, her friends following her quickly.

Once they'd finished laughing.

As they strolled across the yard, Mr. Muggins following at their heels, Daphne tipped her head ever so slightly toward the first man before them. "Whoever is that?"

"Which one?" Tabitha asked, shielding her eyes.

Harriet laughed. "The one who looks like a pirate."

For indeed there was a gentleman who did resemble a privateer of old — from his rugged, tanned countenance, his untamed crop of dark hair, to the nonchalance of his dress. He leaned heavily on a cane but at the same time gestured wildly as he conversed with another man.

"That is Captain Bramston," Tabitha told them.

"Bramston?!" Harriet gasped. "*The* Captain Bramston?"

All three ladies gazed over at England's newest hero. Daphne knew the name well, for his naval daring had figured prominently in the papers for years, and his prominence had continued once he'd been sent home to London to recuperate.

"He is a cousin or some such to Lady Juniper and Lord Henry, on their mother's side. He also brought his sister, Lady Clare," Tabitha supplied as they continued past the captain, who doffed his hat and winked as they passed.

"So he's not a Seldon, then," Daphne remarked.

Harriet let out a low whistle. "He's handsome enough to be one."

"And a bit devilish," Daphne noted, wondering if perhaps behind all the man's bluster lay Dishforth's sensible soul. It didn't seem possible, so she moved to the next possible candidate. "And who is that with the captain?"

"Believe it or not, the Earl of Rawcliffe," Tabitha told them.

"Rawcliffe?" they both gasped, their gazes pivoting back to the man who, in Kempton, was as infamous as he was absent. The earl held the living that had been Tabitha's father's until his death, and that Tabitha's uncle, Reverend Timmons, now held.

"Yes, he's back in England. Has been since the beginning of the Season. Preston mentioned seeing him at White's, and so I invited him," Tabitha confided. "Imagine my surprise when he accepted."

The man noticed their attentions and bowed to the three of them.

Daphne sighed. There wasn't a spinster in Kempton who didn't dream of being the mistress who restored Rawcliffe Manor to its former glory, the grand Tudor mansion having sat empty for far too many years. *If he were Dishforth . . .*

She slanted one more glance at the Earl

of Rawcliffe and considered the possibilities.

No wonder Lady Essex and several other ladies from Kempton — the Tempest twins and even shy Miss Walding — hovered about in the man's orbit.

As they continued to move along the outside of the crowd, Daphne discarded several of the guests as unlikely candidates: Harriet's brother Chaunce, too much a Hathaway to sit down and compose a letter; Roxley, too much a gadfly even to think of such a thing; and the Earl of Kipps? Easily dismissed, for he had pockets to let.

Kipps needed an heiress. Not something one sought by placing an advertisement in the *Morning Chronicle*.

As they got to the front of the crowd, Daphne spied Lord Henry off to Preston's right, and discovered, much to her annoyance, that he was watching her.

She wet her lips and glanced away, that wild tremor racing through her limbs, the one that always ran rampant whenever she looked at him.

She had to imagine that when she found Dishforth, her entire body would tremble so, and so she glanced around at the crowd of gentlemen, waiting for one of them to inspire such a passion.

A slight shiver.

A spark?

And yet there was nothing.

"Daphne," Harriet whispered. "Smile. That scowl you are wearing will have Lady Essex over here with her vinaigrette, convinced you have need of it."

"I am hardly scowling," she whispered back, doing her best to smile and not look at Lord Henry. "Do you know what all this is about, Tabitha?"

"Preston will explain," the future duchess said, nodding toward her soon-to-be husband.

The duke leapt onto a mounting block and held up his hands. "Here is the challenge for today. A treasure hunt."

There were cheers and some bits of muttering. Gentlemen cast mischievous glances at the ladies, while fans fluttered over the prospect of such a task.

The duke continued, "Each pair will be provided a map and instructions for where their treasure is hidden, and all you have to do is find it and return before anyone else."

"However are the teams to be decided?" Fieldgate asked, sending a wink over at Harriet.

"By lots," he told them.

This took everyone aback, and this time

the muttering grew louder.

"Yes, but —" Roxley objected.

"No objections or you will not be eligible for the prize," Preston told his friend.

"A prize?" whispered Daphne.

"Yes, just listen," Tabitha told her.

"The winning team will have the first choice of dancing partner for the unmasking waltz at the ball."

Daphne took a deep breath. How utterly romantic. If she were to win or Dishforth did, they could be together for the unmasking.

She saw it so perfectly in her imagination.

"Miss Spooner," he would whisper, his fingers gently tugging at the laces of her mask, and when it fell away, they would see each other for the first time.

But much to her chagrin, as she imagined the moment, it wasn't just any handsome features staring down at her but Lord Henry's.

She wrenched her eyes open and shuddered.

"Whatever is the matter?" Harriet asked.

"A chill," Daphne replied.

"I am beginning to think you do need Lady Essex's smelling salts," Harriet muttered back.

"I daresay it is going to rain," Tabitha

added. They both looked at her. "Well, Daphne always shivers just before it starts to rain."

"There's nary a cloud in the sky," Harriet said, crossing her arms over her chest and giving Daphne a searching glance.

"It might rain," Daphne said, not wanting to reveal the true cause of her trembling.

And this time, she didn't look in *his* direction. Rather she scanned the rest of the crowd and noticed ladies off to one side near Lord Astbury. One of them wore a fine apple green silk that Daphne had seen in a draper's shop in London. She'd nearly died over the cost — it had been prohibitively expensive — and now here was a young woman who not only could afford it but could also wear it done up in an ordinary day gown.

"Tabitha," Daphne whispered. "Who is that lady —" She nodded toward Lord Astbury. "The one in the apple green silk?"

Sparing a quick glance in that direction, Tabitha's nose wrinkled. "Miss Nashe. And of course, Lady Alicia Lovell with her."

"Miss Nashe? The heiress?" Harriet said, gaping unfashionably at the lady.

"The one and the same," Tabitha replied, but it was clear she did not like the girl. Though Tabitha was an heiress herself, she hardly played the part as Miss Nashe apparently did, from the French ribbons in her bonnet down to the fine calfskin of her boots. "Lady Juniper insisted she be invited. And you can't ask Miss Nashe without including Lady Alicia."

And they all knew why. Wherever Miss Nashe went, glowing reports in the columns were sure to follow — as they had all Season. Where Miss Nashe shopped. Who she danced with. At what times she rode in the park. To be snubbed by Miss Nashe was as good as being ruined.

And of course, there was always her dearest friend, Lady Alicia, right there, with her impeccable bloodlines and connections, though sadly none of Miss Nashe's blunt.

Meanwhile, Preston was holding up two velvet purses. "I have the names of all the ladies in this pouch" — he held the first one up high and then hefted the other — "and the men in this one. I shall pull the name of a lady and then she will pull the name of her partner. Then the team is free to choose the carriage of their choice and be on their way." Preston handed the pouch with the men's names to Tabitha, then reached inside the sack with the ladies' names. "Miss Hathaway," he called out.

Harriet shrugged and walked forward.

After a moment of trepidation, she shoved her hand in the sack and pulled out a name, holding it up for Preston.

"Fieldgate."

The man came stalking forward, grinning like a lion. He took a map from Preston, caught Harriet's hand in his and walked triumphantly toward the racing curricle in front.

And thus it was for the next few minutes, couples being paired up, the field of potential partners narrowing and the faster carriages disappearing quickly.

Even Lady Essex gained a partner, Lord Whenby, an older gentleman who left her blushing with whispered promises as he escorted her to one of Preston's more daring phaetons.

Much to Daphne's dismay, all too quickly it came down to her, Miss Nashe, Lord Astbury, and none other than Lord Henry.

Worse yet, the choice of carriages was down to an old curricle and a pony cart. Not exactly the sort of fleet conveyances that would carry one to victory.

Fixing her attention on Lord Astbury, she considered his potential as Dishforth.

He was rumored to be educated and scholarly, and it was said he kept to himself in London. All points in his favor.

And he was handsome. Ever so.

Yet . . . rebelliously her gaze strayed in the other direction.

For there was Lord Henry, grinning with rakish delight at Miss Nashe, as if he was convinced of their pairing. The girl fluttered her lashes at him and smiled, just slightly.

Truly? This was the sort of preening lady that Lord Henry found intriguing?

Once again, Daphne felt a smug satisfaction in her convictions that Lord Henry couldn't be the man she sought. Her very sensible Mr. Dishforth would view the showy and overly resplendent Miss Nashe with prudent horror.

No, there was no earthly way Lord Henry could be Dishforth.

Just then, Daphne realized that Preston was calling another name.

"Miss Nashe."

Daphne stilled as she watched the heiress step forward.

Her fate, her very future, was being decided by Miss Edith Nashe.

The girl fished around inside the bag for what felt like an eternity until Lord Henry said, "Miss Nashe, it is but a slip of paper — take one." His words came out impatiently, almost testily.

"I hardly know which one to choose," she

said, smiling at both gentlemen and obviously immune to the censure.

Good heavens, pull out Lord Henry's name and be done with it, Daphne wanted to shout. That, or just tug off her boot and clout the simpering fool with it, like she'd seen Harriet do once to one of her brothers.

Lord Astbury was far kinder. He smiled warmly. "You have both our hearts in your dear hand, Miss Nashe."

Daphne didn't know why, but she slanted a disgruntled glance at Lord Henry, for she very rightly shared his impatience. And to her surprise, he was looking at her with the same look of utter exasperation.

Whatever is wrong with her?

How am I to know? I would have pulled the name by now.

She wrenched her gaze away. However was it that every time she looked at that man, he had a way of entangling her?

But this time, Lord Henry wasn't entirely to blame.

"Yes, well, here goes," Miss Nashe said and pulled a name from the bag.

CHAPTER 6

Miss Spooner, I must make a confession. I rarely dance. It is not that I am against dancing, it is just that it all seems so contrived. The asking, the sets, the observation of so many rules and requirements. Haven't you, my dear girl, ever wanted to dance where you may? To dance under the stars, to even dare to dance in the rain?

Found in a letter from
Mr. Dishforth to Miss Spooner

"We are most certainly not lost," Lord Henry insisted.

"We most certainly are," Daphne corrected. "I have visited this area on more than one occasion and I know for a fact we are going in the wrong direction." She shook out the map and pointed at it. "Do you see the curve to the river? And there is the bridge marked here." Her finger stabbed at the map. "We must turn around and go back in the other direction and take this turn . . ." Her finger tapped the paper again. ". . . the one I pointed out earlier."

Mr. Muggins, who had, against everyone's orders, planted himself in the back of the pony cart and remained there still, looked from Lord Henry to Daphne and then back to Lord Henry again.

Lord Henry's brow furrowed as he studied the map. "This can't be correct," he said, turning it this way and that and ignoring both Daphne and the dog.

How had everything turned out like this? One moment she'd been convinced she was going to be spending the afternoon with Lord Astbury — doing her utmost to determine if he was Mr. Dishforth — and the next, that infuriating Miss Nashe had claimed the marquess.

Oh, it was all by chance she knew, but what rotten chance this, especially since Lord Henry had gotten them lost.

"See, there is the river and that is the bridge," she said again, pointing at the map. "We will never find the treasure at this rate."

Instead of seeing the sense of what she was saying, he turned the map yet again, as if that would help.

Daphne gave up, scrunching herself into

the corner of the narrow seat the pony cart afforded them. Which still left them wedged together, his muscled thigh brushing intimately against her skirt with each jolt of the road.

The wrong road, she wanted to shout.

For turn around they must. By Daphne's reckoning they were nearly to Langdale. Crispin's house, to be exact. And most likely already on Dale land.

Oh, wouldn't that turn all her plans to naught if they ran into Cousin Crispin.

And as if only to thwart her plans further, from up ahead came the sound of horses' hooves and the whir of wheels from a quickly moving carriage.

Mr. Muggins let out a low growl, a harbinger of the disaster about to whirl into their path.

Round the corner and over the bridge came an expensive phaeton, the sort a gentleman of means and with a penchant for driving owned.

There was no mistaking who it was coming toward them — Crispin, Viscount Dale, in all his handsome glory. The holder of the family title, the golden boy of a handsome family.

There wasn't a female Dale cousin or close relation — or even those, like Daphne, whose place on the family tree was on the sort of branch that should have been trimmed off generations ago but was left on for the sake of family unity — who didn't hold a torch for Crispin Dale.

Devilishly handsome and charming, with a rakish demeanor, he left the female half in a state of awe and wonder by simply walking into a room.

Daphne wouldn't have been surprised if the sun had burst forth from the gathering clouds and shone down on his fair head, if only to illuminate his way.

Crispin barely spared them a glance, for Lord Henry had already guided the old nag and cart over toward the side of the road, but when he came nearly upon them, he took a closer look and immediately pulled his matched set to a stop, the flurry of dogs that had been racing after his carriage all tumbling to a halt in a wild, raucous chorus of barks.

At first, she thought Crispin had noticed her and was stopping to rescue her, but rather her relation had his dark gaze clapped on Lord Henry Seldon.

And he looked none too pleased to find him on Dale land. Even if they were neighbors.

So Daphne kept her chin tucked in and

hoped the brim of her bonnet would shelter her face.

Just perhaps, just maybe, Crispin wouldn't notice her. Might not even remember her.

"Sir, you are lost and should turn around." The strained comment held all the welcoming tones of a judge about to set down a long sentence.

For Daphne knew exactly what Crispin truly meant. *Get off my land, you bounder.*

"Hardly lost, sir," Lord Henry replied with every bit of haughty disdain that only a Seldon could manage. "Merely taking a tour of the surrounding countryside. But you are correct, we should turn around. There is nothing of note ahead. Or so I've heard."

Daphne tucked her head down further. Oh, good heavens. She didn't know what was worse — the Seldon pride or the Dale vanity, because one surreptitious glance revealed that Cousin Crispin appeared ready to toss down the gauntlet.

"Oh, my good God!" Cousin Crispin sputtered. "What the devil is —"

Daphne cringed, for certainly her masquerade was up. He'd spied her and was even now —

"What the hell is that mongrel doing to my best hunting bitch?!" he exclaimed.

She stilled. And then glanced over her

shoulder where Mr. Muggins had been sitting in the back of the cart.

Save now the cart was empty.

Beside her, Lord Henry chuckled. "My lord, if I have to explain *that* to you, I can't see how the Dales have been so prolific over the years."

"Sir, get that beast off my dog!"

No! No! No! Daphne didn't even want to look. But she did anyway.

Oh, Mr. Muggins! How could you?

"Not my beast," Lord Henry was saying, leaning back and tipping his head as he glanced at the oversized terrier, who was happily repeating the original scandal that had brought the Dales and Seldons to blows. "Hers," he offered, jerking his thumb at Daphne, for which she covered her face with her hands.

"You think this is amusing?" Crispin asked, straightening up into a position so starched that Daphne thought he might snap.

"It does have a certain irony," Lord Henry said. "Don't you agree, *Miss Dale*?"

A stillness descended around them. Daphne thought quite possibly the world was about to be ripped asunder as she looked up and met the gaze of Crispin, Viscount Dale.

187

He rose up slowly in his seat until he was towering over the occupants of the pony cart, lending him an almost unearthly air. "Daphne Dale?"

"Yes, ah, a good day to you, my lord," she offered.

Crispin couldn't have looked more shocked. Well, save the expression he'd worn while Mr. Muggins had been ruining what might have been a profitable litter of pups. "Daphne, what are you doing —"

Henry intervened. "She's with me. Fine day for a drive, isn't it?"

Both the Dales ignored him.

"Cousin, get down out of that . . . that . . ." Crispin shuddered as he looked over at the poor conveyance that was barely able to amble along. ". . . contraption," he finally managed, "and come with me. Immediately." He moved slightly to show her the space where he expected her to join him.

Daphne glanced from one man to another. And much to her chagrin, she caught a wry light in Lord Henry's eyes. A most defiant shimmer that called to her.

Oh, she was a Dale through and through, but she hadn't come this far to be ordered about like an errant child.

Even if she was behaving like one.

"I will not," she told him, folding her

hands in her lap and facing her cousin, the very head of her family, with all the defiance of, say, a Seldon.

Heaven help her.

"Perhaps you did not understand me, Daphne," Crispin said. "You are not keeping respectable company." The viscount's gaze swept first over Mr. Muggins, who had finished his business and hopped back into the pony cart, and then continued to Lord Henry.

The arch of his brow said all too clearly he considered them both mongrels.

"I don't like your implication," Lord Henry leveled.

"I do not like your intentions," Cousin Crispin countered. "Whatever could it be that you are doing so far from Owle Park with a young lady of good name and character —"

Thankfully, Lord Henry had the good sense not to snort over this, as he had at the engagement ball.

"— I don't care to know, but understand this, my cousin is coming home with me *now* so she can be returned to the sanctity and safety of her parents' keeping." He paused and glanced over at Daphne. "Who, I suspect, have no idea their daughter is here."

Lord Henry shot a quick glance at her, as if to watch her deny this statement. Almost immediately his eyes widened as he spied the panic she couldn't hide.

There it was. The cat was now out of the bag.

He knew she'd lied. To him and to her family. Thankfully though, he didn't know why she'd gone to such great lengths.

Oh, bother! It wouldn't be long before he went digging for the truth. Lord Henry just seemed the sort who would want to know the very why of something.

Including her secrets.

To add to the already ominous air around them, the dark clouds that had been threatening all afternoon were drawing ever closer.

Crispin glanced over his shoulder as the wind freshened, bringing a brisk change to the air and the hint of the rains to come.

"Now, now, Daphne," her cousin said in the smooth, polite tones one used with an unruly child. "I'll see to it that you are inside before the weather turns. It would be a dreadful shame for that lovely gown to be ruined." Then he did exactly what she feared he might.

Gave her the Dale smolder.

That tip of the head, the half-lidded smoky glance that could lure a dedicated and lifelong spinster out of her corset.

It was a snare no woman could resist. Except, so it seemed, Daphne.

You are not like other ladies, are you, Miss Spooner? For that I am most relieved. Most ladies bore me to distraction.

Mr. Dishforth's words came forth from who knew where. Perhaps the Fates had brought them along with this unseasonable bout of rain. But they gave Daphne the wherewithal she needed to do the last thing Crispin Dale expected.

Defy him yet again.

"No, my lord. I think not," she told him, settling into the narrow seat of the pony cart as if it were Lady Essex's well-appointed barouche. "I am most comfortable here."

"Cousin, I order you to get out of that cart," Crispin said, smolder replaced by a furious glare.

"And I, Cousin, politely refuse." She managed a firm smile that belied her quaking insides.

"Daphne Dale!" he commanded. "You cannot be left alone with this . . . this . . ."

"I am of age, my lord," she pointed out, "and can therefore make my own choices. I will not be bullied by you" — she glanced over at Lord Henry as well — "or any man." Daphne looked up at the gathering clouds framing Crispin's towering figure. "You have my answer, my lord. You'd best hurry to Langdale without me, or you'll find your jacket ruined."

"We shall see about that!" he said, plunking down in his seat and gathering up the reins. "Consider this choice carefully, Daphne, for once made it cannot be undone — just as many other things cannot be salvaged. You must see how you have no other choice but to return with me."

Daphne shook at his implication that she was as good as ruined. "I disagree."

"You cannot refuse me," he shot back.

"I think she has," Lord Henry told him, taking up the reins to the cart and clucking a bit at the tired nag. The poor horse was hardly a matched set of bays chafing in their traces, but you couldn't tell that by Lord Henry's demeanor. "Now, it is time you ceased badgering the lady and let us get on our way before the rain catches us."

Crispin's brow furrowed. "If that is your choice, Daphne."

"It is."

"So be it," he said. "But hear me well, Seldon," he added, turning his stormy gaze toward Lord Henry. "This lady's welfare is in your hands. See her safely back to Owle Park. Immediately."

"I have no desire to be drenched," Lord Henry replied, neglecting to mention Daphne's welfare, much to Crispin's chagrin.

He straightened. "I shall hold you to your word, sir, that Miss Dale is returned without any hint of dishonor."

Lord Henry bowed slightly in agreement.

Crispin turned to her, his gaze flitting for a second to Mr. Muggins, who hovered close to her shoulder. "Do not think this is the end of this, Daphne." With that said, he wheeled his carriage around in a tight circle and drove off as if the hounds of hell were nipping his heels.

Or rather, Mr. Muggins after another of his prized hunting dogs.

"Yes, well," Lord Henry said as the dust of Crispin's carriage began to settle, "best get you back before he has time to fetch a halberd and settle this in some medieval fashion." He glanced at her. "I've never fancied a pike through the chest."

"I hardly think he'd choose halberds when he is an excellent shot," she said, settling her hands primly into her lap. Then, after Lord Henry had turned the cart around — certainly not with Crispin's skill, but well enough — she turned to him. "He has a right to be concerned."

Lord Henry snorted.

"You are a Seldon."

"And you are a Dale."

"What is that supposed to mean?"

One of his brows tipped into a high arch.

"Yes, right," she agreed, recalling how this very same disagreement had gotten them into trouble at the ball — a path neither of them wished to travel down again . . . or so she thought.

"I might add though —" Lord Henry began.

Daphne set her jaw. Of course he couldn't leave well enough alone.

But what Lord Henry said next shocked her. Utterly.

"If you were my cousin, I would not have left you in my care but followed you back to Owle Park to make sure you were well chaperoned. Your cousin is an overly proud fool." He gave a disapproving shake of his head and said no more. Not that he needed to.

He was right, of course. And she glanced over her shoulder, where there was no sign of Crispin racing to her rescue.

Daphne drew her shawl around her shoulders a bit tighter, hoping to stave off the shivers. And this time it had nothing to do with the impending rain.

"You did give your word, as a gentleman," she reminded him.

"Do you trust my word?" he asked, not looking at her. "Because I hardly trust yours."

She flinched. As well she should.

"Yes, of course my family approves," he mimicked from earlier. "My family doesn't mind in the least." He glanced over at her. "Is that still your story?"

She pressed her lips together and refused to speak. She certainly wasn't going to tell Lord Henry why she had dared to come to a Seldon wedding.

Why she had defied her entire family.

"Yes, well, when the Dale clan arrives, armed to the teeth and looking for blood, I for one am not going to stand firm over your folly," he declared. "If I have any say in the matter, they will find you at the front gate, with your bags packed and a note pinned to your pelisse with directions to the nearest madhouse."

After a few moments of driving in silence, Daphne let out a long sigh. "Are you finished?"

"Yes, quite," he admitted.

"Then you should know that you missed

the turn back there." She nodded toward the narrow track that ran off the road. "If you continue on this course, we shall be lost. Again."

"Not in the least. This is a shortcut," he told her. "I promised to see you safely back to Owle Park, and I shall. No matter what you opine, I am a gentleman and a man of honor."

Now it was Daphne's turn to let out a snort.

Pompous, arrogant know-it-all. He was going to get them lost.

And just for those reasons, she didn't argue the fact. She rather liked the idea of proving him wrong.

Utterly.

At least she did until the clouds opened up and emptied their bounty all over her lovely new gown.

The folly appeared on the rise before them just at the point when Henry was about to have to concede to Miss Dale that she'd been correct.

He'd gotten them lost.

Utterly.

But then they had turned a corner, and as he'd dashed the rain out of his eyes, there it had appeared — the stone rotunda his grandfather, the seventh duke, had built after his Grand Tour.

"Come now, let's get out of this," he said, pulling the horse to a stop and catching hold of her hand.

Her fingers were like ice, and he glanced over at her.

Just as her cousin, Lord Dale, had predicted, her gown was drenched, ruined. Ignoring the twinge of guilt — for no gentleman should let a lady end up in such a state — they dashed toward the covered pavilion, hand in hand, dancing over puddles and around the larger rivulets of water rushing over the path.

Mr. Muggins had needed no urging and was already ahead of them, shaking the rain out of his fur in a wild flurry of droplets.

By the time Henry and Miss Dale had climbed the wide steps and gotten out from the drenching downpour, the dog had already found a dry spot beneath one of the benches and lain down, head on his paws.

As for the two of them, they came to a halt in the middle, and save for the heavy pattering of rain all around them, it was as if the countryside had stilled.

Henry didn't know quite what to say or do — but when he glanced over at Miss Dale, he realized two things.

He hadn't let go of her hand.

Nor did he want to.

How could he? She looked utterly divine. Like one of the goddesses a temple like this might have been dedicated to — a nymph who currently stood before him in a pique of rage.

Not that she left the decision up to him. She wrenched her fingers free of his grasp and stalked over to Mr. Muggins.

Apparently a wet hound was preferable company.

Well, he would tell her that he'd had other plans for this afternoon. His sights set on finding another lady.

A proper lady. A sensible one.

Might have found her by now if it hadn't been for Preston and his cork-brained treasure hunt.

Which had left him with the ungodly luck of being paired with Miss Dale.

Miss Dale! The most insensible woman in all of England. Or at the very least, the one who drove him to the edge of madness. Why, he'd nearly kissed her at Preston's engagement ball, and now he was lost with her in his company.

The woman was determined to lure him into some scandalous mire.

He glanced over at her to see what sort of

mischief she was making now — only to find her unpinning her sodden bonnet, which, once freed, she tossed down on the stone bench. Her shawl followed, as did her gloves. Thus divested of her wet outer garments, she paced around the edge of the columns, circling him like a vengeful griffin.

He suspected he was about to be flayed alive. Nor could Tabitha's mangy beast of a dog be counted on to save him.

"Go ahead," he told her, bracing himself.

She paused and glanced over at him. "Pardon?"

"Go ahead," he said, holding out his hands, as if to be locked away.

Miss Dale shook her head. "Whatever do you mean?"

He wasn't fooled. Hen did this all the time. Lured him into confessing his wrongdoings so she didn't have to lay them out for him and waste her time listening to him deny them. "Just say it."

"Say what?" she asked, then resumed her pacing.

Truly, this was becoming more difficult than it needed to be. Besides, her circling was making him dizzy.

" 'I told you so.' " Whyever couldn't a woman just come out and say a thing? Rather they had to drag out an accusation, like a painful thorn.

She blinked and gaped at him, as if the realization of what he was getting at finally hit her. Huffing a sigh, she went back to her pacing. "Lord Henry, I have far more important troubles at hand than to waste my time crowing over your wretched sense of direction."

And with that said, the pacing began anew. This time with a more determined *click* to her steps.

"Whatever has you in this state?"

She came to a blinding halt. "Crispin, of course!"

What she left out, but truly had no need to say, was, *The one we would not have crossed paths with if you had listened to me and taken the correct road.*

"Oh, yes, him," he managed, shuffling his boots a bit. He'd been doing his best to forget their encounter with Lord Dale.

"Yes, *him.*"

The sarcasm stung, but then he'd lived with Hen all these years not to be a bit immune.

It was what she said next that left him flummoxed.

"He'll ruin everything!"

Then, much to Henry's chagrin, she resumed pacing. Did she have to go in a

200

circle? He was going to get nauseous.

But something else struck him. *"He'll ruin everything"?*

Henry perked up, feeling the scales of justice tipping back into his favor.

As he'd suspected, the lady had a secret.

He strolled out of her path and sat down on the bench beside her ruined hat, though not too close. The muddled mess of silk was letting off a regular brook of rainwater.

"What will he ruin, Miss Dale?"

She stumbled to a stop and cast a glance over her shoulder at him. No longer the vengeful valkyrie, her eyes widened, then just as quickly narrowed to hide her alarm.

Ah, yes, the lady had a *big* secret.

"Nothing."

Yes, he knew that tone as well. When a woman said "nothing," it usually meant "everything."

Henry glanced down at the state of his boots and said nonchalantly, "I thought you said this morning that your family approved of your attendance."

She flinched and put her back to him.

"So they don't?"

Her shoulders hunched up as if to shield her from his prodding.

He got to his feet. "Does anyone know you're here?"

She whirled around. "Everyone will now."

Henry had to admit, he rather admired her plucky defiance — save when it was aimed at him. But her defiance was also entangling him in a mess of epic proportions.

Whyever had she gone to such great lengths to come to Owle Park to begin with?

Meanwhile, Miss Dale took one of his sister's favorite tacks: turning the tables. "This is all your fault."

If he'd had a sovereign for every time Hen had used that phrase . . . "My fault?" he ventured.

"Yes, yours." The lady crossed the space between them and stopped right in front of him. "If you had but followed the map —"

So much for that accusation remaining unsaid . . .

"— we would not have run into Crispin. And now . . ." Her words failed her as she gave into a bout of shivers.

He looked at her again, and this time, noting more than just the state of her ruined gown and the shape of her comely figure, he also realized she was chilled to the bone.

Some gentleman he was!

Shrugging off his driving coat, he wrapped it around her shoulders, ignoring her wary gaze and her attempt to brush his gallantry aside and slip out from his grasp. He held onto the lapels and straightened it so it covered her.

Protected her.

Then he looked into her eyes and saw a wrenching light of despair and felt — for whatever reason, for he was hardly the cause of this misery — a twinge of guilt.

He'd done this to her. Worse yet, a nudge of conscience said it was up to him to fix all this.

He let go of the lapels and backed away. He'd never been one to melt over a lady's languid gaze, but Miss Dale had a way, what with those starry blue eyes of hers, that pierced his sensible hide like no other woman had ever done.

She'd done much the same thing to him on the dance floor at the ball.

Hell, from the first moment he'd spied her.

She'd led him astray that night with those comehither eyes of hers, led him off course.

Taking up the clearly discernable path of puddles she'd left around the marble floor of the folly, he began to pace. The mess on the floor was in stark contrast to the unnavigable path she was treading upon his heart.

Henry shuddered against such a notion

and concentrated on the moment at hand, stealing a glance at the lady and her wrenching expression.

His fault, indeed! It wasn't. And yet . . .

For about the thousandth time since breakfast — hell, since the engagement ball — he'd reminded himself of two things.

She was a Dale.

And she was none of his concern.

Oh, but she is. And that was the rub. Somehow she'd become his problem, no matter how much he denied it or the lady herself protested. His problem. Or was she?

I'll have you know, Lord Henry, I am nearly betrothed to another.

Henry latched onto the confession she'd made the other night at the ball. Nearly betrothed . . .

What else had she said about the man? Ay, yes. *A gentleman of standing.*

Henry skidded to a stop. Turning, his gaze narrowed, and he said, "Him! He's your nearly gentleman." He shook his head to clear his muddled thoughts. "Your nearly betrothed."

She crossed her arms over her bosom and gaped at him. "Whatever are you going on about?"

"Crispin Dale. He's your nearly betrothed.

The one you were crowing about the other night."

"My lord, I never crow," she said, and then having taken in the full weight of his accusation, her eyes widened before she laughed. "Me? Betrothed to Crispin?" Her giggles turned into a loud series of guffaws, leaving her with her hands clasped over her stomach as if she'd never heard anything so amusing.

"Whatever did I say?"

"How little you know of the Dale clan." She tittered again. "Me engaged to Crispin? Ridiculous."

Henry didn't see why such a notion was so foolish. "How so? He rather seems your sort."

"My sort?" Her gaze wrenched up, all of her hilarity evaporating. Once again she was all wary suspicion.

"Yes, your sort," he said, adding his own imperious stance to hers.

"Whatever does *that* mean?"

Henry shrugged. "Overdressed. Fussy. Wealthy." He left out "an overreaching prig."

"That description could be applied to most of the men in the *ton,*" she pointed out. Tipping her chin up, she added, "Yourself included."

"I am not fussy," Henry shot back.

"If you insist," she said, shrugging a shoulder.

"I do." Not liking the course of this conversation — damn the lady, she had a singular knack for turning the tables on him — he shifted the tide back in his favor. "Still, I don't see why Lord Dale is not your sort."

She shook her head as if the answer would be obvious even to the inhabitants of a nursery. "He's *Crispin.*"

Whatever the devil did that mean?

Miss Dale huffed a little sigh and retreated to where her bonnet lay in a limp pile. Then she began ticking off what apparently was Dale canon. "He's Crispin, Viscount Dale. The Dale of Langdale. The head of the family."

Again Henry hardly saw why any of this precluded that starched and overbearing jackanape from being her "perfect gentleman."

She must have seen the confusion in his eyes, so she went on. "Crispin Dale can have his choice of the most beautiful and eligible ladies in London."

Henry had the suspicion he would never understand any of this, and yet, against his better judgment, he asked, "So why not you? You're beautiful."

The words, just like his suddenly vacant good sense, tumbled out into the space between them.

Words. They were only words. A simple statement of fact.

You're beautiful.

Disarming words. For they held an unmistakable air of confession to them. Even he knew it.

Worse, so did she.

Her gaze flew up to meet his, as if she expected to find him laughing at her.

Just as she'd laughed at him.

And she said as much. "Now you're teasing me."

Henry straightened. Ever the Seldon, he'd waded into this mire, and instead of retreating for the safety of the bank, he plodded further into the depths.

Why wouldn't he? Before him stood a lady who could have been mistaken for a watery nymph. Her fair hair coiled in long curls down from her head, her fair skin made even more translucent by the chill in the air, quite in contrast to the luscious pinkish rosy color of her cheeks and lips.

Only the smattering of freckles across her nose gave any indication that she was not some ethereal creature come to tempt him. Lure him to his doom.

Unfortunately for him, Miss Dale was all too real.

And she tempted him more than he cared to admit.

She repeated herself. "Lord Henry, it isn't mannerly to tease a lady so."

"Miss Dale, I do not tease." Taking a deep breath, he took another step — figuratively. For if he did it literally, he would have been straying dangerously close to temptation. "You are a beautiful woman. Too much so."

They stood there — and once again Henry had the sense of being lost within their own world — with the only sound the pattering of rain all around them. The deluge was beginning to let up, and now the drops competed with the large plops of water dripping from the trees and shrubberies that hid them away in this quiet corner of Owle Park.

Neither of them moved, just stood there, expectantly.

It was the sort of moment that was more Preston's forte than Henry's, but that didn't mean he didn't know what to do . . . or rather what he'd promised not to . . .

She pursed her lips as she watched him, her lashes fluttering softly. "Lord Henry, I —"

He didn't want to hear what she had to

say. Didn't want to hear her protest. Or a confession of her own.

So he did the only thing left to him.

The same thing that his rakish ancestors had always done so well.

Daphne might be from Kempton and considered a bit naive — rightly so — but she wasn't so inexperienced with men that she didn't recognize the rakish gleam in Lord Henry's eyes as he declared her "beautiful."

Too much so.

Her heart took a tremulous leap. And wrapped as she was in his greatcoat, surrounded by the fine wool and the masculine air that clung to the threads as if it was woven in . . . bayberry rum and something so very male . . . she couldn't help but feel surrounded by him.

Then she looked again into the piercing blue gaze of Lord Henry Seldon and knew . . . knew down to the squishy soles of her boots why every Dale lady was warned to give the Seldon males a wide berth.

Because the light of passion burning in his eyes left her trembling . . . shivering despite his warm coat around her shoulders. Probably because of it.

For it was like having the man himself holding her.

Almost. For she knew what that was like. All too well.

Just then the rain stopped. As if the heavens had decided the green fields had had enough and that was that. The steady patter abruptly ended, broken only by the occasional *drip* and *plop,* leaving Daphne standing and staring at this man in a still air of wonder.

Did he truly think her beautiful?

One more glance told her the truth. *And more.*

Not only was Lord Henry telling the truth — he did find her beautiful — but the gleam in his eyes also said he found her desirable.

Her legs pressed together and she gathered her arms around herself, either to ward him off or to hold fast to the delicious sense of yearning that was spiraling through her.

Desirable. Oh, such a notion brought with it a heady, wondrous feeling. Made only that much more dangerous because it came from someone as rakish and dangerous as Lord Henry.

Oh, Harriet could claim all the way to Scotland and back that Lord Henry was a dull stick, an anomaly of the Seldon bloodlines, but nothing could be further from the truth. Daphne saw him exactly for what he was, in his true light.

For here she stood, with her toes curled up inside her damp stockings, her soaked boots, and it was all she could do not to take a step closer to him.

She needn't. He did it for her.

Coming closer and reaching out to push a stray tendril of her hair off her face. His fingers brushed over her cheek, her temple, and she shivered.

"You're chilled," he whispered.

"Not in the least," she admitted. Not when he touched her like that. Her insides seemed to catch fire.

"No?" he asked again, teasing another strand out of her eyes.

Teasing her.

All the denial Daphne could manage was a slight shake of her head.

He reached down and took up her hands in his, holding them together as if they could ward off any chill.

But the thing was, she was no longer cold.

"Your fingers are like ice," he said, bringing them to his lips, blowing slightly on them, the heat of his breath a shock to her senses.

He glanced at her, waiting for her protest, some word. As she should. As she would, once she remembered how to breathe.

You are a beautiful woman. Too much so.

211

She hardly knew what to do, other than stand there and let this handsome man work his rakish magic on her.

His warm lips stole over her fingertips. As he drew them closer, she followed, leaning up against him, his coat falling open.

And then it was as if all the barriers between them fell away.

For one moment she was there, enclosed and safe in his coat, and the next she was in his arms.

And hardly safe.

Daphne had moved without any thought, save one.

This is where I belong.

In this man's arms. Oh, it shouldn't be so. But it was.

Still, she looked up, ready to protest, searching for the scolding words she should be casting out, and finding only one thing in her heart . . .

Surrender.

It was that starry, dangerous moment at the ball all over again, save there was no impending threat of family, friends or fire-breathing chaperones.

No boundaries. No barriers. Nothing but this spark that could not be denied.

He bent his head down and claimed her lips with his.

Daphne sighed. Good heavens, how could one desire a thing so much without ever having known it could be so?

His lips teased her mouth, nipping at her lower lip, nudging her to open up to him.

And when she did, everything shifted.

The spark burst into a bonfire of desire, and Lord Henry tugged her up against him and deepened his kiss. His tongue slid over her lips, tasting her, moving over her own.

Daring her to dance. To dance where she may.

Meanwhile, his hands roamed over her, beneath his coat, over her curves, tracing the line of her hips, curving around her behind, igniting a firestorm in their wake.

His coat slipped from her shoulders and she trembled as it puddled around her feet.

Not from the chill in the air. Hardly. How could she be cold when she was on fire?

Longing, deep, dangerous longing, filled her. Uncoiling inside her, leaving her tangled and tight, and delirious.

This was not a kiss, it was an awakening.

Daphne tried to breathe as she clung to the man holding her. Raw, untamed passion unraveled within her as he touched her, as his kiss deepened.

If she shivered before it rained, Daphne now trembled before the storm of desire

Lord Henry unleashed with his kiss.

Her nipples tightened as she found herself pressed against the wool of his jacket. Daphne moved against him like a cat, letting her senses come alive as her body contacted his. Her hands opened across his chest, and she let her fingers fan out over the muscled planes.

He continued to kiss her, hold her, explore her, his lips leaving hers to kiss her neck, the hollow of her throat, and then back to her lips, returning to her eagerly, hungrily.

His hand caught hold of her backside and drew her closer, right up against him, and Daphne's lashes fluttered open as she realized just how much of a rake Lord Henry was . . . and in that same moment, the sharp trill of a warbler burst through the stillness.

It was as if the bird's song brought with it a reminder. Cousin Crispin's warning.

Consider this choice carefully, for once made it cannot be undone.

Cannot be undone . . .

Half mad with desires she was only beginning to understand, but knew would lure her to her ruin, Daphne wrenched herself away from this man who had suddenly stopped being merely a Seldon.

And something oh-so-much-more treacherous.

No, desirable. Very much so.

"Miss Dale, I —"

She held up her hand. "No. Please don't say a word." For she didn't know what she feared more: his words dousing the fire between them or his saying something utterly unforgivable . . . like apologizing for his behavior or calling it a mistake.

"It's just that —"

"Please, Lord Henry!" This time she pleaded. "Can we not speak of this?"

For a moment they just stood there, naught but an arm's length between them. And like it had earlier, that spark started to kindle anew as she stole a glance at him. For there in his eyes was the truth.

He wanted her back in his arms.

And, oh, how she wanted to return. To that breathless place where there was only his lips on hers, his arms around her, and passion . . . nothing but passion between them.

But then it was as if he heard his own warning, and his eyes widened as if he had just connected the woman before him with the woman to whom he'd pledged earlier to keep his distance.

Much to her chagrin he took a hasty step back. "Yes, yes, I suppose it is for the better."

They stood there for some time, separated by silence and wariness until Lord Henry asked quietly, "What will he do?"

So quietly that she barely discerned that he'd spoken, for she was still lost in her tangled thoughts, this sudden passion.

Daphne glanced up, blinking. "Pardon?"

"What will Lord Dale do now?" He bent over and picked up his greatcoat, this time handing it to her instead of settling it over her shoulders himself.

Oh, yes, Crispin. She'd nearly forgotten. Shrugging on the coat, she slanted a glance at Lord Henry. It was easy to see why the threat of her relatives was so far from her thoughts.

His blue eyes still held a smoky hue, his tawny hair loose from his usual queue — giving him a pirate air. Without his driving coat, he cut a rakish figure, standing there in his dark jacket, plain waistcoat and breeches. Polished boots encased his muscled calves. And that chest, oh, she knew that chest so well now, for her hands had splayed across it, explored it.

She blushed at her wayward thoughts and looked away.

"Crispin?" he nudged.

"Oh, yes," she stammered. "Most likely, he'll write Aunt Damaris."

"Damaris Dale?" Lord Henry exclaimed, his words followed by a great shudder.

Apparently her great-aunt's infamy extended even outside the family.

Daphne continued on with the likely scenario. "Then there will be a flurry of correspondence as to what must be done."

"That could take a week or so," he offered, most likely trying to appear helpful. That, or calculating the necessary fortifications that would need to be made to Owle Park.

"And then someone will be dispatched to fetch me home." She made her way back to her sad, lonely bonnet and picked it up. The pink bow lay flat, and the silk flowers that had looked so jaunty earlier were now all well past their bloom.

The whole thing was a shambles.

Just like her plans to find Dishforth.

"Oh, dear!" she gasped, her hands coming to her still swollen lips. Lips that she'd vowed only for another.

However had she forgotten her stalwart, her steady love so quickly? So utterly?

She glanced over at Lord Henry and found him studying her, a bevy of questions mulling about behind the furrow of his brow, the intensity of his scrutiny.

One not to leave any stone unturned, as

she feared, he asked, "Why did you come here, to Owle Park, if you knew this would happen?"

This? Their kiss? She looked at him and realized he'd meant — much to her embarrassment — something else entirely.

Why had she come? Why had she risked so much?

Without even thinking, she said the first words that came to her. For they answered both her reasons for coming to Owle Park and perhaps her unfathomable reasons for kissing him.

They were Dishforth's words, and once again, her mysterious lover seemed to know her better than she knew herself.

"Lord Henry, haven't you ever wanted to dance where you may?"

CHAPTER 7

Mr. Dishforth, may I be forward? I am
going to be, without hearing your answer, because I know what you would
tell me: speak from your heart. And I
shall.

Do you have a wen?

Found in a letter from
Miss Spooner to Mr. Dishforth

"What the devil were you thinking?" Preston asked. No, more like lectured.

No, actually, bellowed.

Henry did his best to stand his ground in
the spot of shame that was a well-worn
patch in front of the fireplace. They were in
the family salon in the back of the house,
far from the guests. Which unfortunately
gave Preston all the freedom the duke
should desire to unleash his displeasure with
his uncle.

It was rather an odd position for Henry to

be in. Up until a month or so ago it had always been Preston standing uncomfortably at attention, forced to listen to his relations chastise his behavior.

But here he was, and Henry found it nearly impossible to keep from shifting from one foot to another while Preston and Hen took turns chiding him.

"What were you thinking?" Hen wailed.

"Dishforth made me do it," he muttered.

"Dishforth? Who the devil is he?" Great-Aunt Zillah demanded from her prime location — the large chair by the fireplace.

The Dales had Damaris, and the Seldons had Zillah.

"Well?" the old girl demanded. "Who is this Dishforth?"

Preston and Henry shot accusing glances at Hen, since she'd insisted their only other relative be invited. While the Dales were as prolific as a colony of rabbits, the Seldons had never been overly fruitful.

"He's no one, dear," Hen told her.

"No one?" Zillah huffed. "You can't fool me. There's a note on the salver for him even now."

Henry caught himself before his head snapped to attention and he let out an eager "There is?"

Instead, he spared a glance at his nephew

220

and sister and gave a sad shake to his head. *Poor old girl. Going at long last.*

"Henry! A Seldon does not blame others for his misdeeds," Zillah admonished, wagging a long, thin finger at him and proving that she wasn't as infirm as Henry would like the others to believe.

"Yes, precisely," Hen agreed.

"It started to rain. Nothing more," Henry told them. For about the tenth time. It was the truth and yet no one wanted to believe him.

Gads! Had it been like this for Preston all these years? Glancing over at the duke's glower, which held a triumphant air to it, revealed that this turnabout wasn't all that unpleasant for the notorious Duke of Preston.

Then again in his favor, having listened to Preston "explain" his side of his less-than-respectable conduct over the years had taught Henry a thing or two about confession.

Taking a page from Preston's example, he used enough of the truth to be believable.

"I got lost."

Hen and Preston glanced at one another and had to shrug in concession. There was no arguing Henry's poor sense of direction.

Not that Zillah was about to yield the

field. "That gel looked tumbled when you brought her back. Tumbled, I say!"

Yes, we all heard you the first time, Henry thought with a flinch. Slanting a glance over at his great-aunt, an ancient crone if ever there was one, he knew there were volumes of old family stories about Zillah's flamboyant past. Yet looking at her now, Henry found it impossible to believe she even knew what tumbled would look like, let alone be able to still discern it.

Why, not even Hen knew how old Zillah was. And the lady herself? She wouldn't have revealed her age to save the king or the whole of England. For all they knew, Queen Elizabeth was most likely reigning when Zillah was born.

Probably been her impudent dog who had caused all the fuss between the Dales and the Seldons to begin with.

"Tumbled," Zillah repeated, before her head nodded back and she let out a loud snore.

Henry shook his head at the others, even as he knew it was an impossible position to defend.

Daphne had looked tumbled, for she'd very nearly been.

So had he — though not in the same way. Never mind that kiss — well, not that he was ever going to forget it, for it alone had been enough to knock him over — but when she'd stood there before him in that state of enticing dishabille, all wet and disheveled, her hair tumbling . . . yes, tumbling . . . down in wet curls, making her stunning confession, she'd turned his world upside down.

Haven't you ever wanted to dance where you may?

He'd staggered back as if she'd slapped him. Dishforth's words. Coming out of her lips.

No, not Dishforth's, but his words.

How the devil had she known to say that? Pure chance? A mockery by the gods of love?

And before he'd been able to react, before he'd been able to demand an explanation from her, haul her back into his arms and kiss her until she was willing to explain how she knew such a thing, Preston, Hen and Tabitha had driven up, all too clearly witnessing the spectacle of the two of them — drenched to the bones, gaping at each other in wonder.

Then everything had sped forward so quickly that it was as if the thread binding them together with those words had been whisked back onto the spool from which it had come.

In the blink of an eye, Miss Dale had been bundled off in Preston's carriage and Lord Henry had been left with the pony cart to trot obediently behind, with only Mr. Muggins for company. That, and the one burning question that had Henry at sixes and sevens.

Could that minx be . . . ?

No, he'd told himself over and over. *Impossible.*

Miss Spooner was a respectable lady. Sensible. Well-bred.

With a tart pen and a passionate nature, Dishforth would have added. *Don't you recall what she wrote to us?*

I am a tangle of shivers since I read your last letter. Promise one day we will dance under the stars. Dance where we may, just as you wrote. I would dance with you, sir. Wherever you may.

Henry had glanced up at the carriage before him, where all he'd been able to see had been the back of Miss Dale's fair head.

No! . . .

And yet . . . what if Miss Dale was his Miss Spooner?

Henry had shaken that thought off just

like Mr. Muggins had shaken the rain from his wiry coat — quickly and efficiently.

There was no way the impetuous beauty in the carriage before him was his Miss Spooner.

Would you mind if she was? a voice like Dishforth's had nudged.

Indeed I would, he'd told himself, ignoring the way his body had thrummed to life as he'd recalled how she'd felt in his arms, her gown clinging to her full breasts, the rounded lines of her hips beneath his hands.

He hadn't given her his coat out of some duty of chivalry. He'd done it to hide those damnable curves of hers — at least that had been his reasoning the second time around — for the sight of her could have turned even the most sensible of fellows into the most Seldon of rakes.

Even him.

Ah, those curves . . .

"Ahem," Hen said, clearing her throat and wrenching him back to the present.

Henry glanced around and found all three of them looking at him. "She was not tumbled," he told his self-appointed tribunal.

"She was wearing your coat," Preston pointed out. Being a rake of the first order gave him a rather unique familiarity with the subject.

If anyone could spot tumbled, it was Preston.

But Henry wasn't a proper and sensible gentleman for nothing. "She was soaked," he told his nephew. "Would you rather have had me leave her shivering? Or worse, catch her death?"

"Whose fault would that have been?" Hen mused.

Preston ignored her and continued on. "How the devil did you get so far afield as it was? Another few miles and you'd been over the boundary."

The boundary.

Demmit! Henry had hoped to avoid that subject. And to his consternation, his guilt must have shown on his face.

"Henry! No!" Preston exclaimed. "You didn't."

He managed a deep breath and knew there was no choice but to confess it all.

The boundary part. Not the kiss. Nor about Miss Spooner. Or his suspicions as to who she might be.

Stealing a glance over at Zillah, he reordered his list. No confessing about the kiss. Especially not the kiss.

"Well, if you must know —" he began.

"No!" Preston groaned.

"Yes, I fear so," Henry admitted.

Hen, scenting a growing scandal, sat up.

"Whatever are you going on about?" Zillah asked, her head snapping up to attention. Apparently her nap was over. "I will not be left out!"

Ignoring her, Henry lowered his voice. While a set down by Hen and Preston was one thing, Zillah was known to take umbrage for months. Years. Decades.

And while no one would venture a guess as to how long the old girl might have left, knowing Zillah she'd give it her all and last another quarter of a century, if only to make good on a grudge.

"I had a bit of a dustup with the viscount," he admitted. He didn't have to say which one.

"You not only crossed the line but you also managed to happen upon *him*?" Preston said, raking his hand through his hair and beginning to stalk about the room.

"Yes, I fear so," Henry told him, his gaze following the duke warily.

"What is this?" Zillah demanded, her hand cupped to her ear.

His sister was more than willing to enlighten her, for it hadn't taken her long to catch up. "Apparently, Henry strayed across the boundary onto Langdale, Auntie."

Zillah's eyes widened. And then she let fly. "Lord Henry Arthur George Baldwin Seldon! How could you? There are just three rules we Seldons live by —"

Oh, no, Henry winced. *Not the rules.*

She held up her bony fingers and ticked them off in order. "A Seldon serves his king. He does his duty by his family. And he never, I mean ever, crosses *that* line."

"Yes, right, but it isn't well marked," Henry said in his defense, not that any of them were listening.

"What happened?" Preston demanded in a voice that reminded one and all he was the duke.

Henry related Crispin's demands and Miss Dale's obstinate refusal to acquiesce.

"I despise that man," Hen said, shaking her head.

"You made much the same observation about Michaels," Henry reminded her.

Hen's nose wrinkled. "At least he wasn't a Dale."

"Might as well have been," Zillah muttered.

They all ignored her, no matter that they agreed.

"What do you think will come of this?" Preston asked.

"Miss Dale believes he will write Damaris Dale."

All four Seldons shuddered at the mention of that lady's name.

"How unfortunate burning witches has gone out of fashion," Zillah said, spitting at the coals in the grate like one would to ward off an evil spirit.

No one argued with her.

Henry weighed his next words carefully. There was still the matter of Mr. Muggins's indiscretion . . . but perhaps that would be better mentioned after dinner. And after Preston had partaken in a brandy or two.

"Miss Dale believes that once her family is apprised of her whereabouts, someone will be dispatched to bring her home."

Hen got to her feet. "Are you suggesting her parents are unaware she is here?"

"So it seems."

His sister sank back down into her chair, white-faced at the very thought of it. "Whyever would she come here against her family's wishes?"

"Tabitha is her best friend," Preston said, raising a defense for Miss Dale. For whatever reason, he held a soft spot when it came to this particular Dale, for this wasn't the first time he'd championed her cause. "I suspect she was willing to set aside tradition to see her best friend married."

Hen nodded in concession, but Henry held his tongue.

He wasn't about to voice his own suspicions until he had some concrete proof.

If Daphne Dale was . . . was . . . her . . . his Miss Spooner . . . Henry stilled. No, it couldn't be true. Even if he'd been all but convinced as much the night of the ball. Yet now he knew that had been a grave mistake, one he didn't want to repeat.

All he had to do was prove Miss Dale's uncanny choice of words was mere happenstance.

Like her choice of that blasted red gown.

Or her sudden inexplicable appearance at a Seldon house party.

Henry flinched as the evidence began to mount against him.

Zillah, who'd been nodding again, jerked back awake. "Whyever are we discussing Damaris Dale?"

"Her niece is here," Hen explained. "Miss Dale. You met her earlier."

"Dale?" Zillah shook her head. "I thought her name was Hale." This time she turned her wrath on Preston — a deliverance of sorts for Henry. "Good heavens, young man!" she bleated. "That you have to lower yourself to include Dales just to fill out your

house party convinces me you've brought this family to the very depths of shame."
She squinted at Preston, then at the others, and then sort of nodded off again.

Much to everyone's relief.

"How long do we have?" Preston asked quietly, sneaking a glance at their great-aunt to make sure she was still dozing.

"A fortnight at the most, I imagine," Henry said.

"Unless Crispin Dale decides to come storming over here beforehand, if only to make a scene," Hen pointed out.

She needn't sound so pleased with the notion. Then again, there wasn't anything Hen loved more than a good row.

Hence her disastrous marriage to Lord Michaels.

"Why not just send her packing now?" she continued.

Preston shook his head. "What? And cause more scandal? Besides, Tabitha is over the moon that her 'dear Daphne' was allowed to attend. I won't ruin her happiness."

"If this disrupts your wedding, you might be of another opinion," Hen pointed out.

"It won't," Henry said, straightening up. Like it or not, until he could prove otherwise, Daphne Dale had become his problem. "I swear I shall see to all this myself."

231

"Well, then I suppose there is nothing left to be done," Hen said, in a way that left her brother and nephew fully advised that she was washing her hands of all of it.

"Nothing to be done?" Zillah exclaimed, waking once more. "The Dales are at our doorstep! Preston, fetch my father's flint-lock. The pistol, not the Brown Bess. I know how to load it."

And no one doubted that she did.

"Miss Nashe, you've made quite the collection of conquests at dinner this evening," Lady Essex declared. The ladies had all retired to the sitting room to await the gentlemen, who were partaking of their port and cigars.

Dinner had been a lengthy and painful affair as far as Daphne was concerned.

She'd been seated at the far end of the table, wedged between the new vicar, who'd eaten as if he might know something the rest of them were not party to — that this might be the last supper — and Harriet's brother, Mr. Chaunce Hathaway, who worked doing who-knew-what for the Home Office. It was impossible to determine the particulars because he rarely spoke.

So Daphne had had little to do over the various courses but follow Chaunce's silent example and study the room.

If anything, it had given her time to clear the peel Lady Essex had rung over her on the dangers and perils of straying so far afield with a gentleman, even if he was a dull stick like Lord Henry Seldon.

Dull stick, indeed, she would have liked to have told the old girl. Try wolf in sheep's clothing.

Had he truly kissed her like that, or had she imagined it all? It had happened so fast. His lips upon hers, his hands exploring her, leaving a trail of desire that had continued to whisper and tease her every time she'd dared slant a glance in his direction.

How could a kiss from the wrong man — and yes, there were no doubt in her mind that Lord Henry Seldon was entirely the wrong man — have left her feeling so . . . *undone*? Right down to the soles of her boots.

Thank goodness she'd come to her senses when she had and remembered who and what she was.

Miss Daphne Dale. A proper miss. A sensible lady. In love with another.

Whom you've never met. Never kissed . . .

There were more important things than kissing, she'd told herself.

Though, for the life of her, she hadn't

233

been able to think of one. Not when she looked at Lord Henry.

Which she had done her best not to do. Especially since he'd been seated beside Miss Nashe and making a great show of it — in all his handsome glory, teasing her (and Lord Astbury) for winning the treasure hunt. And when not showering his charms down upon the heiress, he'd been flirting outrageously with Lady Alicia and even sending a few charming sorties out to Lady Clare.

Wretched man! Certainly Mr. Dishforth would never behave in such a rakish manner.

Yet as dinner had progressed, Daphne had realized her search for Mr. Dishforth might not be an easy matter.

However would she discover which of these gentlemen was Dishforth short of standing up and just asking the man to reveal his identity.

Daphne's fingers had curled around the arms of her chair and she'd been about to push herself to her feet and do just that — demand to know who Mr. Dishforth was — but she'd stopped short when she'd realized Lady Essex had her steady gaze fixed in her direction.

"Bother," Daphne had muttered as she'd

slumped back into her seat, for publicly admitting to such a folly a would be exactly the sort of unladylike display that would have Lady Essex shipping her back to Kempton in irons.

If only she'd been seated beside Lord Astbury. After all, he was, as Tabitha pointed out, the most likely candidate.

He was certainly handsome enough, as Phi avowed the man was. But then again, all around the table were handsome fellows — Captain Bramston and his craggy, rugged features and dark eyes; Lord Rawcliffe, with his aristocratic bearing; Kipps, who was hailed as the most charming and dashing Corinthian who had ever graced a London ballroom; and even Lord Cowley, who was known more for his academic leanings but still had a poet's bohemian air about him.

All of them fit Phi's nearsighted description of the elusive Mr. Dishforth. Even worse, Daphne supposed she would also have to include Lord Henry on that list — for he was also handsome.

Too handsome.

Still, it wasn't as if he could be Dishforth. . . .

But don't you wish he were, a wry voice had whispered in her ear as she'd recalled that dangerous kiss in the folly.

Thud. Thud Thud. Lady Zillah Seldon pounded her cane to the floor, bringing Daphne's attentions back to the sitting room. "In my day, I was considered quite the catch, just as you are, Miss Nashe. Best not waste your opportunities. Another Season, gel, and you'll be on the shelf."

"My lady, I have no idea what you mean," Miss Nashe demurred, her fan fluttering delicately even as her eyes narrowed.

Lady Alicia came to her friend's rescue. "Miss Nashe has a way of stealing the heart of every man in the room. She cannot help it."

Daphne tamped down the urge to gag. Truly? This is what they taught at the Bath finishing school these two had gone on and on about while at the table?

A Bath school offers a lady a chance to shine above all others, Miss Nashe had said, letting her gaze fall on the ladies who hadn't had the privilege.

Which had singled out all the guests from Kempton. Save Lady Essex. But then again, Lady Essex had gone to her finishing school in the previous century. And not in Bath, but a perfectly respectable establishment in Tunbridge Wells, not that Daphne would expect Miss Nashe to agree.

"You could hardly miss Lord Henry," Lady Essex said in her forthright manner. "He was clearly vying for your attentions."

"Oh, yes, my dear," Mrs. Nashe enthused. "And the Earl of Kipps couldn't tear his gaze away from you."

"You quite held every man's attention, my dear," Lady Clare said, a slight pinch to her nose as she said the words.

"They are all such excellent gentlemen," Miss Nashe preened ever so slightly now that she had the notice of the entire room.

"Most excellent," Lady Alicia echoed in fervent agreement.

Daphne glanced over to where Harriet and Tabitha stood, and then at the large vase of pink and white roses on the table beside them. *Oh, wouldn't Miss Nashe look so much better with a bit of a soaking?*

Harriet glanced at the vase as well and covered her mouth to keep from laughing, while Tabitha gave a slight shake of her head. *That would never do, Daphne.*

Ever the vicar's daughter was Tabitha.

But then again, Tabitha had stopped Daphne on more than one occasion from doing much the same thing — dashing something over a lady's head. Make that most Thursdays, at the Kempton Society meeting, where the horribly well-to-do Miss

Anne Fielding was always preening and prancing about Lady Essex's salon, what with her new hat, or travels to Bath, or the well-appointed carriage her father had promised.

Daphne's gaze narrowed as she measured this latest incarnation of her old nemesis. Either the room was not lit as well as it should have been, or good heavens, Miss Nashe bore a startling resemblance to Miss Fielding.

It was one of those moments that every lady of modest means and limited connections knew only too well.

When she realizes she is doomed to be surrounded by the Miss Fieldings and Miss Nashes and the rest of their ilk forever.

For there it was. Daphne's Achilles' heel. Raised a Dale on stories of her family's lofty place in society, in England's history, and yet . . . the Kempton Dales were hardly considered fashionable.

For the most part, they were overlooked and oft-forgotten.

Still, she'd come to London with such grand plans — and a bit of pin money her mother had set aside over the years. With a few new gowns, and the right introductions, she would find her chance to shine bright, to show one and all that she was a Dale worthy of recognition.

But in London she found herself shuttled to one side and then the other as just another girl from the country with no dowry and a lack of good connections.

Nor were her Dale relations much help. Whyever would Great-Aunt Damaris put Daphne forth when there were cousins aplenty with hefty dowries to dangle over Society?

The Daphnes and Phis of the family were left to wrestle for the affections of family leftovers, such as the Right Honorable Mr. Matheus Dale.

And while Daphne had spent most of her years dreaming of a lofty marriage to a man with an equally elevated income, it had taken Tabitha's engagement to, of all people, the Duke of Preston to make her realize it wasn't rank or money that made a good marriage.

Just one glance at how Preston looked at Tabitha quite stole one's breath away.

Then along had come Mr. Dishforth, and Daphne had stopped worrying over her lack of dowry or connections. She could only hope that one day, when they met, he would look at her as if she was his entire world. Never mind that she was only poor Daphne Dale of the Kempton Dales, or that she came with naught but a hundred pounds; he would love her for who she was, who she dreamed of being.

Yet it was nigh on impossible not to feel that familiar stab of jealousy, that niggle of worry that Miss Nashe and her money would steal away the only thing she had left: the pending affections of Mr. Dishforth.

That didn't seem so much to ask. Just to let her find her Dishforth.

Miss Nashe, now having moved to the very center of the room — for certainly someone in the corner might not be able to see her if she remained sitting on the settee — continued her discussion with Lady Essex on the virtues of the various gentlemen.

"What of Lord Astbury?" Lady Essex asked. "How lucky for you to be paired with him today. And to win so quickly. Why, it was almost as if he couldn't wait to bring you back."

Miss Nashe turned slightly and smiled. "The marquess is ever so clever and was most determined to win. For my sake. And of course he was most conscious of my social standing. I believe he could drive to China and back without getting lost." She shot a speculative glance in Daphne's direction.

Daphne didn't rise to the bait.

What was it Harriet always said? *Just because someone throws a hook in the water doesn't mean you have to bite.*

Daphne had no intention of paying Miss Nashe any heed, let alone biting at anything she tossed out.

"Such a lovely prize," Harriet rushed in to say. "A pearl necklace."

Miss Nashe fingered the strand around her neck. "Yes, quite quaint. Mother insisted I wear it."

Daphne glanced over at Tabitha, who had chosen the prize. *Don't bite . . .*

"Now Lord Astbury can choose whomever he wants for the unmasking ball," Lady Alicia enthused, having missed the undercurrents around her. She smiled at her friend, confident that Miss Nashe would be that cherished prize.

"But remember, only from the available ladies," Miss Nashe said with a coy flutter of her fan, implying that she would not be among that group.

And neither will I, Daphne vowed. *I'll find Mr. Dishforth. Tonight if I must. Even if I have to stand up and demand he step forward.*

Which she hoped she didn't have to resort to.

"I find it all so romantic," Lady Alicia continued. "Especially how Lord Henry and the Earl of Kipps were vying over you at dinner."

While nearly always the picture of composure, Miss Nashe snapped a dark glance at her dearest bosom friend. One could only assume that Lady Alicia had let spill a confidence: that the heiress had set her cap for one of them.

Lord Henry or the Earl of Kipps.

But like any Bath-educated heiress who hoped to rise quickly in society, Miss Nashe recovered quickly. "I do so prefer a man who is handsome and well turned out." She paused to make sure everyone was looking at her when she said, "I thought Lord Henry looked quite dashing tonight, while the earl is so . . . so . . . strikingly noble."

"Most decidedly," Lady Essex agreed. "If anything, it simply becomes a matter of whether a lady prefers the security of wealth and connections —"

Meaning Lord Henry.

"— or the addition of a coronet to one's jewel case."

Which would make the lady the next Countess of Kipps.

Miss Nashe didn't so much as nod in agreement, but let a sly smile tip at her lips. She had made her decision as to which man she wanted, but she was keeping her choice a closely guarded secret.

Yet given the gleam of avarice in the girl's eyes, Daphne could make a good guess as to her intentions. To catch the earl's eye and his hand.

Despite the fact that Kipps had pockets to let — through his own imprudence and recklessness — he was an earl.

Foolish chit. Lord Henry is twice the man Kipps will ever be, Daphne thought, the vehemence of those words resounding through her like the echoes of St. Edwards's sturdy bell.

Yet what if she does prefer Lord Henry over the Earl of Kipps?

The question prodded at Daphne more than she cared to admit.

And as if to tug at that nagging thread, Harriet and Tabitha joined her on the settee.

"Lord Henry," Tabitha whispered.

"No, I wager Kipps," Harriet countered. "As Benedict might say" — referring to her brother in the navy — "half pay will never suit Miss Nashe."

Meaning a mere second son, with just an honorific title like Lord Henry, was not up to her lofty aspirations.

"What do you think, Daphne?" Tabitha asked, smoothing out her skirt even as the door opened and the gentlemen began to arrive, sending a nervous flutter of fans and whispers through the sitting room.

"I think you should have stricken her from the guest list before the invitations went out," Daphne said, smiling politely at the heiress across the room.

For the better part of the evening, Henry had done his ingenuous best to discover Miss Spooner's identity.

And to prove that the lady's similarities to Miss Dale were a ridiculous coincidence.

However, his search had been for naught.

Lady Alicia had only wanted to discuss Miss Nashe's charms. Miss Nashe had only wanted to discuss, well, herself. And since he'd known Lady Clare since childhood and knew that she had vowed since her broken engagement several years earlier never to marry, he sincerely doubted she had taken up Miss Spooner's pen.

He paused for a moment beside the pianoforte and gazed across the room, where Roxley and Miss Hathaway were playing a fierce game of backgammon — something it appeared they had done before, given Roxley's accusations of "Harry, you always cheat."

Henry found he rather envied the earl's

easy friendship with the affable, albeit cheating, Miss Hathaway. A far sight more enjoyable than prowling the room in search of a phantom miss.

"I see you've settled on your conquest," came a pert comment from his right.

Henry glanced over and found Miss Dale on the opposite side of the instrument. How had he not seen her standing there before? Yet there she was, in that same red silk gown she'd worn the night of the engagement ball, her blonde hair all piled up atop her head save for a few stray curls that tumbled down.

Tumbled.

He cringed, for suddenly he found himself wary of that word and all its implications. Especially since it carried with it echoing refrains from Zillah's scold.

That gel looked tumbled when you brought her back. Tumbled, I say!

Looking at Miss Dale now, Henry would argue that the lady always looked slightly undone, from her fluttering lashes to that impossibly tousled hair. She was temptation in all its incarnations.

Worse, everywhere he'd turned this evening, she'd caught his eye, what with the sway of her hip as she walked, the curve of her smile, the rare light in her eyes when she laughed — really laughed, not just the polite noise she'd made for Lord Crowley when he'd recited some nonsense verse he'd written lately.

And now here she was, teasing him from across the pianoforte.

"My what?" he asked.

"Your conquest," she repeated, then shook her head. "Oh, dear, I forgot who I was talking to. A flirtation. A dalliance, a trifling." She listed every definition a lady could politely use.

Those words — *conquest, flirtation* and *dalliance* — from any other person would have been ridiculous, but from Miss Dale, they seemed to hold a challenge within them. As if she knew of what she spoke.

Which she did. For look how he had behaved earlier. When it had been just the two of them.

Shaking off that memory — one that left his blood thick and throbbing through his body — he instead focused on her accusation.

That he was about to make yet another conquest.

As if he was the only one who'd spent all evening flirting. She ought to look at the wake behind her. Why, she'd dallied with nearly every man in the room, having moved from Kipps to Bramston, then Astbury, and even Crowley. Taking turns around the room with them, laughing at their jokes, fluttering her lashes at them, her gloved hand atop their sleeves, then moving to her next conquest.

And he was about to point out her expertise on the subject, but she was already nattering on.

"— I don't suppose she is the dallying type, though she rather seems *your* sort."

"My sort?" Henry's gaze followed hers toward the trio of ladies by the window.

Of course, there sat Lady Alicia, Lady Clare and Miss Nashe — the trio he'd spent the night dancing attendance upon.

Henry decided the best course of action was one of innocence. "Whoever do you mean?"

"Why, Miss Nashe, of course," she said, tipping her head as she took another examining look at the heiress.

"Whatever does *that* mean? My sort, indeed," he puffed before he remembered what he'd said about Crispin Dale earlier.

Not that Miss Dale was going to let him forget as she turned his own sword on him, making a perfectly timed thrust into his chest. She leaned closer as she made her move. "Overdressed. Vain. Wealthy."

He had the feeling she'd left out a few. Given the arch of her fair brow, he had to imagine that "overreaching mushroom" was a possibility.

Henry knew Miss Nashe was exactly the "sort" a second son like himself sought for a bride — wealthy, gracious and lovely, beloved by the society columns — but there was one impossible hurdle that not even her dowry could tempt him to leap.

The girl herself.

Still, he feigned surprise. "Miss Nashe? You think her vain?"

"You don't?" Miss Dale's nose wrinkled. "Why, look at her! Even now she is regaling poor Lady Clare and Lady Alicia with tales of her social prowess."

Given the set of Lady Clare's jaw, Miss Dale was probably correct, but Henry wasn't going to admit such a thing. Instead, he asked, "However can you hear what is being said? They are all the way across the room."

Miss Dale's chin rose. "I have a talent for these things."

Of course she did.

"You do?" he asked against his better judgment.

"Yes, watch," she said, glancing over at the trio. The next time Miss Nashe opened her mouth, Miss Dale supplied the words.

"Oh, the expectations placed on one when one is mentioned daily in the social columns are exhausting."

Henry coughed on the fit of laughter that nearly choked him. "She would never say such a thing," he argued as he tried to compose himself.

"No, no," Miss Dale told him. "She isn't finished. Listen —"

Then modulating her tones and clipping her words, she matched Miss Nashe's overly educated enunciation perfectly.

"Yet I endeavor to provide proper and edifying on dits *so as to inspire the lesser of my peers to learn from my grace and status. It is my gift to Society."*

And demmed if Miss Nashe didn't finish and smile at the end of Miss Dale's lines, as if indeed she was conveying such a condescending speech to her audience.

Henry snorted back another fit of laughter and turned his back to the trio, for it was devilishly hard to look at Miss Nashe and not hear Miss Dale's recitation.

Meanwhile, his impish companion grinned with wicked delight. "I told you."

Henry had to admit that the one thing he rather liked about Miss Dale was the fact that she didn't suffer from a lack of straightforward honesty. And so he replied in kind. "She is rather impressed with herself."

Miss Dale covered her mouth to keep from laughing aloud. "What a terrible thing to say, Lord Henry."

"You started it," he shot back. "But I confess that after listening to her go on for half an hour as to how she'd modernize Owle Park if she were Tabitha —"

Daphne's eyes widened with outrage. "Change this house? Whatever for?"

Her annoyance echoed his own. He tipped his head closer. "Apparently it is not the first stare of fashion."

Miss Dale clucked her tongue. "It isn't supposed to be. It is a family home." And she didn't stop there. "Owle Park is delightful. Rather surprising, actually."

"What do you mean?"

"Well, it isn't what I expected," she said, glancing away, a bit of a blush on her cheeks.

"What did you think you would find, Miss Dale? Remnants of the Hell Fire Club in the dining room? Stray virgins lolling about awaiting pagan sacrifice?" The color on her cheeks confirmed just that. Henry laughed. "You did, didn't you?"

"It is just that one hears such tales, and then one supposes . . ."

"Disappointed?"

She paused for a moment and then glanced up at him, a twinkle in her eyes. "Slightly."

They both laughed, and it seemed the entire room stilled and looked over at them.

Henry stepped away from Miss Dale, probably a bit too quickly, for it made him look guilty . . . of something.

Not that he had anything to feel guilty about. And yet there was Zillah, her dark eyes blazing with accusations. *Not again, you foolish boy!*

He edged a little farther away from Miss Dale before his proximity prompted his great-aunt to come over and give the entire room a recitation of the Seldon family rules.

With nothing of note happening around the pianoforte, the other guests finally went back to their previous pursuits. All too soon, the din of quiet discussions, exclamations from well-played hands, and Roxley's occasional expletive followed by a "Harry, one of these days I'll catch you cheating," left Henry to draw a sigh of relief.

As if he'd lucked out this time. Better than earlier, when he'd gained an earful.

He glanced over at Miss Dale. "You weren't in too much trouble, earlier that is, were you?" he asked quietly.

"A bit," she said with a sigh. "And you?"

"Oh, yes." He had her attention now.

"Rang a peel?"

"Quite."

She nodded in understanding, then lowered her voice. "They don't know about —"

She had no need to say the rest . . . *the kiss.*

"No!" he shot back. "You didn't mention —"

Miss Dale shook her head slightly. "No."

"Best forgotten," he advised, though he knew it would be some time before he could. Forget, that is.

"Yes, precisely," she agreed, rocking on her heels.

"Terrible mistake."

"Exactly," she shot back.

Rather quickly, he noted. Too quickly.

Did she have to agree *that* fast?

When he looked back at her, he found her studying Miss Nashe once again.

"Are you supplying more lines for the drama over there?" he asked.

"No," she said with a slight shake of her head. However, the tip of her lips said quite another.

Henry shot her a wry glance.

"Well, perhaps," she admitted.

"You are a devilish minx, Miss Dale."

"You disapprove?"

Henry sighed. "Sadly, not in the least."

Once again, their eyes met, and it wasn't just their gazes that entangled. It was something altogether more dangerous.

Henry's blood came rushing through his veins as he remembered how it had felt to take her in his arms, kiss her madly, passionately. For no other reason than she thought him a rake.

And given the light in her eyes, she still thought him one.

Then she bit her bottom lip and tugged her glance away. "We need to stay apart," she reminded him.

Henry glanced up and around the room, feigning disinterest. "Yes, I suppose we must."

"Need I remind you, I am nearly engaged elsewhere —"

"Yes, your most excellent gentleman," Henry mused.

"Yes, him." She stole a nervous glance around the room, and suddenly an entirely new possibility occurred to Henry.

The answer to the Gordian knot in his life: Why the devil was Miss Dale here at Owle Park?

Actually, he'd never quite believed her declaration of having a betrothed. Or a nearly betrothed, whatever that nonsense meant.

But now . . .

Henry turned to her, a wide grin turning his lips. He had his answer. He'd bet his fortune on it.

"He's here, isn't he?"

Daphne's heart nearly stopped.

Lord Henry had not just asked that question.

"Well, is he or isn't he here?" the man pressed.

Yes, apparently he had.

Daphne wasn't a member of the Society for the Temperance and Improvement of Kempton for nothing. For when not gathering baskets for the poor spinsters in the village or planting flowers in the graveyard, they also practiced deportment at Lady Essex's urging.

Therefore Daphne could give even a Bath-educated lady like Miss Nashe a run for her money when it came to being utterly composed.

Even when one felt like running in a blind panic.

She straightened and collected herself as best she could. If only she could still her hammering heart. "I am not discussing *him* with *you.*"

He leaned in, indecently close, like the wolf that he was. "Whyever not?"

The nearer he got, the more Daphne's resolve and composure began to waver. Bay rum and a hint of port invaded her senses. It was like being surrounded by his coat all over again. Yet this wasn't just a greatcoat enfolding her but the man himself.

The one who'd kissed her breathless. Touched her until she'd trembled. Ignited a fire in her once temperate heart.

Oh, but she was too close to finding her perfect happiness to let Lord Henry Seldon ruin everything. For that is what Seldons were unsurpassed at: ruin.

"My affairs are none of your business," she told him as tartly as Lady Essex did when she scolded her nephew, Lord Roxley. Adding to this, she folded her arms over her chest to show him just how firm she was in her resolve.

And not, as one might think, to ward him off from breaching what little control she could still claim.

Unfortunately, her tone had no effect on the man. Her words, on the other hand . . . they seemed to urge him on.

"So it is an affair —" he said, his eyes sparking with mischievous delight.

"Not in the way you would assume," she told him. "Ours is a coming together of the mind and the heart. Far outside of the realm of your base encounters."

"Is that what we shared earlier, a 'base encounter'?" he asked.

Daphne shook with anger. "I told you, I am not discussing that."

He glanced down at the music rack, absently thumbing through the sheets. "I suppose there really isn't much to discuss now, is there?"

She sucked in a deep breath, trying to hold back the scathing remark that so wanted to come bursting out.

"So tell me this, Miss Dale," he continued, edging still ever closer, his hand sliding along the top of the pianoforte until it was nearly around her hip, "why aren't you at his side right this moment?" He looked around the room as if he was trying to imagine where she rightly belonged, even as he took another step toward her.

"Whatever are you doing?" she asked, for he had her trapped, cornered in every sense of the word.

"Testing a theory." He took another step, leaving naught but a whisper between them.

In front of the entire party? Good heavens, could he now see how this looked?

"We agreed to keep our distance," she reminded him.

"Yes, I suppose we did," he conceded, but that didn't stop him from leaning in, his hips nearly against hers, the wall of his chest but a sliver away from her breasts.

Daphne tried to breathe, but he was ever so close, ever around her. She couldn't breathe without drawing him in, couldn't move without touching him.

Didn't dare look up at him, for then it would be too much like those reckless, dangerous moments in the folly.

Too close to deny that she desired his kiss. With all her heart.

Whatever was wrong with her? It was Dishforth who should ignite such a fire inside her, not Lord Henry. Never Lord Henry.

Oh, Mr. Dishforth, where are you?

"My lord," she managed, daring to look up at him, "I hardly think this . . . this . . . is keeping our distance."

He grinned. "Miss Dale, you have two choices: go and seek your perfect gentleman" — he nodded toward the crowded room — "or better yet, let's see if he shares your opinion of me and will rescue you from my nefarious attentions."

And with that, Lord Henry dipped his

head down as if he was about to steal a kiss.

Right there. In front of everyone.

His breath teased over her ear, sending a clarion cry through her. He was going to ruin her.

Let him.

Daphne panicked. At least that is what she vowed later to Lady Essex and Harriet and Tabitha.

She put her hands on his chest, an attempt to push the loathsome beast away, but the moment her fingers splayed across his jacket, she found herself entwined by the same magic that had wound around them at the folly.

Indeed, it was a dangerous kind of folly that Daphne and Lord Henry soon found themselves in.

Especially when Lady Zillah Seldon chose that moment to wake up a bit and take stock of what was happening around her.

CHAPTER 8

No. I most certainly do not.
                    Found in a letter from
            Mr. Dishforth to Miss Spooner

The next morning
"What aspect of the very simple vow that we agreed upon — to keep our distance — eludes you, Lord Henry?"

Henry came to a blinding halt in the middle of the breakfast room, his thoughts too focused on the business at hand, that of uncovering the identity of Miss Spooner, to notice that the room was not empty.

And the complaints weren't over yet. "Good heavens, I even got up an extra hour early to escape you, and still you cannot leave me be? This is unconscionable."

He cringed. *Miss Dale.* His gaze swept the grand table, and at the very end he found the sole occupant.

Which also meant they were alone. Once again.

Splendid.

That always went so well for them, he mused as he gauged their surroundings.

Well, not completely alone, for Tabitha's huge beast of a dog lay at her feet. Mr. Muggins gazed up at him with a crooked smile that suggested the big terrier wasn't the least shocked at Henry's arrival. Contrary to Miss Dale's horrified greeting, the dog got up and ambled over, nudging Henry's hand with his wiry head and then looked up at him with those great big brown, adoring eyes.

Of course, the dog was also looking over at the platter of sausages on the sideboard, as if to suggest that Henry might also make a good footman and fetch him a couple. Just between friends and all.

Some chaperone. Once fed, the dog would surely look the other way at any goings-on.

Of which there weren't going to be any. None whatsoever. Last night had been disaster enough.

"What are you doing down here so early?" Miss Dale continued, shooting a wry glance at Mr. Muggins, one that suggested she found the dog's attentions downright traitorous.

"I had thought to avoid you," he said, setting his papers and writing box down at his chair near the head of the table. At least the chit had chosen a spot well away from his.

"Harrumph!" Miss Dale sputtered, her teacup rattling in the saucer as she set it down.

Ignoring her glower, he went to fetch a plate from the sideboard. Mr. Muggins followed, tail wagging happily.

"You don't intend to stay?" she protested as much as she questioned.

"You could leave," he pointed out as he slowly filled his plate, stopping before the platter of sausages. "So we might avoid another near catastrophe."

"That was hardly my fault," she pointed out. "And speaking of last night —"

Oh, must they? His ears were still ringing from the peal Hen had rung over him. The one she'd begun the very moment she'd been able to decipher what Zillah's shrieking had been about.

Fortunately for him, his great-aunt's ranting had managed to pull every pair of eyes in Zillah's direction and give him enough time to set Miss Dale well out of reach. By the time anyone had been able to make out what had the lady in such a lather — *he's going to kiss her* — all the evidence had been quite to the contrary.

Henry had been standing at one end of the pianoforte, feigning interest in the music sheets, and Miss Dale had stood at the other, studying the painting of the sixth Duchess of Preston.

"Kiss who?" he'd said, laughing. "No one but you, Zillah." Then he'd bussed the old girl on the cheek and winked at the crowd as if to say, *Poor dear, half out of her wits.*

However, his ruse hadn't fooled Hen. Or Preston. And as such there had been another family dustup in the back salon, where he had spent a good hour explaining that Great-Aunt Zillah had had it all wrong: he hadn't been kissing Miss Dale. He'd finally gained a reprieve when he'd reminded Hen and Preston of the previous Christmas when Zillah had ordered 'round Bow Street because she'd thought there were Dales hiding in the basement.

Sadly, that was not the end of it, for Hen had spent the next hour giving him a thorough wigging on which ladies were proper prospects for the second son of a duke and which ladies weren't. It didn't take a member of the Royal Society to know on which side of that argument Hen placed Miss Dale.

Besides, he hadn't actually kissed Miss

Dale. Just meant to call her bluff.

Nor did it appear that Miss Dale had fared much better as a result of Zillah's tirade.

"— I had to endure another lengthy lecture from Lady Essex —"

She had him there. Lady Essex could probably put even Hen to shame when it came to delivering a blistering scold. Henry was ready even to offer some condolences when she went on and said, "— despite my reassurances to her that your overly licentious nature casts no spell on me —"

Now, just a bloody moment. His licentious nature?

Henry stormed down to the end of the table. "My nature?"

"Yes, yours," she said. "You are determined to mire me in ruin, and I won't have it. I have my future to think of. I understand that you can't help yourself —"

"I am not the one with the made-up suitor," he shot back.

"Made up?" she said, her hands balling into fists. "I'll have you know that my dear —"

But to his chagrin, she stopped herself before the name slipped out.

Henry arched a brow and gave her the most quelling Seldon stare he could manage. The one his father often used to silence the entire House of Lords.

Not that it daunted Miss Dale. Not in the least.

"My situation is none of your business," she finished.

He smiled, because this time she hadn't said "affair."

"Who is he?" Henry asked. "This suitor of yours?"

Her lips pressed together, her brow crinkled.

"Then I return to my original theory that he is a figment of your imagination. For whyever would any man let you wander about if you are his true love?"

"Because he is secure in my affections and I in his," she said.

Now it was Henry's turn to scoff, for in business he knew that when an opponent boasted or protested overly much, it was because they hadn't a firm conviction beneath them.

Miss Dale got to her feet. "Of course you wouldn't understand. As a Seldon, how could you? You have no sense of what true love means."

"Oh, not that rot again," he complained.

"Oh, yes, that again," she shot back. "How am I to think otherwise when you persist in trying to ruin me at every turn?"

"Ruin you?" Henry laughed. "Oh, if that isn't a lark!"

"A lark? That's what you call it?" Miss Dale stood her ground. "You use every opportunity you can gain to take advantage of me."

Henry had had enough. He stalked over until they were nose to nose. "Then why do you linger, Miss Dale? Why do you stay?"

"Linger?" she sputtered back.

"Yes, you. Always lingering about as if you want me to kiss you. Again."

She took a step back. "Oh, I never! Want to kiss you? I'd rather take my chances with Mr. Muggins." She crossed her arms over her chest and glared at him.

Mr. Muggins, who still manned his spot at the sideboard, looked from Henry to Miss Dale and then back at Henry again, and gave his head a tousled shake, then another pointed glance at the sideboard. *Enough talk of kissing. Sausages, anyone?*

Henry gave up on both of them and went back down to the end of the table, where he'd left his writing box. "Lingering!" he muttered in accusation.

"Hardly lingering, I have correspondence to attend to," she said, sitting back down and folding the letter she'd been writing, her jaw set with obstinate determination.

Stubborn chit. Standing her ground despite everything that had happened between them.

Could happen between them. Could ruin them both.

Oh, Zillah might rail on and on about the Dales and their failings, but Henry couldn't fault them for their bottom. Daphne Dale's audacity in the face of ruin was nothing less than impressive.

Like how she'd faced down her cousin. Or last night, when she'd been about to dump him on his backside. (He was now more than convinced she had been the one who'd tripped him at the ball.) Audacious, dangerous minx! Those traits alone should have warned him off. But no, he rather admired her mettle, nor did it stop him from prodding her a bit to test it.

"Writing your parents to inform them where you are?" he asked, the epitome of polite and measured concern.

"Harrumph."

Apparently not. Yet Daphne Dale never liked to leave a question unanswered.

"If you must know —" she began.

"Truly, I hardly care," he shot back.

"Then whyever did you ask?"

Henry paused. He supposed he had asked.

"Merely being polite."

"You needn't be," she told him. "I have much to attend to this morning."

And indeed, she had what looked like a long list before her and a stack of letters. It all appeared as organized and orderly as the stacks Henry preferred for his business matters.

And a twinge of curiosity prodded at him. *Whatever was she about?*

Not that he was going to pry. Not into Miss Dale's business.

"Yes, well, so do I," he said, hoping that was the end of it.

It wasn't.

"Whatever do you have to write about?" she asked. "Other than your usual daily apologies to the ladies you've wronged."

Henry pressed his teeth together and ignored her jab; instead, he decided to retort with something more shocking — the truth.

"I will have you know, in addition to helping Preston manage the ducal estates, I have my own houses and properties, which require close attention." Henry couldn't help himself; he puffed up a bit, for her face was a mix of skepticism and shock.

"You do?"

He nodded. Most people — apparently Miss Dale as well — just assumed that

267

because he was a second son, he was barely worth noting, save as a conduit to the duke . . . that is, when Preston's favor was being curried.

"Properties? As in a house and lands?" she asked.

This question from any other miss might have implied that she was measuring him for a trip to the parson's mousetrap, but from Miss Dale it was completely and utterly a test to see, he suspected, if he knew one from the other.

"Three houses," he told her. "One is quite productive — good wool, and a coal vein has just been discovered on the other."

She sat back and looked at him as if he'd fallen from the sky and just landed in front of the buffet. He could almost see the calculations going on behind her furrowed brow.

Three houses? However could that be?

"And you don't have a steward or an agent who handles these matters?" she asked.

Not an unusual question, for most men handed over the care and maintenance of their estates to others — as Preston would have if Henry hadn't been there.

"No," he told her as Mr. Muggins jostled his elbow. Henry looked down at the hound, who gazed up at him with the most adoring gaze, as if Henry was the only one on earth who could save the poor beast from starvation. And even though he knew better — for hadn't Preston warned one and all not to feed Tabitha's dog or there would be no end to the dog's attentions — he stole a glance over at Miss Dale, who was even now looking over a letter she held. Before she looked up, Henry slid a sausage from his plate, and the quick-witted terrier snatched it out of the air.

The *snap* of the dog's jaws brought the lady's gaze up.

"Uh, well, I find," Henry said, quickly filling the space with words to cover his momentary weakness, "that if you want a task done right —"

"You must do it yourself," Miss Dale finished.

They looked at each other — a sense of mutual understanding coiling between them. Both of them shifted uneasily at the discovery for it should be evident that they held nothing in common.

Or so they wanted to believe.

Miss Dale brought her napkin up and patted her lips. "I often find the same is true with a gown. If you want it just so, you must do the work yourself."

"Yes, quite," he said, a bit of a shiver running down his spine. Not for the world would he have admitted he held the same conviction.

Not about gowns, per se, but a task none the less.

"Yes, well, don't let me delay you," she told him, taking a sip of her tea and going back to her correspondence.

And normally he would have done just that, gone on with his business matters and letters, but with Miss Dale at the other end of the table, he found his attentions wandering.

Like how was it that no matter the time of day, she always looked enticing? This morning it was a pale blue muslin concoction and her hair tied up simply with a matching ribbon.

One the same color as her eyes.

And why was it that he noticed those things? He couldn't tell you the color of Miss Nashe's eyes, or even the shade of Lady Clare's tresses, but with Miss Dale . . .

Henry took a deep breath and told himself he'd never really paid much attention to such things before he'd begun corresponding with Miss Spooner.

Take Miss Dale. How was it that a lady could look so perfectly refreshed, so utterly composed at such an early hour? He ran his hand over his chin, which he'd shaved himself, his valet, Mingo, having gone off in a fine fettle over something to do with the laundress and cravats, so he knew he was hardly well turned out.

No wonder he'd thought she might be Miss Spooner when they'd met in London. Outwardly she was everything he'd imagined the lady to be — pretty, self-assured and determined.

Just not possessing some of Miss Dale's other traits — stubborn beyond all reason, presumptuous, and all-too-desirable.

Very much desirable.

Henry wrenched his gaze away from the object of his study and began to put his papers in order. There was an inquiry for the properties he held in Brighton, questions from his solicitor about a shipping venture, and a few other questions about improvements he intended for Kingscote, the house and lands he'd recently purchased.

They all required a measure of discipline and concentration, but he found himself distracted to no end by the scratching quill at the far side of the table.

Good heavens, didn't she possess a single pen that could write a line without making such an infernal noise?

Miss Dale looked up at him. "What is the matter now?"

"Your quill — it is making the most interminable screeching."

"Really? I hadn't noticed." And then, as if that was the end of the subject, she went back to writing her letter, scratching at it all the much louder, if that was possible. Why she sounded like a hen poking about in the gravel.

Oh, yes, Hen had been right about one thing last night — he was going to pick up Preston's scandalous role in the family . . . starting right this moment by strangling Miss Dale.

Henry pushed his chair back and started down the table, albeit to sharpen her quill, not to throttle her, when Miss Dale was saved by the arrival of a third party to their breakfast.

A witness, as it were.

"What a cozy setting," Miss Nashe declared, having stopped in the doorway to survey the scene before her.

Henry whirled around and then took stock of what exactly the lady was seeing — him hovering at Miss Dale's elbow — and so he straightened and bowed to the heiress.

She acknowledged him with one of her wide smiles and came into the room. It was then that Henry noticed that the girl had brought with her an ornately decorated writing box.

"Here I thought myself so unique, getting up early to catch up on my correspondence, only to find myself in such crowded company," Miss Nashe said. "But we make an excellent trio, do we not?"

Henry had the sense the girl was including him and Mr. Muggins and not the other lady in the room. Apparently so did Miss Dale.

"Yes, rather," she remarked, glancing up at Miss Nashe.

Was it Henry's imagination, or was Miss Dale once again making up lines for Miss Nashe?

Oh, the expectations placed on one when one is mentioned daily in the social columns is exhausting.

He stifled a laugh, and both ladies looked up at him. "Ah, nothing. Just that dog of Tabitha's. Um, he's looking at my plate again." He waved a hand at Mr. Muggins. "I shall not share my breakfast."

"And don't ever," Miss Nashe advised. "Dogs become horrible beggars when they are allowed in the dining areas." She glanced again at Miss Dale as if she held her responsible for this crime.

Miss Dale smiled at Miss Nashe as she reached over to her own plate and slid a sausage off it for Mr. Muggins, which the dog caught with practiced ease.

Ah, so that was how the lines were going to be drawn. Henry had the sense of being caught between the English and the French.

And not for every farthing he possessed would he declare which side was which.

Miss Nashe sniffed, then delicately turned her back to Miss Dale, snubbing her. She settled her writing box on the table and began to carefully select from inside everything she needed. "I have so many letters to catch up on. Why, the attentions afforded me never seem to end."

Henry didn't dare look down the table at Miss Dale. She'd have that wicked light in her eyes, and he knew, just knew, he would be able to hear exactly what the lady was thinking. Still, he couldn't keep himself from chuckling, and when both ladies glanced up at him, he waved them off and made his way to his seat. "I just remembered an invitation I must turn down. Regrettably so."

Miss Dale made a most inelegant snort, but from Miss Nashe he received nothing but sympathy.

"Oh, my dear Lord Henry, I so understand your dilemma. Isn't it a trial to be so pressed upon from every corner of Society?" she mused.

"Yes, I suppose so," Henry agreed.

There was no need to look in Miss Dale's direction to discover her thoughts. Her pen was screeching anew, as if carving her sentiments into the very table.

"Oh dear heavens, how your pen scratches, Miss Dale," the other girl said with a delicate shudder. "Miss Emery always said at school that using a less than sharpened quill shows a disregard for one's composition. A lady's handwriting must be delicate and precise, so as to distinguish her from her lessers."

The heiress's censorious words would have been easy to dismiss as utter snobbery, but within the lady's admonishment rang something Henry hadn't considered.

What had that pompous chit just said?

A lady's handwriting . . . so as to distinguish her from her lessers.

That was it. Gazing down the table at the two ladies quietly writing their letters — well, one of them quietly composing — his heart pounded.

Handwriting. Miss Spooner's distinctive script. Why hadn't he thought of it before? Why, he could spot her scrawl from across the foyer.

And here were two examples right before him. Henry began to push back from the table, but he had to stop himself.

Demmit, he had no good excuse to go ambling down to the other end of the table to peer over Miss Nashe's shoulder to see if her handwriting matched the very familiar hand of Miss Spooner.

And what about Miss Dale's?

He cleared his throat in an effort to force that thought out of his head. No, he wouldn't venture that far in his quest. Stealing a glance down the table, he found her bent over her page, her teeth nipping at her bottom lip as she was lost in her composition.

Scratch. Screetch. Scratch.

Henry shuddered. The infernal noise was enough to peel the gilt paper from the walls. And yet . . . he had to admit that *delicate* was not the word he would use to describe Miss Spooner's determined penmanship.

And watching Miss Dale write was like watching a mad artist paint. Her words flowed from her pen with passion and . . . dare he admit it? . . . purpose and determination.

Just like he'd always imagined Miss Spooner at her desk, writing to him.

No, no, no! It couldn't be. Not her.

Henry took a deep breath, for he knew exactly what he would have to do if it was Miss Dale: Hie off to London as fast as he could and then pay his secretary an indecent amount of money never to let him compose another letter ever again.

Well, he wasn't ready to flee just yet, not before he'd scratched Miss Nashe's standing from his shrinking list.

Slowly and with as much nonchalance as he could possess, he rose from his chair and, looking around for an excuse, picked up his half-finished plate and wandered over to the sideboard to refill the empty spots.

"Miss Dale, do you have a spare piece of paper?" Miss Nashe was saying. "I need to make a list for my maid, and the coarse sheets you seem to prefer appear perfect for such a task."

"Yes, of course," Daphne told her and fished out an extra sheet of paper for the girl.

As Miss Nashe walked down the side of the table, Henry saw his chance.

But then, as it had with everything else in his search for Miss Spooner, Fate intervened.

Or rather Hen did.

"Henry! There you are!" she said in that

exasperated tone of hers. "I've been searching all over for you."

"Just a moment," he told her, the page
and his answer nearly in his sights.

"I will not be put off. Zillah is causing
another commotion. I have assured her you
want nothing to do with that wretched Miss
—"

At that moment Hen stopped her grand
entrance and spied the rest of the occupants
of the room. "Oh, my, Miss Dale. And dear
Miss Nashe. How charming," she said,
shooting a glance at Henry that said she
was anything but.

Charmed, that is.

Henry took this momentary diversion to
start for the other end of the table, but Hen
was too quick for him.

"Oh, don't think to escape through the
butler's pantry. You will help me with Zillah, or I will move her to your wing of the
house." She bustled over to his side, one
hand coiling into the crook of his elbow like
an anchor line. In the blink of an eye, he
was being towed from port, a reluctant ship
against the tide.

And when he stole one last glance at the
room, he found both ladies watching him
leave.

Miss Nashe with a smile that encouraged

him to return.

From the far end came the wry glance of Miss Dale, one that wished him well on his journey.

And if he didn't know better, she hoped it would be a long and hazardous one.

Daphne drew a deep breath as Lord Henry was hauled from the room, and she did her best to ignore the knowing glance that Miss Nashe tossed in her direction.

Yet the heiress was hardly done with just her snide expression. After several minutes, she set down her pen and pushed her "urgent" correspondence aside. "Lord Henry," she announced, "is certainly a creature of strong habits if both our maids have discovered his penchant for an early breakfast and correspondence."

"Our maids?" Daphne said, not quite catching on.

"If we are both arriving here at this ungodly hour to catch him," she supplied, one brow tipped in a challenge.

Daphne's mouth fell open. "Oh, goodness, no! You don't think that I . . . that is, I have no desire to —"

"Miss Dale, everyone at this house party is discussing your blatant attempts to en-snare Lord Henry." Miss Nashe's nose turned up slightly. "A girl in your situation and a man of his wealth and lands, why wouldn't you set your cap so far above your station?"

For a moment Daphne was too shocked to take in the more insulting parts of what Miss Nashe was saying. How was it that this girl knew all about Lord Henry's wealth, as if his holdings were common knowledge?

Perhaps she knew as little about the Seldons, as she'd accused Lord Henry of knowing about the Dale dynasty. Well, she'd make sense of all that later.

Right now there was a more insulting matter to be dealt with.

"Above my station?" she echoed.

"Well, of course," Miss Nashe said in all sympathy.

For her. Daphne Dale of the Kempton Dales.

"Miss Dale, you seem quite intelligent despite your lack of finish and must know the only reason you are here, in this company, is because of Miss Timmons's dear and simple affection for her former friends."

Former friends?

"But if it were any other lady marrying the Duke of Preston, you would never have been invited."

There was some truth there, Daphne

would admit. She was a Dale at a Seldon wedding after all, but she doubted that Miss Nashe, with her *cit* origins and new money, had any notion of the Dale and Seldon relations.

Or therein lack of.

"Surely you can see how embarrassing your pursuit of Lord Henry is becoming —"

"My pursuit?"

"Yes, well, it can hardly be called a courtship when the man has no interest in you," Miss Nashe declared. "I fear for what little credit you do possess, for there will be nothing left of it when you leave here, unattached and so very humbled."

Daphne's blood boiled. Oh, whyever had she promised Tabitha not to dump anything over Miss Nashe? Worse yet, she was so furious that she couldn't find the perfect retort, the right words to send Miss Nashe packing.

Meanwhile, the other girl was gathering up her belongings, tossing them haphazardly into her expensive writing box and, worse, taking Daphne's silence as agreement.

Mr. Muggins, hoping for a sympathetic handout, stirred, his gaze flitting from the heiress to the sideboard.

"Leaving so soon?" Daphne said, finally finding her tongue and her own pitchfork.

"What of your multitude of admirers?"

Miss Nashe glanced up as if she'd all but forgotten Daphne. "Excuse me?"

"Your correspondence? Your admirers? Won't they be watching their posts for some tiding from you?"

The girl smiled. "Why, Miss Dale, that is why I have a secretary." Her smirk finished the sentence. *And you clearly do not.*

And when she left, Daphne noticed she had not taken the sheet of paper she had borrowed.

"Horrid mushroom," Daphne said, glancing over at Mr. Muggins.

The dog seemed to agree. For certainly there had been no sausages from Miss Nashe.

"As if I am chasing Lord Henry!" Daphne shook her head. "Nor am I lingering after the man."

Lingering after him! As if she might want his kiss. Which she did not. Not in the least.

She glanced over at Mr. Muggins. "I don't," she told the dog. "Not at all."

And why would she? Lord Henry left her all a tangle. Furious one moment, and the next . . .

Well, Daphne didn't want to consider what came next. Not with him.

For there was Dishforth — steady, reliable

Dishforth. And he was ever so close. He'd never leave her at sixes and sevens. Never tower over her and accuse her of lingering.

He was all that was comfortable and sensible and right about a gentleman. And Lord Henry, for all his protestations and Miss Nashe's claims of his desirability, was none of those things.

He is so much more.

That thought stopped Daphne cold. How could she even think such a thing? This was what came from not keeping to their vow to stay out of each other's company. Well, no more, she promised herself.

Again.

She reached for her pen. This time she meant it. To that end, she snatched up the unused sheet of paper and wrote the only words that needed to be said.

Glancing over at Mr. Muggins, she said, "This is the solution to everything." With that, she addressed it with the one name that could save her from the lonely depths of humiliation to which Miss Nashe had described with such glee.

Dishforth.

He would rescue her. Save her from Miss Nashe and her ilk.

And from Lord Henry . . . and the other sort of ruin he represented.

■ ■ ■ ■

Hen's attempt to pull Henry into another one of Zillah's tempers came up short when they crossed paths with Benley in the foyer.

"Ah, my lady," the butler intoned. "A word with you if I may. About the masquerade costumes." He waved his hand over to the stack of trunks piled up in the corner.

"Excellent," Hen declared, letting go of Henry and marching over to survey her newly arrived treasures.

Taking advantage of his sister's diverted attention, Henry backed out of the foyer and beat a quick path toward the morning room, determined to investigate Miss Nashe's handwriting.

Oh, and that of Miss Dale's as well.

But when he came up to the room, he could hear Miss Nashe's voice, slightly raised from its usually well-modulated tones.

Something about the pinched notes gave Henry pause, and so instead of returning to the room, or getting caught lolling about the door, as if he'd been eavesdropping, he slipped into the butler's pantry to the side.

The footman standing near the slightly opened door gave a bit of a start. Apparently Henry wasn't the only one intrigued by the conversation inside.

Instead of chiding the man for listening in — how could he when he had every intention of doing the very same thing? — he whispered to the fellow, "Will you go see if cook has some more scones baked?"

Thus dismissed, the footman yielded the prime spot at the door, and Henry stepped up to where he could hear Miss Nashe saying in a smug, loud voice, "A girl in your situation and a man of his wealth and lands, why wouldn't you set your cap so far above your station?"

Henry bristled with annoyance. How dare this mushroom accuse Miss Dale of such toady behavior, when clearly it was Miss Nashe who was scraping and clawing her way above her lot in life.

Miss Dale was, after all, a Dale, something Henry could appreciate.

For while the Seldons and the Dales might disdain each other, never once when England had been threatened had the two families ever shirked their duties. They'd stood shoulder to shoulder at Agincourt, in the fields of Flodden, and at Bosworth and Blenheim.

Something the Nashes couldn't claim.

Miss Dale had the blood of heroes in her

veins. So who was this Miss Nashe to snub her? Who was this dressed-up *cit* who had Society all a-dither? Quite frankly, he'd rather kiss a Dale.

Henry paused. Oh, bother. He already had.

And it seemed the puffed-up heiress wasn't done.

"Miss Dale, you seem quite intelligent despite your lack of finish and must know the only reason you are here, in this company, is because of Miss Timmons's dear and simple affection for her former friends."

Once again, Henry held back from bursting into the room, for he was quite certain, nay he was completely positive, Miss Dale would give this chit the set-down she deserved.

He stole a peek in the room, listening to Miss Nashe's haughty opinions, and never once did Miss Dale bat an eye or give way to the dark emotions that were certainly bubbling up in Henry's chest.

No, she sat there, serene and calm. Hands folded in her lap, her expression bland.

Then he remembered something his mother had told Hen on more than one occasion, especially when faced with the censure that often came of being a Seldon: *A true lady never lowers herself to argue with her lessers. A well-bred lady always rises above the rabble.*

And apparently it was a dictum that Miss Daphne Dale held as well. But of course she would. She was a lady.

Just then, Miss Nashe gathered up her belongings and went marching from the room, as if she held the higher ground.

He was about to push the door open and congratulate Miss Dale on her noble composure when he heard her sputter, "As if I'm chasing Lord Henry!" There was once again the indignant rattle of china. "Nor am I lingering after the man."

Henry felt a bit chagrined. She needn't sound adamant. And bother it all, who the devil was she talking to?

Taking a peek, he found her ruffling Mr. Muggin's bristled head, confessing her secrets to the mutt.

Go in there, a very Seldon voice inside him urged.

"And say what?" he whispered back. Because if he went in there now, he knew what he'd find out.

For hadn't his list of possible suspects gone down to a single name?

A name he dared not say aloud for fear his heart would hear it and refuse to let go.

CHAPTER 9

I'm ever so glad. I try to be above such
things, but I will confess a longing for
silk gowns and a handsome partner in
life.

> Found in a letter from
> Miss Spooner to Mr. Dishforth

Somewhere in Owle Park, someone was
playing a piano. Not the distinct tinkling of
a lady at the piano-forte, but a grand piano
being played with passion. The music — full
of longing and desire — lured Daphne from
her determined course to find a copy of *Debrett's.*

Whoever could play with such fire?

She wandered through the maze of halls
and wings with Mr. Muggins at her heels.
The terrier cast more than one glance at
her that said very clearly that she was going
in the wrong direction for sausages.

When eventually the notes grew louder,

Daphne found herself filled with both the exhilaration of the music and the thrill of discovery as she approached an open doorway. Since she didn't want the music to end, she stopped just short of entering and instead took a furtive peek inside. Immediately she reeled back.

She gaped down at Mr. Muggins, who had planted himself at her feet.

No! It couldn't be.

Taking a deep breath and realizing she didn't trust her eyes, she took another longer look, and there it was, Lord Henry sitting alongside his ancient relation, Lady Zillah, at a grand piano.

He stopped abruptly and turned to his great-aunt. "That is how it is played," he said to her.

"You still have a knack, Henry," Lady Zillah replied.

"I should," he laughed. "It was you who taught me my first notes. So I don't mind helping you with this piece."

"I find it keeps my mind sharp," the lady said, nudging him aside a bit and taking up the keys herself. "But this one has been bedeviling me for months." As she played — with surprising skill — Lord Henry turned the pages for her.

Daphne knew she should leave them to

their practice, but the music was so lovely, and the scene so curious and intimate. It was as if she was seeing not only Lord Henry but also the entire Seldon family for the first time.

The music didn't stop Lady Zillah from nattering on. Loudly. "Henry, you could be out shooting or riding, whatever are you doing hanging about with an old lady like me?"

He smiled at her. "I was lured from my duties when I heard you playing. You don't play all that often anymore, so it is a treat to hear you."

Daphne thought the real treat was hearing Lord Henry play. Zillah was good, but Lord Henry played with such a hidden passion.

Rather like the way he kissed.

"My goodness, I never knew you'd inherited your father's flair for flattery," Lady Zillah teased back. "Always thought you more an Oscroft than a Seldon."

"Thank you, Cousin Zillah," he replied. "My mother despaired that neither of her children appeared to hold any of her family's traits."

"I hardly meant it as a compliment," she shot back. "You are too nice by half. Respectable and kindhearted; look how you've managed Preston's estates all these years, kept the entire family afloat — and nary a scandal to your name. I was starting to doubt you were truly a Seldon." Lady Zillah's pronouncement came out in a scolding voice, but there was a spark of pride to the lady's eyes as she glanced at him.

"Nary a scandal to his name?" Daphne mouthed to Mr. Muggins.

Told you, Mr. Muggins's large brown eyes seemed to say.

No, the lady must be wrong. As was this mangy terrier, whose opinion of Lord Henry had been formed in the breakfast room. Over a purloined sausage.

No, they were both wrong. Lord Henry was the most scandalous man Daphne had ever met.

And how many gentlemen have you met, Daphne Dale? Mr. Muggins seemed to be asking.

Well, if she was being honest, she'd really never met any until she'd come to London with Tabitha — for certainly her Dale relations didn't count.

Inside the room, Lady Zillah wasn't done with her assessment of Lord Henry's character. "I had lost hope of you, my dear boy, at least until this house party."

Daphne turned toward the door again. Oh, she knew she shouldn't be eavesdropping, but she couldn't help herself. What

291

else had Lord Henry done?

Besides kiss her.

"Whatever were you doing last night?" Lady Zillah was saying, even as she nodded toward the music sheets.

Lord Henry leaned forward and flipped the page. "Not that again."

"Yes, that again. And this time I will have a straight answer from you."

He heaved a sigh. "Aunt Zillah, do I need to remind you this is a house party? Occasionally one loses one's head. I do believe it is expected."

"Oh, of course it is. But not with one of *them.*"

One of them. Oh, Daphne could well imagine who Lady Zillah meant. Because while she might call Lord Henry barely a Seldon, Lady Zillah was a Seldon through and through.

Then the old girl confirmed her suspicions. "If only I'd been consulted about the invitation list beforehand," she complained. "Dales! Here in Owle Park! Why, it is unforgivable."

"Yet you stay on," he teased. "And it is only one Dale."

"Mark my words, they are like squirrels. Feed one and you will be feeding the lot before a week is out."

Daphne pressed her lips together. Oh, he was a devilish rake to bait the old girl so, and at the same time, her heart beat a little faster to hear him do so.

It was almost as if he was defending her right to be here.

Almost.

"What was your sister thinking?" Zillah demanded.

"Hen?" he asked, feigning innocence.

Daphne had seen him do the same thing, acting as if he hadn't a clue what one meant, but he didn't fool her any more than he was deceiving his elderly aunt.

"Of course, Hen. What other sister do you have?" she snapped, then reached over to flip the music sheet herself, glaring up at him as she did. "I would expect better of Henrietta. She's a rare woman with refined taste, and I daresay this invitation to a Dale was not to her liking." She cocked a brow at him, as if to dare him to naysay her.

Instead, Lord Henry remained his usual composed self. "Miss Dale is Tabitha's dearest friend, and Preston speaks quite highly of the chit."

Daphne waited for him to add his vote for her, but there was none forthcoming.

Not that she had expected as much. Not really.

Well, perhaps a little.

Meanwhile, Lady Zillah was off and running at such a challenge. "*Bah!* Preston's opinion, indeed! Not that I give much countenance to what he thinks — he's spent the last five years dallying about like a second son."

"If you recall, Cousin Zillah, I'm a second son, and I don't see you giving me such short shrift — in fact, weren't you just singing my praises a moment or two ago?"

"I *was,*" she warned him. "That is until I saw you return from that carriage ride with that girl looking quite tumbled —"

"She was drenched from the rain," he protested. "As was I, something no one seems to have noticed."

I did, Daphne would have told him. *I noticed.* His shirt plastered to his chest, his breeches tight against his . . .

Inside the music room, Aunt Zillah remained unimpressed. "If I say she looked tumbled, then she looked tumbled, Henry Seldon! And don't tell me what I did or didn't see, because I know what I saw! Just as I did last night."

"Oh, why can't she leave off on last night," Daphne whispered to Mr. Muggins, who had given up hope that they would continue on to the kitchens and now lay on the carpet with his head atop his paws.

"Rather than berate my luck at having to partner with Miss Dale for the scavenger hunt, you might try being civil to the gel and get to know her."

Lady Zillah's fingers stopped, sending a discordant note jarring through the room. "Be civil to a Dale? You are mad." She shook her head, turned her attention back to her music and played a few bars before stopping again.

Lord Henry wasn't done. "I think you would find you have much in common."

"With a Dale?" Lady Zillah squawked.

"With her?" Daphne whispered furiously.

"Never!" they both said in varying tones.

"I disagree," Lord Henry said, picking out a few notes. "Miss Dale is an opinionated and spirited lady. Rather like you, my dear aunt."

"Bah! She is nothing like me," Lady Zillah replied, but this time she didn't sound as offended.

Lord Henry continued. "She's also loyal to Tabitha. Helped Preston win her hand. And has risked much to come here for their wedding. As a Seldon, you should be able to respect such loyalty."

Lady Zillah pushed his hands aside and

began to play again, as if thinking over the matter.

Daphne considered his words as well. "He thinks I am spirited and loyal," she told Mr. Muggins.

Don't forget opinionated.

The music stopped again. "I don't care if she cured the king of his madness, I cannot be civil to a Dale. Not after the way Dahlia Dale behaved at my debut ball!"

"Good heavens, Zillah, that was how many years ago?"

"Don't you be impudent with me! Why, I remember it like it was yesterday! I was nearly betrothed to . . . nearly betrothed to . . ." Lady Zillah's fingers pounded down on the keys. "Botheration, what was his name?"

"Lord Monnery," Lord Henry supplied. "And here — this is how you do the bridge. I'll make a note here on the sheet."

Daphne glanced inside to spy him writing notes on the sheets.

"Yes, yes, Monnery," Lady Zillah said, glancing over at the notes and nodding her thanks. She played through the portion, this time perfectly, before she stopped again. "*Harrumph.* Nearly engaged I was, until that toothy bit of muslin Dahlia Dale came along and quite stole him away."

"I hardly think it was as you say," Lord Henry remarked as he turned a page and pointed to the place for her to continue.

"I haven't forgotten any of it," Zillah told him.

Save the man's name, Daphne would point out.

"That gel ensnared my nearly betrothed with her Dale wiles. Quite ruined him, because a fortnight later she threw him over. Fickle, scandalous creature that she was. Just as that bit of Dale muslin here will ruin you."

Daphne blew out an exasperated breath. Seldons! What an overly dramatic lot. And whoever was Dahlia Dale?

She ran through her family tree, searching all the branches, and then came to a stop.

Oh! That Dahlia Dale. The one Great-Aunt Damaris kept a portrait of — displayed in a dark corner in one of the back hallways.

The one Cousin Phi had remarked upon before a crowded room of Dales by saying in all innocence, "Daphne rather takes after Cousin Dahlia, don't you all think so?"

And had been met with stone-faced, horrified shock.

Oh, yes, that Dahlia Dale.

Inside the music room, the debate continued. "Aunt Zillah, if I recall the story cor-

rectly, you didn't want to marry Monnery
—"

"Of course I didn't want to marry Monnery. He was a nincompoop."

"So you might consider that this Dahlia Dale did you a favor," Lord Henry suggested.

"Stealing my nearly betrothed from me at my debut ball? Hardly!" Lady Zillah shook her head furiously, the keys of the piano taking the brunt of her indignation. "Bad form runs through their blood like scandal does ours," she declared, as if one trait was better than the other.

And Daphne knew exactly which trait Lady Zillah found superior.

"What concerns me most is how you were dangling after her last night," Zillah continued. "I won't have you beguiled and entangled by that minx!"

"Zillah!" Lord Henry protested.

"No, hear me out! You are far too innocent in these matters —"

It took every bit of Daphne's restraint not to snort. Lord Henry? Innocent?

Obviously the name of the old lady's lost love wasn't the only thing she was a bit addled about.

"— I fear that girl has you in her crosshairs. She's using you, if only to appear more eligible than she actually is. That's how they do it."

"Zillah —" Lord Henry's voice held a warning tone.

"And she will only ruin your hopes of making an advantageous match. Who is this Daphne Dale? She's not even one of the better Dales."

"There are better ones?" he teased.

"You know exactly what I mean. I'm surprised she hasn't been fawned off on that old warhorse, Damaris, as a companion. That's what they do with the ones who have no hope of a match or have *fallen*," Zillah told him, wagging a finger in warning. "Mark my words, that gel wants to see you entangled."

Daphne couldn't breathe. For even as the lady said the word — *entangled* — all she could imagine was being in Lord Henry's arms again.

Entangled. Enticed. Enthralled.

But not for long.

"You needn't fear for my sake," Lord Henry was saying. "I have it on good authority that Miss Dale is all but betrothed."

"What's this?" Lady Zillah said in that loud, impertinent voice of hers.

Daphne didn't think the lady was hard of hearing, rather she just liked making people repeat themselves.

"Daphne Dale will not be a Dale for long," Henry said.

"Once a Dale —"

— *always a Seldon,* Daphne mused.

Henry struck a balance between the two of them. "Yes, yes, I know."

"So if this gel has someone else on the hook, whyever are you dangling after her?"

"I'm not."

Daphne huffed a bit. Well, he needn't sound so adamant. Or so put out.

"Good," Lady Zillah said. After a few moments, she spoke up again. "There is that lovely Miss Nashe —"

Daphne discovered there was adamant and then there was *adamant.*

"Good God, no!" he burst out.

So Lord Henry hadn't been taken in by Miss Nashe's winsome smiles and precise manners. Daphne pressed her lips together to keep from smiling smugly.

If only she could be the one to tell Miss Nashe. . . .

"Oh, she's an ill-bred mushroom, I'll give you that," Lady Zillah conceded.

"You can say that again," Lord Henry enthused.

"But she has the loveliest dowry," the lady added, cackling with open avarice.

Daphne wished Miss Nashe and her lovely dowry to perdition.

And so, it seemed, did Lord Henry.

"Zillah! I have no interest in that girl. She could have a king's ransom at her feet and I would still find her unworthy."

The old girl seemed unimpressed. "Well," she sniffed. "A fortune like that belongs where it can be well served. Not lining a merchant's pockets."

"I don't want it in mine," he told her in no uncertain terms. "I have no desire to marry some sow's purse. Mark my words, Zillah, when I wed, I will marry as Preston is doing — when my heart is engaged and the lady is my perfect match."

"That's an overly romantic notion for the likes of you. Hardly sensible," Lady Zillah noted.

"Perhaps I am only now realizing how much of a Seldon I truly am," Henry told her.

And this time, Daphne grinned and knew she needed to slip away before she was discovered. Yet her escape was delayed when Lady Zillah spoke again.

"You say Miss Dale has another in her sights?" she prodded, obviously unwilling to let go of the subject.

"Yes, Aunt Zillah."

"*Harrumph!* That didn't stop Dahlia Dale."

Daphne spent the rest of the morning in a bit of a tangle about what she'd overheard.

Lord Henry defending her? It seemed too much.

But more to the point, how could anything Lady Zillah had said about him be true?

Throughout nuncheon, served alfresco in the walled garden outside the orangery, she'd found herself stealing glances at him and trying to see him as his aunt had described him.

Nary a scandal to your name . . .

Too nice by half . . .

Respectable . . . kindhearted . . .

Oh, she'd give him the kindly part. She'd seen him at breakfast slipping a sausage to Mr. Muggins when he'd thought she hadn't been looking.

And she'd done her best to reconcile the man at the ball, at the folly, the one who'd kissed her, the rake who'd teased her last night, with the gentleman before her — the one of property and means, who didn't flaunt his good fortune.

Rather, spent his time caring for his family and was beloved by them in return.

She'd become so married to the notion that he was naught but a rake that she felt

as if she was seeing him with new eyes —
for here was a man with fine manners and a
reserve to his behavior.

And true to his confession to Zillah, he
went out of his way to avoid Miss Nashe's
blatant attempts to catch his eye.

Daphne had to admit — that point alone
rather won her over. Not that she wanted to
be won over by Lord Henry.

Still, she couldn't forget what he had said
earlier. *I will marry as Preston is doing —
when my heart is engaged . . .*

A frisson of something oddly close to
jealousy ran down her spine, leaving her
wondering what it would be like to be Lord
Henry's perfect match.

The very thought left her insides quaking,
a fluttering bit of breathless need racing
through her. All at once.

His kiss . . . his touch . . .

Daphne felt herself being lured from her
plans. Her very sensible plan.

Why wait for happenstance, or even a
planned assignation? There was only one
way to catch Mr. Dishforth, and that was in
the act. Which was why she was here — hidden in the alcove in the foyer where the
salver sat.

Waiting for him.

She was ever so determined to uncover

his identity. Before . . . Before . . .

The determined clop of boots down the hall brought her gaze up. But when she parted the curtain slightly, to her chagrin it was Lord Henry coming.

The thump of his boots woke up Mr. Muggins from his dozy state, and the giant dog jumped up and barked.

"No, Mr. Muggins, no," Daphne whispered, but the terrier was already halfway out of their hiding spot, barking happily, his tail waving exuberantly enough to shake the curtains back and forth.

"Ho, there, boy," Lord Henry said in greeting, "whatever are you doing in there?"

Daphne shrunk back and closed her eyes.

"Up to no good, eh —" Lord Henry was saying, parting the curtain. "Miss Dale!"

Daphne's breath stopped in her throat. Perhaps he'd just go away. When she opened one eye, he was still there. So much for her prayer that he'd evaporate into thin air.

He pulled the curtain back further. "What the devil are you doing hiding back there?"

She tried to say the words she usually did when faced with Lord Henry and his pompous demands — *wretched, awful man* — but instead found herself listening for that piece of music he'd played, remembering what he'd looked like when he'd pulled her into his arms and kissed her in the folly.

Thoroughly, passionately. Rakishly . . .

Oh, that would never do!

Dishforth, Daphne! she reminded herself. *You must find sensible and reliable Mr. Dishforth.*

"Miss Dale?" he said in a voice etched with concern.

Smoothing out her skirt and glancing up at him, feigning a look of surprise at his untimely arrival, she stepped around him. "Oh, Lord Henry! Whatever are you doing here?"

"On my way to the ballroom to choose my costume for the masquerade. I would have thought you would have been down there first thing, like all the other ladies."

"I was delayed —" she replied, stealing a glance at the empty salver, then wrenching her gaze away. Bother, she'd forgotten about the costumes. "— by Mr. Muggins." She reached over and gave the traitorous terrier a scratch on his wiry head. "I believe he spied a bird."

"Inside the house?" Lord Henry asked, stepping back and studying her.

Daphne laughed, perhaps a little too hysterically. Drat it all, she was so terrible at lying. "No. Of course not. It was . . ." She glanced around. "Outside. Yes, outside. Just beyond the window." She turned back and smiled at him. "Mr. Muggins and feathers! He is the very devil."

Lord Henry's brow wrinkled. "Yes, so Tabitha mentioned. Went so far as to ban them from the house party."

"Good thing," Daphne advised. "Just ask Lady Gudgeon."

"I heard about that. He chased her across Hyde Park until he'd brought her hat to ground."

"He did."

"Rather wished I'd seen that," Lord Henry admitted. "Never been overly fond of Lady Gudgeon."

"Apparently that is a sentiment shared by many," Daphne said.

Just then, Miss Nashe and her mother came strolling through the foyer on their way to the rooms set aside for the costumes. Both mother and daughter wore identical expressions of disapproval. They glanced at each other and Daphne could well guess what passed between them.

See. I told you she's set her cap.

So you did.

Then Daphne glanced up and realized Lord Henry had edged closer to her, almost protectively. Then once the pair was well and gone, he shuddered.

306

"Allow me to escort you, Miss Dale," he said, holding out his arm. "I fear the path ahead is plagued with trolls."

Since she hadn't any plausible excuse for hanging about the salver, and no desire to enlist his help in finding Dishforth, there was nothing Daphne could do but accept his offer and lay her hand down on his sleeve.

As she did, he reached over and laid his other hand atop hers, and the moment they touched, it was as it had been in the folly all over again — save without his lips covering hers.

The magic, the heat, that spark that lit inside both of them every time they touched.

Daphne yanked her gaze away from his hand and looked straight ahead, concentrating on her raison d'être.

Find Dishforth. She must find Dishforth.

Or . . . or else . . .

Well, she knew what "or else" meant.

Ruin. At the hands of this very rakish man. No matter what his harridan of an aunt claimed.

"Any word from your family?" he asked.

"Pardon?"

"Your family?" he nudged. "I just assumed you were hovering about the salver in case

307

any word of their impending approach arrived." He laughed a bit, as if this disastrous notion was something worthy of waiting around for.

"I wasn't hovering about the salver, as you put it, and no, I've had no word from my family."

"Truly?" he asked.

And she hadn't the least idea if he meant, *Truly you haven't heard from your family?* or *Truly, you weren't hovering about the salver?*

Nor was she inclined to delve into either subject.

So she did the next best thing. She ignored him and hoped he'd leave well enough alone.

But then again, this was Lord Henry, and he was apparently as tenacious as Mr. Muggins when he spied a feather.

"And here I thought you were hiding from the impending doom of your family's likely arrival," he teased.

Daphne glanced over at him. Had he suddenly gone mad to joke about such a thing?

"Hardly," she replied with the same haughty disdain that was Lady Essex's trademark. "As I said, Mr. Muggins spied —"

"Miss Dale, you needn't gammon me." He shook his head and made a *tsk, tsk* sound. "If you wanted to escape your chaperone, you'll get no objections from me, nor sanctions. Far from it."

"Well, I wasn't."

"If you say so," he mused. "But if you were —"

"Which I wasn't," she shot back.

"Miss Dale, you are at a house party, not locked away in a London town house. If you want peace and quiet, Owle Park affords far better choices than a dusty alcove."

"It wasn't dusty in the least."

He laughed. "So you were hiding in there."

Daphne notched up her chin and refused to be baited further.

"I would have suggested — if you had come to me —"

"Which I wouldn't —"

"Yes, well, I think we've covered that. But as I was saying, next time might I suggest the rose garden, the orangery, or even the maze. All far superior choices for peace and quiet, if that is what one is truly seeking."

Daphne made a little sniff.

"I could show you around this afternoon," he offered. "If you would like, so that the next time you are in need of solitude you'll have the perfect spot at the ready."

Show her the perfect spot for a secluded interlude? She'd just bet he would. Probably knew every such venue within a five-mile radius — that is, if he didn't get lost along the way.

"No, thank you," she replied, of half a mind to report his offer to Lady Zillah. Then they'd see how Lord Henry would spend the rest of the house party.

Trussed up in the cellar.

"Are you certain?" he pressed.

"Decidedly so," she told him, gritting her teeth. Not a rake, indeed! She went back to her original theory: Lady Zillah was firmly planted in her dotage.

"Well, if you find yourself with a free moment, do not hesitate —"

"I have previous plans," she told him, which they both knew was a lie. This was a house party, and the schedule was posted every day by Lady Juniper.

The remainder of the afternoon was completely and utterly open for such entertainments.

"Yes, well, if you change your mind —"

"I won't."

"So you say," he said in an offhanded manner, which only piqued her temper all that much more.

They walked down the long hall, and Daphne began to feel a momentary bit of triumph. Here she was with Lord Henry, and she wasn't bothered by it in the least.

He hadn't any hold or sway over her.

None whatsoever.

Save for the hammering of her heart and those dangerous tendrils of desire that seemed to entwine around her every time she touched him . . .

Those notwithstanding, she had everything under control. Now all she had to do was find Dishforth.

Sensible, nearly reliable Dishforth. She could only hope he kissed as well as he was pragmatic.

Leave it to Lord Henry to nudge her off her confident, lofty perch.

"About your gentleman —" he began.

Daphne came to a staggering halt. "Oh, good heavens. Must we?"

"Yes," he told her, crossing his arms over his chest. "I fear I might have wronged you."

Now he was having a lapse into regrets? Now?

"I would rather not discuss this with you!" she declared, continuing down the hall without him.

He followed, his long stride eating up the distance she'd tried to create, and once again he was at her side. "I think we should discuss him."

"You might think so, but I do not."

Lord Henry caught her by the arm and stopped her. "I merely want to know if I've caused difficulties between the two of you."

Daphne lowered her voice. "Good heavens, Lord Henry, haven't you the least notion of propriety? Besides, there was nothing last night to cause anyone a moment's concern."

"Are you certain?" he asked, drawing closer.

"Yes." She went to turn and flee again, but she came up short as he held her fast.

"I must know who he is."

She shook her head. Vehemently. "Oh, no, I think not."

"Not?"

"Not!"

"Then I'll be forced to guess."

Daphne threw up her hands and this time was free to make her escape. That is, until Lord Henry reined her to a stop with his first conjecture.

"Fieldgate," he called after her.

Daphne's feet stopped. Fieldgate? Just like that? With nary a thought?

Daphne felt a spark of ire burn to life inside her. She glanced around the hall. Wherever was a spare pike when a lady from Kempton needed one? "No, it is not Lord Fieldgate."

At least not so far as she knew.

"Oh, good news that," he said, sounding like a man who had just received a king's pardon.

Taken aback by his concern, Daphne's heart tripped a beat.

"Why is that?" she asked, thinking she might hear a declaration of how Fieldgate was a complete rotter and unworthy of her.

No, unfortunately, Lord Henry's relief was for an entirely different reason.

"Fieldgate is a deuced good shot. Wouldn't think twice about putting a bullet through a fellow if he thought his honor had been impugned."

Daphne's mouth fell open. That was what he was concerned about? That Lord Fieldgate might take offense and demand satisfaction?

Not a word about her honor? But rather that Fieldgate was capable of laying him low?

Shuttering her lips, she grit her teeth. Fieldgate, she would like to tell Lord Henry, wasn't the only deuced good shot under this roof.

Lord Henry sighed again and, seemingly with all his problems solved, started down the hall, this time without her hand on his sleeve.

Daphne found herself hurrying to catch up.

"Hmm," he was musing, glancing over at her as she stormed back up to his side, most likely warned by the determined click of her boots. "If it isn't Fieldgate, then who? Kipps?" He studied her for a moment, then shook his head. "No, never. He's too impractical for you."

Harrumph! "Must you continue this?"

"Decidedly," he told her, as if he was surprised she would even protest. "This is my nephew's house. Wouldn't do to have some untoward scandal happening under his roof —"

She cocked a brow at him. Untoward scandal? As if a Seldon wasn't quite capable of providing enough *on dits* to keep even the most jaded gossips busy for a month.

They were nearly to the ballroom, where a flurry of activity could be heard.

"Hen loves a good masquerade party," he said, surveying the chaos before them. "Just like our mother did."

"Lady Salsbury," she said, before she realized it.

"Yes, she was Lady Salsbury before she married my father." He grinned at her. "An aficionado of *Debrett's?*"

Daphne flinched. For she had spent a

314

good hour this morning — after her side trip to the music room — searching the pages in the dated volume she'd found on the shelf for any reference to the name Dishforth. That had been Tabitha's idea.

But much to her chagrin, Daphne's time had been spent reading the entire section devoted to the Seldon family.

Including Lady Salsbury.

"I believe Tabitha mentioned your mother," Daphne said instead. "Your sister has given her some of your mother's jewels — the ones she wore as the duchess."

Lord Henry nodded. "Of course. Hen is thoughtful that way."

"Yes, it was thoughtful of her to have all these costumes sent down from London."

"Perhaps. Mercenary, more like it. She's also had the ones here brought down and aired. She's in quite a state to ensure the entire party is well garbed, since invitations have gone out to all the local gentry and there is an entire throng coming down from London." He paused for a moment. "She wants the reports and gossip to speak only of a glowing success."

"I doubt she will fail," Daphne said diplomatically.

Lord Henry let out an impatient snort. "Will be a terrible crush is what it will be.

Stand warned, you won't know who you are dancing with, a local knave or a knight with no title."

Ahead of them, there was a clamor of excited voices.

"Ah, the costumes," he said, sounding less than enthused. "You are destined for a shepherdess or worse, I fear."

"Not in the least," Daphne told him. "Tabitha and Harriet promised to save me from such a fate."

"Good news that. For you do recall that Miss Nashe beat you there, and we both know how ruthless she can be."

Once again, Daphne had the sense of him riding to her rescue, like a Lancelot to slay the evil queen — a costume Miss Nashe ought to consider.

Lord Henry leaned over. "I deplore masquerade balls."

"So do I," she agreed without thinking. And there it was, another moment when she discovered something else in common with Lord Henry.

It gave her shivers, as if to tell her to pay attention to this man. But that was madness. For certainly her reasons — disliking old, mangy costumes and overdone Aphrodites — could hardly be the same reasons as his. And just to test her theory, she asked as casually as she might, "What are your reasons?"

"Graying matrons done up as Aphrodite and some old costume my sister thinks will be 'divine' on me but instead smells like a horse blanket."

Daphne cringed. Oh, good heavens. Truly, how many times did she have to tell herself that she and Lord Henry held nothing in common, only to have that dratted man prove her wrong?

Or right.

She wasn't too sure which it was.

Before he could say more, Lady Juniper came bustling out. "There you are, Henry. Good heavens, you'll end up being the Nave of Hearts if you don't go in there and claim a costume." Suddenly she spied Daphne at his side and her brows rose slightly. It was clear on her face that while she might be the widow of Lord Juniper, she was a Seldon at heart.

Her? What the devil are you doing with a Dale?

But if anything, Lady Juniper held good manners in high regard, and she whisked the shock off her face to say in a polite, albeit a bit strained, fashion, "Yes, well, there you are, Miss Dale. The ladies are choosing their costumes across the hall in the morning room. The light is better in there." She pointed the way, but her strained expression seemed more inclined to pointing toward the front door, which opened to the driveway, which joined the road back to London.

But before the lady could do more, there was a clamor inside the morning room, and she had to rush off to solve yet another emergency.

Daphne went to follow, but Lord Henry caught her by the arm.

"You have no intention of telling me who you were waiting for, do you?"

She shook her head. "No."

"Then so be it," he said. But instead of letting her go, he pulled her closer. "But know that I think whoever he is, he's a demmed lucky fellow if he's won your heart." He bowed over her hand and placed a lingering kiss on her fingertips. Then having released his grasp and flashed a smoldering glance, not unlike the one from last night — the one that had left her trembling — he disappeared into the ballroom.

And left her alone. To find her Dishforth.

Then suddenly he was back at her side. "You had best leave Mr. Muggins out here in the hall," he told her.

"Why?" Daphne felt as she always did

when he arrived at her side . . . a little taken aback. Just as she had the first moment she'd laid eyes on him.

"As I recall, my mother had a particular costume she loved — a water sprite, I think it was, but the hemline is done in blue feathers." Then he leaned over and whispered, "If you find it, offer it to Miss Nashe."

And then her Lancelot was gone. Yet again.

Offer it to Miss Nashe.

Daphne pressed her lips together as she walked into the morning room. Why that wretched, awful man! How devilish of him to put such a notion in her head.

But demmed if she didn't take a quick, furtive glance around the room for just that gown. The one with the feathered hem.

Better that than consider what else Lord Henry had just said.

But know that I think whoever he is, he's a demmed lucky fellow if he's won your heart.

She couldn't help herself; she looked over her shoulder. *Whatever did he mean by that?*

Had he been teasing her, like he had when he'd suggested she offer the feathered costume to Miss Nashe?

Or had he meant every word?

But before she could consider anything else, Harriet and Tabitha came bounding forward and towed her across the room, the

319

entire space awash in gowns and props and splashes of color. The other ladies were holding up velvet gowns made for a princess, fairy gowns of changeable silk that shimmered in the light, and gaudy ensembles that spoke of the gilded times from the previous century.

"We saved the best costume for you," Harriet told her, guiding her past the others, including Miss Nashe and her mother, who appeared affronted by the meager choices left them.

"I must confess, we came down early and hid it before Miss Nashe arrived," Tabitha said, her eyes dancing with mirth. "This costume is perfect, and I wasn't about to let her wear it."

Daphne made a note to mention to her old friend that just because she was marrying a Seldon, she needn't take on their mischievous ways. But it wasn't until they got to the far corner and Harriet dug the dress out from beneath a pile of silks and brocades that Daphne became convinced that Tabitha had utterly forgotten her vicarage roots.

She and Harriet thought this the perfect gown?

From all around the room, there was a chorus of gasps and then a round of "ah's."

For indeed the costume was stunning.

And utterly scandalous.

"Cleopatra?" Daphne managed, eyeing the diaphanous silk and shaking her head at the deep V that made up the front of the gown. "You want me to dress as the Queen of the Nile?"

"Why not?" Tabitha asked, looking over at the costume as if the gown had come from Mrs. Welling's stodgy shop in Kempton.

"Because that gown is . . . I would look . . . I cannot," she said, shaking her head. She looked over at Harriet. "You should wear it. Your coloring makes you a better Cleopatra than I."

"Me?" Harriet blushed and shook her head. "Oh, no, I couldn't. No, I cannot. Besides, you have more nerve. And Tabitha and I are in agreement that once Dishforth sees you in this gown, he will no longer remain in the shadows. He'll have no choice but to come forth and claim you."

Claim her? If he didn't take one look and judge her to be a reckless jade, that is. That gown would give poor, sensible Dishforth apoplexy.

Though whatever would it do to Lord Henry? a wicked little voice whispered.

Tabitha joined in. "Would you prefer that we offer the gown to Miss Nashe?"

The three of them turned in unison and looked over at the girl, who stood with her mother frowning at the last remaining costume, a shepherdess gown with far too many flounces. Poor Miss Nashe looked as if she would like to stick the crook she was holding into someone, if only to gain a better costume.

Namely Daphne.

Harriet leaned in and whispered. "Do you want her to arrive at the ball and be the Queen of not only the Nile but of the night as well?"

If only her friends didn't know her so well. Daphne took another glance at the gown and knew the woman who wore it would never be forgotten.

And even though she had no doubts she'd be in Mr. Dishforth's arms tonight, there was a small part of her that worried that the ardent plea she'd penned this morning and had left in the salver would not bring him out of hiding.

However, such a gown . . .

Taking it from Harriet, she walked over to the large mirror that had been brought down from one of the bedchambers and held it up to herself to gauge how it would fit.

Perfectly, if Harriet and Tabitha's grins

were any indication.

And Daphne knew with all her heart that if this gown didn't bring Dishforth out of hiding, he'd end his days wondering why he hadn't summoned the nerve to claim her.

Then again, as she eyed the scandalous, seductive silk one more time, she had to wonder if it was Dishforth or Lord Henry she was trying to tempt.

"Oh, maman! Here is the perfect gown!" Miss Nashe cried out in triumph, holding aloft a gorgeous green silk — a nymph's costume — hemmed in feathers.

Tabitha sucked in a deep breath. "No. Miss Nashe, you mustn't —"

Daphne whirled around and clapped her hand over Tabitha's mouth.

Harriet, seeing Daphne's intent, stepped in front of her friends and then chimed in. Loudly. "You had best take that away, Miss Nashe, before Lady Clare arrives."

The implication being that Lady Clare, who outranked all of the other unmarried ladies, could claim it as her own.

Something not even Miss Nashe and her bountiful dowry could protest. Not unless she wanted to appear the grasping mushroom.

Meanwhile, Tabitha was trying to wiggle free of Daphne's grasp, her eyes wide and furious. "Ohmmm — waaa —"

Miss Nashe, gown in hand, hurried from the morning room, her mother in her wake. That was when the barking commenced.

CHAPTER 10

Do you ever make mischief? I know we agreed to live a sober, sensible life, but sometimes one must laugh.

Found in a letter from
Miss Spooner to Mr. Dishforth

"Well, I think I have apologized for everything, save the entire Irish race," Tabitha declared as she came into their room to change before supper. She shot Harriet and Daphne pointed glances. "It should be the two of you down there groveling."

Harriet glanced up from where she was ensconced on the settee reading the latest *Miss Darby* novel. "Apologize for what?"

Daphne bit her lips together, but it was no use; she couldn't hold back the laughter.

Which turned out to be doubly contagious.

Tabitha quickly shut the door and, leaning against it, began laughing until tears were running down her cheeks.

"Did you see her face?"

"That first bark! He did warn her."

"Who would have thought her so fleet?"

"Or so vulgar?"

They all laughed again, this time falling onto the settee around Harriet and laughing until they could barely breathe.

Mr. Muggins sat at their feet, looking askance at each of them.

He saw nothing humorous in any of it. There had been feathers afoot, and as far as the Irish terrier was concerned, he'd saved them all from a fate most dire.

For the moment Miss Nashe had paraded out of the morning room with her prized costume, she'd been met by Mr. Muggins.

Now some might have seen that confection of green silk, French lace and dyed feathers as the most beautiful costume ever.

They, however, were not an Irish terrier with attitude.

It had taken Mr. Muggins about two seconds to decide that particular gown was a menace to Society.

Miss Nashe, who wasn't about to relinquish her prize, found herself very quickly backed up against the opposite wall with the gown clutched to her bosom. Not even when faced with a half-mad dog would she release her hold on her prize.

Instead, her screams — sharp, shrieking tones that Lady Essex would later say were inherited from the gel's fishwife forebears — had brought the entire house running.

Not that Mr. Muggins was going to let anyone near. Not when there were feathers afoot.

"That was a standoff for the history books," Harriet declared.

Tabitha shook her head. "I still don't see how she was able to make it nearly to the stairs before Mr. Muggins caught her."

Mr. Muggins wasn't the only one in the girls' room looking askance over the entire scene. Daphne's maid, Pansy, stood by the clothespress, her mouth set in disapproval over their unladylike display. She sniffed and went back to sorting out Daphne's gowns.

Thus chastened, the trio of friends did their best to look remorseful, for certainly they would have to make it through dinner and the rest of the evening without falling into another case of the whoops.

"Oh, my goodness," Tabitha exclaimed, bounding to her feet, "is that the time?"

Pansy glanced over at the mantel clock. "Yes, miss." She then shot a pointed stare at her mistress, for the maid knew all too well how long it took Daphne to get dressed.

"No, it cannot be!" Daphne declared. "I've hardly had time to choose a gown!"

And she had every reason to find the perfect dress. For after the dust had settled on what Lady Essex had declared "the feather incident," Daphne had discovered a single note in the salver.

Tonight. Yes, my dear Miss Spooner. Tonight.

Dishforth had replied to her. Promised to meet her.

Daphne's hand went to her belly to soothe her restless nerves before she once again surveyed her choice of gowns. The blue one she was wearing would not do, she could see that now.

Oh, to finally meet Mr. Dishforth. This was exactly why she'd come to Owle Park, and now it was to happen.

It had to happen. Why, she'd spent the rest of the afternoon composing list after list of the perfect things to say when she met him.

My dear Mr. Dishforth . . .

At last we meet . . .

I am speechless . . .

No, no, that would never do. If she was truly speechless, she wouldn't be able to manage that much.

Oh, dear, whatever was she going to say?

*When we meet, mere words will never be
enough, my dear Miss Spooner.*

Ah, yes, leave it to Mr. Dishforth to have
the perfect answer for such an awkward
situation.

She turned from the pile of gowns on the
bed and hugged herself. Everything would
be perfect from here on out.

Whirling around, she faced her maid.
"Where is my green gown?"

"Another one, miss?" Pansy asked. "You
look pretty as a picture in that one."

"No, this shade of blue won't do."

"Do what?" Harriet asked. Suffering no
case of nerves, Harriet had dressed with her
usual casual efficiency in a modest gown
and had had Pansy pin her dark hair up in
a simple crown of ringlets.

"Nothing," Daphne told her. "I have the
right to change my mind."

"No one is arguing that," Tabitha said.
"But look at the time."

"Oh, bother!" Daphne said. None of her
gowns seemed to be right. Not for tonight.
She paused, taking another look at the apple
green muslin she'd had made in London
just a few weeks earlier and that Pansy had
fetched from the clothespress. But it was
too much like the gown Miss Nashe had
worn yesterday. As a day dress. "No. This

just won't do."

Tabitha and Harriet exchanged a glance, and then Tabitha shooed Pansy out the door.

They all loved Pansy dearly, but the girl was a bit of a gossip.

Once the door was closed and they were all alone, Tabitha turned to Daphne, hands fisted to her hips. "What is so special about tonight."

Harriet sat up. "Is it Lord Henry?"

"Lord Henry?" Daphne sputtered. "Whyever would you say such a thing?"

Harriet looked to Tabitha for help. When none was forthcoming, she waded in. "It is just after last night —"

"Oh, not that again," Daphne complained.

"Daphne!" Tabitha chided. "We saw you. The two of you. If you think no one noticed, you are very wrong."

"There was nothing to see," Daphne told them with every bit of resolve she possessed. As if that was the end of the matter.

Harriet snorted. "If nothing means Lord Henry was about to kiss you, then yes, I suppose we saw nothing."

"He was not . . . I would never —" Daphne stammered.

Oh, whyever did it have to be Harriet and Tabitha accusing her? They knew all her secrets and her failings.

Primarily that she was a terrible liar.

So she went back to her choice of gowns, for she was at her wit's end as to which one to wear for her assignation with Mr. Dishforth. She picked up one, then another, discarded them both and picked up a third. Well, the green muslin would just have to do. She was about to shrug out of the blue silk she was wearing when she found that her friends were not finished with her.

"Daphne, whatever is the matter with you?" Harriet said, rising to her feet and taking the green muslin out of her grasp. "That is the sixth gown you've tried on tonight."

"I always change my mind," Daphne protested, trying to retrieve the dress, but Harriet held it out of reach and then passed it along to Tabitha, who put it behind her back.

"You change your gown three times before dinner," Harriet pointed out. "Never six."

"I just want to look perfect tonight," Daphne told them.

"What is so important about tonight?" Tabitha repeated, holding the muslin just out of reach, a tempting prize being offered for an honest answer.

Which Daphne was not about to concede. "Nothing. It is just that . . ." She stammered

331

for a moment, then found her lie. "Miss Nashe was going on and on about her gown for this evening, and I would so like to outshine her —"

She had told them what the heiress had said over breakfast, so perhaps . . .

"This has nothing to do with Miss Nashe," Tabitha said, seeing right through the ruse. "Besides, I think the score between you and Miss Nashe is quite even now."

"Oh, goodness," Harriet exclaimed. "It's Mr. Dishforth, isn't it?" Then her friend's eyes widened. "You've discovered who he is, haven't you?"

While she had hoped to keep her meeting a secret — after the disaster that was the engagement ball — she realized she very much needed their help this one last time.

"Nearly," Daphne confessed.

Henry, who was never late for anything in his life, was late yet again.

Hen was going to have his hide on a platter for such a lapse — or call for a surgeon from London to have him gone over.

At least he had a partial excuse for his tardiness, he mused as he stood at the crossways of two long halls.

Demmed if he could find his way through the ambling maze of passages and wings that made up Owle Park. Unfortunately, this had been Preston's childhood home, not his.

Getting lost, his sister would expect, but she'd have been shocked to discover the real reason behind his belated arrival: Henry had had Loftus replace not only his cravat — twice — but his boots and his coat as well. The poor valet had finally given up on his usually affable employer, throwing his hands in the air and muttering something about the country air having gone to his lordship's head.

So he was a bit distracted. Why wouldn't he be, when tonight his entire life would change?

We must meet. Tonight. In the library. After dinner. ~S

Yet he'd been taken aback as he'd read the sparse lines, sensing an urgency behind them.

On one hand was Miss Spooner, a lady, not just a week ago, he had welcomed meeting.

That is, until he'd crossed paths with Miss Daphne Dale.

Now? Well, he didn't know what to think. Did he want to be Miss Spooner's sensible gentleman, a role he'd always found agreeable, or did he want to be the rake he saw reflected in Miss Dale's engaging glances?

Miss Dale, indeed! What an impossible notion.

No, no, he needed to discover who Miss Spooner might be and move cautiously forward from there. For he had told Zillah the truth: he would not marry just to be married. Not for money, or business, or status.

He'd follow his heart. A rather insensible notion for a man who prided himself on being practical. And he had the very impractical Miss Dale to thank for this change of heart.

That didn't mean he knew what to do next. He'd spent a good part of the afternoon pacing circles around the fish pond wondering what the devil he was going to say to the chit.

Especially when every time he imagined entering the library and it was none other than Miss Dale who turned around to greet him.

Demmit, whatever would he do then? For he was already half in love with her.

Oh, why try to fool himself. There were no halves about it.

He was in love with Miss Dale.

And he could even pin it down to the exact moment when she'd succeeded in stealing his heart.

When he'd been watching the spectacle this afternoon. Oh, he hadn't been eyeing Miss Nashe's epic dash through Owle Park with Mr. Muggins on her heels. No, his gaze had been fixed on Miss Dale.

Miss Dale, with her lips pressed together so it appeared she was as beset and concerned as everyone else. He hadn't been fooled. She'd had her mouth clenched shut to keep from laughing.

Much as he had.

And when she'd spied him watching her, she'd mouthed two words: *Thank you.*

In that instant, Lord Henry Seldon fell in love.

Head. Over. Heels.

With a Dale. He'd been so bowled over, so thunderstruck, that he'd barely been able to get out his answer.

You're welcome.

Then she'd grinned at him and slipped back into the milling crowd, taking his heart with her.

As he'd stood there, utterly blindsided by this accident of fate, he realized he'd been in love with her for far longer. Probably since the first moment he'd clapped eyes on her at Preston's engagement ball.

Love. What an ass he'd been all these years

on the subject. Love, he now realized, was utter chaos. A maelstrom against the sagacious.

No wonder a bewitching minx such as Daphne Dale had inspired his once sensible heart to take flight.

In a panic, Henry had fled to the music room, hunted down a pen and paper and dashed off a response to Miss Spooner.

Tonight. Yes, my dear Miss Spooner. Tonight.

Henry had never fallen in love before, and panic had seemed the most sensible response.

Miss Spooner would restore his equilibrium, bring him back to his senses.

Yet now, as the time drew closer, he wasn't sure what he would do. However would he know if he was making the right choice. If Miss Spooner was the right lady for him?

And his answer seemed to come as he rounded a corner and collided with another.

A lady, in fact.

"Oh, dear heavens!" she cried out as she slammed into him, his perfectly pressed jacket now creased beyond repair.

Henry caught hold of her, and the moment his arm wound around her waist, his fingers caught hold of her elbow and he steadied her, he knew.

Miss Dale.

He looked down at her, and for a tremulous second, they gazed into each other's eyes.

One could have dismissed the night at the ball as mere chance. The afternoon in the folly as, well, folly. But Henry couldn't deny that each time he looked into Miss Daphne Dale's wide, innocent blue eyes, his heart stopped.

The entire world stilled, at least for him as he took in her silken wisps of blonde hair escaping from her nearly perfect coif, her pretty, full lips that were just made for kissing — no, make that devouring. It wasn't panic that filled his veins this time but desire.

Hot, hard desire.

Henry wanted nothing more than to sweep her up in some medieval, high-handed manner and carry her off to the highest reaches of Owle Park.

There, he'd seduce her. Make love to her. Find solace for this restless, aching need racing through him that he knew, just damn well knew, she was the only woman capable of easing.

Of course, finding his way might be a bit of a bother . . . and might require he put her down to ask directions. But once they got there . . .

"Miss Dale," he whispered. *Daphne.*

"I'm late . . . and a bit lost," she murmured, her gaze never leaving his, her lashes fluttering as she spoke.

He had the sense she wasn't just talking about finding the dining room — that the two of them were on the same errant course. One that kept tossing them together only to pull them apart.

Never mind that she was a Dale . . . oh, he couldn't deny that was a rub. Henry could almost hear his forebears rising up to protest such a coupling . . . or how Aunt Zillah would take the news.

Perhaps that was exactly why Miss Dale was so devilishly tempting.

"I'm rather lost as well," he confessed, looking down at her and resisting the urge to brush an errant strand of her blonde hair out of her eyes.

She shook her head as if she didn't believe him. "How can you be lost?"

"I've never been here," he told her, not even realizing that he had drawn her closer until he felt the rustle of her gown against his hips, or how his words might have a second, more important, meaning.

"Never?" Again the question was so laden with so many implications.

Layers Henry didn't dare peel back. Even for a peek. "Yes, well, Preston grew up here. Until . . . until . . ." He paused, but one look at the sudden sad light that flickered in her gaze told him she knew the horrible story as well.

How Owle Park had been Preston's childhood home until his entire family, save him, had perished from fever, leaving him orphaned and the heir all in one fell swoop.

That cold, haunted memory stopped them both. Sent a chill between them as if the ghosts in this house had better sense than they did.

It was enough to give Miss Dale the impetus to step out of his grasp, wavering still, but this time, he suspected her trembling stance wasn't from their collision.

"There, see," she said, glancing down at her feet and smoothing her skirts. "No damage done. So sorry to have . . ." Again, she glanced up at him, this time almost warily.

"No, truly, it was my fault," he told her.

Then it started all again, that awkward silence, followed by the compelling need to close the gap between them.

Henry sensed that if they dared, if they took that one step to close the chasm, there would be no turning back.

Miss Dale drew a deep breath. "I suppose

we should find the dining room," she suggested, glancing right and left and not at him.

So it was decided. Which was for the best. "Yes, quite," he agreed. After all, he was to meet Miss Spooner tonight.

Sensible, practical, perfectly acceptable Miss Spooner.

The sooner, the better, he realized as his body continued to thrum with reckless desire. So he started down the hall, Miss Dale at his side.

Right where she belongs.

Henry cringed and decided to take a different tack. "Are you in trouble over —"

"That incident which should not be named?" she asked, her lips twitching into a sly smile.

Oh, how it called to him. Henry shrugged off that notion and continued doing his utmost to maintain an orderly veneer. "Yes. Truly, I should never have suggested it. If I had known your daring side —"

"Daring had nothing to do with it," she told him. "Nor did I. It was all Miss Nashe. Well, nearly all Miss Nashe."

"Then you had something to do with it," he pressed.

She glanced away. "A small part. Hardly worth mentioning."

"Hardly?"

"So slight," she demurred. "The lady found the gown all on her own and was most insistent on making it hers."

"Yet you didn't warn her?"

"Tabitha might have tried," she admitted.

"Might have?"

"She might have been able to do so if my hand hadn't been covering her mouth."

Henry, despite his better nature, burst out laughing. How could he not? The scene was rife with irony: Miss Nashe in all her haughtiness and dear Tabitha, ever the vicar's daughter, trying to do the right thing.

And then there was Miss Dale.

"Wicked girl!"

She slanted a glance at him. "You shouldn't sound so admiring over it."

He straightened, for he shouldn't. Admire her, that is. "Whyever not?"

"Lady Essex says there will a grand scandal over it."

"You can count on it," he told her. "Benley has been laid low with all the posts leaving Owle Park this afternoon. Not one of these gossipy harpies wants to be the last one to make her report."

"And you don't mind?" she asked.

Henry shook his head. "Quite immune to it."

"I suppose you are."

"And you?"

"My mother would have horrors over my part in all of it, but thankfully no one will ever know," she admitted.

"Save me," he said, waggling his brows at her. He couldn't help himself.

"Oh, dear heavens, does that mean I'm indebted to you?" she asked in mock horror.

"Your secret is safe with me," he told her in all solemnity.

"I believe you. I even trust you. Which I never thought I'd say about a Seldon." She needn't sound so shocked.

"No? And how many have you met?" he asked.

Miss Dale laughed. "Only you and Preston. Oh, and Lady Juniper and Lady Zillah."

"I do believe, then, you have met all of us."

She turned and gaped at him. "That's all there is? Just you four?"

He nodded. "Well, we've never been a prolific lot, like you Dales."

"Which is rather ironic," she pointed out.

"How so?"

"You Seldons are considered quite licentious, and yet there are so few of you left."

"Perhaps we are not as licentious as we seem," he said with a rakish wink that made her blush. He rather liked it when she did — it wasn't so much because she was embarrassed but because she thought him a rake.

"Please do not tell Zillah I admitted as much," he added hastily. "She takes great pride in our scandalous reputation."

"She must be ever so disappointed in Preston, now that he's reformed." Then she slowed slightly and lowered her voice. "Was he as scandalous as they say?"

"I do believe Preston was under the impression that was how he ought to behave — not how he truly is."

"So I am beginning to see," she admitted.

"Still, you don't approve."

"Tabitha's engagement to Preston took us all by surprise," she said. "It was just so sudden, so . . ."

"You are being diplomatic," he said, folding his hands behind his back.

"Yes, well, as a Dale —"

"Yes, yes, say no more —"

"No, I must. You mistake me," she said. "While of course I can hardly approve of the match — for he is —"

Henry arched a brow and waited for her answer, if only to see how far her diplomacy could take them.

"He is Preston," she finally said.

True enough. That had been enough this past Season to have even the most upstart mushrooms giving the entire Seldon family the cut direct.

Then Miss Dale surprised him. "Yet he does love Tabitha."

"Passionately," Henry added.

"Yes, that he does." And it was that — the very envy in her voice — that cut him to the quick.

And now it seemed it was a sentiment he shared with Miss Dale.

Yet she wasn't done. "Tabitha would never choose any man who wasn't deserving, and it is as you say, that the duke loves her passionately, but I fear . . ."

They had come to a stop.

"Well, what I mean to say is . . . that is . . . do you think —" she began, then she looked up at him and finished, "is passion enough?"

Oh, very much so, he wanted to tell her.

That thought, that conviction made without even blinking, came straight from his heart.

For all he could see was Miss Dale undone, in his bed, beneath him. Passion? She left him in its throes by walking into a room. To spend the rest of his life that way?

Henry would never have believed how alive passion, desire, could make one feel.

Until now.

Good God, he hoped when he walked into the library it was Miss Dale there. Never mind the dustup such an affair would result in. He wanted to be her rake. To be the passion in her life. To have her always.

Damn tradition. Damn the lines.

Yet she took his silence all wrong and started walking again. "Everyone speaks of love as if it was so easy to understand, as if it makes sense," she was saying when he caught up.

"It doesn't?" he asked as he joined her.

She shook her head. "Preston is . . . well, he's Preston. And Tabitha is . . . goodness, she's a vicar's daughter. Yet they fit. They make the other whole. How can that be?"

Henry spoke without thinking, his restraint and sensibilities having fled in the face of Miss Daphne Dale, and without those confining boundaries, he said, "That would rather be like you and me falling in love."

What had Lord Henry just said? The words rang through Daphne with such a deafening clang that it took her a moment or two to make sense of them.

That would rather be like you and me falling in love.

Them? In love? It wouldn't be the oddity that was Tabitha and Preston's impending marriage; rather, if they — she and Lord Henry — were to fall in love, it would be . . . why, it would be . . .

Heavenly. The word came unbidden into her thoughts, carried by the memory of his kiss.

If Daphne didn't know better, she suspected she was already in love with Lord Henry Seldon.

No, not suspected. Knew.

Oh, it was too impossible to believe. Her. In love. With a Seldon. If a postal engagement was scandalous, this was . . . beyond ruinous.

"What an unmitigated disaster that would turn out to be," she told him with a shaky laugh, starting down the hall again.

Fleeing was more like it.

He laughed a bit as well. Was it her, or did his amusement sound as forced as hers? She glanced back at him. "Yes, wouldn't it be?" he said. "Can you imagine Zillah's reaction?"

Daphne made a great show of shuddering — though a good part of it wasn't all acting. "Yes, imagine that. And my Great-Aunt

Damaris."

Lord Henry paled. "Yes, I would think it would be prudent to write to her."

"Wouldn't save us," Daphne confided. "We have a saying that if you sneeze in Scotland, Aunt Damaris will hear it in London."

He laughed. "Zillah has much the same uncanny sense of disaster."

"Yes, our falling in love would be a disaster," she said, slanting a glance at him.

But oh, so heavenly . . .

Daphne drew a deep breath. She had to stop thinking like that. Tonight she would find Mr. Dishforth, and she would fall in love all over again.

Not all over again, she told herself. For the first time. The very first time. Because with Mr. Dishforth it would all make sense. They already fit.

Just like Tabitha and Preston.

At least she thought they did. Hoped they would.

Then she would have to stop finding herself in these impossibly perilous interludes with Lord Henry.

No more chance encounters. No more shared jests.

No more kisses.

She looked again at him. *Would it be so*

wrong to kiss him one more time?

Yes, decidedly.

Bother! Her conscience was starting to sound like one of Tabitha's uncle's sermons.

"Miss Dale, is something amiss?"

Daphne found that she'd come to a stop without even realizing it. Lord Henry stood a few paces further down the hall, staring at her.

What had he asked? If something was amiss?

Well, yes, everything! she wanted to tell him.

"No, nothing," she said, hurrying to catch up and continuing toward the dining room. To get through dinner and then slip away to the library.

Where she was destined to find true love. Yes, that was it. True love.

Still, whatever had Lord Henry meant when he'd said, *"That would rather be like you and me falling in love"?*

Did he think it possible? Was he merely joking? Daphne needed to know before she set foot in that library, but however did one ask such a thing?

"Miss Dale?"

Daphne looked up and realized that yet again, in her woolgathering, she'd come to a stop. And here was Lord Henry looking her up and down as if she were standing about in her shift.

"Yes? Is there something wrong?" She feigned innocence and glanced down to make sure her gown was in order — and that she hadn't gone out only in her chemise, as she'd dreamt the night before the Seldon ball.

"No, no," he said. Then he made a sweeping examination of her ensemble. "But you've done something different tonight."

This was promising.

"My hair," she said, hoping Pansy's arrangement of Grecian curls was still as orderly as it had been when she'd left her room. And yet, here was Lord Henry with his brow furrowed and looking at her with his lips in a sour purse. "Don't you approve?"

"Approve?" Henry glanced at it again. "Uh, well. It isn't for me to say."

Whyever did he look so uncomfortable? She glanced down again, for she had the feeling her petticoat was showing.

But her search showed nothing but her pale green muslin laying perfectly smooth down to her hemline. So if it wasn't her petticoat . . . perhaps . . .

She tipped her head just so, letting the collection of curls fall over one bare shoulder. "I would so love a man's opinion. Does this arrangement suit me?"

"Yes," he ground out. "Perfectly so."

He hardly sounded inclined to kiss her. More as if he was in some state of discomfort. Oh, this would never do.

"And this gown?" she asked, holding out her skirt just so.

"Yes," he replied. "Miss Dale, believe me when I say you would look perfectly amiable in sackcloth and ashes."

Amiable? That was hardly the description she'd been hoping for.

"I am so pleased that you approve," she said, knowing all too well that she didn't sound pleased. And before she had to explain her pique, she started back down the hall.

Perfectly amiable, indeed! Oh, she'd never felt so foolish in her life.

"Whatever is wrong?" Lord Henry said, his stride leaving him capable of catching up with her all too quickly.

"I took great pains to appear to advantage tonight, and you find me just amiable?" she complained.

Having Hen for a twin, Henry knew an argument that could not be won from twenty paces.

And this was just such a mire.

"What I meant was —" he tried.

She waved her hand in dismissal. "Never mind."

Ah, yes. Unwinnable. But that didn't mean . . .

"What is so special about tonight?" he asked.

Her steps faltered slightly. "No reason."

Henry took a glance at her. He hadn't done business in London all these years not to know when someone was bluffing.

Or had something to hide.

And given the distracted flutter of Miss Dale's long lashes, he would guess the latter.

But before he could press forward with an inquisition, she turned the tables on him.

"You've taken pains tonight as well," she said, giving him a thorough once-over.

"H-h-hardly," he faltered.

Miss Dale smirked. "Your cravat is tied in a waterfall, is it not?"

He glanced down at himself. "I suppose it is. Loftus, my valet, rather insisted I —"

"Yes, I suppose so. He must have grown tired of your usual Mailcoach."

"I allowed it because I truly didn't think anyone would notice," he demurred, trying to fob her off. How the devil had she pulled the rug out from beneath him?

But Miss Dale wasn't done with her perusal. "And your boots. They have extra polish. Perhaps His Grace's valet did them — for that gloss makes you look quite the Corinthian."

Henry looked down at his boots as if this was the first he'd noticed them. He'd actually asked Loftus to redo them, which had nearly put his proud valet to tears. "He must have convinced Preston's valet to share his infamous concoction for boot black."

"Or he pinched it," she teased.

"Loftus? He'd quit in shame first!" Henry avowed.

She laughed merrily, and after a few moments, so did Henry.

"If I were a wagering sort," she mused, "I would say you have done all this in preparation for an assignation tonight."

Henry came to a blindiing halt. "That is utterly ridiculous," he told her. "Whatever do they teach young ladies in these Bath schools?"

"I wouldn't know. You will have to ask Miss Nashe — if that is who you are meeting."

"I'd never —" At least he hoped it wasn't Miss Nashe. Good God, if it was, he'd be on the first ship out of the London pool.

No matter its destination.

Miss Dale eyed him up and down again. "Yes, there is no doubt in my mind, you are angling to catch some lady's eye tonight."

Angling? If anyone was angling . . . "One could say the same of you." His hands waved at her hair and her gown. "What with all this. Whomever are you fishing for, Miss Dale? Are we all to discover the identity of your most excellent gentleman tonight?"

Touché. Her eyes widened and her mouth fell open to protest, but just as quickly snapped shut.

However, Henry's triumph — and his resolve — were short-lived, for as they continued on down the gallery, Miss Dale came to a blinding halt. "Who is that?" She pointed up at the painting towering on the wall.

"My grandfather," he told her after taking a closer look. "Actually, I was named after him."

She drew closer and read the plate on the bottom of the frame. "Henry George Seldon, the seventh Duke of Preston. *Hmmm.* You favor him," she said, looking at his grandsire and then at him.

Henry took a step back and shuddered. "I should hope not."

"What do you mean?"

"If family rumors are to be believed, he was a terrible scoundrel. Wild Hal, he was known as," Henry said, turning from the portrait and the mocking, rakish gaze of the seventh duke.

"Truly? A Seldon who was a scoundrel? Why, I never," she teased, that light in her eyes glowing with impish delight. As she stepped back to get a better look at the imposing portrait, her skirt brushed against his thigh, reminding him how much she enticed him.

Suggesting that he had more in common with his forebear than he'd ever realized. That was all it took, that ever-so-brief moment, a glance at her, and he was lost.

For there was in her smile and nod of approval evidence that she saw in him that same enticing light that had made the previous Henry Seldon the most notorious courtier of Queen Anne's court.

Some even said he'd dallied with the old queen herself. Then again, hadn't Owle Park come into the family about then? And wasn't Lady Essex encamped in the room known as "The Queen's Chamber"?

"I am hardly in the same league," he protested aloud.

Miss Dale shot him a wide-eyed glance, a bit startled by his outburst. After another glance at the seventh duke, she grinned. "In my opinion, the resemblance is uncanny."

Her words held all the notes of a suggestion. Admiration, even.

But mostly, they held the one thing Henry couldn't resist. Not from her.

A dare.

Henry turned to her and closed the gap between them. He had every intention of gathering her up in his arms and running away with this tempting miss, but Lord Henry Seldon had yet to master one very important part of being a rake: timing.

"Finally! Someone to help me find the dining room," came Zillah's booming voice from behind him. "Confounded place gets me lost every time."

Then out from behind Henry stepped Miss Dale.

And from the look on his great-aunt's face, Henry sent up a prayer that the lady didn't know the way to the armory any better than she did the dining room.

CHAPTER 11

Tonight, I will find you, my dearest Miss Spooner. And no longer shall we be separated by pen and paper. Nothing will ever keep us apart again.

> Found in a letter from
> Mr. Dishforth to Miss Spooner

In the dining room, where the men were enjoying their port and cigars after dinner, Henry heaved a sigh that he'd survived so far. Now all that was left was to escape without too much undo notice.

Though he wouldn't be surprised to find Zillah outside the door waiting for him.

The look she'd bored into him in the hallway, a combination of guilt and fury that said, *Not her again.* It had been enough of a censure to have him on edge all through dinner.

Lost in thought, he hadn't even noticed that Preston had wandered over until the duke said in an oft-handed fashion, "What the devil is the matter with you?"

"Me? Why, nothing," Henry told him, drawing himself up into a composed stance.

At least that was how he was supposed to look.

Preston's brow arched upward. "Henry, I've known you all my life. And you've never looked so havey-cavey as you do tonight." His nephew paused and studied him closer. "If I didn't know better, I'd think you have an assignation in the works."

"Why does everyone think that tonight?" Henry said far too quickly.

"Aha!" Preston snapped his fingers. "So you do!"

"Ridiculous!" Henry said, resorting to a lawyer's trick of neither confirming nor denying the truth.

"So who else thinks you've got a lady love stashed away above stairs?"

"No one —"

Preston gave him the Seldon stare, a glower that could wrench even a king into confessing his most dire secrets. And while Preston hadn't quite mastered the dark glance, he was — much to Henry's dismay — acquiring an admirable knack for it.

"Oh, bother," Henry complained. "First there was Loftus."

"Rather telling, my good man," Preston remarked.

"How so?"

"A valet knows these things. If Loftus believes —"

"Loftus knows nothing."

Preston's expression remained for the most part entirely bland. Save for the knowing twinkle in his eyes. "Because there is nothing to know?"

"Exactly."

Preston snorted. "And who else suggested, besides myself, that you might be engaging in some after-hours entertainments?"

Henry cringed.

"Oh, come now, Henry. You know I'll ferret it out of you eventually. And if I can't, a casual, inopportune comment in Hen's hearing will most likely —"

Good God, no! Not Hen. Preston wouldn't dare.

Slanting a glance at the duke, Henry had his answer. Hadn't he resorted to much the same tactic to rein in Preston's antics from time to time?

"Miss Dale," Henry ground out.

Preston's eyes widened, as if he wasn't too sure he'd heard him correctly. "Did you say —"

"Yes, I did."

"And she thinks —"

"Yes."

"And she said as much?"

Her words came back in haunting clarity. *I would say you have done all this in preparation for an assignation tonight.*

Henry nodded.

"Why that saucy, shocking little minx," Preston said, shaking his head. "These chits from Kempton, egads, they have the most forward manners. Say whatever occurs to them."

"Who are you to complain? You brought them into this house by agreeing to marry one of them."

The duke grinned. "So I did."

Henry hoped that was the end of the matter.

Of course it wasn't. This was Preston, after all, and he was rather enjoying his new role as a reformed rake.

Rather too much.

"So who is it you are meeting — because I must say, you are going about it in all the wrong way. In over your head, if I were to judge." Preston leaned against the wall, arms crossed over his chest.

Henry took a sip of the brandy, then, remembering its potency, he set down his glass.

If he was going to muddle his way through all this, it wouldn't help his cause to be, well, muddled.

"Come now, Henry, you've been as secretive as a cat of late. Haunting the post, up all night composing letters, hardly commenting when I wagered at White's the other night —"

"I've had an inordinate amount of business to attend to, what with —" Henry paused. "Just a moment, you were wagering at White's?"

"Never mind that," Preston demurred. "I want to go back to this 'business' of yours. That is what you're calling it? *Business?* Really, Henry, if you are going to be a Seldon, then at least you call it what it is."

"And what is it?"

"An assignation. An affair. A mistress." Preston grinned. And if Henry didn't know better, he'd say it was with a bit of familial pride.

"It isn't that at all," Henry said, once again resorting to a solicitor's meandering ways. "Besides, I've had mistresses in the past."

Preston sighed, looking a bit bored. "Yes, but you've hardly ever been in a fix over one of them."

"I am not in 'a fix.' "

"So you keep saying, but let us look at the facts." Preston held up one hand. "Late nights." He ticked off one finger. "Haunting the salver." Another fell. "And composing business letters that should be the domain of your secretary, but for whatever reason you are insisting on composing them your-self so they remain private." The third finger went down, and it was as if a spark lit inside the duke as he tallied the facts at hand.

Henry watched in horror as the duke silently mouthed that last word again, as if testing it. *Private.*

Preston shook his head. "No. That adver-tisement! Oh, you didn't?! It cannot be."

Without a ducal glare to call upon or the practiced gambler's instincts to help him, Henry's expression must have given Pres-ton every bit of confirmation he needed.

He caught Henry by the elbow and towed him to the other side of the room, well out of earshot. "Tell me you didn't answer one of those demmed lonely hearts letters."

Gone was the mocking light in Preston's eyes, his larkish demeanor having fled. Panic marked his every word.

Because for all their teasing and ribbing back and forth, they were family. And they were all they had.

And Henry knew this, even as he suddenly

longed to confide in someone. Because it was exactly as Preston had said: he was in over his head.

Not just with the letters and Miss Spooner. There was Miss Dale as well.

"I had no intention —" he began.

Preston paled. Actually grew a bit white. His mouth opened as if he had something to say, but nothing came out.

Henry couldn't have shocked his nephew more if he had claimed to have taken up with the Princess Royal.

"But it isn't like you think," he continued hastily on. *In for a penny, in for a pound . . .*

"Hen doesn't —" Preston began.

"No!" Henry shuddered.

"Yes, of course not. If she knew, she would have wrung your neck by now." Preston scratched his chin and drew a deep breath. "Tell me everything."

Knowing this was the best course, Henry spilled the entire story, starting from the moment the letter had fallen from the basket until he'd arrived at his present predicament.

Though he left out everything to do with Miss Dale. There was confession, and then there was finding one-self being carted off to Bedlam.

And Henry knew the difference.

"Do you know which of the ladies it is?"

"That's just it," Henry confessed. "I haven't the slightest notion." So this wasn't quite the truth either. He could hardly tell Preston that he suspected it was Daphne Dale.

Rather hoped it was. Then again, it could be Miss Nashe.

His dismay must have shown on his face. But luckily for Henry, if there was anyone who could see a way out of this mire, it was Preston. And it turned out he had just the solution.

"And you say this gel is in the library, right now, waiting for you?"

"Yes. At least that's the plan."

"That's excellent news," Preston said, his eyes once again alight with mischief.

"Excellent for you, perhaps — you aren't the one who has to endure the surprise and possible shock of it."

"Who says you have to go into the room not knowing who your Miss Dishes —"

"Spooner."

"Yes, yes, Spooner. Who says you have to go in uninformed? You always are going on and on about how one can't go into a partnership without knowing exactly who you are doing business with —"

"Certainly," Henry agreed. "But what

does that have to do with finding out who Miss Spooner is?"

"Everything," Preston said, nodding toward the door. "Let's go see who this lady love of yours is."

Henry caught him by the arm. "You are not going in there with me."

"I have no intention of doing that. Would make you look like an utter coward, arriving with a second and all. But I would think a man of your business inclinations wouldn't mind arriving forearmed."

"Preston, whatever are you going on about?"

And so the duke told him.

Daphne didn't know whether she was disappointed or relieved when she entered the library and found no one in there.

"If anything, I have a few moments to compose myself," she said to Mr. Muggins as they both looked about the large, well-appointed room.

It was all as it had been this morning when she'd penned her note to Dishforth. Bookshelves lined three of the walls, interrupted by several large paintings and a grand fireplace. French doors let out into the rose gardens. There was a map desk in the middle of the room, a collection of settees and a grand chair near the fireplace, and a few chairs and stools scattered in the corners, the sort that encouraged settling in for a cozy read. Thick carpets and green velvet curtains gave the large, rambling room a sense of studious decorum.

But at night, the corners were cast in shadows, and the room held an intimate, cozy appeal, the sort a Seldon could appreciate.

Well, she certainly hadn't invited Mr. Dishforth here for *that*.

Smoothing out her skirt and doing her utmost to compose her nerves, Daphne tried to gauge the best place to sit and wait — a spot from which she would be seen at best advantage. But no matter where she tried — lolling on the settee, modestly composed on a straight-backed chair or feigning a bluestocking's interest in some old, dusty tome — she felt only one thing: utterly foolish.

Mr. Muggins suffered from no such nerves. He plopped down on the rug before the hearth and let out a contented sigh.

Since she couldn't very well follow his example, Daphne decided a dignified pose might be the best. Until, that is, she looked up at the portrait she'd found herself standing beneath.

"You!" she gasped, gaping accusatorially at the face looking down at her.

Lord Henry. Well, not her Lord Henry.

Not that he was *hers,* per se. But . . .

Oh, bother, just stop, Daphne, she chided herself. How was it that scoundrel always left her so tangled up?

"I don't care what he says," she told the painting of Henry Seldon, the seventh Duke of Preston, "the resemblance between the two of you is uncanny."

The seventh duke had no reply other than that mischievous smile that could not be contained in oil and paint, or dimmed with age. As she gazed up at the rogue, she had the feeling that even now, His Grace was looking down at her from his gilt-framed prison and taking a lascivious delight in imagining her clad only in her chemise.

Daphne whirled around and put her back to the painting. "You devil!" she scolded over her shoulder.

Oh, good heavens, what was wrong with her? She was going mad if she was talking to paintings.

Stealing a glance over her shoulder, she found the duke still grinning at her, but all she saw was Lord Henry's face — as he'd held her tonight in the shadowed hallway and looked to be about to tell her something.

No, rather, show her something.

Well, the seventh duke would know.

"Your grandson hasn't fallen so far from the tree," she told the old duke. "He nearly ravished me in the hallway earlier."

Nearly.

But he hadn't. And what the devil had she been doing letting herself fall into his arms?

If she'd had any sense, she would have found her footing far more quickly and extracted herself from his grasp without a moment's delay.

But she hadn't. Instead, she'd lingered.

Yes, lingered. Just as he'd accused her before.

Dangerously waiting to see if Lord Henry would prove his heritage and make good his Seldon name.

By kissing her.

Daphne's insides quaked just thinking about that moment. His lips so close to hers, her breasts pressed to his solid chest, his arms coiled around her — holding her fast.

Lord Henry had left her feeling completely undone. As if her hairpins had all fallen out, her gown had been stripped away and she'd been his for the ravishing.

"He may argue to the contrary, but he is no different than you," she accused. "Well, I suppose you would have finished the task." Daphne paced before the painting, stealing glances up at the old duke, infamous for his affairs.

Which had been left out of his lengthy description in *Debrett's*.

Of course they didn't put such things in *Debrett's*. If they started including all the noblemen's mistresses and affairs, well, there wouldn't be enough paper in England to chronicle all that.

Was that why Lord Henry hadn't kissed her? He was saving himself for another?

"Well, he was rather done up tonight," she told the duke. "Handsomely so." She paused. "As if he had an assignation."

Daphne, well used to filling in lines for others, could well imagine what the duke might say.

Ah, you are correct, my lovely little delight. The perfect cravat. The shine to the boots. The light in his eye. No, our Henry hasn't fallen too far from the Seldon tree. When he didn't kiss you, I'd quite feared —

Daphne's insides turned from that melting sort of memory of being held by Lord Henry into something more like boiling oil.

"And whyever didn't he?" she demanded

of the duke. "Kiss me, that is?"

The rogue had no reply, but the glint in his eye suggested that he would not have failed in such an endeavor.

"I wonder who she is?"

Jealous?

"Not in the least." Daphne's brow furrowed. "I suppose I should be thankful. He would have ruined everything."

If he hasn't already . . .

"You see," she continued, for apparently it was quite helpful to have an understanding, yet completely impotent, rogue to confide in, "he's got me questioning everything about — well, about someone else. Someone I thought would be the perfect choice."

But there was the rub. What if Dishforth wasn't like Lord Henry? Didn't leave her so unsettled, so filled with this restless passion that seemed to have a voice of its own, constantly demanding to be let out?

"Well, that wouldn't do," Daphne muttered. She couldn't discard her reputation, her virtue just to discover what might be possible with a rogue like Lord Henry Seldon.

You might be surprised how perfect it is to be kissed by a rogue. . . . To let your passions run away unfettered . . .

She glanced back up at the portrait, for

369

she could have sworn the old duke had just nudged her with such a scandalous thought.

Let him run away with you. . . .

"Oh, do be still," she scolded the duke. "You are only complicating matters."

For weren't things complicated enough? Any moment now, the door to the library would open and in would come Mr. Dishforth.

Dishforth no longer, she corrected. She'd know exactly who her sensible gentleman was.

And what if it is Fieldgate?

Daphne slanted a glance at the painting. "That is hardly helpful, and I doubt it is him."

No, she couldn't imagine Viscount Fielding ever using the world *sensible,* let alone knowing how to spell it.

Then what about that earl? The one with that awful shock of ginger hair? Oh, he's spilled a bit of his wild oats and gotten himself into a bit of financial trouble, but what young man hasn't? He could be a sensible sort, with the right woman.

Daphne nodded in agreement. Kipps was an earl. And he did have his heart in the right place trying to find a bride to save his family.

"Why would a money-strapped earl use

an advertisement to find a bride?" she posed, and when the seventh duke had no answer, she crossed the earl off her list. Yet again.

Astbury?

Daphne shook her head.

Bramston?

She laughed. The captain was quite dashing, but hardly the sort to sit down and compose such heartfelt missives.

Cowley?

Daphne bit her lower lip. He was rather the most likely choice. But oh, dear, whatever would she do if it was him?

Indeed. Can't imagine him giving you a good thorough tumble.

"That would hardly be a proper consideration for choosing a mate." Daphne stole a glance at the woman hanging in the portrait next to the duke. The seventh Duchess of Preston.

Little do you know, her satisfied expression seemed to say.

Daphne ignored her. Hadn't that particular Preston duchess been an opera dancer?

The duke continued to grin. *Rawcliffe? Could be him. All that scandal around his first wife's death has left him a bit of a pariah in Society. Certainly a passionate fellow when riled — they say he finished off Lady Raw-*

cliffe in a fit of rage by . . .

"That is hardly helpful," Daphne pointed out. "Now, however am I to get that image out of my head if it is indeed Lord Raw-cliffe who comes through that door?"

The duke hardly appeared penitent, loung-ing in his frame and smiling at her with that look of scandalous delight.

There's always my grandson, he offered. *Could be him.*

Daphne snorted. "I doubt he would know what a 'rational meeting of minds' entails. Lord Henry, my Dishforth? I'd rather eat my gloves."

Before or after he kissed you?

Preston led Henry down a passageway that wound behind the walls of Owle Park, hold-ing a single candle aloft to gauge where they were.

As if one could tell in such a narrow, dark space, Henry thought.

"I had forgotten these were here," Preston was saying, almost as if he was reminding himself, "until you started on about meet-ing this chit in the library. These tunnels run right alongside the wall where the seventh duke is hanging on the wall. Freddie and Felix used to take great delight in scar-ing the living daylights out of me from inside here. Had me utterly convinced the house was haunted until Dove showed me how to get in here. Then I had my revenge. Oh, how they howled." He chuckled at the memory.

Henry's gaze flew up to Preston's back. It was the first time he could ever remember the duke speaking of his long-lost brothers and sister.

Then again, it was miracle enough that Preston had reopened Owle Park, and now here he was happily reminiscing about the family he'd lost nearly overnight.

It was as Hen claimed; they owed a great debt for the healing touch Miss Timmons had brought to his life. Their lives as well, for Preston was now happily settling into his role as the duke and the head of the family.

Perhaps too much so.

"Henry, I still can't believe you answered one of those letters," Preston whispered, swiping his other arm in front of him to clear out the cobwebs.

"I'm rather at a loss to explain it myself," he admitted, hoping the spiders had long since fled. Henry really loathed spiders.

"I wager we find Miss Walding in the library," Preston said over his shoulder.

"Miss Walding?" Henry shook his head.

"Unlikely."

"Better than Miss Nashe." Preston shuddered. "Last time I leave the guest list up to Hen."

Henry didn't bother to point out that the next guest list Preston had to review would have been compiled by his bride. Nor did he have time to, for Preston stopped and turned, put a warning finger to his lips, then pointed at a small slat in the wall. Shielding the candle with his hand to hide the light, Preston nodded at Henry to slide it open.

Taking a deep breath, and steeling himself against a major disappointment, Henry stepped up to the hole that had been hidden there.

In that moment, the entire guest list ran through his thoughts.

Lady Alicia, Lady Clare, Miss Nashe, Miss Walding, the Tempest twins, Miss Hathaway . . . right there, Henry stopped himself.

For in his mind's eye, he imagined only one woman in the library.

No, not imagined. *Desired.* With a thunderous, loud rumble of desire that rushed through his veins like an avalanche.

Daphne Dale. With her willowy ways and impertinent manners. With her rosy, delectable lips, a mouth made for kissing, and a body that left a man with nothing but the most lascivious notions.

Why, that damned gown she was wearing tonight fit her like a glove and left him speechless. Yes, that was all he needed — a bride who would leave him in a perpetual state of dismay and desire.

No, his Miss Spooner was on the other side of this wall, and she would be a sensible, proper lady who would make an excellent partner with whom to live a perfectly prudent life.

That was what he wanted.

Until, that is, he peered through the opening.

And immediately reared back. "Good God, I'm ruined!" he gasped, albeit as quietly as he could.

He found himself with his back to the opposite wall, his chest pounding.

"I'm done for," he whispered, his frantic gaze fluttering up to meet Preston's.

Because he knew in his heart that this was exactly what he wanted. Wasn't it?

"Who is it?" Preston asked in the same hushed tone.

Henry couldn't say the name. Honestly, didn't know if he could even speak.

He merely nodded toward the opening. *Be my guest.*

Preston slanted a quizzical glance at him

and then took a look. He had much the same reaction and reeled back from the hole as if it were on fire. "We're all done for!"

The duke reached over and closed the slat. Then he pointed that they should beat a hasty retreat, handing Henry the candle so he could lead the way.

If only it was that easy.

"Better you found out now," the duke whispered. "At least you are braced for the meeting ahead."

Meeting?

"What the devil do you mean?" Henry asked.

"When you go in there," Preston nudged him forward.

"I'm not going in there." Was Preston mad? That room was no longer the library. It was the Coliseum, and he was about to be cast into the ring for lions to devour.

No, he wasn't going. Not willingly. Not unless Preston had a Roman legion to prod his every step.

He wasn't about to go in there and make a bloody fool of himself. She loved another, not him.

She was expecting her most excellent gentleman . . . not him.

Then the totality of all of it tumbled into place.

Oh, good God, she was expecting Dishforth. Her most excellent gentleman was . . . him.

Henry felt one of Hen's megrims coming on. Hen never suffered from the complaint, but she demmed well knew how to give them.

"You have to go in there and tell her," Preston whispered. No, more like commanded.

Henry took back his sentiment that Miss Timmons was to be commended for her reform of the duke.

A reformed duke was a pain in the ass.

Namely, his. Henry shook his head, as recalcitrant as a child.

Go in and face Miss Dale? Alone? In the library? With that grinning portrait of the seventh duke looking down at him in disappointment that he didn't have the lady's gown up over her hips and her crying out in delight?

No. He wasn't going to do that.

But Preston had another notion. "You owe the lady the truth. Honor demands it. Anything less would be cowardly."

Henry flinched. Damn Preston. Any moment now he was going to be dredging up the family code of honor, like Zillah would.

They'd gotten to the panel where they'd

377

entered the tunnel and Preston reached over him, feeling around the wall for the latch.

"You never know," he was saying. "Miss Dale might find the entire situation amusing."

Hope sprang up in Henry's chest. "You think so?"

Preston shook his head. "No. Not in the least."

CHAPTER 12

There is nothing I can say that will gain
your forgiveness for my unpardonable
lapse.

> Found in a letter never sent by
> Miss Spooner to Mr. Dishforth

Henry took a deep breath and pushed open
the door to the library, striding into the
middle of the room. Feigning a measure of
shock and surprise, he said, "Miss Dale!
Whatever are you doing here?"

"Lord Henry?" Her face was the epitome
of horror. "What are you doing here?" she
finally managed, after — he guessed —
she'd gone through a myriad of questions.

You're Dishforth?

No, it can't be true.

She glanced at the door, then her eyes narrowed. *How the devil am I going to get rid of
him?*

Henry watched her as she moved around

the settee in the middle of the room, strategically placing it between them.

A good plan, but it was hardly the gulf that Henry suspected they needed if they were to truly keep their distance.

"My lord! What are you doing here?" This time her question was a demand.

"What am I doing here?" He forced a puzzled expression onto his face. "Why, I came to get a book, why else?"

"A book?"

No woman had ever sounded so relieved in her life.

To make good his point, he strolled over to the bookshelf and pulled one down. After thumbing through it for a moment, he looked around the room and proceeded to settle into the large chair by the fireplace.

Mr. Muggins opened one eye, examined this new addition to the room, thumped his tail a few times in approval and went back to sleep.

Miss Dale did not share the hound's opinion. "What are you doing?"

"Thought I'd read a bit before I settle down for the night."

"Well, you can't!"

He glanced up from the page. "Pardon?"

"You mustn't," she told him.

"I mustn't what?"

"Read that book! Not here."

"It is a library, is it not?"

"Yes."

"And this is where one normally finds a book to read, is it not?"

"Yes."

"Yet I can't read it here?"

"No."

"Whyever not?"

"The light is poor." She glanced around, searching for more coin to add to her lie. "Wouldn't you be more comfortable in your own room?"

"No." He stuck out his legs and tucked his boots atop the ottoman. "I rather prefer to read in here. I find this room quite agreeable." Then he went back to the pages before him.

And while he wasn't reading, he was counting. *One, two, three, four, five . . .*

"You need to leave."

He glanced up. "Leave?"

"Yes," she said. "Immediately." She pointed toward the door.

Henry closed the book and tossed it atop a nearby table. "Miss Dale, I have the distinct impression you want to get rid of me. Whatever are you about?" He glanced at her from head to toe. "Are you waiting for a gentleman? Some late-hour assignation?"

Her mouth fell open, but she recovered quickly. "What a scandalous suggestion, my lord!"

But, he noted, she hadn't denied it. "Is it?"

"Yes! Don't you recall that I am nearly betrothed?"

"Oh, yes, that," he mused, waving his hand in dismissal.

"Yes. That." Her gaze flitted from him to the door and back again, as if she could will him out of his seat.

Henry settled in deeper. "Still, I suppose when one finds a lady alone in the library at this hour of the night — when she should be safely ensconced and chaperoned in the salon with the company of the other ladies all around her — one might assume that she is —"

"Oh, good heavens! Only a man of your inclinations would assume such a thing."

He ignored the slight she'd thrust into his midsection. "Then what *are* you doing here, Miss Dale?"

Her lips pursed together and her brow furrowed as she scrambled for an answer. "A book. Of course. That's why I came here."

Yes, of course. "And you came here alone?"

"I was on my way up to bed."

Bed. That word landed between them and caught them both in its snare, its implications.

"Alone?" He couldn't help himself. He followed the seventh duke's example and leered.

Just a bit.

"Of course," she huffed. "As I was trying to explain, I have a megrim." And then, remembering her malady, she pressed her hand to her brow. After a few moments of this dramatic repose, she opened one eye to see its effect.

He gave her his best imitation of Zillah's stare — the one that said all too clearly that the preceding statement was a steaming pile of horse manure.

"Well, it isn't a truly horrific one. Yet. Just the beginnings of one," she corrected, fingers going to press her forehead as if that could stem the rising pain. "After making my excuses to your sister and Lady Essex . . . in fact, it was Lady Essex's suggestion that I retire early —"

"Who am I to disagree with my sister and Lady Essex?"

"Who, indeed?"

"That doesn't explain how you ended up here, alone, in the library."

"As I said, I came here to find a book."

"To read?"

"Of course!"

"To help ease your megrim?"

Miss Dale stilled, like a doe cornered. Then she turned ever so slowly, her chin chucked up and her eyes full of determination.

He had to admire her daring. Her continued battle to maintain this charade.

"Not to read this evening, my lord," she replied.

"No, of course not." He shook his head, the master of concern and care.

Lying little minx.

"As you know, I like to arise early —"

Yes, he knew.

"And I thought that if I awoke refreshed, I might like to read before I came down for breakfast." She finished with a triumphant smile, her chin tipping upward, daring him to refute her story.

He had to admit she had bottom.

But was a terrible liar.

Henry glanced up at the seventh duke's portrait hanging over her shoulder.

What the devil are you waiting for?

Henry blinked. Had he just heard that?

"Pardon?"

"I didn't say anything," she told him before she glanced over her shoulder. Henry could have sworn she flinched as she looked at the notorious rake.

There was little doubt in Henry's mind what the duke would advise his namesake to do.

Get up. Take that bonny bit of muslin in your arms and declare yourself. It's that simple.

If only it was. For now that he was faced with telling her the truth, he realized he wanted Daphne Dale to choose him for being him — not the man who had written those ridiculous letters.

Dishforth, he would tell Miss Dale, is a right proper prig.

No, Henry wanted her to defy everything that was sensible and proper. Demmit, defy her family as he would his, and choose him. Lord Henry Seldon.

So he began with the first of the seventh duke's instructions. He got up.

Miss Dale regarded him warily, her fingers digging into the settee before her. "Are you leaving?"

She sounded rather hopeful.

"No," he told her, crossing the room toward her.

She backed up until she stood right beneath the previous Henry Seldon.

"I came for something," he told her as he stopped before her.

"Can I help you find it?" she offered, standing her ground. *So you'll be on your way.*

"Yes, I believe you can," he said, reaching out and hauling her into his arms. Rakish step number two accomplished. "Miss Dale, I have something to tell you."

Overhead, Henry thought it was the duke's turn to flinch.

Honesty? With a woman? Are you mad? Wait just a bloody moment, did you say Dale —

Henry blotted out any more notions of seeking his grandfather's advice.

He could do this on his own from here. Thank you very much.

"Lord Henry?"

He looked down at her. "Yes, Miss Dale?"

"Did you know you have a collection of cobwebs on the shoulder of your jacket?"

He glanced over. "I shall advise my valet to be more careful in future."

"Indeed, in fact —"

"Miss Dale, there is something I must tell you —"

"Now?" she glanced frantically at the door.

"Yes, now."

"I really don't think this is a good time."

"I disagree," he said. Then Lord Henry Arthur George Baldwin Seldon proved he was every inch the grandson of the seventh duke.

Daphne didn't even have a chance to protest.

Not that she would have.

When Lord Henry's lips met hers, she surrendered. To every bit of good sense, to any hope of a future that wasn't marked in ruin.

For here he was, his lips hard and demanding. She opened up to him, and his tongue danced and slid over hers, enticing her to come along on this passionate exploration.

How could she deny him?

Her shawl fell to the floor. Whether she'd shrugged it off or he'd brushed it aside, she didn't know, she didn't care, for his fingers were sliding along the edge of her bodice, over her collarbone, twining into her hair and, finding the pins there, plucking them free until her hair tumbled down.

As it cascaded down, he moaned — growled, really — a sound both greedy and delirious. It was filled with desire and passion entwined in a deep earthy need that vibrated through her limbs, as if he'd touched her with his longing.

She answered back, pressing herself against him, her breasts against his chest, her hips swaying, a feminine reply that said she'd heard his call.

And still he kissed her. Long, hard, demanding.

Devouring her.

He held her fast, up against him, and there was no doubt the entire man was in the same state as his kiss.

Long. Hard. Demanding.

A sigh, a moan rose up from her depths, her hips brushing his as she drew even closer, as a desire to be right up against him, to draw him inside her, shivered through her.

His hands roamed over her, cupping her breasts, his thumb rolling over her nipple. It tightened into a bud beneath the muslin of her gown, and then the fabric was teased from her shoulders, leaving her bare to his touch.

Daphne shivered, but where the cool air touched her skin, Lord Henry's lips followed.

She arched as his hot breath, his tongue washed over her shoulder, leaving a trail of desire in its wake. Then his head dipped lower, while his hand cupped her breast and brought it up for him to explore, to kiss, and then taking her nipple into his mouth, he sucked on it — leaving her gasping for air.

However could such a thing feel so good?

Oh, but it did, leaving her rising up on her tiptoes and clinging to his shoulders as he suckled one side and then the other, until even her breath was shuddering, coming in and out in ragged gasps.

He paused for a moment, and Daphne opened her eyes — when had she closed them? — and found him smiling at her.

Oh, what a smile. Full of dark, smoky passions. Full of possession. Like all Seldons, he had the coloring of a lion — that tawny hair, those dark eyes — and right now he looked every inch the great beast, hungry and ready to claim his stake.

Without asking, without a word, he swept her up into his arms and carried her across the room, kissing her as he went. When they came to the wide, deep gold brocade settee that sat in one of the shadowed corners, he laid her down and followed quickly, covering her with his body.

Daphne reached for him, her arms winding around his neck, her lips seeking his, her fingers twining in his hair, holding him, so she could find her way right back to that delicious, trembling state.

His body rocked against hers, as if seeking solace, seeking entry.

Between her legs, her body was tight and trembling, coiled with longing, and every time he slid against her, her insides quaked.

Yes. Yes. Please!

And so when she felt his hand draw her skirt up, a momentary shiver of panic ran through her.

Whatever was he going to do?

His fingers brushed over her small clothes, then slipped inside, brushing over the curls at her apex, then teasing past the folds and finding the taut nub beneath.

Daphne arched against his hand, her mouth opening in a wide O even as his fingers stroked her, beguiled her, sliding deeper, and then he slid a finger inside her — right into her, filling her, stretching her, drawing the wetness from her and sliding it back over her.

Back and forth he moved inside her, out, even as he kissed her, his tongue sliding over hers, sucking her into him, breathing her out. Her bare nipples rubbed against his shirt.

When the devil had he taken off his jacket? His waistcoat? She couldn't remember.

She didn't care. For the linen of his shirt brushed over the sensitive points, only adding to the building fires inside her. It was all building so quickly, his touch — insistent and teasing, drawing her upward. His kiss, demanding and insistent.

Come with me, love. Come with me, his body cried out to hers. *Come see what we can find up here.*

She rose with his touch, with his kiss. Let him lead her upwards, where there was no air, no light, just his touch and her need.

Her hips were moving on their own, urging him to touch her faster. Deeper. Harder.

The darkness burst into light, her mouth opened to cry out, but no words came out. Shattering waves rushed through her, tossing her, crashing over her, until she had gone as high as she could.

And when she began to fall, fluttering in the wind like a feather on the colliding currents, there was Lord Henry, holding her, whispering to her, teasing her still so the waves of pleasure continued until she was spent.

That was also when she heard the footsteps in the hall. The sharp trod of boots sending a warning refrain through her muddled senses.

She blinked once, then twice, and looked

up at Lord Henry.

He grinned at her with a lion's share of pride at what he'd done. What he'd drawn from her.

But her passion was replaced with panic. Dishforth!

Oh, what had she done? What had Lord Henry done to her?

Pleased you immensely, I imagine.

Good heavens, would she ever be able to get the seventh duke out of her head? Oh, yes, it had been a pleasure.

But it was also ruinous. She had pleaded with Dishforth to come, and this was how she repaid his loyalty? By letting him find her entwined with another man?

Putting her hands to Lord Henry's wall of a chest, she shoved with all her might and toppled him off the settee.

He landed on the carpet with a thump and a curse. "What the devil —"

"Oh, do be quiet," she whispered. "He's coming —"

"No, he's not," Lord Henry complained, rubbing his backside. "Whoever it is, they've gone."

"Gone?" Daphne glanced briefly over her shoulder at him and then did a quick shake of her gown, righting the hem in place and tugging up her sleeves. "No, that cannot be.

Oh, what have I done?"

"Daphne, wait," he said. No more Miss Dale. She was Daphne. As if she was his.

But she couldn't be his. Not now. Not ever.

"I cannot. Oh, however did I let this happen?" she moaned, and then fled.

Out the door and away from the pleasures and utter ruin that was Lord Henry Seldon.

But it was too late. For even as her slippers padded up the stairs, she knew.

It was far too late for Dishforth. Or any other man.

Now that she was ruined.

Lord Henry went to follow Daphne out of the library, but he found his path blocked by his nephew.

"Looks like she took the news hard," Preston said, glancing up the stairs where Miss Dale had disappeared. "So much so that all her hairpins fell out."

"Um, yes," Henry managed.

"What went on in there?" The duke looked over Henry's shoulder into the shadows of the library. "She didn't break anything, did she? Like Hen did when that scoundrel Boland threw her over?"

Henry shook his head. Though he had rather feared she'd take up the pike on the wall. All that Kempton nonsense coming back to haunt him.

No, that cannot be. Oh, what have I done? Her words full of anguish, her expression rife with a rising anger. Once she got done blaming herself, then she'd aim her fury at him.

Rightly so.

"Then what did she say?" Preston asked again.

"Um, well," Henry began, shuffling his feet and wishing himself in a thousand different places.

Like in the lady's bedchamber finishing what they had started.

"You did tell her, didn't you, Henry?"

"Tell her? Oh, that."

"Yes, *that.* Did you tell her or not?"

Henry shook his head.

Preston caught him by the arm and towed him back into the library, closing the door behind them. "Whyever not?"

Henry cursed Preston's newfound respectability. "I . . . that is to say . . . it's rather complicated . . ."

Preston, pacing before the aforementioned pike, came to an abrupt halt. "You can't continue this! You have to tell her who you are."

Henry shook his head. "I can't!"

"Why not?"

"She despises me now," Henry told Preston. "She'll hate me more so when I tell her the truth."

And that was putting it mildly. Especially now . . .

Preston's brows furrowed into a line of confusion. "Why do you care what she thinks of you?"

The confession came out before Henry could stop the words. "Because I love her."

There was a moment when Preston just stood there — most likely weighing whether or not he'd heard Henry correctly — but then the words registered and the duke sank into the large leather chair.

It creaked and protested.

"No, Henry," he said, shaking his head. "Not her."

"Yes, her."

"She's a Dale." It was a statement that in any other circumstances would have been self-evident.

"I couldn't help myself."

"One says that over too much wine. Or betting on a nag that any man can see is going to run dead last. But not with one of them."

A Dale.

Henry raked his hand through his hair.

"You like her," he pointed out.

"Liking her and pulling all the pins out of her hair is an entirely different matter."

"She's so demmed gorgeous." As if that explained the circumstances. Nor could it be resolved by telling Preston that he'd done all that because Daphne Dale was aggravating and opinionated and tempting and delightful.

All at once. No, he'd stick with "gorgeous."

"Of course she is," Preston was arguing. "All Dale women are, and that's the rub. Gorgeous, tempting pieces. Then once you find yourself leg-shackled to one of them, you'll end up like Cornelius Seldon," Preston said. "You do recall the story of Cornelius Seldon, don't you?"

"Yes," Henry ground out. Zillah used to tell them of Mad Corny's final trip to Bedlam as a bedtime cautionary tale.

It had given Henry nightmares for years. Until . . .

"And what about Lord Kendrick Seldon? Do you recall how he ended his days once he'd crossed the line?"

Henry's gaze wandered up to the pike. Kendrick had been the source of his remaining childhood nightmares.

Preston wasn't done. "I can't believe

you've fallen in love with her. What were you thinking?"

Apparently the ruinous interlude in the library was excusable, but falling in love with her, well, that was another matter altogether.

"When and how did this happen?" the duke continued. He glanced around the library. "And I assume this began before tonight?"

Henry nodded. Since it seemed a night for disclosures, he told Preston nearly everything.

About his mistake at the engagement ball. The encounter in the folly.

Meanwhile the duke had gotten to his feet and was once again pacing. "If Hen finds out —"

"Oh, good God, no," Henry added, coming to his senses.

"Now you see that? After you've gone and —"

"Demmit, Preston!" Henry said, getting to his feet as well. "It isn't like I set out to ruin her."

It was bad enough she was ruined, but she'd left him aching for more. Left him gobsmacked with the white-hot truth: he'd never stop wanting her.

"You cannot pretend this did not happen,"

the duke told him. "There are consequences to these things. There always are." If anyone would know that, it was Preston. "The Dales will be out for blood."

"However do you think they will find out?" Henry shot back.

"Someone always finds out," Preston said, again with the surety of a practiced rake.

"It isn't as if she is going to tell her family this." No more than Henry had any intention of telling Hen.

Preston groaned, hand to his forehead. "Of course she won't say anything directly. But someone will hear of this. Mark my words."

"Not from Miss Dale. She's in love with someone else." Henry paused. "She's convinced he's the only man for her."

The duke turned and studied his nephew. "In love with whom?"

"Dishforth," Henry said. "She is in love with Dishforth."

"Dishforth?" Preston's eyes widened as he tried not to laugh. "That is a tangle."

"Do not remind me. I loathe the fellow."

"You are the fellow."

"Yes, and I'm a wretched bastard in both cases," Henry admitted.

Preston did laugh this time. "When you tell her that Dishforth is naught but a figment of your imagination, she'll probably be inclined to share your loathing — so you'll have something in common."

"This is hardly funny," Henry told him, finding nothing amusing in any of it.

"I never said it was. But you must admit" — Preston shook a little, then composed himself enough to finish — "she's in love with another man who happens to be you."

"Oh, good God, you are not helping."

"I suppose I'm not," Preston said. "But when you do tell her, I might suggest telling her in a letter. Especially if she takes after Kendrick's Dale bride."

Henry groaned. "She'll hunt me down. Determined minx."

Preston went over to the sideboard and filled two glasses with brandy. He handed one to Henry.

Henry raised his glass in a mock toast. "Demmed Dishforth. Bloody, rotten fellow."

"He's supposed to get us out of fixes, not make our lives a tangled mess," Preston mused.

Henry glanced over at him. "What did you say?"

"Dishforth. He's ever so unreliable, and such a horribly unfeeling creature," he said, using the line Hen had once given their nanny about one of Dishforth's alleged crimes. It had become one of those oft-repeated sayings between the three of them.

What a horribly unfeeling creature Mr. Dishforth can be. Ever so unreliable.

"That's it!" Henry said. Raising his glass, he added, "To Dishforth, may he prove himself such a horribly unfeeling creature that she'll have nothing to do with him."

Daphne hurried up the stairs and down the first hall she came to, only to discover she was on the wrong floor, and in the wrong wing.

Glancing around, she realized she was standing in front of the music room, and from inside came a crash of the keys.

She whirled around and found Lady Zillah making a beeline for her. The lady seemed to have lost most of her infirmities; fiery determination marked her every step.

"You there!" the lady said, shaking a bony finger at her.

There was no hope of fleeing now.

Lady Zillah came to a stop before her and took in her disheveled appearance with a quick glance and a very loud snort. "Bah! Get in here, Miss Dale. I will have a word with you."

Daphne found herself rooted in place, for

inside the music room was a large fireplace, and even though it was August, there was a good blaze roaring away.

"Don't keep me waiting!" Lady Zillah chided as she turned back toward the piano. "Any niece of Damaris Dale would have better manners than that."

She would if she wasn't so uncertain whether or not the crone before her wasn't about to pop her in the fireplace.

But Daphne was also Damaris's niece, so with her head held high, albeit missing hairpins, she strode into the music room as if this was to be merely a friendly chat.

Lady Zillah sat with her back ramrod straight, and she took another look at Daphne before she began with the honesty for which she was famous.

"If you think that rapscallion nephew of mine will marry you even now after he's obviously tumbled you —"

"My lady!" Daphne burst out.

"Was it him, or wasn't it?" Lady Zillah demanded. When Daphne refused to answer, Lady Zillah took her silence as confirmation.

The interview went rather downhill from there, and ended with Lady Zillah stalking out of the music room in high dudgeons.

But that wasn't the worst of it.

CHAPTER 13

Come with me, Miss Spooner. Run away and be my bride. I shall await your answer at the inn in the village. My coach and my heart await you.

Found in a letter from
Mr. Dishforth to Miss Spooner

Early the next morning, with Dishforth's latest note tucked into her pocket, Daphne stole down the stairs. The entire house was quiet, save for Mr. Muggins, who continued to dog her every step.

Literally.

She turned to the Irish terrier and scratched his head. "Sit here, Mr. Muggins. And wait for Tabitha."

And then she closed the front door behind her and went down the drive, taking a deep breath and committing herself to the plan before her.

The one outlined in Dishforth's note, the

one she'd found waiting for her, having been slipped under her door during the night. So he had discovered her identity after all.

Yet it was his words that took her breath away.

He loved her still, despite their missed chances, and hoped she'd understand.

Daphne had read those lines twice. Perhaps three times. He loved her. Still.

And as she read the rest of his letter, she knew exactly what she had to do.

Yet with each step she took down the long, winding drive, she wondered if this was the wisest course.

Whatever would her family say?

Daphne took only one glance over her shoulder back at Owle Park and then vowed not to look again.

Whatever her doubts about Dishforth, she had no such qualms or doubts now of his intentions toward her. He wanted to marry her.

She got to the gate and shifted her traveling valise from one hand to another as she crossed under the imposing stone arch, with its colonnaded towers on either side.

"Giving up?"

Daphne paused, for she knew that voice as well as she knew the owner's kiss.

Lord Henry.

There was a crunch of gravel behind her, and she turned to find the rogue pushing off the base of the column, where he'd apparently been lounging about.

Morning had barely arrived, yet here he was, with his coat flung open, no cravat, his shirt open in a V at the neck and his waistcoat undone. Dusty breeches and scuffed boots showed the wear of a cross-country trek, while his usually properly combed mane of hair was tied back in merely a simple queue.

She'd never seen him so undone. So entirely at ease. So perfectly handsome.

Had he been up all night? she wondered. Not that she had much time to consider it as he came forward much as he had last night — a lion stalking through his territory, eyeing her as one might easy prey — until he stood before her, blocking her escape. "I asked if you were giving up. Going home, perhaps?"

Daphne tried to get an answer out, but all that she could manage was a stammering "Yes . . . no . . . eventually." And then she shifted her valise again and went around him.

Persistent rake that he was, he followed and kept up with her easily. "If that is the case, I could call for a carriage."

She shook her head. "No thank you, my lord." If she thought that was enough to deter the man, Lord Henry continued to match her pace.

For a while they walked in silence, Daphne continuing determinedly along, Lord Henry doggedly following her.

He rather reminded her of Mr. Muggins.

Finally, tired of this ruse, she couldn't take it anymore. "Whatever are you doing, loitering after me? Haven't you something more important to attend to?"

He shook his head. "No, not in the least. Found myself awake early this morning. Couldn't sleep, so I decided to come down here and watch the sun rise."

Daphne glanced over her shoulder. "And so it has, so now shouldn't you be seeing to your breakfast?"

He grinned at her. "Actually, it didn't show its bright face until you arrived."

"Pish!" she replied. "Really, Lord Henry? Comparing my arrival to the sun?" She shuddered and shifted her valise again, but she found it removed from her grasp and the gentleman carrying it for her. He didn't say a word, but the stubborn set of his jaw precluded any opposition to his assistance.

"It is a long way to London," he noted,

nodding up the empty road before them. "I can still call for a carriage."

"I'm only going to the village."

"There is no mail coach through the village."

"I have a ride."

"You do?"

She nodded.

"Who?"

Daphne huffed an impatient breath. If that was the way he wanted to do this . . . "None of your business."

"Miss Dale, are you eloping?"

This time she merely shook her head, as she did when Pansy brought her the wrong gown. And she kept walking.

With the wretched lout stalking along beside her.

"Let me see, sneaking off from a house party at an early hour," he mused. "No need for a coach, mail or otherwise. And a small valise" — he gave it a heft, as if weighing it — "with the necessities for a three-day journey. *Hmmm,* then I can only assume you are indeed eloping."

"Oh, bother. Yes. I am."

"Hardly proper," he told her.

"But necessary," she shot back.

"Necessary?"

"As if you have to ask," she said. She

leaned over to retrieve her valise, but he held it out of her reach. Thwarted, but refusing to give up, Daphne continued on.

Lord Henry followed. "Why is this elopement suddenly so necessary?"

She came to a grinding halt, hands fisting to her hips. "Since you ask, any moment now Cousin Crispin and an entire host of Dales will arrive here demanding my removal, and I will be whisked away in shame."

"Shame?"

"Utter ruin," she corrected. "Then there will be a family conclave and I will be married off to the first Dale they can find to take me in my tarnished state."

"Tarnished?" He looked her up and down as if searching for a blemish.

She gave him a withering glance.

To which he smiled. "Never tarnished, Miss Dale. Not to me. To me, you shine brightly."

"Harrumph!" And this time she managed to regain the possession of her valise, marching onward toward a fate of her own making. Though she knew the necessity of making a good show of it.

"Go away!" she told him, like one might a stray dog.

"No."

"No?"

"No," he repeated. "As a gentleman —"

"A gentleman! Bah!"

"A man of honor?"

"Piffle!"

He came around in front of her, once again blocking her escape. "What about a fellow in good standing —"

"Please, Lord Henry," she begged, pointing down the road in the direction from which they'd come, "go back to Owle Park, where you belong. To your life. Leave me to mine. Please."

"No," he repeated stubbornly. "Not until I know you're safe." He paused for a moment, and when she glared at him, he continued, "I wouldn't be able to live with myself if something untoward happened to you. And there it is. You might not think me a gentleman or a man of honor, but I won't let anything or anyone harm you."

She nodded in acquiescence.

They continued walking on, and as they entered the village, Daphne spoke up again. "Aren't you needed elsewhere?"

Henry considered her question for a moment and then shook his head. "No. Not that I can think of."

One of the shopkeepers who was opening his business for the day doffed his hat to them, and Henry nodded politely back. "I'd rather spend these last few minutes with you. That, and I would be remiss if I didn't stay and ensure this gentleman's intentions toward you are honorable."

Daphne stumbled and stopped. *"You* are going to discern *that?"*

"You needn't sound so incredulous," he replied as he kept walking. "It takes a rake to know one," he called back over his shoulder. "I'd be doing you a favor. I owe you that much, Miss Dale."

Daphne hurried to catch up. "I would prefer you leave well enough alone."

He slanted a glance at her. "I suppose you are going to insist."

"I am."

He sighed again. "But I could ensure —"

"Not one word, Lord Henry!"

"Oh, good heavens, Miss Dale, you are a trying creature. But if I must remain silent —"

"You must," she insisted. "You will not say a word to the gentleman who is awaiting me at the inn."

He crossed his arms over his chest. "If that is your heart's desire, Miss Dale, I will promise with all my heart not to say a word to the gentleman waiting for you."

"Swear?" she pressed.

"Upon my honor," he told her.

Satisfied, she continued on, her eyes fixed on the inn at the end of the row of shops and houses.

Out in front sat a shabby-looking carriage.

"How odd," Lord Henry remarked.

"Odd?"

"I thought this most excellent gentleman of yours would have some elegant barouche to carry you off in style and comfort."

Tucking her chin up, she told him, "Thankfully, he is not the sort to be overly extravagant — he disdains such showy pretensions. Some might call him thrifty and sensible. Qualities I quite admire."

As they got closer to the carriage, it was obvious it was a tumbledown affair.

Lord Henry let out a low whistle. "As long as he doesn't do the same thing to your dress accounts."

She shot him a furious glance.

"I must ask," Lord Henry continued, "however did you fall in love with this man? Because a lady would have to be in love to dare a journey in that rattletrap."

"I did, and I will, because he has been nothing but honest and forthright with me." Was it Daphne's imagination, or did Lord Henry flinch?

When she started for the inn's door, he

called after her, "Well, good, you've gotten that off your chest."

Against her better judgment, Daphne stopped. "Excuse me?"

"That bit of pique. It brightened you up a bit. I fear you were starting to look a bit pale. A man likes his bride with a starry-eyed gaze and a bit of a blush to her."

She glanced over at him, feeling a lot of her color rushing into her cheeks. "I've already taken up too much of your time. Good-bye, Lord Henry." She stopped short of adding, *Good riddance.*

Lord Henry ignored her, went over to the door and pushed it open. "Miss Dale, wild horses couldn't drag me away from witnessing your happy union."

From over Daphne's shoulder, Henry winked at the innkeeper. *This is the one I told you about.*

The man barely nodded, giving Henry a nearly imperceptible answer. *Gotcha, gov'ner.*

Even the lad on the stool by the fire knew his role, for he said not a thing.

Henry had been most honest with Miss Dale when he'd said he'd gotten up early and gone for a walk. He had. To this very inn to set up the tableau which was about

411

to play out.

It was all he could do not to grin.

For in the next few minutes, Daphne would find out that Dishforth had departed, and he, Henry, would be right there to soothe her broken heart. The perfect time to make his case and show her exactly why he was the only gentleman for her.

And such a plan might have worked if he had tried it on someone a little less determined, a far sight more malleable than Daphne Dale.

Certainly there should be a furrowed look of concern on her face — for here was the common room, empty, with no sign of Dishforth. Shouldn't she appear, at the very least, a bit crestfallen?

Not Miss Dale.

She marched up to the serving board and nodded politely to the innkeeper. "Sir, I am to meet a gentleman here. Where might he be?"

The innkeeper bore a patient expression. Truly, in Henry's estimation he was on par with Keen in his acting ability. "A gentleman, you say?"

"Yes, he said he would be waiting here for me," she explained. "His coach and four are outside. Will you please summon him and let him know that Miss Dale is here."

The man's gaze narrowed. "A coach and four?"

"Yes, the one outside."

Shaking his head, the innkeeper said, "The coach outside belongs to the inn. We let it out. Do you need a coach, miss?"

"No, I don't need a coach," she said. "The gentleman I was to meet was bringing his. Might he be summoned, please?"

Lord Henry leaned against the wall, arms crossed, and watched her with nothing less than awe. What a determined slip of muslin she was.

The innkeeper shook his head. "Miss, there is no one else about. Just you and his lordship." He nodded toward Henry, who did his best to look mildly concerned — at least for her sake. Besides, everything was working perfectly. All the innkeeper had to do was explain —

She frowned at Lord Henry and leaned closer to the innkeeper so her query wasn't so public.

Not that it wasn't easy to hear.

"I am looking for a gentleman." She leaned closer still. "Mr. Dishforth."

"Mr. Dishforth?" He scratched his chin.

"Yes, a gentleman of some respectability. He was to meet me here."

"Oh, that gentleman," the innkeeper said,

snapping his fingers. "I fear, miss, he left."

"Left?"

"Yes, he already left. In a hurry, you might say."

Miss Dale stepped back from the board. "But whyever would he have left?"

"I can't say, miss. He was here and then he was gone." The innkeeper shrugged, then picked up a tankard and began polishing it with a cloth.

Truly, Lord Henry felt guilty about this deception, but it was better this way. Certainly it had to be.

"He left?" she asked, then shook her head. "He can't have left. He wouldn't have left. You are mistaken."

Of course she wasn't going to believe that her loyal Dishforth would abandon her, so Lord Henry had taken the precaution of adding another player to this scene.

"Oh, aye, miss," the lad by the fire piped up. "The grand gentleman left, oh, say, an hour ago. Mayhap two it was."

"No, he wouldn't have," she told the boy, tears brimming up in her eyes. "He wouldn't have left. Not without me."

My dearest, beloved Miss Spooner. When we meet at the inn, we shall never be parted ever again.

414

And it was that very promise broken that left her wide blue eyes all undone with grief. Those tears also managed to unravel everything Henry had devised.

Because the lad by the fire was as stricken by them as if he had been the one abandoned. And so he improvised, if only to stop her crying — or so he later claimed, for he supposed his efforts would help the cause.

"He didn't leave alone," he told her. "He left with a woman. A right fancy one. He wasn't the right one for you, miss. Not in the least."

The room stilled. Completely and utterly. As if there wasn't even a whiff of air in it. Not even the fire made a crackle. For there, in the middle of all this silence, was this grand bouncer, this unthinkable addition to Henry's carefully wrought plans.

A grand herring of a fish tale that had one and all gaping — each for their own reasons.

And of course, it was Daphne who recovered first. "He left with a lady?"

"Yes," the lad told her. "Oh, a beautiful, fancy lady." He glanced over at Henry, as if expecting a nod of encouragement. And, not even waiting for that, he barreled on. "The lady, she wept when she arrived and found him here. Then the gentleman, a more handsome fellow you can't imagine,

415

he called her his 'perfect love' and begged for her hand in marriage. When she said 'yes,' he kissed her. Right here." The boy pointed at his cheek. "Then she wept some more, and finally he summoned his driver and they left." And if that wasn't enough, he hastily added, "Oh, it was a grand sight to witness. The lady and gentleman so handsome and riding away in such a grand carriage. One fit for a king."

Henry sank onto the nearest bench. For what could he do? Confess right now as she gaped dumbfounded at the lad and looked ready to faint? Tell her he'd lied and deceived her, if only to gain her hand?

But Henry soon found out that he didn't know Daphne Dale all that well.

She whirled to the innkeeper. "That carriage, the one outside —"

"Yes, miss —"

"It's for hire, isn't it?"

"Yes, miss, but —"

"Then I would like to hire it."

"You, miss?" He glanced up at Henry as if he didn't know what to do first. Other than toss his romantically inclined stable lad down the nearest well.

Henry straightened, a terrible suspicion knotting in his gut. *No. She wouldn't.*

"Yes, I would like to hire it," Daphne told

the man, drawing out her reticule and pulling out the necessary coins. "I'll need the fastest set you have so I can overtake Mr. Dishforth."

Oh, yes, she would.

"You want to overtake him, miss?"

"But of course," she replied.

Henry got to his feet. "Miss Dale, you cannot think to go after him —"

"But I must. There has been a terrible mistake, and I must save him."

"Save him?" Henry and the innkeeper said at the same time, like a disbelieving chorus.

Henry's Shakespearean comedy had taken a horribly tragic Greek turnabout.

Miss Dale gave them both a look of utter indignation. "But of course. Who else can save him but me? Someone must tell poor, simple, misled Mr. Dishforth that he has eloped with the wrong bride."

Chapter 14

Miss Spooner, I have never been in love before. You'll excuse me if — at some point — I make a terrible muddle of all of this, won't you?

> Found in a letter from
> Mr. Dishforth to Miss Spooner

Owle Park
Eight hours later

"I'm coming with you."

Preston found Hen, valise in hand and jaw set, blocking his path to the front door. He looked over her shoulder to where his traveling coach waited in the drive beyond and frowned.

Hen's expression was just as grim and determined. "He is my brother and I will see his reputation put to rights."

"His reputation?" Preston shook his head. He didn't have time for this.

Suddenly Zillah came marching up and

took a stand beside Hen. "Well, of course, Henry's reputation! He's obviously been lured. Perhaps even drugged." The old girl glanced up at Hen. "I've never believed that nonsense that Cornelius Seldon went willingly with that mad-as-a-hatter Doria Dale."

Tabitha looked ready to leap into this squabble, if only to defend her bosom bow, but Preston cut her off. They would all need each other in the coming days and weeks, and this sniping didn't serve anyone.

"You two," he said, wagging a finger at Hen and Zillah, "need to reconcile yourselves to the fact that Henry is in love with Miss Dale —"

When they both looked ready to erupt in a bevy of protests, he summoned his most ducal glare.

Which, to his shock, actually worked. At least for now.

"Be advised that the only course for Henry and Miss Dale is to see them married. To each other," he finished, making sure to close any loopholes.

"Married?!" This might have been a duet of protest, but a third voice had chimed in.

For there on the front steps had suddenly appeared none other than Crispin, Viscount Dale. "Married?" he repeated. "Over my dead body."

"That can easily be arranged," Zillah muttered.

Out from behind Tabitha came Mr. Muggins, who, spying his former adversary, let out a warning growl.

"Now what is all this?" Crispin demanded. "Where is my cousin?"

"Gone!" Hen told him. "She lured my dear brother to his ruin."

"Lured? Daphne?" Lord Dale sputtered with indignation. "More like she was kidnapped!"

"Kidnapped!" came yet another protest from behind Crispin. "Where is my dearest niece?"

This was probably the first time Damaris Dale had ever uttered that phrase in reference to Daphne, but it wasn't something the Seldons would know.

The tall, willowy figure of a matron came up the steps and took her place at Crispin's side. In her wake hurried a slight young woman in the plain hand-me-down gown of a companion. She maintained a respectful distance a few steps down.

"I said, where is my niece?" the older woman repeated.

All three Seldons stilled, chilled to their marrow.

"Damaris!" Zillah hissed.

420

The Dale matriarch flicked a glance in her direction, then sniffed. Loudly. "Zillah. I didn't think you were still alive."

The pair eyed each other like old sparring partners, until Damaris's gaze wavered over toward Mr. Muggins.

"Still breeding mongrels, are we?" She sniffed at the overgrown terrier. Then, having had enough of the Seldons, Damaris turned her attention to the viscount. "Where is our Daphne?"

"Gone," he bit out. "Stolen by Lord Henry."

"The ruinous, evil fiend!" she announced before she turned to her companion. "Summon Bow Street. Send word to Derby Dale in the Home Office that we have need of him. I'll have Lord Henry Seldon dragged and tried through the courts until he's —"

"Aunt Damaris, this is not helping," Crispin told her.

And wonders upon wonders, she stopped and bowed her head slightly in deference, though she hardly looked pleased at being interrupted.

Then Harriet Hathaway, who up until now had been watching the drama play out from the grand staircase, waded into the fray. "Daphne hasn't run away with Lord Henry but with Mr. Dishforth."

"Dishforth?" they all said in a loud chorus.

Especially Hen, whose eyes went wide at the mention of the man's name.

The duke cringed. Oh, demmit, this was going to be the devil's own puzzle to explain.

Not that he had an explanation to give. He was of the same mind as Damaris Dale and inclined to send Bow Street after Henry. Or some sturdy hands from Bedlam.

"How the devil —"

"Who the devil —"

"When I catch this rogue!"

Everyone set up a clamor demanding answers, save Preston and Hen. And Tabitha noticed. "What do the two of you know of this Mr. Dishforth?"

Hen and Preston shared a guilty look.

"Preston!" Tabitha said in a tone that would stand her good stead once she was his duchess. "Who is this Dishforth?"

"There is no Dishforth," Preston admitted, while Hen threw her hands up in the air and began pacing in tight circles as if she was trying to unravel all of this.

"But there must be," Harriet insisted. "Daphne has been corresponding with him. Mr. Dishforth placed an advertisement in the paper seeking a wife. And Daphne answered it. They have been exchanging letters ever since. Here is one of the letters he wrote just recently."

Hen rushed forward and took the paper from Harriet. After a quick glance, the color rushed from her face. "Oh, no! This cannot be. Not Dishforth! The demmed rogue."

"Why, he seemed quite respectable when I met him," Damaris's bespectacled companion piped up.

When all eyes turned on the girl, she blushed deeply, already regretting her hasty words. "I warned Daphne this would all turn out bad," she said in her own defense. "Tried to convince her —"

"We will discuss this later, Philomena," Damaris told her.

Hen, meanwhile, had turned back to Preston and was shaking the note under his nose. "You know what this is, what this means."

"What does it mean?" Tabitha asked, her solemn question lending a moment of calm to the rising panic in Hen's voice.

"It's Henry's handwriting," Preston told her, told all of them.

"Oh, I knew it all along!" Harriet declared. "Lord Henry is Mr. Dishforth. How perfect!"

Though as it turned out, no else seemed to be sharing her joy.

423

Especially not Damaris Dale. She rounded on Preston. "Now, Your Grace, explain all this. Immediately." Her cane came down with a sharp rap.

Preston didn't have time, for Hen, having added it all up, now turned on him, fury in her eyes. "That abominable advertisement of yours! This is all your doing," she blasted, wagging an accusing finger at the duke. "You *and* Roxley." She cast a disparaging glance at the earl, who was lounging on the stairs.

Roxley shrugged, as if he hadn't the slightest notion of what she was saying. But he also did so as he took two steps back up the stairs, distancing himself from this growing scandal.

And then Preston explained all he knew — about the ad, about Henry's part in all of it — with Tabitha, Harriet and Philomena filling in Daphne's portion.

"I should have known *you* had a hand in this disgrace." Lady Damaris wagged an aggrieved finger at Preston, sparing Roxley just a shuddering glance for his part. "Now tell me once and for all, where has your uncle taken my niece?"

"Gretna Green, I imagine," Preston told her.

Damaris's eyes widened, then narrowed

into two tight slits. "I should have known. This is all my fault for turning a blind eye to Daphne's stubborn determination to keep such company." This was followed with a scathing glance at Tabitha.

"Never fear, Aunt Damaris," Crispin told her, taking her hand. "I shall get our Daphne back." Then he turned to Preston. "And woe be it to Lord Henry when I get my hands on him."

"Is that necessary?" Preston demanded. "After all, we have every reason to believe they are in love."

Honestly, he had no idea if that was true or not, but it was a far sight better than unleashing another civil war between their families.

Besides, the Seldons were sadly outnumbered.

"Love! *Harrumph!*" Damaris wagged a bony finger at them. "Be well reminded of what happened to Kendrick Seldon when he lured Miss Delicia Dale into an ill-advised elopement."

With that said, the old girl turned and stormed over to her carriage, Crispin and Philomena in her wake.

Roxley had come down the steps to stand beside Preston, most likely to gain a better vantage point. He leaned over and asked,

"Whatever happened to this Kendrick fellow?"

Preston told him, though not loud enough for anyone else to hear.

But the meaning of his words were clear as Roxley blanched, then flinched, his hand going to cover the upper part of his breeches, as if to ward off such a fate.

The Hornbill & Cross, Manchester Road
Twenty-four hours later

"And that's the whole story," the posting lad told the overflowing room at the inn in Bradnop. He had arrived from Swinescote with the tale, having heard it from the lad who rode between Swinescote and Mackworth. "There isn't a soul up and down the road who hasn't heard of them. The runaway lovers. They say the lady is ever-so-pretty. She has eyes like June bells."

There were sighs from some of the ladies, guffaws from the old duffers with their half-filled tankards.

"I don't get them toffs," a gruff old drover said from his stool near the fire. "Why doesn't he just tell 'er there is no other fellow? That this Dishworth —"

"Dishforth," the lad corrected.

"Eh, Dishworth, Dishforth, what does it matter if the plain truth is he don't exist?"

426

"Oh, but Sulley, he does," the serving girl told him. "Didn't you listen to Timmy's tale? Dishforth is this Lord Henry, and he must love his lady ever so much to go to such lengths to win her heart."

Spitting into the fire, Sulley shook his head. "Well, this lady is going to find out the truth soon enough, that she's been right deceived, and see if she doesn't toss this fellow into the nearest ditch."

There were nods about the room, including a solemn one from the innkeeper's wife, who swung her ample hips easily through the crowded room as she refilled pitchers. "Right you are, Sulley," she agreed as she topped off his cup.

Sulley grinned at the crowd and raised his tankard in triumph. Such a sight was a rare thing to see, considering Sulley had always been one of the most cantankerous coachmen on Manchester Road.

"Don't you be taking on airs, John Sulley," she scolded. "It is as fine a tale as I ever heard. And deservin' of our help."

"Help?" he sputtered, sending froth all over the front of his coat.

"Yes, help," she said, casting a firm glare about the room. "We are going to help this gentleman win his lady love."

"How can we do that, Mrs. Graham?" the

lad asked, sitting up straight on his stool, eyes alight with the promise of mischief.

"By getting Mr. Dishforth to Gretna Green."

"I think you've been drinking a bit too much of your own brew, missus," Sulley told her. "There is no Mr. Dishforth."

"There is now," she said. And then she explained exactly what needed to be done.

Simple. Miss Dale thought Dishforth a simpleton.

Lord Henry crossed his arms over his chest and leaned back in the seat of the hired carriage, glaring at the countryside whirling past.

To make matters worse, he had the sneaking suspicion she was utterly correct.

Dishforth was a simpleton. Which meant in actuality that he — as in Lord Henry Seldon — was a fool.

For what sort of man would find himself dashing toward Gretna Green with the woman he loved, but not, as one might suspect, with the intention of making a runaway marriage but to stop a man who didn't exist from eloping with the figment of a stablehand's overly fertile imagination?

The entire scenario was giving Lord Henry a severe megrim.

But obviously not one painful enough to get him to confess the truth.

For God's sake, tell her everything, he could almost hear Preston's stern voice saying.

Lord Henry blew out a breath. Oh, yes, that would be sensible. *Miss Dale, you are chasing after a phantom. I know this because I am your beloved Dishforth. I have led you on this merry, ruinous adventure in hopes of your coming to your senses and realizing that I am the only man for you.*

She'd kick him out of the carriage. Most likely on a blind corner. With some sharp object imbedded in his back — if she was feeling merciful.

Worse, he'd end up like Kendrick Seldon.

Henry flinched and then shuddered.

However had he gotten so mired into this tangle?

He glanced across the carriage to where Daphne sat, serene and calm, hands folded in her lap and eyes bright as she looked out the window.

She was the epitome of beguiling — one fair curl peeking out from beneath her bonnet, fluttering slightly in the breeze, a sprinkle of freckles across the bridge of her nose, and those lush pink lips of hers, the curve of which tempted a man to haul her close and kiss her senseless.

Well, tempted him, at the very least. Tempted him more than he cared to admit.

He knew what the seventh duke would tell him to do.

Kiss her, then follow it with a rousing session of tupping. That solves any number of difficulties with the female persuasion. A good tupping always does.

Henry would argue that it had been kissing that had gotten him into this mess.

But who could blame him? She possessed the wiles of a courtesan and the eyes of a siren. One look, one glance and she'd entangled him, with no hope of escape.

At least not alive. He grimaced again.

"Lord Henry, is something on your mind?" she asked, peering up at him from beneath the brim of her bonnet.

Here it is . . . your chance. Screw up your courage, man, and tell her.

But while he was a Seldon through and through — for wasn't he leading her to complete ruin with every passing mile? — the Seldons had one weakness.

They were horrible at confessing the truth. Especially when it came to love. His only hope was that she would grow weary of this chase and call it off. Disavow Dishforth. And then the field would be clear for him to . . .

Him to do what?

Henry had no idea. But he'd cross that bridge when he came to it. For truly, how far would Miss Dale go for such a pompous nit as Dishforth?

He shook his head and smiled at her. "No, nothing, Miss Dale. Nothing at all."

Two days later

"You do not seem overly distressed that we are stranded," Lord Henry posed as they stood beside the road and watched the posting lad and coachman ride away with their horses.

"Travel is fraught with such mishaps," Daphne replied, hoping her sense of relief as she watched them disappear around the bend wasn't overly apparent.

"Don't you think it odd that all four horses suddenly went lame?"

"I suppose it can happen; in fact it has," she replied, nodding at their own horses happily trotting down the road and hardly looking lame.

"Still . . ." Lord Henry kicked a stone across the road, his jaw set.

Perhaps she should feign a demeanor fraught with worry and concern for Dishforth, or, more to the point, over her certainly lost reputation.

For here she was stranded out in the middle of nowhere with Lord Henry Seldon.

All alone.

Where anything could happen.

She slanted a glance in his direction. *Anything.*

And yet nothing was. Much to her growing annoyance.

If anything was leaving her fraught with worry, it was Lord Henry's suddenly honorable and gentlemanly behavior toward her.

"I will say, though," she offered, "that if one must be stranded, it is in a perfectly lovely spot."

Indeed it was. For there was a large oak on the other side of a rock wall, and beyond its sheltering shade were wide meadows dotted with wildflowers. There was even a wide, clear stream dividing the valley laid out before them.

Lord Henry glanced around and huffed another sigh, picking up the basket and crossing the road.

Daphne chewed at her lower lip and went over the last few days in her head. Through all the changes of horses, all the miles, all the hours of traveling so intimately together, not once had Lord Henry attempted anything untoward.

He'd been the epitome of a gentleman.

Wretched beast.

Hopefully this delay would be enough to nudge him into confessing the truth.

That he was Mr. Dishforth.

A few days earlier at Owle Park

"Was it him or wasn't it?" Lady Zillah demanded.

Something inside of Daphne — most likely that bit of her that had left more than one relation shaking their head and likening her to Great-Aunt Damaris — refused to yield.

She took a few steps forward and smiled at the lady politely. As if she were a Fitzgerald or a Smythe and not this Seldon crone.

"Pardon, my lady?"

"Harrumph!" Zillah snorted. "You have Damaris Dale's pride all over you."

"Thank you, my lady."

"That was no compliment."

"I shall take it as one, all the same."

"Bah! He's a fool to even glance in your direction. And what's worse is that you know it."

Daphne didn't reply, for even to acknowledge the lady's accusation was to give it credit.

Where none was deserved or wanted.

Lord Henry! She didn't know whether to shout with joy or cry her eyes out. She was head over heels in love with him and all but promised to another.

"He'd have none of my advice to leave you be. Quite the opposite, he's determined to make mischief where it doesn't belong."

Meaning with her. With a Dale.

"So I am asking you, since for some folly of a reason Preston will not, to leave Owle Park before you have that boy in knots." Daphne opened her mouth to protest, but again Zillah obviously had been looking for an opportunity to make this speech and had it all planned out. Thus, she continued unabated, "You will make your curtsy, apologize profusely and leave immediately. I will not see him bedeviled another day."

"I have no reason to leave. Whatever would I say?" Daphne posed.

"Lie," the lady said plainly. "You're a Dale, after all. It should come naturally."

Daphne sucked in a deep breath, every bit of indignation she possessed coming to the forefront.

While Lady Zillah's age and rank required Daphne to give the lady every bit of respect she possessed, in her estimation, Lady Zillah deserved none.

But there was no time to utter even the quickest of retorts, for Lady Zillah had turned back to the piano and was gathering up her music sheets. She *tsk tsk*'d over each one. "And after Henry was so kind to make all these notations for me," she complained, glancing down at the pages she held. "For another time when I won't be disturbed."

Then she flounced off with all the arrogance that only the daughter of a duke could possess.

And as she swept past Daphne, her skirt held to one side so as not to even graze a Dale, one of the lady's music sheets slipped unnoticed from her grasp.

Though not unnoticed by Daphne. Leaning over and snatching it up, she was about to call after her.

Truly she was — not even the wry thought of crumpling the page and tossing it after the old witch's head had lasted overly long — that is, until she looked at the page, heavily annotated as it was.

Daphne stilled and gaped down at the bold, broad, sure hand that had written all over Lady Zillah's music sheets.

A script Daphne knew all-too-well.

For not only did it belong to Lord Henry

but it also belonged to another.

Mr. Dishforth.

Back on the road to Gretna
So Daphne hadn't dashed out of the inn in a wild state, determined to save "poor Dishforth" as she'd professed.

She'd done it to force Lord Henry's hand. To get him to confess the truth. Declare himself.

Because until he did so, how could she?

And now here she was, nearly to the Scottish border, ruined beyond redemption, and not one word had Lord Henry uttered. Oh, this had become a ruinous, ridiculous farce.

One of your own making, Daphne Dale.

And worse yet, it seemed the lie that was Dishforth's elopement had spread up and down the road that led to Gretna Green.

Every inn they stopped at, every posting house, every tollgate, there was some new addition to the story . . .

The beauty of Dishforth's faux bride-to-be.

The man's kindness and gallantry toward his lady love.

And his extravagance. Buying pints all around in one inn to toast his good fortune. Tipping the posting lads ungodly amounts to hasten their dash to Scotland.

Daphne and Henry always seemed to have

"just missed the pair."

Funny, that. Ridiculous lies, all of them. But every time one of these bouncers landed in their lap, she watched for Lord Henry's reaction, for surely now he would say or do something.

But each time he listened attentively and did nothing.

Daphne ground her teeth together. Whenever was he going to put an end to all this? She couldn't imagine it would be much longer, for at least she'd had the presence of mind to actually pack a valise.

She'd gone down to the inn outside of Owle Park half expecting him to make a full accounting of himself and then beg her to elope.

And when he hadn't, and he and the innkeeper and that terrible boy — goodness, whoever had thought to include such a wretched liar in their plans? — had gone on about Dishforth's departure, she'd had no choice but to force his hand.

And instead of telling the truth, he'd gone along with her madcap scheme.

For what reason, she couldn't fathom. Not once had Lord Henry looked ready to confess during these last few days, not when it meant wearing the same clothes day after day or even when he'd had to subject himself to the ministrations of whatever hapless servant could be pressed into duty as "his lordship's temporary valet."

She almost pitied him, for the shave he'd gotten this morning looked as if it might have been done by a blind man.

Nicked, battered and rumpled, and still he wouldn't confess.

And whyever not? She'd spent nearly every waking minute trying to answer that one question.

What was it Lady Zillah had said about him? *You are too nice by half. Respectable and kindhearted.*

Was he not telling her the truth — that he was Dishforth — simply because, as a man of honor, he wanted to avoid hurting her?

Or might it be a way of avoiding a scene when she discovered his deception?

Certainly she was avoiding the moment when he discovered she'd known of his duplicity all this time and could well have put her foot down . . . including saving him from that butchering barber . . .

One thing was for certain: it made little sense that Lord Henry was attempting to avoid marrying her by running off with her all the way to Gretna Green.

Which left her right back at the beginning of this terrible muddle, to the one possibility that tended to haunt her in the middle of the night:

What if he was simply waiting for her to cry off? To beg him to turn the carriage around and take her back?

Waiting for her to disavow Dishforth so they could return to Owle Park, where she would be whisked away by her family in a complete state of ruin and he could go about his normal existence — his Seldon reputation affirmed and no one overly shocked as to his hand in all this.

After all, he was a Seldon and allowed a few scandals.

And her? Well, she'd be ruined and shuttled off to the farthest reaches a Dale could travel.

Yet when Daphne looked at Lord Henry, or caught him studying her — on those rare moments when he thought she wouldn't catch him — she felt, oh, how she wondered how he could remain silent.

If only . . . if only . . . he'd kiss her again.

Then she'd be able to know . . . she was sure of that.

But he hadn't tried. Not once in these past few days.

Apparently such mischief was only for the confines of Owle Park.

She glanced down the now empty road

and sighed. At least they had the basket the innkeeper's wife had packed for them this morning — even though they hadn't ordered one. The thoughtful lady had insisted, saying that it was impossible to know what was ahead but anything could be faced better with a full stomach.

So Daphne had accepted the proffered basket gratefully.

Looking back, one might suspect the lady had known what was in store for them.

But how could she have known? Ridiculous, romantic notion, really.

As if the entire Manchester-to-Glasgow road was conspiring for them to fall in love.

Fall in love. Too late, she would have told them all.

Glancing over at Lord Henry, where he was bent beside a hedge examining something — she frowned, for romance was in very short supply on this misguided and unwitting elopement.

But when he turned around, she realized how wrong she was. In his hands, Lord Henry held a fistful of forget-me-nots.

He walked over to her — well, a Seldon never just walked, they had this way of striding about as if the very soil beneath their boots was theirs to command.

He handed the flowers over without so

much as a word, and she took them.

Now he's going to confess, she thought, biting her bottom lip in anticipation. *Now he will finally tell me.*

And she dared to look up.

The moment their gazes met, it was so magical — wasn't it to him? — that it left her trembling. Her heart hammered, her throat went dry, her every limb was a-shiver, as if calling out to him to sweep her into his eager grasp.

But once again, Daphne found herself disappointed.

"Yes, well," he began, before he turned from her, took up the basket and headed over to the low stone wall by the side of the road. He nodded toward the flowers clenched in her hand. "Perhaps those will last until we reach Gretna. They can be your wedding bouquet when you find Dishforth."

Like the music sheet back at Owle Park, the forget-me-nots very nearly ended up being tossed at a Seldon's head.

Very nearly.

Since Lord Henry had made off with the basket, she had no choice but to follow. He'd climbed over the stile and plunked down in a spot under the large oak and was plundering the basket like a pirate by the time she joined him.

"Ah, tarts!" he exclaimed as if he'd just found a cache of Spanish doubloons.

Tarts. The rogue. He knew those were enough to lure her closer. Spread about was a tin — tea, most likely — along with apples, a wedge of cheese and a small round loaf of bread.

"Come sit," he bid her. "The view is most excellent."

It was. The Cumbrian countryside rolled all around them, with a scattering of green trees here and there, while the lush green meadows carpeted the valley before them.

"He's a fool, you know," Lord Henry told her as she sat down. "To have eloped with the wrong woman." He handed her a tart.

As she broke it into pieces, she mused that Dishforth wasn't the only fool.

"He was deceived," she replied. "Poor Dishforth is not a worldly sort." She smiled fondly into the distance, as if dreaming of her simple, foolish lover. When she glanced back, she found Lord Henry's brow furrowed.

"He's what?"

"Not very worldly, not whatsoever," she told him most emphatically, liking the way her words made his eye twitch ever-so-slightly with indignation whenever she praised Dishforth's less than stellar qualities. "He's a sensible man, but he's also overly romantic, which, I suspect, is why he was so susceptible to this Jezebel who has him in her clutches." She clucked her tongue at the injustice of it all. "However, I don't fault him for it."

"You don't?" Lord Henry looked up from the apple he was eating.

"No, not in the least." She dug into her pocket and pulled out a letter. "Just listen to this —" Daphne read the lines from a poem inscribed there.

"I find that most well put," Lord Henry told her, sounding just a tad too defensive.

"Yes, but —" She paused and sighed.

He sat up a bit. "But what?"

"Well, those lines are hardly original," she confided, carefully folding the letter.

"I found them quite stirring."

"Really? I found them overly familiar. Indeed, I asked Harriet's brother, and he laughed — told me every boy at Eton learns those lines. A schoolboy's sentiments." She shrugged.

"A schoolboy's —" he began.

She leaned forward and cut him off. "I don't like to admit this, but I fear you are right and Mr. Dishforth will turn out to be an overly simple man. Otherwise why else would he be so easily duped, as you said before."

"Overly simple?"

"Yes," she said with a smile. "Ever so much so."

This time, when Lord Henry straightened, he let his apple fall to one side. "And you like that?"

"Of course. A simple man will not overrun me or attempt to deceive me. I think he sounds the perfect husband."

"Doesn't sound so to me. Not if he's the sort to pass off schoolboy lines."

"Not everyone can have your dash and polish, Lord Henry." She smiled at him, met his gaze and waited.

There was a moment when neither of them spoke. "I have dash and polish?" he managed.

"Yes." Again waiting for some sort of inspired declaration from the man.

Instead, he leaned back against the tree, his hands behind his handsome head.

Daphne wasn't in the mood to let him preen for long. "Oh, you needn't be so proud of the fact. That is also one of your faults. Seldon pride."

"I've always thought the Dales possessed the lion's share of that trait, leaving hardly any for the rest of us."

"I'll admit we are a prideful lot," Daphne told him, "but then again, we have much to preen over."

"*Bah!* Dales!" he mocked.

"*Harrumph!* Seldons!" Daphne met his gaze with an arrogant one of her own, and before she knew it, they were both laughing uproariously at the ridiculousness of it all.

"How long have our families been at each other?"

She shrugged. "Forever."

"Over a litter of mongrel pups."

Daphne looked aside and blushed, for she wasn't supposed to know that, but of course she did.

"Foolish, isn't it?" He looked at her, his glorious eyes filled with something that was far from mockery, far from the usual Seldon disdain, and Daphne's heart skipped and tumbled as it always did when he looked at her that way.

"Very much so."

He thrust out his hand. "Then a truce is in order!"

"A what?" she managed, looking down at his hand and willing herself to take hold of it. For as much as she bemoaned his unwillingness to declare himself, now she was just as hesitant to take what he was offering.

"A truce, minx. Yes, a Seldon-Dale truce.

I declare all hostilities between our families hereby null and void." He pressed his hand closer, and Daphne took it.

What else could she do?

And as his large palm wound around her smaller one, she felt as she always did around him — engulfed.

She looked down at their intertwined hands. "I don't think I shall be counted as a Dale after this."

He laughed and let go of her, leaning back again in that lord-of-the-manor way of his. "I suspect the seventh duke will haunt me to the end of my days, but it is a fate I am willing to risk."

He was? Willing to risk the censure of his family for her? Was that what he was saying?

"Why?" she asked.

"Because, Miss Dale, you and I are alike."

At this she laughed.

"We are," he insisted. "Whether you approve or not."

Daphne stilled, for she was quite convinced he was about to haul her into his arms and kiss her. He was, she just knew it.

And then he blinked, as if remembering something, and turned around as quickly as the moment had begun. "Yes, well, if we are so alike, I suppose you are as famished as I am."

And so they returned to their meal in silence, each lost in their own thoughts.

Henry ran through a thousand different ways he might nudge Miss Dale into admitting that Mr. Dishforth was not the man for her.

It wasn't until he spied a fine house rising in the distance that he thought he might have the perfect entree. This was not some tumbledown relic but a gentleman's house — a respectable home. The sort a lady like Miss Dale would admire.

"Such an excellent house. I wonder who lives there?" he asked with a nonchalant wave of his apple in that direction.

She glanced at it and shrugged.

"Does Mr. Dishforth have such a residence?" he asked, all the while examining the apple in his hand.

"I don't know," she admitted.

"What do you know about this rogue?" he pressed, glancing in the basket again as if the answer really wasn't *that* important to him.

"Oh, plenty," she replied from the other side of the blanket, where she sat picking at the grass blades.

"Such as . . . ?"

She huffed a sigh, then looked over at him.

"He lives in London. With his sister. She must be a most gracious and delightful creature, for he is ever so fond of her."

Henry had made the mistake of taking a bite of apple at that point, and he nearly choked.

Miss Dale was not done. Why, it was as if the lady had compiled an entire dossier on the man. "He also cares for a nephew, who is a dreadful trial —"

Henry couldn't argue with that.

"So Dishforth must be a great blessing to his family."

Henry tried to appear thoughtful. "Can he keep you?"

"Keep me?"

"Yes, afford a wife?"

She sniffed at this. "What a vulgar thing to ask."

"Yes, well, silks don't come cheap." Well he knew. He'd seen enough of Hen's bills.

Her chin chucked up. "I hardly think new gowns will be on my mind when I am Mrs. Abernathy Dishforth."

"Abernathy?" This time he'd had the presence of mind not to take another bite from his apple.

She glanced up at him, a quizzical look on her face. "Yes. Didn't I mention his name before?"

"I suppose I forgot," he mused, trying to remember if he'd ever used a first name — which he was quite positive he hadn't.

What the devil? Was she just making this up as she went along?

"Abernathy," she sighed. "Such a romantic name. Though Harriet is of the opinion he must have a wen."

This brought Henry right up. "A wen?!" Not that again.

"Yes, right in the middle of his forehead," she said, pointing to her own. "Further, it is Harriet's opinion that such a name, Abernathy Dishforth, is the sort one gives a child who will grow up prone to eating paste and tattling. But I doubt that he could be that dreadful."

Henry ground his teeth together. First his letters were classified as simple, and now this? A wen-sporting looby with a penchant for eating paste?

"It might not be his true name," he pointed out.

"It doesn't matter to me what his name is," she replied, once again absently picking at the grass blades.

"It might well," he muttered.

"What was that, Lord Henry?"

Here it was, the opportunity to confess everything, and yet his pride wasn't about

449

to reveal that he was her paste-eating simpleton of a lover.

"Nothing," he ground out.

Miss Dale shrugged. "I suspect given Abernathy's sensible opinions, he must be a gentleman reduced to trade."

There was no way he'd heard her correctly. "Reduced to wha-a-at?"

"Trade."

He couldn't help himself; he shuddered. "And this isn't a problem for you?"

She smiled. "Trade isn't as ignoble as it used to be. Perhaps with the help of my Dale relations, he might be elevated. Knighted, perhaps."

Henry closed his eyes. He still was unconvinced he'd heard her correctly, but he had no desire to explore her theories as to why she thought Dishforth was in trade.

His pride couldn't take it.

So he tried another tack. "Have you considered what you'll do if you and Mr. Dishforth don't suit?"

"We already do," she said with such supreme confidence that Henry wondered how he could ever change her mind.

But it was Miss Dale who took pity on him and changed the subject, albeit unwittingly.

"Is your house like that one?" she asked,

nodding toward the residence he'd pointed out before.

He looked at it again. "Yes, the one in Sussex is most similar, but the one in Kent is a rambling pile. If you like Owle Park, you would love Stowting Mote. It's an amazingly old keep, with a hodgepodge of Tudor additions tacked on. It needs a thorough cleaning and some renovations." He glanced at her.

"Two houses, Lord Henry?"

Lord Henry grinned at her surprise. "Three, actually."

"Three? Oh, yes, I quite forgot. You had mentioned that the other day, hadn't you? I don't know why I didn't remember." She paused. "Rather unusual, isn't it? A second son with three houses?"

"It isn't as if I won them at cards or dice, or came by them in some illicit manner."

"I didn't mean —"

"No, no. After all, I am naught but a spare. And a suspected Seldon wastrel at that."

"I thought we'd declared a truce on that notion."

"Yes, indeed. My apologies."

"None needed," she told him. "I would think having three houses would make you quite a catch."

"That is why I don't nose it about Town." He picked up the loaf of bread and tore it in two, handing her one half. "Besides, there is more to a man than his property and income."

"There is?" she teased, nibbling at her half of the loaf.

"You are a dreadful minx."

"Well, property and income — you did say income, didn't you?"

"Yes. An indecent one, if I do say so myself."

"Now you are just showing your —"

"Pride?"

She nodded.

"I suppose I am."

She looked again at the house in the distance. "I've always dreamt of being a mistress of such a house."

"And why wouldn't you?"

"I'm from Kempton, to begin with."

"Yes, Preston mentioned some nonsense about the lot of you being cursed."

"Well, there hasn't been a happy marriage in quite some time."

"I think Preston and Miss Timmons will change all that. Suppose it will cause a flurry of courtships in your village."

She laughed. "I doubt it. Traditions are so very difficult to surmount. Sometimes it is a divide that cannot be crossed."

"Yes, I suppose so," he admitted. He thought not of Kempton but of them. Seldon and Dale. "But you aren't amongst such narrow-minded spinsters. Surely you came to London with the hopes of —"

He resisted teasing her. *Snaring a husband . . . Catching a fellow in the parson's trap . . .*

"I had rather hoped that Mr. Dishforth —"

"Ah, yes, we always end up back there," he said, weary of the subject. "Still, you are a Dale — and one of the loveliest. I can't imagine you'll be a spinster for long."

"Me?" She shook her head. "I am merely Daphne Dale, of the Kempton Dales. I am considered a rather poor relation and hardly one of the family's beauties."

He leaned back and studied her. "Then they are all blind."

CHAPTER 15

In the light of day, will you come to
regret this?

Found in a letter from
Mr. Dishforth to Miss Spooner

Lord Henry's statement, nay, confession,
took Daphne's breath away.

Had he truly just said that? Did he mean
it?

Apparently he did, for he pushed off the
trunk of the oak, against which he'd been
leaning, and crossed the seemingly impossible valley that had sprung up between
them.

His hand reached out and cupped her
chin, and he drew her closer until his lips
captured hers.

*Protest, remind him of Dishforth, make him
tell the truth first. . . .*

Objections fluttered through her thoughts
before they were caught on a wayward

breeze and lofted far from reach.

His kiss, his touch left her without any reason. Just desire. Heart-pounding, inescapable desires.

He'd claimed her with his kiss before; now his hands, his body captured her. He edged up the blanket, covering her, one hand still cupping her chin, the other on her hip — pulling her ever closer — until she found herself on her back, his body covering hers.

All the while, he kissed her, deeply, insistently. The demanding sort of kisses that claimed not just the woman but her soul as well.

And Daphne inhaled, drew him in, her fingers clinging to his shoulders, her mouth open to him. Everything about him seemed to touch her — his tongue teasing over hers, his hands as they roamed over her, his hips pinning her to the blanket beneath them.

He'd gone from the tentative rogue in the folly, to the seducer in the library, to a man determined.

His touch wasn't teasing and light, it was insistent, as if his desires had been bottled up and were now bursting forth like champagne.

That one kiss, that one moment where he'd made that fateful decision to cross the blanket, to breach the divide between them, now saw his every desire unleashed.

Having started with a kiss, his lips continued their assault over her neck, behind her ear, leaving Daphne breathless, her insides quaking.

She tried to gasp, to speak, but her mouth could only open, and what came out was a mew of pleasure. *"Ahhh."*

He continued to tease her with his trail of kisses, his lips nibbling at her neck, and down along the edge of her bodice, as his fingers slipped beneath her gown and freed first one breast and then the other, leaving them bare to his touch.

Now it was his turn to moan as he sucked one of her nipples deep into his mouth, leaving it puckered tight and Daphne's hips dancing upwards, strafing against the hard ridge beneath his breeches, as if seeking relief from the anxious, dangerous passions building inside her.

And then that wayward breeze ran over her legs — for she hadn't even noticed that he'd brought her skirt up, and he had lost no time finding that nub between her legs, beginning to work his magic yet again.

Her legs opened to him, her body already wet and ready for him.

And then his kiss delved lower, his lips against her thighs, his breath hot against the curls at her apex, and when his fingers parted the way, his kiss at her very core, his tongue curling around her, washing over her, Daphne's hips bucked, her heels digging into the earth beneath them, seeking something solid to hitch her to the earth, for she was truly rising again, but this time ever-so-fast and furiously.

Panting and anxious, she could only cling to the blanket, his tongue insistent over her, lapping at her, urging her to let go, to find her release.

"Ah, ah, yes, ah," she gasped.

He caught hold of her hips and drew her closer, as if he knew exactly what her soft cries meant, knew the translation.

And the cure.

He trapped her close and sucked deeply, leaving Daphne rife with desires. With need.

There was nothing left for her to do but let go.

When she did, those anxious, dangerous spirals he'd coiled inside her burst open, tendrils flung out in all directions, wayward branches whipping this way and that as if tossed by this tempest of pleasure he'd unleashed. Above her, the dappled sunshine blinked and winked through the oak leaves like a thousand points of fireworks, fluttering and flashing even as her body danced and tossed with wave after wave of passion.

Lord Henry didn't stop there, he continued to kiss her, continued to tease her until she was spent and shaken. And only then did he let go. He cradled her, soothed her with kisses to her lips, to her shoulders, with whispered promises of the delights to come.

Daphne could hardly believe him. More? Was that possible?

But when she looked into his deep, passionate gaze, she knew Lord Henry was a man of his word.

And deed.

Henry wanted nothing more than to bury himself between her legs and slake this desperate need that had burned in his veins since the night of the engagement ball.

He'd wanted her then. He wanted her now, but with such a different longing. To have her always. To tell her everything and for her to understand.

But right now, all he could do was make love to her.

The starry light in her eyes called for him to give in to his pent-up desires. Unleash the fires she stoked within him.

But he wasn't about to rush this afternoon.

Entwined as they were, he knew instantly

the moment her body stirred back to life, for her hips were once again brushing up to explore against him, her fingers trailing down his back, her fingernails taut against his skin.

He loved the way she teased him, like a cat on points, all nails and arched, ready to be tamed.

And then she surprised him, her hands moving to the top of his breeches, opening them, and as he had before with her bodice, she reached inside and let her fingers curl around his rock-hard manhood.

Where it had been straining against his breeches, now it pulsed to life in her grasp. He rolled off her and they lay face-to-face so she had room for her explorations and the leisure to tease him.

Henry tried to breathe as hot sensations of desire shot through him.

Her touch, at first tentative, became stronger, running up and down his length, her mouth coming to join again with his as her touch became more hurried, her tongue teasing at his.

Now it was Henry's turn to groan, for with each stroke, he grew harder, his body tightened. Her fingers toyed with a glossy bead that had formed on the head, and she used it to torture him as she slid her hand back and forth, his length now slick.

"I want you, Daphne," he gasped. "I want to be inside of you. I need to be inside you."

He reached down and began to tease her back to life, until she was once again panting with need, then he rolled her on her back and shifted himself until he was right at her cleft.

"I want you as well," she whispered.

"Who do you want, Daphne?" he asked as he began to enter her, slowly, opening her and then moving out.

Her mouth opened. "You, Lord Henry. I want you. And only you."

And then he entered her, breaching her virgin's barrier and filling her.

She gasped, her eyes fluttering open wide at this invasion.

"It is only like that once," he told her. "Now remember how it was when I touched you, when I kissed you." Then he began to stroke her, slowly, until her once soft mews of pleasure became more urgent cries.

As she reached her peak for the second time, Henry's own climax shot through him emptying him into an abyss of pleasure.

They spent the remainder of the day in each other's arms, making love again, and eventually, hand in hand, they wandered from their blanket haven and explored the meadows beyond, gamboling through the waist-high grasses and wildflowers like children.

As they strolled back to the tree, Daphne said, "Tell me about this house of yours. This Stowting Mote."

He grinned at her, reaching over and brushing an errant strand of her hair away from her face. "It has a moat."

"A moat? Truly?"

"Indeed. The water surrounds the entire house, and you can fish from any window."

She laughed at him. "Now you are teasing."

"I'm not. The house is truly surrounded by a moat — it is centuries old, with the last real renovations done about the time Old Bess was queen. But the gardens are good, and it has a lovely orchard that spreads up along a wide lawn in the front."

"It sounds romantic," she told him.

"Hardly," he admitted. "The moat needs to be drained and cleaned, and I imagine once I start mucking around, I'll find all sorts of places that need shoring up."

"Whyever did you buy such a place?"

Lord Henry shrugged and glanced off in the direction of the lovely house in the distance. "Stowting Mote has always been a family home. A unique one, granted. Families have lived there for generations, and then come and gone. And yet the house still stands. I suppose I just wanted to be part of that, that legacy of generations, to belong to that history."

She nudged him. "You are an incurable romantic, Lord Henry Seldon."

He dropped her hand and struck a horrified pose. "Insults will land you in the moat, Miss Dale."

She reached over and took his hand. "Then I expect you will fish me out."

"I might."

"Wretched, awful man," she taunted him back as they resumed their walk to the spot under the tree.

They gathered up the blanket and the remains of the basket and strolled down the hillside toward their carriage. About the time they got to the rock wall, the sound of hooves echoed down the long lane.

Their postilion, their driver and fresh horses came round the bend.

"So soon?" Daphne mused, rather saddened that their perfect afternoon was ending. She knew all too soon that she and Lord Henry would have to have a coming to the truth, a full confession of sorts. She only hoped he would forgive her as much as she was willing to look past his stubborn pride.

He had been right earlier: they were alike. Too much so.

"I thought you were in a hell-fire hurry to get to the border?" Henry posed. For he was no longer Lord Henry, he was her Henry, and she his Daphne.

Daphne tucked up her chin defiantly. "I've been known to change my mind," she told him as he helped her over the low stone wall.

"Truly?" he replied as he climbed over, basket in hand.

"Yes."

He paused. "Name one occasion."

She laughed. "I don't despise you as much as I first did."

Henry barked a laugh and caught her by the hand, bringing it to his lips. "That's good, for you are rather stuck with me now."

"Am I?" she shot back, turning her attentions to the driver and lad, who were even now guiding the horses into their traces.

Henry didn't press the matter and, following her lead, turned his attention to their long-awaited driver. "Almost thought you'd forgotten us."

"Terrible time getting new horses, my lord," the man explained. "Everyone seems to be headed north today."

"How odd," Daphne remarked as she climbed into the carriage. "We haven't seen a soul all afternoon."

As the carriage rolled down the road, Daphne laid her head against Henry's shoulder, suddenly finding herself exhausted. The gentle swaying of the carriage and Henry's steady, solid presence beside her left her ready to slip into dreams.

Besides, it was growing dark, and the shadows made it easy to close one's eyes.

"Minx, whatever are you going to do?"

"Hmm?" she replied, half awake.

"When we catch up with your Mr. Dishforth?"

Daphne raised her sleepy gaze to his. Still? He wanted to continue this charade? She sighed. "I'll tell him quite simply that I forgive him his foolish pride."

"His what?"

"You heard me," she murmured and snuggled closer.

"Whatever do you see in this bungler?" Henry pressed, sounding a little more than vexed by her continued allegiance to her other lover.

"Many things," she said. And when he nudged her a bit, she knew he wanted to hear more. "His loyalty to his family. His kindness. His words — they encouraged me

464

to break with the past and dare to dream that I might dance where I may."

She could hear the soft groan of frustration rumble through his chest. Well, he'd asked.

"And you discovered all this through his letters?"

She shook her head. "No, Henry. A lady reads between the lines."

"What will you tell him about me? About us?"

"The truth. He'll understand." She sighed and sunk closer to a soft refuge of dreams. "I imagine he'll thank you for bringing me."

Henry sputtered. "Thank me? How can you be so sure?"

Sleep started to steal at her senses, but she opened one eye. "Because he loves me."

"Are you certain?" he whispered.

"Yes."

And she was, as she drifted off to sleep in his arms.

They arrived at the inn just after dark, and Henry hated to wake her up. Then again, everything Daphne had said as she'd drifted off to sleep had left at him at a loss.

What the devil did she mean that Dishforth would love her still?

He would have thought, well, he'd just assumed that once they'd . . . they'd . . . made love, she would have made her choice.

Apparently not.

"Are we there?" Daphne said, her eyes opening. "Are we in Scotland?"

"Hmm," Henry mused. "No. Just a few miles from the border. Seems we will need to stop here for the night."

She sat up and stretched. "Just as well. It has been a busy day. I don't know about you, but I'm famished."

Henry got out and helped her down, and once again, to his amazement, rooms were at the ready and Daphne was whisked off in the efficient hands of a sturdy-looking maid.

It had been like that all the way up the road — as if their every stop had been anticipated. But then again, he'd never dashed off to Scotland before, and mayhap that was how things were done on the Manchester Road.

Then again, the cheeky innkeeper two nights before had handed Henry a second bill.

"For Mr. Dishforth's expenses, if you please, my lord." And then the fellow had slanted a glance at Daphne and made a greedy waggle of his brows, as if to say, *Best pay up, for it would be a shame if the lady was to discover the truth.*

Still, having rooms at the ready and a hot supper on the table was worth a few inconveniences.

And a bit of blackmail, he mused, wondering what Mr. Dishforth had needed with a hot shave, two bottles of Madeira and laundry.

No, this had to end. Now. This very night.

"How would you like your supper, my lord?" the innkeeper asked as he came forward.

Supper? Yes, that would be perfect. He'd tell her over an excellent meal. He glanced up at the inn. At least he hoped it would be decent.

"Quickly," Henry told him. "And in a private dining room, if you will?"

He'd tell her everything. Beg her to marry him, carry her over the border in the morning, make her his wife and then they could go into hiding until the worst of it blew over.

Not a very noble stance, but utterly sensible, given the Dale and Seldon tendencies to overreact when one of their own defied that line that kept them apart.

Well, it was a line no more for him.

"A private room? Of course, my lord! And a fine supper for you and the lady. Quite in order. Why, Mr. Dishforth ordered up that exactly, just last night," the innkeeper said.

Then the man leaned closer. "And Mr. Dishforth also said your lordship would have no complaints in covering his expenses."

Henry tried to muster his most withering glare, but it was of no use on such a weathered innkeeper, who rubbed his hands together in glee as he hurried off to get everything prepared.

Following him into the inn, his boots tramping along, Henry knew one thing was for certain. After tonight, he would lay the past to rest and there would be no more of that unreliable, horribly unfeeling creature, Abernathy Dishforth, ever again.

Daphne was halfway down the narrow staircase when a voice in the common room below halted her steps.

"I am seeking word of my cousin — she is traveling toward Gretna Green in a disastrous match. It is imperative I find her."

Crispin!

Daphne whirled around, scrambling to flee up the stairs, but her path was blocked by the maid who had dressed her hair with such care.

"Oh, dear!" she exclaimed.

"Gar! What is it, miss?" the maid said in her thick northern accent.

"My cousin! He's come to find me, stop me," Daphne whispered, even as she pushed her way past the girl and ducked higher up the stairs and out of sight.

"No! He can't," the girl exclaimed just as vehemently. "Not when you've come so far."

"Exactly," Daphne agreed. "I just need one more night."

"Leave it to me," the girl said, rushing down the stairs.

Daphne peered down the stairwell, just enough to listen.

"Not one of you has seen her? This is quite possibly the only posting inn that hasn't," Crispin was saying with that edge of suspicion that sounded very much like Great-Aunt Damaris's probing, skeptical tones when she sensed a scandal.

"You there, miss," Crispin called out as the maid came down the stairs. "Have you seen my cousin, Miss Dale? She's about your height and has fair features. I think she would have come through here not but an hour or so ago."

"Oh aye, sir, I've seen her," the girl declared.

There was a stirring in the room, not unlike the tremble in Daphne's heart. Perhaps the maid had landed at the end of the stairs, seen Crispin's fine presence and sensed a reward that would compensate for her duplicity.

But how wrong Daphne was.

For hadn't this been the same girl who'd said every lady deserved their happy ever after?

"Yes, sir, I saw her. We all did. She and the gentleman — they came through here about an hour ago. So in love, it about left me in tears."

"Love! Bah! That scurrilous Seldon has her deceived."

"Then whyever was he looking for another way across the border — so as to keep the likes of you from finding them?" Then the girl gasped and flung her hand over her mouth as if she wished she could have stoppered the words.

But it was too late. Crispin leapt upon her lie like a bird after bread crumbs.

"Another route into Scotland?" Daphne could almost hear the starch in Crispin's neckcloth creak as he straightened to his full height. "What other route?"

"Oh, now you've done it, lass," one of the patrons complained. "Done and given those poor lovers away."

The girl sniffed loudly. "I didn't mean to!"

"Too late now," another complained. "Aye, sir, there's another route. But it will cost you."

"Cost me?" Crispin's outrage was palpable.

"Aye, cost ye. The other lord, he was willing to pay for someone to guide him, if only not to get caught, so if it was worth it to him . . ." The man left off, the room growing still with anticipation to see what would happen next.

"I shan't be blackmailed," Crispin declared. "This match is ruinous for the lady, and as gentlemen all, you should be stepping forward to aid me, as you would ask for aid if she were your kinswoman."

"Mine don't run off," another fellow joked. "Wish they would. Should count yerself lucky, milord."

There was a rough volley of laughter at Crispin's expense.

"The route!" he demanded.

"Pay up," the man said, "or spend the night and find it in the daylight yerself. Personally I think you ought to try — but I don't fancy finding you and your excellent carriage at the bottom of the ravine."

There were nods all around.

"Yes, well, then, name your price," Crispin said in a of huff. "But whoever takes me had best know what he is doing, for I must catch them before they are married. Or worse."

Daphne stilled as a price was arranged and a fellow came forward to ride along with Crispin's driver.

What followed was a whirlwind of activity and shouted orders, then the creak of the door and the sound of it slamming shut. Not until there was a neigh from the horses and the carriage rumbled out of the yard did Daphne come down the stairwell, only to find the grinning maid waiting at the edge of the steps.

"Oh, thank you," she said to the girl who had brazened such a scheme. "I just need tonight to tell him everything. To explain everything. To get him to forgive me all of this."

"Exactly what do you need to explain, Miss Dale?" came a familiar voice. "And what do I need to forgive?"

Henry didn't wait for Daphne to answer; he caught her by the arm and hauled her toward the room the inn-keeper had set aside for their supper.

He towed her quickly, afraid his temper would boil over before they reached the privacy of the dining room, well away from prying ears and eyes.

But he didn't make it. For the moment Daphne had expressed her relief, "to get him to forgive me all this," the truth hit him squarely between the eyes.

She knew. She knew the truth.

He'd never felt such a fool!

"All this . . . the carriage, the chase, your worries and your countless concerns over Mr. Dishforth — you knew!" he burst out just as they gained the room but before the door could be shut.

Daphne reared to a stop. "Which you could have ended at any moment."

Yes, she did have to point that out.

"How could I? You called that idiot —"

"You mean I called *you,*" she corrected, hands fisted to her hips.

"Yes, yes. You called Mr. Dishforth a simpleton. You claimed you loved him."

At least she had enough decency left to look slightly guilty. Not for long, though. "The point being? My lord, you could have stopped all this with one single confession."

"My confession? What about yours?" He threw up his hands. "I should point out that this folly has left you ruined."

She huffed a sigh. "As well I know."

" 'I know'?! That is all you have to say? This coming from 'Reputation is everything, sir. A man's reputation is his shining

473

grace.' "

She pinked around the edges as he quoted from one of her letters. As well *she* should. And as if she could feel the heat in her cheeks and what it revealed, she turned her back to him.

"Ruined!" he continued to rail. "Further, you have left me with no alternative but to marry you — if only to save your reputation and mine."

Oh, that spun her around, her eyes alight with fury. "Why would you bother? As a Seldon, don't you think that goes against Society's expectations?"

"Don't tempt me, Miss Dale." But honestly, all she did was tempt him. Just by breathing, she had him tangled in the crosshairs.

"Oh, am I 'Miss Dale' again? What happened to 'my dearest Daphne'?"

"That rather leapt out the window when you fell asleep in my arms murmuring love notes to that looby Dishforth instead of to me. The man, I will point out, that you love."

She waved a hand at him as if he spoke utter nonsense.

Henry was past caring who heard him or how his voice carried. "Haven't you a thought as to how all this reflects on me?

Until I met you, I was a gentleman. Now your family most likely thinks I've kidnapped you — stolen you away for nefarious reasons."

"There is no arguing that," came a voice that stopped them both.

Crispin, Viscount Dale. Hell and damnation, he'd returned.

Daphne turned first, and then Henry.

Being first, Daphne had the privilege of seeing her cousin send a bruising fist into Lord Henry's face.

Henry, on the other hand, never saw it coming.

CHAPTER 16

I will not be parted from you. I will find
you, my dearest love. This, I promise.

> The last letter ever penned
> by Mr. Dishforth
> (well, nearly the last one)

When Henry came to, it was to the faces of
Preston and Hen staring down at him.

"What happened?" he moaned, pushing
aside the beefsteak resting over his eye and
trying to sit up.

Preston pushed him back down. "You
were blindsided by Dale."

"The brute," Hen complained. "Loathsome, horrible man!"

Dale?

Then it all came back to him. The argument. Daphne's gasp as she turned around.
And then the blackness.

This time he managed to struggle up to a
sitting position. They were in the private

dining room he'd ordered up. The dinner still sat on the sideboard, untouched.

"Where is Daphne? Where is she? I must speak to her —"

Again, Preston pushed him back down onto the settee. "She's gone, my good man. Spirited off by her cousin."

"Gone?" Henry shook his head, pushing past Preston and going for the door. "We have to go after them. We have to stop them!"

"Can't."

Henry turned to his nephew. "Can't or you won't?"

"Can't," Preston told him.

"Shouldn't!" Hen enthused. "You are well rid of her, if you want my opinion."

"Well, I don't," Henry told her. Hen looked ready to open her mouth and contradict him, but he cut her off. "Not another word, Hen. Need I remind you what you told Preston and me after you married Michaels?"

Her brow furrowed as she recalled her words. "The situation is hardly the same."

Preston grimaced and looked about to argue, but one glare from Hen stayed his retort.

"I am going to marry Daphne Dale and you had best get used to it."

Henry's adamant announcement sent Hen staggering back, as if he'd struck her. "Never," she told him. "Besides, she's well and gone, and by tomorrow she will be too far from your reach to ever discover again. See if they don't hide her away."

"I'll catch them before they reach Black-ford," Henry swore, wrenching open the door as much as holding onto to it to steady himself.

"Can't," Preston repeated.

"Whyever not?" Henry asked, a thousand thoughts going through his head. How he'd been an ass. A fool. He should have told her. She loved him and had known. Probably, knowing Daphne, she'd been testing him.

Of course, she had. Given him any number of chances to come clean.

And he'd failed her.

"Because the viscount took all the horses with him. Gave the innkeeper a ridiculous amount of money to allow him to take all the mounts. There isn't a nag to be had — save my cattle, but they're dead tired and need to be rested." Preston shook his head. "Tomorrow. We'll catch up with them to-morrow. I promise."

But Crispin proved to be a wary adversary

and thwarted Henry's chase at every turn, bribing the tollgate keepers to delay them unnecessarily, hiring up all the changes at nearly every post, and driving at an indecent speed to beat them back to Langdale.

Daphne found herself locked in her cousin's carriage, and only let out to use the necessary. And when she'd nearly managed to slip away once, her determined cousin had caught her, tossed her over his shoulder and carted her right back to her prison.

"Lord Henry will save me," she told Crispin over and over again, her frantic thoughts going back to the last time she saw him, laying on the floor of the inn.

She didn't even know if he lived, and she doubted Crispin cared that he might have committed murder.

"He'll come and save me," she insisted.

"He can try," was all Crispin would say in return.

But by the fourth day, Daphne had no idea where Henry might be. She was exhausted and battered from being tossed about the carriage, furious beyond measure at Crispin's high-handed ways, and wishing over and over she'd told Henry everything that beautiful afternoon beneath the oak tree.

"Oh, Henry, come find me," she whispered up to the stars night after night, hoping one of them would take pity on her and carry her message to her love.

But when Crispin's carriage rolled into Langdale, she knew her chances of rescue were dimming. So close to Owle Park, and yet they might as well have taken a ship to the Orient.

Lord Henry would hardly expect Lord Dale to bring her right back to the original scene of the crime.

Nor did she have any hope of effecting an escape.

Especially when she was let out to find not only Great-Aunt Damaris on the front steps but also the Right Honorable Matheus Dale beaming down at her as if she had just stepped out in her finest, most fashionable London garb.

Matheus Dale? Oh, they wouldn't.

It seemed they would.

Not that anyone was going to explain their plans to her, not that they needed to. Given the haze of tears on Phi's face, Daphne had her answer.

And late that night, Phi came to her door, to the room where they'd locked her in "for her own good."

"Cousin?" Phi whispered as she scratched quietly at the door.

"Phi?" Daphne sat up, then rushed to the door, kneeling before it, her fingers pressed to the solid oak barring her escape. "Whatever is going to be done? They aren't going to —" She couldn't even finish the thought. *Matheus Dale?!* She shuddered.

"Yes, I fear so!" Phi whispered back. "But they are awaiting a Special License."

"Get me out," Daphne begged.

"I cannot. Aunt Damaris has the key well hidden."

Daphne sank deeper into the door. "Oh, Phi, I love him. With all my heart, I love him."

"I'm so sorry, Daphne. So very sorry."

And then Phi was gone.

Two days passed, with Daphne's only contact being a surly old maid who had no use for pleas or entreaties.

Once Matheus came to the door to invite her downstairs to sup, and she tossed a vase at the panel in a defiant reply.

As night fell that second day, Daphne heard an odd sound. A *ssssh* that whispered loudly in the silence. She glanced over at the door and spied a note that had been shoved beneath.

Daphne leapt upon it, her heart hammering. And indeed, when she turned it over, she found it addressed to:

Miss Spooner.

She hugged it close, and then just as quickly ripped it open.

Open your window, my love. Let me in.

Open her window? Good heavens, she was on the third floor.

Yet when she got to her window, hauling back the heavy drapes, and then pulling and yanking the sash open, there was Lord Henry climbing up a rope that seemed to dangle from the roof above.

He swung himself into the room. "Minx!" he cried out as he opened his arms to her.

Daphne rushed to him. "How did you . . . Whatever were you thinking? . . . Oh, I am ever so glad you've come."

"Yes, to all of that," he told her, smoothing back her tumbled hair. "But first this."

And then he kissed her, and all her worries and fears and the buckets of tears she'd shed were all forgotten. The moment his lips touched hers, she knew that everything would be as it should.

When they paused, if only to gasp for breath, she rushed to ask, "How did you know how to find me? Let alone —" She waved her hand at the open window as if she still couldn't quite believe it.

"The stable lad," he told her, kissing her brow and her cheeks, as if he couldn't get enough of her.

"The stable lad?"

"Yes, the one from the inn who told that horrible bouncer about Dishforth."

"Whatever has he to do with all this?"

"Apparently he feels quite wretched over his poor dissembling —"

"Oh my! He didn't get sacked, did he?"

Henry shook his head. "Seems he's a dab hand with horses, but not much for telling a lie."

"He is that," Daphne said with a laugh and then covered her mouth. "We must be quiet."

He nodded and lowered his voice. "The boy came up to Owle Park this afternoon and offered to help."

She shook her head. "I don't see how he could."

Henry's eyes lit up with mischief. "His sister works here. She's a chambermaid. Knows the house inside and out. She smuggled him and the rope up to the roof. Couldn't manage the key. Still, it was all I needed. Some way to get inside, to get to you."

"To rescue me," she said, grinning at him. Her own knight-errant. Then she realized something else. "However do you intend to get me out?" She looked in horror at the rope hanging outside her window.

She rather preferred a rescue that involved the backstairs and a hasty retreat in a good carriage.

"I'm going to climb back out —"

Daphne was already shaking her head. "I can't . . . I'll never be able to —"

"You don't have to. Roxley is going to come to the front door and insist you be released."

"Whyever would Crispin release me just because the Earl of Roxley insists?"

"Once we are married, he'll have no choice but to let my wife go."

"Married?" she gasped.

"Yes, married," he told her, his gaze searching her gaze for some sign of agreement. So to press his point — and also to reassure her he hadn't gone stark raving mad — he opened up his coat and dug out a piece of paper. "I've a Special License. All you need to do is sign it and the vicar will marry us."

Daphne wasn't too sure she'd heard him correctly. Get married? "Henry, I haven't a vicar handy."

"Ah, but minx, I do."

Daphne gazed up at him with disbelief in her eyes. He had to admit it was a madcap scheme, but surely she would appreciate that point.

"Well, I haven't the vicar just yet. I will in about an hour," Henry told her. "Didn't know how long it would take to climb that wall, so Preston is waiting with the fellow just on the other side of the line and will be here at the top of the hour." He nodded to the mantel clock.

"So we have some time to wait?" Daphne asked in a low, sultry voice that caught his attention like a lure.

"Um, yes," he managed, his throat going dry. But as she came gliding into his arms, he found the words to murmur in her ear. "You wicked, tempting minx."

"I've missed you," was all she said before she rose up on her tiptoes and kissed him. Claimed him.

"And I, you."

Murmuring apologies and words of love, they fell into her bed, a tangle of limbs and kisses. The moment he touched her, he was lost — hard and delirious. His lips kissing her, claiming her. His hands stealing away her gown so she was naked beneath him.

Gloriously naked and his.

Her legs opened to him and she took him inside her with little prelude. It was a hot, fierce joining. A reunion and a promise. He thrust deeply and swiftly into her, as if he'd hungered for her for years instead of just days.

And beneath him, Daphne writhed with joy, her hips meeting his thrusts, her legs winding around him, holding him closer as she rocked against him.

When she began to cry out, forgetting even their perilous situation, he covered her mouth with another kiss that contained his own deep growl of possession as he came, filling her with his seed, thrusting and thrusting until he was spent.

It was hasty, hot and quick.

But neither of them minded. They had a wedding to see to. And the rest of their lives to make love.

Beneath Daphne's window, Preston was waging another sort of battle.

"This is highly irregular, Your Grace," the vicar complained as he looked up at the happy couple standing in the window. He was new to his posting and still fresh from his recent ordination. "The lady looks . . . well, she appears to be . . ."

"Tumbled, I'd say. And thoroughly," Roxley said, filling in where the blushing vicar wouldn't.

If the man of God wasn't blushing before, he turned a deep shade of scarlet now.

"Then I'd say it is best we see them married in all due haste," Preston pointed out.

"Yes, I suppose so, Your Grace," the vicar said, looking up at the window and around the darkened yard.

Preston had to imagine no amount of divinity school had prepared the poor fellow for this.

Roxley leaned forward and added to the argument. "Might I emphasize the haste part. The Dales aren't averse to letting their dogs loose. Rather large ones."

The man squirmed at the dilemma before him, tugging at his collar. "Still, this is a rather difficult moral position, if I must say."

Preston got to the point. "Do you find your living at Owle Park difficult, sir?"

The man gulped. "No, Your Grace. Not in the least. Why, it is quite comfortable and —"

It was then that the man caught the duke's meaning.

But Preston wanted to make sure the man understood. "Marry my uncle quickly and quietly before he ruins Miss Dale." They all took another glance up at the bride and groom.

"Yet again," Roxley added with a grin.

EPILOGUE

The Elephant and Whistle Inn
The Manchester and Glasgow Road
Fifteen years later

"Henry, I believe we stayed at this inn," Lady Henry Seldon commented as she climbed out of their carriage, looking around the yard. "Indeed, I am positive." She smiled brightly at her husband, enchanted by the notion.

"Ever the romantic, my dearest Daphne," Lord Henry said, kissing her hand and then her lips. How was it he could never, even after all these years, have enough of her, his fair wife. Not even five children — four boys and one girl — had changed her in his eyes. They'd only made her more beautiful.

Her blue eyes sparkled as she recognized the lascivious light in his own gaze. She flitted a glance to where their poor beleaguered nanny was guiding the children inside for the luncheon, then back to her husband.

"Tonight," she whispered.

There had been many such nights since their madcap wedding. After Preston had finally coerced the vicar into marrying them, there had been the scene with Crispin and Damaris.

At first, the viscount had been incredulous at Roxley's demands, even when the earl had produced the signed and witnessed Special License, as well as the trembling vicar to attest to the validity of the marriage. But after opening Daphne's door and finding a grinning Henry Seldon in her bedroom, that had been all the evidence Crispin Dale had needed to wash his hands of his sullied cousin.

Oh, their marriage had caused more than just a dustup; even Daphne's parents had refused to acknowledge the newlyweds. Hen wouldn't speak to either of them for months, not until they'd announced that Daphne was increasing. That also managed to ease the tensions with the Dales — for being a prolific lot, the Dales adored children. Lots of them.

Daphne's parents were the first to send their congratulations.

And Zillah? Well, Zillah had been the most shocking.

For they hadn't heard a word from her in

over a year, until the gossip made the rounds that a little Seldon would be making his or her debut in the spring. And then Zillah had arrived, knitting in hand, and with all her trunks.

For while the Dales were prolific, the Seldons regarded babies as something close to the second coming. And Zillah was going to be there when this newest Seldon arrived.

Then Zillah had stayed, she and Daphne finding much in common in their love of the growing brood. The Seldon relic had lived happily with them at Stowting Mote until just this past winter, when the old girl had finally gone in her sleep, a quiet, peaceful ending to a long and scandalous life.

The children missed the old girl and the hours they'd spent with her by the piano listening to her play.

That was the reason for this journey north. Zillah had left them a collection of houses, this last one in Scotland, of all places.

"I had no idea she had so much property," Henry had said, shaking his head when the solicitor had brought her will to the house. Six in all. One for each of their children, and a spare one in Scotland that they'd decided to go visit.

"Shall we?" Daphne asked, tugging his

thoughts back to the present.

"Yes, of course," Henry said. Taking her hand in his, they walked into the public room, only to find the entire place packed, nearly every bench and stool filled.

Henry had never seen an inn so crowded.

"Mama, it's him! It's —" young Harriet whispered as she caught her mother's hand and pulled her forward.

The boys shushed their sister and stopped her rush to tattle, but now the cat was out of the bag.

"Who, Harry?" Henry asked, brushing his hand over his daughter's fair head. "Who is it?"

The children shared a guilty glance until Christopher, the eldest, piped up. "Mr. Dishforth."

"Wha-a—at?" Henry and Daphne said at once.

Harriet pointed to a spot near the fireplace where an old man sat hunched on a stool, the entire room fixed on his every word.

"How can this —" Henry began, but all around them, the crowd added their own *"Ssshh!"* to stop his words, while Daphne gaped in wonder.

"So I stole my dearest Adelaide away from the villainous nobleman who had locked her away, and we rode north —" the old man

491

was saying.

Henry was about to get up and protest when he spied the mischievous light in Daphne's eyes and so he followed her lead and listened to the tale of Abernathy Dishforth and his dearest Adelaide. The story vaguely resembled their mad-cap dash, for this one contained a host of villains: highwaymen, broken wheels, their carriage nearly tumbling down a rocky ravine.

The crowd around them listened avidly, cheering when the couple made it to Gretna Green, and there was hardly a dry eye in the house as Mr. Dishforth related Adelaide's sad passing of late.

Henry leaned forward and whispered in Daphne's ear, "This is the devil who's been dunning me all these years."

For indeed, several times a year, bills from inns and public houses along Manchester Road would arrive addressed to Lord Henry Seldon for the expense and care of one Abernathy Dishforth.

Henry and Daphne had long suspected that someone, a con artist of sorts, had heard their story all those years ago and occasionally put the tale to good use. Now it seemed they'd found the fellow.

"Finally I can put an end to this gull," Henry said.

"Leave him be," Daphne replied, putting a staying hand on his sleeve. "I rather like that our story is told. Look around — who doesn't love a happy ending?"

And indeed, people were smiling and laughing, and a few were dashing aside tears.

Who was Henry to ruin such a tale?

"Papa?" Harriet asked as they returned to their carriage. "Was that really Mr. Dishforth?"

"I daresay we'll find out when they charge us twice," Lord Henry complained.

Daphne laughed. "I think it must be, Harriet. But however did you find out about Mr. Dishforth?"

"Last Christmas. When we went to visit Lady Roxley at Foxgrove," she said, yawning and ready for her afternoon nap. "She knows all about him. Have you heard of him as well?"

"Aye, sweetling. He used to write me letters."

Harriet's eyes grew wide. "Did you write him back?"

Daphne leaned over and whispered in her ear. "Yes, I quite fancied him once. But don't tell your father."